CRY FREEDOM

THE WINDS 1 OF FREEDOM

CRY FREEDOM

~

MARLO SCHALESKY

CROSSWAY BOOKS • WHEATON, ILLINOIS
A DIVISION OF GOOD NEWS PUBLISHERS

Cry Freedom

Published by Crossway Books
A division of Good News Publishers
1300 Crescent Street
Wheaton, Illinois 60187

Cover design: Cindy Kiple

Cover photo: Tony Stone Images

Cover illustration: Linda Benson

First printing, 2000

Printed in the United States of America

Library of Congress Cataloging-in-Publication Data

Schalesky, Marlo 1967–
Cry freedom / Marlo Schalesky.
p. cm. — (The winds of freedom ; bk. 1)
ISBN 1-58134-169-5 (alk. paper)
1. United States—History—Colonial period, ca. 1600-1775—Fiction.
2. Whitefield, George, 1714-1770—Fiction. 3. Delaware Indians—Fiction. 4. Great Awakening—Fiction. II. Title.
PS3569.C4728 C7 2000
813'.6—dc21 99-089206
CIP

15 14 13 12 11 10 09 08 07 06 05 04 03 02 01 00
15 14 13 12 11 10 9 8 7 6 5 4 3 2 1

To Jesus Christ,

my Savior, Redeemer, and Lord.

May this work be worthy of Your name.

and

To my husband, Bryan.

Without your love, support, and great ideas

this book would be only a dream.

Thank you for helping to make my dreams a reality.

SPECIAL THANKS

to my One Heart sisters

for all their prayers, love, and support.

especially to Tricia Goyer,

who read through the manuscript, not once but twice,

to give me invaluable suggestions, critique,

and much-needed encouragement.

to Cindy Martinusen

for her great advice and help with the story's ending.

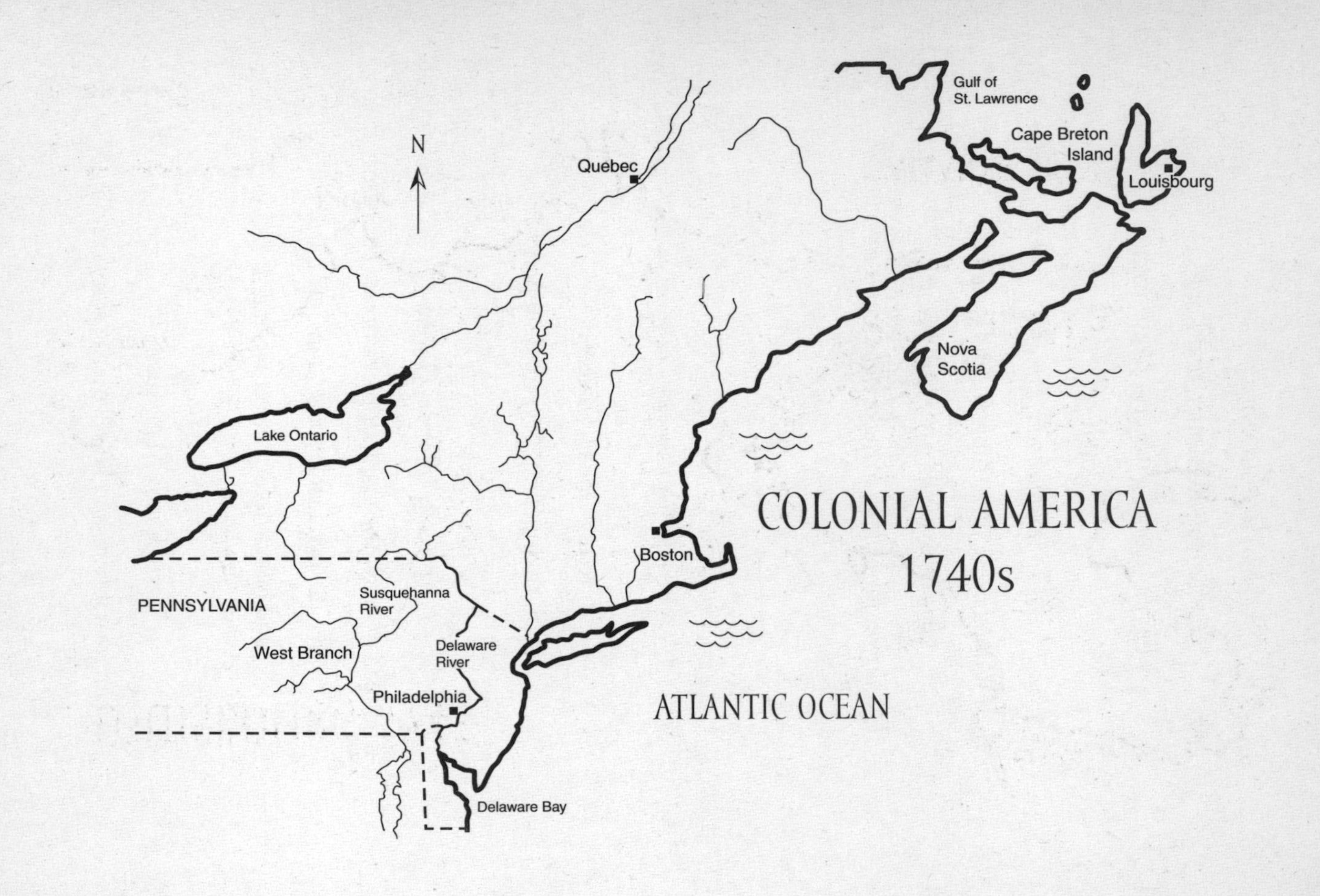
COLONIAL AMERICA
1740s
N
Quebec
Gulf of
St. Lawrence
Cape Breton
Island
Louisbourg
Nova
Scotia
Lake Ontario
Boston
PENNSYLVANIA
Susquehanna
River
West Branch
Delaware
River
Philadelphia
Delaware Bay
ATLANTIC OCEAN

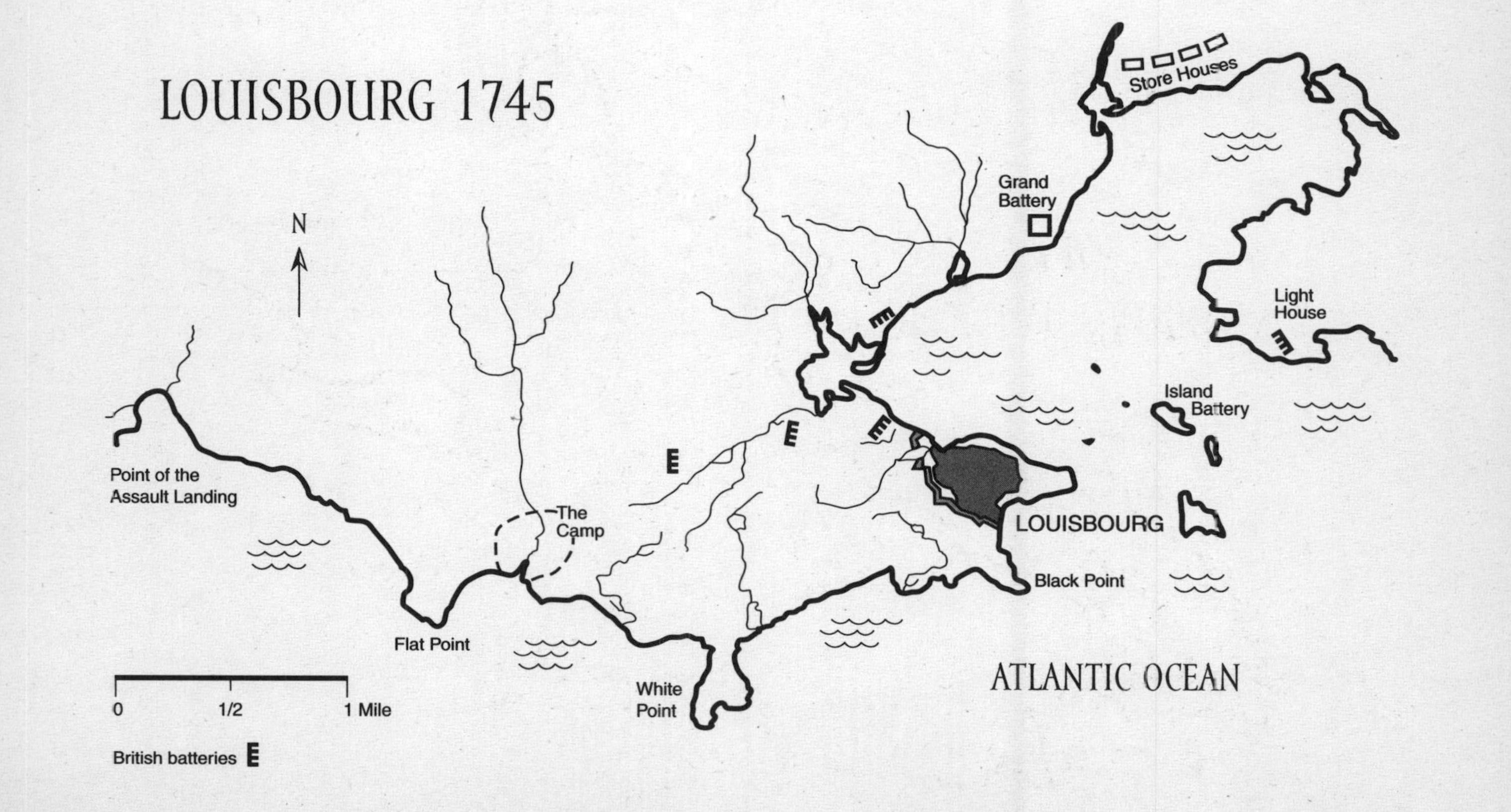
LOUISBOURG 1745
N
Store Houses
Grand Battery
Light House
Island Battery
LOUISBOURG
Black Point
ATLANTIC OCEAN
Point of the Assault Landing
The Camp
Flat Point
White Point
0
1/2
1 Mile
British batteries

If the Son

therefore shall make you free,

ye shall be free indeed.

JOHN 8:36

Preface

The year is 1743, a time of adventure, hope, and betrayal.

In the English colonies a religious revival, which will later be named The Great Awakening, is sweeping through every class of people, drawing the wealthy and common alike into a new and personal experience with God. Through the preaching of a young Englishman named George Whitefield, and others like him, reliance on religious traditions is crumbling as people, awakened to their sinful state, turn to the mercy and forgiveness of the risen Christ.

But as the American colonists find their peace with God, England and France plot for war, the third of four such conflicts waged by the French and British for control of North America.

On the Pennsylvanian frontier, tensions mount as the Shawnee and Delaware ally with the French. Here the drums of war have already begun to beat. French-led war bands advance. Settlers tremble. Brave men, driven by the hope of freedom, grip their muskets in desperate hands.

And, in the midst of it all, one half-breed Indian girl dreams of what it means to be free . . .

PART ONE

Ashes

~

ONE

Pennsylvania frontier, July 1743

The savage cry rent the air in a single burst of terror. It echoed from tens upon tens of invisible throats surrounding the village. Little Cloud heard it, and trembled. It was the sound of their doom.

"Tankawon!"

Little Cloud whirled at his name.

"Where is your father, Tankawon?" Black Hawk shouted. "Only his God can save us now. The enemy is upon us."

The eerie war whoop rose again from among the trees. There would be no escape.

"Shawanowi." The name of the enemy tribe whispered through the village.

Terror clawed at Little Cloud. After only thirteen summers, he was not ready to die. Where was his father? Where was his sister Kwelik? He needed them now. Now, when death screamed from the lips of enemies and mocked his helplessness. Now, when babies stood naked at the entrance of their huts, crying to parents who would no longer heed them. Now, as Black Hawk clutched spear and tomahawk in strong hands, gathering his meager warriors for the fight. Little Cloud needed his father's faith and his sister's. He needed their God.

Only his God can save us now. The words echoed in Little Cloud's mind, playing a dissonant tune to the shriek of the Shawanowi. Before him Crying Wolf grabbed her baby and raced toward her hut. A basket tipped at her passing, spilling bark across the dirt.

Little Cloud stood alone amid the din of approaching madness. He shivered, his eyes wavering on the mud huts that circled the center of the village. Beyond him, in a copper kettle traded from the

French, deer stew boiled untended, the sound of its bubbling lost in the shrill cries of the children. But no one cared. Death was upon them.

Corn meal scattered before Little Cloud as another woman dropped the basket she carried and scooped up her screaming child. Someone wailed. The sound echoed through Little Cloud's frame. He turned his head. A deerskin hung to his right, still curing from a recent hunt. He grabbed it and fled, throwing himself into a corner between a barrel and the side of a hut. He choked as he pulled the skin over his head and peeked from under it. It smelled of dead flesh, like a forewarning of the moments to come.

Around him his people scattered to and fro, their faces pale as they reached for sticks and spears, anything that might serve as a weapon against the enemy. In the village center, tall warriors gathered, their tomahawks hanging from their hands like children's toys.

We are too few. The thought slipped through Little Cloud's mind. *We cannot fight them.*

As if he heard the thought, Black Hawk turned his head. For a moment his eyes rested on Little Cloud. Then he again raised his chin and shouted his own challenge into the trees.

"Oh, God, I don't want to die." Little Cloud choked on the words in a muted sob. He clutched the deerskin tighter. "Make the Shawanowi go away. Rain down fire from heaven to consume them."

As if in defiance of his prayer, a flaming arrow arched from the trees behind him. With a roar it exploded on the thatched roof of his father's hut. The dry grasses blazed high in the fury of their destruction. Little Cloud did not move. His eyes blurred with smoke and fear. Another hut caught fire. Crying Wolf's scream tore through the air as she burst from the hut. Her cry summoned the enemy.

With a final shriek the Shawanowi warriors emerged from the trees and plunged toward the village. An arrow pierced Black Hawk's chest moments before the cruel bite of the tomahawk removed his scalp. Little Cloud watched Black Hawk's eyes roll open in death.

An eerie wail rose above the din of slaughter as a boy ran toward the fallen warrior.

No, Running Wind! Little Cloud allowed the warning to die on his lips unspoken even as he recognized his friend.

Four other warriors fell. Tears of horror gathered in Little Cloud's eyes. His hands trembled on the deer hide.

Still he did not move. Soon he knew they would all die in the flash of iron and blood. If only he could be safe from it. Where was Kwelik? Where was his father? Where was God?

Betrayed! The word shot through Little Cloud's mind as a musket fired near him. Running Wind screamed and fell. Without thought, Little Cloud started toward him. Before he could draw back, the hide was ripped from his hands, exposing him to the enemy. The heat of a burning hut seared his back. He stumbled forward. Behind him a low chuckle sounded in his ears. He turned.

In that moment Little Cloud looked into the face of death and saw that it belonged to a white man.

~

In a meadow far from the village, Kwelik held her breath and willed the world to remain still. Not a movement, not a breath, not a sound but the wild thumping of her heart. There, just inches above her head, lavender wings fluttered in tiny currents of silence. Kwelik's eyes shone with hope. She held her hand motionless, like the ancient oak that towered above her. As if finally comprehending the will of the heavens, the tiny butterfly landed on her outstretched finger and primly flipped its wings behind it. Her delight threatened to spoil the moment as she studied the fragile creature with two orange spots staring up from both wings, like the eyes of an angel. So delicate, so tiny, so free . . .

A throaty bark interrupted the serenity as a huge Irish wolfhound bounded into the clearing and headed for the girl. Kwelik watched the butterfly flutter away and land on a daisy at the far end of the meadow.

"Oh, Lapawin, you've scared him away," she scolded. She threw her arms into the air in frustration and then wrapped them tightly around the old dog.

Lapawin promptly jumped up to place his paws on her shoulders.

Laughing, Kwelik tumbled to the ground and accepted his slobbery kiss. "And it was so beautiful, too. Did you see it, Lapawin?" She rolled over and stared into the afternoon sky. "Someday I'm going to be like that butterfly, free to soar into the heavens and dance through every meadow and smell every flower. Someday God will give me wings."

Lapawin gave her face another sweeping lick, nudging her playfully with his nose. Absently she stroked his bristled fur until he lay his head on her chest. "I wonder what it would be like to dance on the breeze and hear nothing but the melody of God?" she asked, more of herself than of the animal resting by her. With one hand she plucked a dandelion and blew its seed into the air. One by one the feathery seeds were captured by the wind and sent swirling out of sight. "Someday," she murmured, "I'll find out where the wind goes."

She watched as a cloud passed over the sun and momentarily blotted out the light. The shadow passed over her, darkening her dreams.

"Someday, Lapawin," she said, "but not today." She sighed and struggled to her feet, brushing her hands against her buckskin skirt. "Today there's work to be done, corn meal to prepare, deer meat to cook for the tribe. No more dreaming today, as Papa would say. But you'll see, Lapawin—one day I'll mount up on lavender wings and find my dreams."

Kwelik patted the hound on his burly head. "But I'd better do it soon. I'll have nineteen years this fall, and Papa is making plans to marry me off to that arrogant Taquachi." Kwelik shook her head and rubbed Lapawin behind the ears. "You remember him, don't you, boy? You growled at him when he came to see Papa a week ago." She grimaced. "I would have liked to growl at him too, even if he is the third son of Chief Tumaskan. But Papa would say that such behavior is unbecoming to a missionary's daughter." Kwelik lowered her voice to imitate her father's tone. She looked down at the dog and sighed. "Oh, Lapawin, Papa just doesn't understand."

The dog cocked his head as if attempting to comprehend her words.

Kwelik smiled, her sudden laughter swirling into the air like the promise of a song still waiting to be sung. "If you were a man, I'd marry you, and we'd run through the meadows together chasing squirrels and rabbits. We'd find out where the river ends, where the bird flies in winter, where the sun sleeps each night. And there'd be no pompous third son of a chief to stop us. How would you like that, Lapawin? Shall we run away together and see what's beyond these trees, what's out there in the world that Papa came from? Maybe someday, eh?" She let out a long breath. "But not today. Never today."

She shook her head and dared Lapawin to chase her to the stream. She reached the water two strides behind the dog and dropped beside him. Cupping the cool water in her hands, she took a long drink.

Then Kwelik lifted her head and watched a single droplet of water fall and shimmer across the surface of her reflection in a quiet pool beside the stream. She stared at herself—the long black hair of her mother, a Lenape Indian (or Delaware, as the white man called them), and the clear blue eyes of her father, an English missionary. A face out of place in both worlds. Luckily, God didn't care. But everyone else did. Always the outcast. Just like Papa.

His ideas had gotten him banned from his Anglican congregation in England. They could not bear such a personal God as he preached, a God who would know and be known by the simplest of believers. So Papa had taken his faith to the Indians. And River Laughing had believed. On the day they married, the tribe named him Linniwulamen, Truthful Man. From that moment he too was caught between worlds, a legacy he passed to his daughter and son.

Kwelik sighed, traced a dripping finger across one straight brow, and stared into eyes as blue as the summer sky. Skye, the name her father had given her. Skye with Topaz Lights, after a necklace of blue topaz that he had once admired on an English noblewoman. Her mother had always called her Kwelik, the Lenape word for sky. And Kwelik she remained, even though her mother had died three winters past in an influenza epidemic. How she missed her mother—confident, brisk, always with a hint of laughter in her dark eyes. Even in the harsh winter of 1730, she had refused to tolerate fear. The other women shook their heads and said that River Laughing had a fool's hope. But Father knew better. He said she always kept one eye focused on heaven and chased fear away with her laugh. That year the strength of her hope had saved them all.

A frog jumped from the creek and landed in the mud next to Kwelik. Startled, she sat back into a damp patch of clover. "Oh, now look what I've done," she said. She turned toward Lapawin, but he was already several yards down the creek, attempting to capture the perpetrator of the crime. She watched him go, his legs stepping gingerly over the stones at the water's edge. After a few moments, the dog stuck his nose into a clump of tall grass, but he had lost his prey. With a snort of frustration, Lapawin gave up the chase and trotted back toward Kwelik.

She chuckled and dropped one arm casually around him. "We've grown up, Lapawin, you and I. Even the frogs have become too fast for us." She lifted his chin and looked into his drooping eyes. "And yet we've hardly lived at all. What do we have to show for our years? I have read Papa's books a hundred times, it seems. I've studied his sketchings until I could recreate every detail in my mind. But I've never seen a real carriage, a real ship, or even a washbasin." She shook her head. "Sometimes I wonder if Papa's world exists at all."

Kwelik leaned against the dog's side, dropping one hand to trail in the cold water. "I wonder, what would Mama say if she saw me now? Would she understand this longing? Could she tell me why my heart burns when I hold a butterfly in my hand?" Kwelik allowed her eyes to lose focus until the stream, the trees, and even Lapawin faded into a hazy blur of memory.

She could almost feel the stroke of her mother's gentle hand along her hair, just as it was that day in 1730, in the deepest part of winter. The memory swirled around her, enveloping her with its warmth. She had snuggled into her mother's lap, keeping one hand tightly around her waist while clutching the tattered blanket with the other.

"Don't be afraid, Kwelik," her mother's voice had soothed.

From the corner she heard her brother's infant cry as he struggled in Papa's arms. "Hush, Tankawon," Papa whispered as Little Cloud cried out again. He was hungry too.

Kwelik wanted to cry with him, but instead she gripped her mother more fiercely.

"God will not abandon us," her mother said.

Did her mother read her doubt? Could she sense the fear that scraped along Kwelik's nerves like a wildcat refusing to be tamed? Kwelik drew a sharp breath, hiding from the cat's evil claws in the confidence of her mother's words.

River Laughing rocked slowly back and forth, her hand smoothing her daughter's soft hair with rhythmic assurance. "I have prayed," River Laughing continued, "and God knows our need."

"But, Mama, how can He find us beneath all this snow?" Kwelik's voice held a strange mixture of innocence and fear.

"Kwelik, you must be brave enough to believe." Her mother's laugh chased the shadows from her heart. "He sees, Kwelik, even the tiny seed that lies far beneath the ground and waits for the first day of spring." She paused. "Yes, His eyes see right through the snow, through the cabin wall, and into your tummy." River Laughing tickled her daughter's belly until Kwelik forgot her fear and squealed with delight.

"And then do you know what He says?"

"What, Mama?"

"He says, 'What's this? Why, there's nothing in this tummy! I'm going to have to fix that!'"

"What does He do then, Mama? Does He fill it all up with snow?" asked the young Kwelik.

"Well, of course not. He . . ." River Laughing paused again, her voice growing contemplative as it did when she was communicating with God. "Then, my little Wrinkled Brow . . ." She smoothed her finger over Kwelik's forehead and laughed. "Then He gives our hunters a great buck, enough to feed the entire village, just because He loves His little Kwelik and doesn't want her to be hungry anymore."

"Really, Mama?"

River Laughing smiled and squeezed Kwelik. "Really."

Kwelik's father stepped from the shadows. "He has told you this, Wife?" he asked.

"Yes. Tomorrow the hunters must go out. And the women will prepare for the feast."

"I'll tell the clan." Papa never doubted.

Even the biting cold and the village's despair could not defeat her mother's confidence. The next day the men left at dawn. Before the sun had reached its zenith, they returned with the buck on their shoulders and a straggly pup at their heels, a pup that Kwelik had named Lapawin, meaning Rich Again.

~

Lapawin's low cry brought Kwelik back from her memory. He pricked his ears and barked, then raced back to the clearing. There he stopped and looked anxiously at Kwelik.

"What's wrong, boy?" She jogged up to him and rubbed his ears, but he would not be quieted. He gave another loud bark and raced toward the village, not waiting to see whether Kwelik followed.

With a final glance toward the meadow's tranquility, Kwelik hurried after him. As she drew closer to the village, the acrid smell of smoke assaulted her. Tendrils of fear wrapped around her heart, causing it to beat in frenzied confusion. Where were her people? Smoke stained the sky, looking like trails of death.

Just outside their village Lapawin stopped, nosing behind a clump of brush until he found his objective. His desperate whine brought Kwelik to a full run.

Papa! Thomas Ashton lay on his side, an arrow protruding from his chest. "Skye." His eyes rolled back as she leaned over him. "I couldn't save them. Too late." Agony etched his features. He clutched the arrow with spasmodic intensity, then released it.

Kwelik's fingers hovered above the arrow's shaft. "It's deep, Papa. I don't think I can pull it out."

He shook his head and pushed ineffectually at her arm. "Run, child. Shawanowi." Blood trickled from the corner of his mouth. She wiped it away. "Shawanowi attacked us. All dead." His head lolled to one side. "All dead."

"Come, Papa, we'll get help."

"No, Skye." His voice grew stronger, then wavered. "Leave me."

"Never, Papa."

"Obey me, child. I'm going home now. Jesus? Jesus!" His voice faded to a whisper, then grew silent.

Kwelik held him to her breast as the last of life seeped from Thomas Ashton, and peace washed over his weary features. She could almost see his soul following the trail of smoke to heaven. In that moment tears would not come.

An eternity passed in the briefest breath of time. She clutched her father to her chest, unaware of the world around her. All dead.

Kwelik felt the shriek in her gut a moment before it reached her ears. At first she thought it was the echo of her own agony, but no. One lived. Tankawon!

"Let me go!" Little Cloud screamed, his shout followed by a howl of utter defiance.

Kwelik was on her feet, at a dead run, before his voice faded from the air. She reached the edge of the village just in time to see the knife from a warrior's hand flash before the face of her young brother. Kwelik drew a sharp breath. In the carnage that had been her village, five men stood ready to kill Little Cloud, the last of her clan. Only terror stopped her from rushing to her death to save him. She stopped, threw herself to the ground, and watched the knife play around Little Cloud's neck.

Bile rose in her throat as she surveyed the village's destruction. There, not ten yards from her hiding place, lay Black Hawk, his head bloody from scalping. He would have married later that year. Kwelik felt the horror hardening in her chest. Beyond him Running Wind, the boy who helped her hunt berries last winter, stared unseeing at the sky. Even Fallen Leaf, who had just announced her pregnancy during the last moon, had not escaped the brutal bite of the enemy's tomahawk. Kwelik remembered how they had danced and thanked God for the conception of the chief's first grandchild, a babe who would now never see the light of the sun. The others had fared no better. Crying Wolf, Small Sight, Eagle Hunter, Water Dancing—all lay dead among the burning ruins of their village. Kwelik shut her eyes tightly, knowing that the blackness could not erase the scene. Papa was right. All dead. All but Tankawon.

She refocused on her brother, now standing perfectly still in the midst of his enemies. His demeanor wavered between fury and terror as death stalked him too in the sharp edge of a knife. Somehow she must save him. She could not bear to watch him, her brother whom she had taught how to hunt the wild berries, how to sneak up on a bird without it knowing, and how to sing the songs of summer. Her brother who had listened to her stories and always begged for just one more. She would easily give her life in exchange for his. But these killers would not give her that option. One girl could not prevail against five strong warriors unless . . .

Yes! With a deep breath, Kwelik brought her hands to her mouth and let out the fierce cry of a wildcat on the hunt. She let out another cry as the men's heads snapped in her direction. It was enough. Little Cloud sank his teeth into the restraining hand of the Shawanowi holding him and sprinted toward her.

It took only seconds for the men to realize they'd been duped. With one wild war cry, they crashed after their escaped victim. Without looking back, Kwelik pushed her brother in front of her and ran. The sounds of pursuit echoed behind her. Branches slashed her cheek.

Little Cloud was just in front of her, his spindly legs pumping with the desperation to survive. A fallen tree loomed in their path. Without missing a step, Little Cloud, then Kwelik, leaped over it. An arrow thumped into a tree beside them. Neither broke stride.

The next arrow found its mark, driving through Kwelik's leg with a white burst of agony. The tip protruded from her shin as the shaft sank into her calf. She screamed, clutching her injured leg as she fell forward.

Little Cloud stopped. "Get up!" he shouted.

Kwelik lifted her head. "Go!" Her voice carried the intensity of her pain.

Little Cloud hesitated.

"Run!" Kwelik repeated.

Little Cloud obeyed.

Kwelik watched him disappear through the blur of her tears. "Tankawon . . ." His name caught in her throat. With a cry of anguish, she struggled to her feet. Too late. The men were upon her before she could utter another sound. A tall brave with a jagged scar covering one cheek pulled her to her feet and wrenched her arm behind her. She smelled brandy on his breath.

"What's this?" he slurred.

"Aha! A squaw in cat's clothing," mocked a cultured voice from just beyond her vision.

The raucous sound of the men's laughter nauseated her. She shut her eyes. They were devils, all of them.

"Why, it's just a little kitten. Does kitty want some milk?" the voice said again.

She opened her eyes to see a white man, a French lieutenant. He stepped closer, grabbing her hair and forcing her head back so that she stared into the dark slits that were his eyes.

"What's this? A half-breed?" He dropped her head in disgust. From the corner of her eye she saw the flicker of a knife. She ground her teeth in anger and frustration. The mixture of pain and grief erupted into a single flash of fury.

"*Nakowa.*" The word tore from her lips, her voice burning as she spoke it.

"What did she say?" the lieutenant demanded.

"She say, 'snakes,'" the Shawanowi who held her responded.

The lieutenant's hand smacked across her mouth, driving her to the ground. Her vision blurred and tunneled. She tasted dirt mixed with her own blood.

From the edge of consciousness she heard a low growl as Lapawin leapt from the bushes toward the man who had accosted her. With one smooth movement, the lieutenant drew his musket and fired. Kwelik heard the dull thud of Lapawin's body just as the last of consciousness oozed from her battered frame.

TWO

A cool breeze swirled across the clearing and whispered through the leaves overhead, but Jonathan Grant paid no heed. The sparrows, the squirrels, even the trees meant nothing to him at the moment. Only the steady swing of the axe mattered, only the persistent pursuit of his dream. He swung the blade again, his muscles rippling as the head bit deeply into the log before him.

"We've done it, my friend," he called to the black man working near the edge of the clearing. "That's the last one."

A sparrow landed on the pile of cut wood at Jonathan's feet and cocked its head as if questioning the man's confidence. Jonathan quickly surveyed the place he now called home. Two sturdy cabins nestled near the edge of the small clearing while a dozen tree stumps peeked from the grass to give evidence of their work. "It's so different from England," he whispered, "so different from everything I've left behind." He smiled at the thought.

Jonathan paused to stretch before swinging the axe again. If all went as planned, the barn would be finished tomorrow, and their modest homestead would finally be complete. He drew a deep breath and noticed at last the distant rumble of the West Branch of the Susquehanna River as it hurried to join its eastern counterpart.

"I is almost done here, too," Nahum called, running his fingers through his grizzled gray hair before turning back to the log he was carefully shaping into a rafter for the new barn.

Jonathan wiped his sleeve across his forehead and pulled his axe from the final log. "That's it for me. Come, we'll finish tomorrow." Jonathan motioned for his friend to join him under the one birch they'd left in the clearing.

Nahum brushed his hat against his pant leg and strode toward

Jonathan. His sweat glistened with a finely polished sheen as he sat down beneath the birch. "Good work today. Your father'd be proud of you."

"Ha." Jonathan could not keep the bitterness from his voice. "He'd rise from his grave if he could see me now—scorning my precious aristocratic heritage and living like a 'savage.' No, if my father had lived, he would want me to go crawling back to England and kiss the feet of that vile brother of mine." Jonathan snorted in contempt. "I'd become brothers with thc bloody Indians first."

Nahum laughed and clouted him on the shoulder. "Guess I won't be staying awake nights waitin' for that, eh?"

Jonathan allowed a grin to crack the scowl that had darkened his features. "Here, have a drink." Jonathan handed him the water skin and leaned back against the tree. "No, Nahum, we'll make it on the frontier, despite the Indians who don't want us here, despite the tensions between the English and French, and despite my brother."

Nahum frowned. "Queen Anne's War 'tween you and them Frenchies ended nearly thirty years ago."

"The war will never end, Nahum. Not until someone wins. But you and I," Jonathan clapped Nahum on the shoulder as he spoke, "we won't be defeated. We'll make a new life for ourselves here yet. You'll see. An honest life."

"I suppose I believe it when you say it like that. I know you been dreamin' that for all these months now. Beautiful land, this."

"I love it. I don't know why, but it's in my blood." He took a deep breath. "The very air pulsates with hope and with freedom."

"Not for everyone." Nahum's words glanced off Jonathan without effect.

"For me and for you, my friend." Jonathan squeezed the man's shoulder. "For now, that's enough."

Nahum nodded and took another long draught from the water skin. "It's a good life we got, Jonathan. A good life. Ah, sure tastes good." He patted his belly and grinned. "But it don't do much for the empty hole inside."

Jonathan sighed and rose to his feet. "We'd better go cook that rabbit you caught this morning."

Nahum groaned. "What we needs is a cook. Yep, forget the flintlocks and furs. Next time you go to that there trading post, see if you can't buys us a cook. Surely theys got one of those a-sittin' on a shelf just waitin' for us to snatch her up."

Jonathan chuckled. "Imported all the way from South Carolina, just like your Aunt Nellie."

"What do you know about my Aunt Nellie?"

"Just everything you've told me for the last year. I'm almost convinced that I grew up with her, too."

"Yep, too bad ol' Nellie ain't living yet. She'd cook us a rabbit stew that'd make the angels weep for wantin' a taste."

"So I've heard."

"Have you now?" Nahum laughed. "Well, you can just hear it again while I'm dreamin' about it. Never tasted such wonders as Aunt Nellie could make. Almost made it worth listening to her old acid tongue just to smell her cooking."

"A tongue just like the devil himself. I've heard this story. You'd think you could raise her from the dead with all your talk."

"I'm wishin' I could."

"Well, if you manage it, see if you can get some of those cousins of yours, too. We need some extra help, especially with those Indians getting braver every day. There's talk that both the Delaware and the Shawnee of these parts have allied with the French." Jonathan grimaced. "You know how old man Johnson was attacked just last month when they killed his oldest son. He was sure he saw a Frenchman with them."

"A dark day, that. I remember." Nahum scratched his head and gave Jonathan a long look. "Should go to that high-'n'-mighty uncle of yours. He'd give us all the help we be needing. Maybe throw in some soldiers too."

"He won't help us. He fancies himself better than anyone in my family, especially with mother being Irish and all. The only one he doesn't look down his nose at anymore is Richard, since my brother is now Lord Grant and holds one of the richest estates in England." Bitterness laced Jonathan's voice.

Nahum squinted, his eyes boring through the younger man. "Not good to hate your own brother."

Jonathan sighed. "He's my brother in name only. You're more a brother to me than he, Nahum."

"Well, I thank you for that. But you really oughta try that uncle. Maybe he'd help. Never know till you ask."

Jonathan shook his head. "There's no talking to him now that he leads the Pennsylvania Assembly. You'd think God Himself came down and anointed him king, the way he goes around with his fancy clothes and arrogant airs. Can't stomach him." Jonathan ground his heel into the dirt.

"Well, we can't be counting on my ol' Aunt Nellie, though she coulda killed them Injuns with just her fry pan and wicked words. They'da never come back after one look at her."

Jonathan smiled. "No, I don't suppose they would. But they haven't troubled us yet."

~

Jonathan heard the torch hit his cabin floor a moment before he felt the heat. His eyes flew open as he leapt from his bed. His weariness evaporated. Flames licked across the cabin's rug just as a wild war cry rent the air. *Indians!* Dread clutched Jonathan's throat. The fire inside his cabin gained strength. He heard Nahum yell in the distance.

Jonathan grabbed his blanket and smothered the flames. Smoke burned his eyes as he snatched his musket and raced for the door. He paused to slam the shutters of the window shut, cursing himself for failing to latch them against such an attack. Then he flung the door open and raised his weapon.

Jonathan caught his breath. Four, no, five men rode through the night, their voices raw with war cries, their hands brandishing torch and tomahawk. He aimed his musket and fired. The sound of his shot screamed through the darkness.

Smoke cast its gray mantle over the homestead, marring Jonathan's vision and dimming the outlines of the attacking warriors. But it was the scene behind them that caused his stomach to tighten with sick despair. There his new barn roared with the fury of its burning. Flames scorched the sky with tongues of destruction. Nahum stood in the doorway of his cabin, shouting his own challenge at the invading band of Shawnee warriors. Fury and chaos swirled through Jonathan's mind as he reached for more ammunition.

From out of the smoky darkness, a flaming torch spun in Jonathan's direction. Behind it an Indian raced toward him, his upraised tomahawk illuminated in the feral blaze. Desperately Jonathan reloaded his musket. He raised the gun.

Firelight played wickedly off an ugly scar on the brave's cheek as he lunged toward Jonathan. For a moment time held its breath. A howl erupted from the Indian's lips.

The glint of a tomahawk descending. A shot. Silence. And the Indian lay dead at Jonathan's feet.

With a shriek of anger, the band retreated into the night. *Four braves and . . . and one in uniform.* Jonathan's eyes narrowed. *One white man.*

Nahum stepped behind Jonathan and laid his hand on his shoulder. "Nothing we could do. Came too quick. Didn't hear 'em until it was too late. 'Tis a shame, a mighty shame." Nahum dug the butt of his musket into the ground.

Jonathan watched the night swallow up the place where his enemies had fled. Then he turned toward the fire as its flames devoured his dreams.

Finally he turned back to Nahum and spoke. "Look at it. There's nothing left." Jonathan walked over to the barn that was fast becoming a smoldering skeleton. "It took only minutes to destroy what took weeks to build." He brushed his boot over the burning remains of the log that he had cut earlier that day. "This was the last one." A bitter laugh caught in his throat, choking him. He placed his hands on his hips and closed his eyes to the devastation.

"We saved the cabins." Nahum's voice was weak.

Jonathan looked at his friend, looked through him, at nothing. "The cabins." The words meant nothing. He ran a soot-covered hand over his forehead, leaving a streak of ash like an anointing of defeat.

Something glinted from beyond the fire. Nahum glanced at Jonathan and then looked away. Slowly he walked over and picked up a bottle with two fingers. "Look here," he called. Gingerly he sniffed the bottle's opening. "French brandy," he added with disgust.

Jonathan nodded, barely hearing. "A Frenchman. As I told you, the war never ends." He sat down and stared into the embers of his aspirations.

"We needs help." Nahum's words wafted to Jonathan across the dwindling smoke.

"I know."

"You gots to go to that uncle of yours. We ain't got no other choice."

Jonathan's eyes did not waver from the wreckage. He ran his fingers through his brown hair, now dirty with flying ash. "You don't know what it's like being the second son, with no future but that which charity will allow. I chose to escape all that and make my own future." He paused, his voice dropping. "A future that now lies in ashes."

"Don't be looking that way, Jonathan." Nahum's voice sounded far off, spoken from a place Jonathan could no longer reach.

A timber from the barn's roof crumbled into the embers beneath, causing sparks to spray across the ground and die at Jonathan's feet. He stared into the fire, watching the way the last flames licked up, curled around each other, and then fell splashing into the embers. He had seen a fire die that way before, many times. It was so long ago. He didn't want to remember. Not now. Not when his dreams lay shriveled and burned by the savage torch. Not when those dreams meant his freedom, freedom from everything he hated about the old life, about England, about Richard.

Nahum shook his head and sat beside him. "It's too much—the savages, the wilds, no civilized folk. It's more than just a young aristocrat and an old Negro can overcome. We needs help."

Jonathan flashed him a single penetrating look before staring again into the flames.

Nahum lifted his arm to encircle Jonathan's shoulders. "Me and ol' Bessie here," he patted the musket that lay across his lap, "we'll hold 'em off until you get back with a few of them militia boys. We been through a lot, Bessie and me. Won't have no trouble. You go on to Philadelphia now."

"Philadelphia." Jonathan pronounced the word like a broken talisman.

"Bessie and me, we fights for our freedom before. And we fights for ours here. Go. Get us help."

Jonathan did not look at Nahum as he spoke. Nothing existed but the ashes. He could see the fire again. It roared up in his mind, consuming the new barn, then dwindling, smaller, smaller, until it became a fire in an old stone fireplace from a time he wished he could forget. But he could not.

He saw the fireplace, ancient and awesome in its grandeur, built by Sir Frederick Grant more lifetimes ago than even the small village of Lockwood could remember. Jonathan's mind swirled back across the ocean to his childhood home, to England, to Lockwood, to the Grant estate. How often had they sat before that fireplace, the four of them—his father, mother, Richard, and him—with the firelight dancing on their fine silverware as they ate their silent meal?

He had stared into the smoldering ashes then as he stared into them now, losing himself in the strange dance of flame. Only then could he ignore the coldness around him, the coldness that embodied his father, that drove the man to beat his wife and sons, and the coldness that would not be defeated in death, but would later transform Richard into the man Jonathan now despised. How he hated it all.

When their father died in a freak accident just six years ago, Jonathan had thought they would be free. Richard and he would take their battered mother to the new world and there pursue their dreams, dreams they had woven since childhood. Richard, older than Jonathan by five years, would become a schoolteacher and Jonathan a frontiersman. Together they'd care for their mother, and none of them would look back at the Grant heritage they left behind.

But it hadn't turned out like that. Instead, Richard scorned their dreams and became Lord Grant, in position and in personality. With their father there had never been any honor, mercy, or love. And soon in Richard too those traits were squeezed out until there was nothing left but an insatiable desire for power and control, the desire to dominate everything and everyone near him, including his younger brother.

Even as Jonathan remembered it now, it seemed unbearable.

Jonathan had been seventeen then, too young to understand the changes in his brother, too young to fight the cruel accusations that Jonathan had caused their father's death, too young to know that when Richard banished their mother, she would never come back. He'd hoped that life would be different after his father's death. He'd hoped they would be happy. And perhaps they could have been if Richard had not changed. Even now the fury at that betrayal flooded through him, dwarfing everything that had happened since.

Jonathan shook his head, remembering how he had escaped it all, how he'd fled from the iron grip of a dead father, fled from the tightening tendrils of a heartless heritage, fled from the brother whom he had once loved. The colonies had become his refuge, the wilderness, his dream alone. A new world, a new life.

Here he would shed the vanity of his heritage. Here he would be free. In the savage wilderness of the new world, he would find his dream and defeat the devils that haunted him still.

But tonight the devils had won.

THREE

Nausea woke her. Kwelik raised her head from the dirty straw. Pain stabbed through the wound in her leg. Her hair fell in clumps before her eyes, blurring a scene too wretched for her to comprehend. *It isn't true. Oh, God, it can't be true.* But the dank smell of mildew and urine affirmed it—she was a prisoner, thrown into this hole like some kind of refuse. She couldn't bear it. She allowed her head to fall back to the straw. Surely she would awaken from this nightmare soon. She would open her eyes and see her father sitting before the fire, his Bible resting on one knee. Over the flames, fresh bear meat would be cooking, its aroma filling the room. In a moment the nightmare would end.

But it didn't. Slowly, with her head pounding as if in the dance of death, she raised herself to a sitting position. Her hands sank into the damp bedding. She stared blankly at one hand as it rose to push her hair from her face. She felt the blood still crusted there, tasted it on her swollen lip. Kwelik let her fingers linger in disbelief. Was this her face, her blood, her body that screamed in dull pain?

The cruel bite of iron drew her attention to her right leg. She watched her hand travel down as if it belonged to another and numbly tug at the shackle around her ankle. She traced the lock, the wide band, the bolt that held it. She had dreamed of freedom and received bondage.

Three minuscule rays of sunlight drifted in through the slats of wood above her. She squinted into the light. Somewhere out there the sun shone. Yes, she remembered the sun. It was bright and warm and kind. She shivered. Her head lolled to one side as she refocused on the meager hole that was her prison. It was less than five feet wide, she guessed, and about ten feet long, long enough to hold unknown terrors in the far shadows.

Kwelik's eyes widened as movement caught her attention. She willed her vision to clear as a rat scurried across the floor, up one wall, and out a knothole in a plank above. She wished she could follow it—up into the freedom that was the light. She would run and run and never look back. Perhaps then she could escape the enslavement of memories that would not be quieted . . . an arrow protruding from her father's chest, a death trail of smoke, a knife slashing amid the carnage, a shot and Lapawin's whine of defeat.

But would freedom await her outside this pit? Or would she find only another form of slavery? Kwelik forced the thoughts from her mind. All was a blur of terror and pain. No, the pain was real. She fingered the bandage around her leg. The wound burned where the arrow had bitten through her flesh. If only she had some of her father's herb tea to quench it. If only . . .

She shut her mind to the thought and attempted to stand. The ground reeled beneath her as blackness swirled in and out across her vision. She stumbled into the corner and retched until she felt there could be nothing left inside her. The stench of her own vomit mixed with the pungent air as she slumped back onto the pile of moldy straw.

Her thoughts spun in a flurry of confusion. How did this happen to her? Where was she? Where was God? This misery could not be real. Any minute now it would all disappear. It would be mist before the fire.

In a rush of memory, the horror resurfaced. She dug her hands into the straw and allowed great wracking sobs to overtake her. Her father, her village, Little Cloud, Lapawin. She nearly retched again. Her father's words echoed in her head, *All dead*. No, not Little Cloud. She had saved him. She clung to that single fact as a piece of driftwood in the raging ocean of her grief. Tankawon was not dead. She curled back into the straw and allowed darkness to overtake her.

~

Above Kwelik a shadow flickered across the light. How long had she been asleep? An hour, a day, an eternity? She strained her eyes and looked toward the planks above. Was it the rat returning to its hole? No. She sat up, her head clearer this time. A man.

"How's our little kitten?" a familiar voice mocked.

Her stomach turned at the sound.

"Get out of there. There's work to be done. No more sleeping."

Kwelik shuddered and pushed herself back into the shadows. She could feel malice oozing toward her like a tangible thing.

Sunlight flooded into her prison as the hatch was pulled open above her. The brightness assaulted Kwelik's vision. She squinted into the light and moved back further, praying to disappear into the shadows.

A face appeared in the opening. She saw a long, hooked nose and lips that were unusually thin, as if in a permanent grimace of disapproval. She stared into the small, dark eyes of the French lieutenant and then looked away. Did the white man's world breed the hatred she saw? Was that why her Papa had escaped it? She cringed in the corner, as far as possible from the festering disease of this man's hate.

"Half-breed." The lieutenant's voice cut across distance between them. "Get up. You have work to do."

Kwelik looked up into the long barrel of a flintlock musket. Another man stood behind it. She could not see his face. "Climb on out of there now. We don't want no trouble," the man said in French, his voice like the rumble of gravel down a hillside.

Kwelik did not move. She stood transfixed by the musket. She'd heard of what such fire sticks could do to a person, but she had never seen one before. It was said they could rip a hole in your chest large enough to stick your hand in. For the first time, Kwelik wondered what it would feel like to die. How great was the pain? Would the shock numb her senses? Would she see Jesus as Papa had? Perhaps it was not a bad choice.

Impatiently the lieutenant repeated the command, gesturing with his hand as he spoke in the Algonquian tongue. "Climb out."

She did not know what made her try to obey. Maybe it was because the dream of freedom had not yet died. Perhaps it was that fragment of hope that refused to be smothered by her grief. Whatever it was, she gripped the edge of the opening and attempted to pull herself from the pit. Yesterday it would have been a simple task, but today she was too weak. Her arms refused her command. With a groan she landed back on the dirt floor.

"Get up," the lieutenant repeated. "Or do you need a little more motivation?" He grabbed the musket from the other man's hand.

Kwelik was on her feet, her hands again on the planks. She grunted and pulled with all her might. This time she almost made it.

"Guess you're not much of a cat after all," the lieutenant sneered. He ground his boot heel into the fingers of her left hand, still gripping the wood.

With a cry of pain, Kwelik fell back onto the straw beneath.

A laugh floated down from above her and wrapped its chilling fingers around the wisp of hope that still lived in her heart. She sought to shut the sinister sound from her mind, but it echoed there and would not be silenced.

"Here, kitten, try this." A crude ladder made of rope fell through the opening and landed at her feet. Shaking, she grabbed it and succeeded in climbing to the surface.

The French fort was not large. Walls of timber reached to the sky on all sides, defying escape. A few buildings were scattered about, the living quarters to her right and several storage sheds behind her near the middle of the complex. Everything was just as Black Hawk had described it last summer.

On the far side of the fort, a group of soldiers gathered around a small fire. Their laughter grated across Kwelik's nerves. She turned her head, noticing piles of boxes in every direction. She would have liked to see what they contained. Dried food, cloth, or perhaps some of those shiny pots her father had traded for two summers ago? Or maybe they held more of those dreadful fire sticks.

The lieutenant threw a shovel in her direction and set down a bucket of lime. "Enjoy cleaning the latrines," he said as he departed for the far side of the fort.

Kwelik was glad to see him go. The other man pushed her with the butt of his musket until she picked up the bucket and shovel and followed him to the latrine area.

The stench of the latrines made the pit smell like a field of wildflowers by comparison. But she dared not disobey. She did not want to see the fire made by the sticks of death that so many of the fort's men carried. She steeled herself against the nausea and bent to her duty with vigor.

At midday a butterfly flitted through the fort and stopped momentarily to alight on a box near her. She paused to watch it, a lump growing in her throat. She had believed that God would give her wings someday, wings just like the butterfly. Had it been only a fool's hope? No, it couldn't be. Someday she would be free. Someday, but not today. She took a deep breath and gagged. Today she must survive.

And to survive she must cling to her hope. Kwelik clenched her teeth and gripped the shovel's handle until the rough wood made dents in her skin. She must remember that she was not alone. There was One who understood suffering and pain. Jesus Christ. He had been mocked and spat upon. Yet even as He died, He did not waver from the will of the Father. Kwelik determined to think only of Him, despite the cruel jeers of her oppressor. Christ would be her guide out of this nightmare—not the beaver, nor the raccoon, nor the eagle that soared across the heavens. No, God Himself was her spirit guide. She would cling to the remembrance of Him, no matter how distant He seemed, knowing that Jesus, at least, understood her pain and humiliation. He too had suffered, and yet He lived again. She would also live.

At once she was glad for the grime that covered her. It became a shield against the loathsome eyes of her enemies. She retreated into her shell and fought to ignore her revulsion. The hands gripping the shovel were not her own. The matted hair in front of her eyes belonged to another. It was not Skye with Topaz Lights who now cleaned latrines in a French fort. No, she was out in the fields chasing a butterfly. See, it was there now. It fluttered before her vision, taking flight into the summer sky. Lapawin was with her. They wrestled together in the meadow and raced to the stream. The smell in her nose was that of moss growing from the damp rocks at the edge of the water. All was peaceful, calm, perfect. Until Lapawin barked and ran back to the village. If she followed him, she knew what she would find.

What had happened to her innocent dreams? Tears welled in Kwelik's eyes and spilled onto her hands. Had God abandoned her? Where was He? Her people were dead, herself immured in a fate worse than death. Papa always said that God was with you every moment. He lived in His children's hearts, communing with their spirits. His love and mercy were never more than a thought away. So where was He now? She felt no love, only emptiness—no mercy, only affliction.

Kwelik could almost hear her father's voice. She sought to remember its nuances, the way his voice caressed her name. She could not. Even his face was a blur. Was he hidden behind her tears? But the words were still clear. Those could not be taken from her. She repeated them to herself, willing herself to keep believing, to hang on to the truth, to trust the words though everything around her denied them.

No one can love me like God does. There's nothing in this world as glorious as knowing God in my heart of hearts, experiencing Him as my Savior and friend. "For I am persuaded that neither death, nor life, nor angels, nor principalities, nor powers, nor things present, nor things to come, nor height, nor depth, nor any other creature, shall be able to separate me from the love of God, which is in Christ Jesus my Lord." She repeated the phrases.

Ever since she was born, Kwelik had been told of this personal experience with God. And she had believed. She remembered the many times she had spoken with Him, felt His touch, His discipline, and His joy. She had never doubted His presence—until today. Now despite her father's words, her heart felt cold, empty, a barren cavern of agony. Only the voice of grief seemed to echo there.

The promises and assurances faded from her mind, replaced by a single cry: "My God, *my God, why hast Thou forsaken me?*"

FOUR

The tomahawk felt good in Little Cloud's hand. He squeezed his fist around it, feeling the smooth wood against his palm. His heart quivered with uneasy fervor. It was his now. No one would take it from him. He shook the blade at the sky. "It's mine. I won it with bravery." His voice cracked on the last word.

Resolutely he pushed from his mind the fact that he had stolen the weapon from Long Brow's hut that morning. No one knew. No one would suspect him. Not one person in this whole Shawnee village paid any attention to him at all, unless it was time to gather garlic and maple bark, as he was supposed to be doing now.

Sure, Chief Tumaskan and the others welcomed him when he had first stumbled into their village a week before, telling his story of gruesome destruction. He'd hoped they would honor him as a brave returning from battle. It had been a fool's hope. Little Cloud kicked the empty basket away from him.

"Children's work." He spat the words to no one and flung himself to the ground. The basket glared at him, accused him, from a patch of garlic not five feet away. He turned his back and caressed the tomahawk. His destiny was glory and revenge, not the menial task of gathering stinking bulbs.

Little Cloud had traveled far from the village to hunt his ignoble prey. Frustration and shame had driven him past the regular gathering fields. He watched the sun glint off the sharp edge of his weapon. No one could spy on him here. He scowled. They treated him like a child. *Go fetch water for the braves. Stir that pot. Don't let it burn, or I'll flay you alive. Chew this hide. It has to be soft enough to make moccasins for Long Brow, you know. Can't you do anything right?*

He was sick of their talk. But what else could he expect? He had been a coward. He'd watched his village burn, his people die. Yet he had done nothing. Then he'd run away and let his sister be captured by the enemy. She'd been the brave one. She had been the warrior and he the nursling. Perhaps it was right that he was treated like a babe, at the beck and call of his elders.

Little Cloud frowned and ran his finger down the edge of the blade. He was a warrior now. He would not show his back to the enemy again. The white man—he was the enemy.

Yes, it was the white man's fault. He would have resisted the Shawanowi, but the evil sneer from the white man had frightened him. The white man was a devil. Little Cloud dug the end of his tomahawk into the ground, pretending it was the white man's head. He cursed the half of him that shared the white man's blood.

"I'll get that white man," he vowed. "I'll find Kwelik and save her. I'll hear no more talk of peace, of love, of forgiveness."

Little Cloud gripped his weapon fiercely, stood, and held it above his head. He would choose his own destiny—the warpath of revenge. His father's God had betrayed him and his people. He would trust Him no longer. *The God of the white man is dead*, he told himself. He would believe the lies no more.

Savagely Little Cloud yanked a garlic bulb from the ground and threw it toward his basket. Before the next moon, he would prove his prowess. He would throw off the things of the past and become a warrior. Father was a fool. A brave lived to kill or be killed. Next time he, Little Cloud, would be the killer. He threw his head back and faced the sun, solidifying his vow to the gods of the sky and woods.

~

Hook Nose, as Kwelik soon named the lieutenant, checked on her five times that day. Like a bird of prey, he hovered over her and attacked with words of malice. Only once did he allow her to have water. She was glad when darkness finally descended, and she was taken back to the pit and shackled. She fell onto the straw and felt her stomach turn over on itself. Her head bent as she wept, "Oh, God, save me . . ."

Her plea was interrupted by the scraping of the hatch above. A head poked through the opening, surrounded by the glow from a candle. The light reflected from the round face of a boy no more than fourteen years of age, barely older than Little Cloud. His hand trembled, causing the flame to throw wild shadows onto the walls of her pen.

"I-I'm Philippe," the boy stuttered.

Kwelik remained silent, wondering if he was friend or foe. She stared at him, her face void of all expression.

The boy tried again, pointing at his chest. "Philippe. I'm Philippe," he repeated.

Warily Kwelik nodded and backed toward the wall, away from the unmerciful light of the candle.

Philippe's forehead wrinkled in consternation. "Come on now, it's okay. Look." He produced a tin from somewhere behind him. The smell of stale bread wafted over to Kwelik.

"Here, look, I brought you food. Food." Philippe thrust the tin toward her.

Tentatively Kwelik took a step forward and reached up for it.

"There you go," the boy soothed. "It's all I could get."

Kwelik pushed a piece into her mouth and allowed a tiny smile of thanks to brush over her lips.

The boy grinned and bobbed his head. "I brought you some water too." He held a cup in her direction. "Don't let anyone know though. I'm not supposed to come here." He pushed a lock of mousy brown hair from his eyes. "I'll come back later, if I can, with more food." A look of chagrin passed over the boy's face. "Sure wish you could understand me." He sighed, then glanced over his shoulder into the darkness. A tiny gasp burst from his lips. "Oh no, here comes Berneau. I'd better scat." He shut the hatch with only the barest thud.

Kwelik heard his footsteps scamper into the night. For a long time she continued to stare at the place where he had last been. A friend? It seemed impossible in this dungeon of heartache. The boy certainly had a glib tongue. Who knew what secrets would fall from one who thought her ignorant of his language. That, at least, was something to consider.

Suddenly she was glad for all those endless French lessons her father had insisted upon. "Come on, Papa, let's go hunt wildflowers," she'd moan. "I don't feel like studying today. Who needs French anyway?"

Her father would then tousle her hair and point to the lesson in front of her. "The world's changing, Skye," he would say. "The life we live here in our village can't last forever. The world of the Indian is shrinking. Every day it gets a little smaller." His face would then become grave. "You, your children, and your children's children must live in the world that will be."

"What about you and Mama?" she had asked.

"Oh, Skye, we'll be gone by then," he answered.

She had hated to think of that. The thought made an ugly knot in her stomach.

"Listen, child," he continued, "even now the English and French fight for this land. Make no mistake, one of them will have it. You must be prepared to live your life in their world."

"Oh, Papa, you're too serious," she complained. "You know I'd much rather be playing in the meadow or hunting grasshoppers or trying to fly like the sparrow I saw yesterday. It's such a beautiful day." She would cajole and squirm and crane her head toward the door until her father lost patience.

"Skye," he would say, his voice becoming stern, "stop dreaming and concentrate on your lessons."

Then she'd sigh and continue, "*Merci*, *Mademoiselle*. *Merci*, *Madam*. *Merci*, Papa-sage." At that, her father could not keep the smile from sneaking a peek from the corner of his mouth. She could see that smile so clearly in her mind now. But Papa was dead. The knowledge turned like a knife in her gut.

~

By the end of the second week, Kwelik had graduated to peeling potatoes and other roots in the kitchen. The vegetables made her mouth water, but she was not allowed to taste even the scraps. That night in the depths of her prison pit, discouragement hunted her like a cat intent on the kill.

Perhaps it would have been better to have died with the rest. God seemed so silent these days. Had He truly forsaken her? Had her dreams been in error? Had they angered Him? Was this prison a punishment for sins she did not know she'd committed? Her father would say no. Did she believe her father's words?

Remember. Remember. The word pounded into her head with the insistence of a faith that would not surrender to despair. *Remember the buck that came when Mama prayed.* Even now she could almost taste the tangy meat. That buck had been a sign of God's unfailing love for her. She had believed it then. She must believe it now.

Kwelik gripped the damp straw in one hand and squeezed her eyes shut. She fingered the small piece of antler that hung from a leather thong around her neck. It had come from that deer. She saw again her mother's face as she had placed the token around her neck with words spoken low, intense, and searching: *Be brave enough to believe, daughter. God will never fail you.* Those words still laid bare Kwelik's weakness and doubt.

"Oh, God," she whispered, her hand still clutching the antler piece, "give me the courage to believe. Even now, even here." She opened her eyes.

God was out there somewhere. He saw through the walls of the fort into the pit and into her stomach. And, just as in the winter of 1730, He saw that it was empty.

The hatch above her groaned as someone opened it from the outside. Kwelik watched it with growing dread, knowing she couldn't bear another visit from Hook Nose.

But it was the boy's head that poked through the opening. "Hey, I brought you some more food. This time it's potatoes and rabbit. It was great at dinner." He rubbed his stomach and hopped down into the pit.

His quick movement startled Kwelik. She scuttled into the corner, alarmed by his brazen attitude. Was this white boy like all the rest? How could she trust him?

Philippe held out the tin of food like a peace offering. A look of perplexity crossed his face. "I didn't mean to scare you. It's all right."

Kwelik hesitated. Then she took the plate from his hand and returned to her corner, allowing the shadows to disguise her features.

Philippe didn't seem to mind her distrust. He plopped down on the dirty hay and ran his fingers through his hair. "Sure smells bad in here. Guess they don't ever clean it out." The boy's nose wrinkled as he spoke.

Kwelik watched him warily while she ate the remnants of rabbit bones, sucking out the marrow.

"Thought you wouldn't mind some company," Philippe continued. "Been awfully lonely here since Mama died. No one even knows I exist, except if there's a problem with the wall of the fort. Then I'm supposed to report it." His tone turned conspiratorial. "I'll tell you a secret just 'cause you can't understand me anyway." His voice dropped. "There's a board rotted through on the west side of the fort. It's all full of bugs. One little push, and a whole piece would crumble away."

Kwelik's head snapped up. Quickly she lowered it again, attempting to hide her interest. She concentrated on the bone in her hand, her mind racing at the possibilities of escape.

Philippe leaned forward and continued in a whisper, "I think I could squeeze out if I had to. I'm thinking about it too. If Berneau yells at me again, I might just slip out and never come back." He kicked at the straw with his booted heel. "I'd have been gone weeks ago, except I don't have anywhere to go." He paused.

Kwelik searched his face, wondering if it was a tear that was gathering in his eye.

Philippe's voice choked over his next words. "Don't know why we ever left France. My father was going to make it rich in the fur trade. He was all full of hopes and schemes. And I believed him. All he got was a bloody scalp, though, when the Iroquois attacked us. Mama and I made it to the fort, but she died of the fever." This time a tear did escape to trail down his cheek.

Has no one ever listened to the boy? Kwelik crept closer.

Philippe took a deep breath. "So here I am, training to fight for a land that I hate and dreaming of my France all the while. Someday I'll go home again." His eyes held a faraway look so familiar to Kwelik.

Even in her own pain, she pitied the boy. Without further thought, she drew close to him and put her hand over his.

Philippe smiled, sniffled, and wiped his forearm across his nose. "That's the most sympathy anyone's shown me here. And from a half-breed too—English and Indian, twice an enemy, who doesn't even know what I'm saying." He shook his head, a look of determination washing his features. "I'll bring you more food later tonight. I promise," he said. Then he pulled himself out of the pit and was gone, darkness swallowing the place where he had been.

Philippe was true to his word, bringing bread and more potatoes later that night. For the first time in many days, Kwelik fell asleep with a full stomach.

~

Kwelik scrubbed at the spot with renewed vigor. If she didn't get it out this time, Hook Nose would hit her again. The linen shirt felt cool beneath her fingers. She wished she could lose herself in it, forget the boxes crowding in around her, forget the shackle around her ankle, forget the soldiers with muskets who marched near the fort's walls.

"Not good enough." The lieutenant's voice invaded the silence of her thoughts. "What's wrong, kitten? Afraid to get your hands wet?" With that, he tipped the wash basin toward her, soaking her skirt and splashing dirty water over the clean shirts behind her. He stepped toward her, his hand upraised.

"Let her alone, Berneau." Philippe's voice sounded older than his years. He rushed from a nearby doorway and placed his body between Kwelik and her adversary. "Leave her be."

"You taking sides with this half-breed?" The words dripped with hate.

"Better not let the captain hear you say that," Philippe retorted. His voice cracked and sounded boyish again. "He's fathered plenty of half-breeds."

Berneau laughed, the same wicked sound that Kwelik had learned to despise. Before either she or Philippe could react, Berneau stepped around the boy and shoved Kwelik to the ground.

Philippe grabbed the man's sleeve and punched ineffectually at his midsection. "Stop it." He sounded close to tears. Kwelik wished she could comfort him, but she dared not move lest Berneau's fist find her jaw once again.

"Stop it!" Philippe grabbed Berneau's collar and tugged with all his might. "Don't you have someone else to be mean to?"

Berneau lifted the boy with one hand and threw him into the wooden crates that surrounded them. "Who else is there?" He cocked his fist to slam it into Philippe's face.

"Hey, Berneau, get back to your post. Let the boy alone," a man yelled from the wall. "Looks like we got trouble." He pointed his musket over the wall and fired into the trees.

Someone returned the fire. The fort was under attack. Shouts came from all directions as men grabbed their muskets and raced toward their posts. The sound of myriad explosions burst into the air as the defenders fired, reloaded, and fired again. Kwelik covered her ears and sank into the hollow made by two stacks of crates.

"Oh, God, oh, God, oh, God," she whispered. "Save me."

A boom sounded from outside the gates, followed by the distinct whistle of a cannonball. Kwelik heard its scream a second before it hit. The ball landed not thirty feet from her, igniting the ammunition in one of the boxes. The explosion threw her into the crates. They tumbled on her, covering her like a tomb. With a shriek she scratched her way free, only to be stopped by the merciless grip of her shackle. She could feel the heat of the approaching fire. A box burst into flames to her right. A stack of crates caught fire on her left. Trapped! Desperately she clawed at the iron that still encircled her ankle.

The fire raged closer, its malevolent tongue licking the shirts she had so recently washed. Her scream tore through the air. From out of the smoke, the image of Philippe materialized, a hatchet in one hand. Without a word, he cast himself onto her shackle, hacking furiously at the iron binding. A crate crashed near them, spitting fiery embers in all directions. Kwelik smelled the foul odor of burning hair as she brushed the ash from Philippe's head. He did not look up. In a moment it would be too late.

With a shout of triumph, Philippe broke through her shackle and cast it aside. As he yanked her from the circle of flames, the burning crates tumbled into the spot she had just vacated. Her eyes blurred and watered from the smoke. A cough racked her body. She stumbled, her hand automatically reaching for Philippe. He squeezed her arm.

"Run!" he yelled.

"Philippe, come with me." Kwelik stretched out her hand and spoke in flawless French.

Understanding dawned on Philippe's face. The rotten board. He took a step toward her, his hands spasmodically gripping and then releasing his shirt. "I can't," he shouted. "The English will kill me. Go on." He pointed to the west wall. "The board is there, fifth over from the big post. I'll make sure no one sees your escape."

Kwelik turned toward him one last time. "Philippe." She paused, torn between freedom and concern. "Thank you."

The corner of his mouth quirked into a sad smile. "Everyone's always leaving me. And I don't even know your name."

She brushed her fingers across his cheek. "Skye."

FIVE

Kwelik's first breath of freedom filled her lungs like a newfound dream. Bits of decayed timber still clung to her back. She glanced behind her only once, but Philippe was gone. She hoped he'd make it back to France one day, that someday he too would be free. But that was beyond her power. For now the woods beckoned her, as if she were their long-lost child. She raced into their arms, leaving the nightmare behind her.

Or so she thought.

Before Kwelik had taken her second breath of freedom, a hand clamped around her shoulder and threw her to the ground. Again she found herself staring down the wide muzzle of a musket. She stifled her scream and pressed herself into the dirt. She stared up into the stony face of a militia man, his red hair glowing dully in the torch light behind him. Light blue eyes glared into her own. He gripped her collar and pulled her to her feet.

"Look what I found, lads. I believe she be a French spy." Her newest captor did not loosen his grip as he turned toward the trees where another man was emerging.

Kwelik squirmed and sank her teeth into his hand. This time she would not give up her freedom without a fight. His yowl verified her success. For a moment, she was free once more, but his long arm snaked around her and again pulled her tight to his chest.

"Now ye be still, lassie," he whispered in her ear, his moustache brushing her skin, "lest ye want to be feeling the cold bite of metal in your belly." He poked his musket into her side to confirm his threat.

Kwelik slumped against him, defeated.

"What do you have there, Red?" the other man called as he approached them.

"Don't rightly know," Red responded, raising the hand that Kwelik had bitten. "Got the bite of a banshee though. Drew me blood, she did."

"That little slip of a girl almost got the best of our famous O'Malley?" the other man teased. "Lucky all our enemies aren't of the female persuasion."

"I've heard enough of your fool tongue, Williams. Caught her running from that French fort. Now the captain'll want to ask the lassie here a few questions, if I be right. And since ye think yourself so much better than a lowly Irishman, I, your humble servant, will turn the dark-haired lass over to you." O'Malley gave a mock bow, his grip remaining firm on both his captured prize and his musket.

Williams dragged Kwelik back toward the main body of English troops. Her head throbbed. How had this happened to her? Was she not free just moments ago? The trees—had they not beckoned her to safety? But the nightmare would not end. From one captivity to the next. Would God never allow her to be free?

"Keep going, woman," Williams muttered as he jabbed the mouth of his musket into her shoulder.

Kwelik shuddered.

"Retreat, men; it's getting too dark. That's enough for tonight," came a voice off to her right. She turned her head to see a man with his bayonet raised to the pale outline of the moon. In a rush the men pulled back, hauling their single cannon behind them.

The encampment lay a mile upstream. By the time they reached it, night had fallen, and a dozen tiny fires littered the clearing. "Cap'n," Williams shouted, "we got ourselves a prisoner." He headed toward a tent near the middle of the camp. Kwelik could see the vague outline of a man inside. Pulling the flap aside with the end of his musket, Williams pushed her through the opening.

"Think we caught a spy, Cap'n. O'Malley found her running from the enemy fort. He thought she might know something." Williams thrust her toward a cot on the other side of the tent and stood guard by the door, his musket held tightly in one hand.

"Red, eh?" The captain looked up from the maps lying on a makeshift desk. "I suppose he'll be getting up wind for another of those long speeches on the bravery of the Irish. I don't know if I can stand to hear it again." He clapped Williams on the shoulder and turned toward Kwelik. "Well, let's see what we've got." He motioned for her to sit.

Light from a lantern on the desk reflected into her blue eyes.

"So you're a half-breed. Do you speak English?"

Kwelik nodded.

"Good. Let's begin." He placed his muddied boot on the cot and leaned over her. "Why were you in the French fort?"

For a moment Kwelik hesitated. Why should she tell this man anything? And yet why shouldn't she? Perhaps if she answered well, he would let her go. With that hope whispering through her, Kwelik took a deep breath and replied, "A man named Berneau led an attack on my village. He killed my people and captured me."

"You speak well."

"My father was a missionary to the Indians. He married my mother, a Delaware squaw, over twenty years ago."

"Where is this father now?"

"Dead." Her throat closed around the word and refused to tell more.

"She's probably lying, Cap'n. We've seen no English missionaries in these parts." Williams lowered the muzzle of his gun toward her.

The captain waved him off. "Doesn't matter. What she knows about the French does." He turned back toward the cot. "Tell me about their armaments."

Kwelik shook her head. "I don't know. I saw a lot of those." She pointed to the musket held by Williams.

The captain nodded. "How did you escape?"

Kwelik paused. She would not endanger Philippe, not even if they killed her for it. "A French boy had mercy on me." She clamped her jaws shut.

The captain's eyes narrowed. "But how did you get out?"

Kwelik studied the floor of the tent. "Everyone was so busy fighting off your attack that they didn't notice him letting me out." She prayed that he would be satisfied with her incomplete answer.

A breeze fluttered through the tent flap, lifted a paper from the desk, and deposited it at the captain's feet. He stared at it for a moment before leaning over to pick it up. Kwelik watched as he folded the sheet and placed it on the desk.

"Anyway . . ." He turned back toward her. "What was I saying? Oh, yes. How many men did you see? When did they change posts? Which gate has the least posted men?"

The questions went on for two hours, until the captain determined that Kwelik knew nothing more of value.

The captain fingered the blade of his bayonet. "I think that's it, Williams. Take her away."

Williams stood at attention. "What do you want me to do with her, Cap'n?"

Kwelik held her breath.

The captain paused. His eyes flickered to hers and hardened. Then he turned away. "Tie her with the other three. Jennings can sell her with the rest of them in Philadelphia. Tell him to consider himself paid."

Kwelik's head dropped.

"Yes, sir." Williams lowered his gun at Kwelik. "Let's go, squaw."

She stepped outside the tent to see the firelight playing off a band of ragtag men squatting around their respective campfires. Was it a trick of the light, or were their faces as tired and worn as hers? Hopelessness hovered in the air, and she discovered that it was not only her own.

"Hey, what did the captain say? When are we getting out of here?" A man wearing the buckskin of a frontiersman stepped toward Williams. "You were in there long enough. Did he say anything about going home?"

"Yeah," piped up another, "he said we'd be done by now. I want to go home. Got a wife and three little ones. With my luck, the Indians got 'em while I've been off on this fool attack."

Other men, including some wearing the red coats of the British army, mumbled their agreement.

Williams ignored them. "Hey, Jennings, got another one for

you," he yelled to a man at the far end of the camp. "Cap'n says this should cover what he owes you for your services."

Williams threw Kwelik toward the stranger. She stumbled and fell at his feet. On hands and knees, she raised her head to look into his sneering face.

"Led him here without losing a man, didn't I," Jennings growled, "and all he wants to give me is an Indian squaw?" He grunted his disapproval.

"She speaks English. You can get a good price for her—maybe even better than for them." Williams waved toward a group of two men and a woman tied to a tree on the outskirts of the camp.

"Sure, might get a decent price for her in the Carolinas, but I ain't going south this fall. Gotta get up to Boston to make me a deal in tea."

Williams scowled. "Take her or leave her; it's up to you."

For a brief moment, hope soared in Kwelik, then died again as she saw the greed flash across Jennings's face.

"You can get a good price for her in Philadelphia," Williams continued. "Maybe even enough to pay for a new musket. Couldn't hit a Frenchie at ten feet with that one. Maybe a savage though. Never know."

"Humph." Jennings rubbed his hand over his face. "You're lucky I never had to." His laughter erupted in a loud guffaw. "I'll take her."

Kwelik's body gave way beneath her.

SIX

Philadelphia, September 1743

"Silence! I will hear no more lies!"

Jonathan's fist crashed down on the smooth maple of his uncle's desk. Neither man moved as a fine silver candlestick tottered and tumbled to the floor with a muted thud. The seconds froze and crackled along Jonathan's nerves, but he did not allow his eyes to waver from his uncle's rotund face. He studied the small eyes—narrowed further with enmity—the pale cheeks, the drooping chin, the aristocratic tilt of his head. The man had once been handsome. Jonathan noticed the bit of powder that had escaped his uncle's wig to settle in the crack of his nose. Somehow it eased his tension.

"Now may we get back to the business at hand?" Jonathan's voice again held the falsely polite tone he had learned from his father.

"You must learn to control yourself, Jonathan. There is no need for such antics." The smooth, oily intonation of his uncle's words fired Jonathan's anger again.

"The militia, Uncle." Jonathan squeezed the title from between his teeth like an insult.

"Yes, yes," his uncle sighed, drawing his chair closer to the desk. Casually he picked up a quill from its holder, studied the end of it, and dipped it into the inkwell. "I suppose I could sign this paper, and you would get your soldiers. But . . ."

Jonathan clenched his fists and remained silent as his uncle slowly returned the quill to its holder without signing the paper. He watched the half-slit eyes rise to pin him with a look of disdain. "You must learn to bridle your tongue, boy, lest your religion be in vain."

"I claim no such religion." Jonathan's voice was low, controlled.

"Besides, I only said what every civilized man already knows," his uncle continued. "The frontier is for fools, criminals, and vagabonds." The man paused and flicked the end of the quill with deliberate spite. "Tell me, Nephew, which are you?" His fleshy lips pursed in disapproval.

Jonathan leaned forward, his hands gripping the polished surface of the desk. "I, at least, am a man who knows what it means to be one. Surrounded by such fluff and finery, you must think yourself still in England." Jonathan spat out the last word. He leaned closer, his amber eyes blazing with the fire of restrained fury. "You're not in England anymore, Uncle. Remember that."

Jonathan straightened and walked to the window. "What lovely cloth," he commented, abruptly changing the subject to allow his words to sink in. He ran his fingers lightly up and down the window's deep purple drapery and waited.

Outside, horse-driven carriages rattled along the cobblestone street that ran parallel to his uncle's mansion. A man dressed in the simple garb of a Quaker tipped his hat to a group of ladies before respectfully moving on. Jonathan looked up from the scene, his eyes catching the glint of distant sunlight as it reflected off the surface of the Delaware River. He studied the silhouette of a large schooner pulling slowly into the docks. Compared to the open expanse of the frontier, the city seemed crowded and dirty, with merchants, sailors, and urchins scuttling about the streets like so many vermin. Jonathan shuddered and dropped his gaze, refocusing on the purpose of his visit.

This conversation is much like a fencing match, he thought. *Spar, jab, retreat, look for the telltale hint of blood, of weakness, then go in for the kill.* It was the only type of communication his family had ever known. Besides the beatings, of course. Jonathan closed his eyes and sighed. The vision of his mother, her eye colored with a purple bruise, invaded his thoughts. "A simple fall," his father had insisted to the neighbors. A lie. There was always a lie.

Jonathan opened his eyes. He had thought to purge himself through a new life on the frontier, where a man survived by wisdom and might, rather than by smooth words of innuendo and deceit. But here he was, once again in a verbal duel that reeked of the very things he hated about his childhood. Yet it must be done.

Jonathan dropped the curtain and turned back toward his uncle to press his advantage. "No, you're not in England anymore." Jonathan's eyes narrowed. "Beware, Uncle, this is an honest land. It unmasks men like you."

"Ah, a little comfort is good for a man. But perhaps you wouldn't understand that."

"Perhaps not. Tell me, is it such things that make you into a man?" Jonathan paused. "That is not the kind of man I would wish to become." He fingered the drapery again. It was an old argument, an old fight. He was tired of it.

In one fluid movement, Jonathan strode back toward his uncle, his voice dropping in its intensity. "Hear this, Uncle, I will succeed on the frontier. It challenges a man and calls him to greatness. Your world is naught but death."

"Greatness? Bah," his uncle scoffed, motioning to Jonathan's worn buckskin shirt and pants. "You look more like a savage than a man. That is not my idea of greatness."

"You wouldn't know a great man if he walked up and spat in your face. Greatness is more than wigs and fine clothes. It's found in here." Jonathan thumped his fist on his chest. "Something you would not know."

"Wouldn't I?" his uncle sneered. "It's not I begging for help to survive in your precious wilderness. What will a few more men with muskets do for you?" Without looking at Jonathan, he reached for his snuffbox and casually took a sniff. "Ah, yes, much better." He wrinkled his nose and rubbed one forefinger lightly across his upper lip. "It is you who ought to return to England. Run along now, Johnny—run back home to your big brother." His voice did not lose the even, flippant tone.

He studied the snuffbox a moment longer before lowering it to the desk. He smoothed his hand across the maple desktop and then took a cloth and rubbed to a brilliant shine the place where Jonathan's fist had dulled the finish. "Beautiful, isn't it?" He smiled, back to the game. "Some poor carpenter made it from the first tree cut for my estate here in Philadelphia. Do you have such a desk at your home out with the savages? Or perhaps you have forgotten how to read and write?" His eyes flickered up to meet Jonathan's.

Jonathan ignored the jibe.

His uncle tilted back in his chair, his cool, detached voice tossing another taunt toward the younger man. "Or are you afraid to go back to England?"

Jonathan turned away.

"Why did you run away from England, Johnny? What were you afraid of? Your brother? Or your long-dead father?"

Jonathan drew a quick breath. What *did* he fear? Was it only that he knew that his brother would dominate his life? Or was it more than that? Was he afraid that what had happened to Richard would somehow happen to him, that after all his fine words, he too would use his Grant name to cover acts of unspeakable cruelty? Jonathan thrust the latter thought from his mind. "I came here to live my own life. I will not be my brother's minion. I am more a man than that."

"Are you?"

The question caused Jonathan to chuckle. *Thrust. Parry. Dodge the feint. See the opportunity; try for the kill.* "Who is his minion now?" Jonathan's voice was mocking, and he hated it.

His uncle's eyes narrowed. "Careful, boy." His words rasped with the evidence of a direct hit.

Jonathan moved closer. "Is it worth the price?"

His uncle straightened. "Go back to England, Johnny. There's nothing for you here."

"Go back to bondage? Never. Besides," he mimicked his uncle's supercilious tone, "it is no longer my home, as even you must know, but Richard's." Jonathan watched his uncle lick his lips at the opening Jonathan offered.

"Ah, yes." He adjusted his wig, his bored look replaced by intensity as he leaned forward in his chair. "And you fear Richard, do you not?"

Jonathan chuckled again, his stomach turning at the sound of his own voice. The man had too easily taken the bait. "No, not fear, never fear. What kind of man would fear his own brother? No, I only despise him." Jonathan pretended to flick a bit of dust from his sleeve as his eyes added the words, *As I do you.*

But his uncle was not defeated. He rubbed his hand over the desk again, admiring it briefly. His gaze slid to Jonathan. "Go back to England, Johnny. There is no such luxury for you here, soldiers or no."

"This," Jonathan tapped the desk with his forefinger, "is only the luxury of slavery." He ground the last word between his teeth. "I chose this land, Uncle. I was not forced to come."

"Are you sure?"

"I am." Jonathan pulled a wooden chair closer to his uncle's desk and sat in it. He had wearied of the duel. It was a fool's game. "Now," he continued in a voice devoid of expression, "will you ask the Assembly to protect its frontier or not?"

His uncle's heavy sigh filled the air. "Yes, I suppose I can bring your request before them. There is a meeting two days hence. Heaven forbid that I refuse the request of one of my *loyal* colonists." He slurred the word to make it an insult.

The gap between his uncle's front teeth showed as the man gave him a haughty smile. His uncle reached for his watch and snapped it open. Gold glinted in the afternoon sun. "Now is that all? I have important people to attend."

Jonathan nodded once and turned to leave.

His uncle's voice arrested him. "Do not imagine that I will support your foolish fantasy."

Jonathan's jaw tightened as he spun around one last time. "Heed my words, Uncle, I will never return to England. And know this: Neither you with your civilized words of deceit nor the savages with their wild war cries will drive me from the wilderness of this new land." The fine oak door slammed with an air of finality as Jonathan made his exit.

~

When the door had shut, a man dressed in black stepped from the shadows of the parlor to stand in the place Jonathan had just vacated. The man leaned over Jonathan's uncle and spoke in husky tones. "You fool, Archibald. Why do you bait him so? He will never return to England if you goad him."

From behind his desk, Archibald placed his fingers together and pressed them against his lips. "Methinks we have been too lenient with the boy, milord. I can stop the Assembly from helping him, but Jonathan will always be a thorn in your side." He paused, speaking the next words under his breath, *And in mine*. He raised his head. "Unless . . ."

The other man tapped his fingers on the maple desk. "Unless?"

Archibald leaned forward, an odd smile flickering over his features. "Consider this, milord. The death of Lord Grant's brother could work in our favor. Think about it. Jonathan scorned your help. He turned his back on you in defiance and left England. What better way than his death to convince the king that the frontier settlers cannot survive without your help?"

The other man froze, his frown deepening with cold anger. "You may be right, Archibald, but I will not agree to Jonathan's death yet."

The uncle's voice dropped to a harsh whisper. "Did you not hear his words? He must be removed if we are to succeed."

The younger man shook his head. "No, Archibald. Jonathan will come crawling back to me. I will rule my brother yet, and his precious wilderness as well. Doubt it not."

"Yes, milord."

Richard slipped back into the parlor and in a moment was gone.

~

Half-blinded by fury, Jonathan strode down the cobblestone walk away from his uncle's mansion. The thought that such a man had power even in this land made him sick. Yet was he any better, with his haughty tones and barely hidden insults? It was as if he had not been changed at all by life on the frontier.

He slapped his fist against his leg and quickened his pace, wanting to put as much distance as possible between himself and his uncle's estate. He turned east, then changed his mind. He did not want to see the water. It brought him too close to England. He hoped never to set foot there again. Yet even at this distance, its hold remained firm.

He thought he'd severed the chains of bondage during that last conversation with his brother. Even now Richard's words burned in his memory with a fire that threatened his dreams.

"The colonies are naught but a bit of froth on a tankard of ale," his brother had said. "Real power and wealth lie in the land beyond the colonies."

"They say there is no gold." Jonathan's voice had sounded unsure, suspicious.

"Fool!" Jonathan could still hear the derision behind that one word. "What a simpleton you are, Johnny. Power is not in gold but in paper—titles granted by the king of England and the fools in Parliament."

"Titles? Is not Lord Grant title enough for you?"

Richard's face hardened with arrogance. "It is never enough. Oh no, I plan to gain much more. Listen to these titles, Johnny: Governor of the Lands Beyond the Allegheny Mountains, Duke of the New World. What do you think?"

"You want to rule the land west of the Pennsylvania settlements?" Jonathan felt his fists tightening.

"Yes. That land, and more." Richard's words rang with confidence.

"Then I think you are a madman. Surely the king will not agree." Jonathan's voice rose as he spoke.

"I have approached him already. He must only be convinced that the frontier settlers cannot survive on their own, that they need the protection of the crown. And the crown will need me. You will see."

The idea had filled Jonathan with revulsion. "No, Richard. The new world is for men who want to be free." *Free*. The word sent shivers of hope dancing in Jonathan's heart. It was then that he knew what he must do, where he must go. He remembered his next words. "Men like me."

His brother had understood at once. "Stay in England, Jonathan. You owe me that much. Do not oppose me."

Jonathan's jaw tightened as he answered, "No, Richard, I owe you nothing. I am going to the colonies, to the frontier."

"Then you are more a fool than I thought. Somebody will rule those unclaimed lands and the land England will acquire beyond the Allegheny Mountains. So know this: I intend that somebody to be me." Richard had turned and stared out the window overlooking the Grant estate. "Come, Jonathan, we are much the same, you and I. We are like our father. Perhaps I will allow you to rule by my side."

Jonathan's voice echoed off the stone fireplace. "How can you say such a thing? Don't you remember the bruises, the broken bones, our mother's tears? No, brother. I will never be like you. I will never be like Father. Never!"

~

The memory of that conversation made Jonathan sigh. He had thought those words would free him. But even here he played the game of aristocratic arrogance and false words. How he hated it! Yet today he'd fallen into it as easily as he ever had.

He ground his teeth in frustration. *Is there nowhere I can escape the bleating of this infernal city?* The dying sun beat on his back in time with the pounding of his furious thoughts.

He was not worthy of this new land, of the frontier that seemed to call him by name. Yet he must succeed, now more than ever. Only the frontier could purge his blood from the arrogance of his forefathers who used their titles as a mask for savagery. He would not become a man like Richard, like his uncle, or like his father. He would be free.

"Watch yourself, woodsman." An irritated voice penetrated Jonathan's thoughts. He looked up to see a soldier on horseback directly in front of him. Quickly he sidestepped the beast and became aware again of the city around him—women hustling down the cobblestone street, a boy scuttling into the open doorway of a silversmith shop, a single black carriage creaking down the narrow road. He looked at the buildings—small wooden structures huddled together like children afraid of punishment soon to come. He drew a deep breath. The buildings were not familiar. He could smell the Delaware

River. Too close to England even here. He turned down a smaller street to an alley behind an ironworker's shop.

The city air was stifling, closing in around him, heavy, choking. On the frontier a man could fill his lungs with fresh air and take pride in his own accomplishments. There one's enemies were obvious. They did not hide behind maple desks, disguising themselves in fancy clothes and carefully chosen words. There men were brothers and watched each other's backs.

But here brothers spoke of kinship while their eyes betrayed their hate. And yet he had come here for help. He was more the fool. Jonathan grunted in disgust. Still he must stay for the Assembly's decision. He would demand that they hear his plea, but he needed another plan to defend himself against the Indian attacks. If only he knew the tribal mind, their thoughts, their plans.

Jonathan continued his deliberation as the alleys became narrower, twisting between the backs of warehouses and rundown shops. Soon the air lost the smell of the river and instead filled with the scent of dirty linens and molding timber. Cobblestones turned to dirt, and rats replaced the carriages. But only the sound of voices, low and excited, broke through his reverie.

Jonathan lifted his head to see a gathering of some thirty men, their backs toward him. Quickly he shot a glance at the buildings around him. Where was he? He stopped and swallowed hard. His feet had betrayed him.

The men did not seem to notice him, intent as they were on the platform that had been hastily erected against the back of a warehouse. Curious, Jonathan slipped behind two men who glistened with sweat in their cheap finery. He smelled eagerness and fear. Jonathan glanced again at the platform. A black man stood there, his hands tied, a rope tight around his neck. Suddenly Jonathan's own collar seemed too tight. He reached a finger to his neck and adjusted the buckskin.

"A grand servant for men of your quality and taste," the man holding the rope was saying. "How about you, Shillingsworth? What'll you give me?"

Jonathan felt his stomach turn. He'd heard of such things happening from Nahum, but only in the Southern colonies. Such meat markets, as Nahum called them, were not supposed to exist here in Pennsylvania. What had he wandered into? Nahum had given him a loathing for the practice, but to actually witness such a thing . . .

Jonathan watched as the man he assumed was Shillingsworth stepped up to take the rope in his own hand. Next a girl was pulled onto the platform. Her head, instead of falling in defeat like the black man's before her, was lifted, her eyes focused on the sky. What kind of creature was this? Jonathan took a step forward. Slowly the girl lowered her head, and Jonathan was lost in the sky-blue ocean of her eyes.

Seven

A fly. The September sun glinted green and gold off its fat body. Kwelik watched it buzz in a lazy circle above her head before it settled on the rough-hewn platform before her. Slowly it rubbed its spindly legs together and then flew off into the afternoon sky. She watched until the black speck disappeared into the glare of the sun. Her throat tightened. It was not a butterfly, but at least it was free. *Free*. The word groaned through her soul until she thought she would die from the sound of it.

Kwelik allowed her eyes to wander down to the crude rope tightly binding her wrists. She studied the peculiar twine of the fibers, how the colors faded from brown to gold to brown again. Anything to shut out the sound of bidding for the black man now standing on the platform like a sack of human flesh.

The trip to Philadelphia had been brutal, with whips that bit into their backs if they slowed down, foraging for roots they were not allowed to eat, nights of fear, days of pain. But it all paled compared to this moment. A trickle of sweat shimmied down her back, plastering the torn deerskin to her tender flesh. She choked on the nauseating smell of men eager to destroy the last remnants of her dignity.

She refused to look at them, men hoping to purchase prestige from the life of another, to keep the wolves of inferiority at bay. She did not want to see the tattered jackets, once fine, stretched taut over bellies filled with lust. She did not want to see lace handkerchiefs, now worn thin, fluttering out to wipe sweaty brows.

What kind of man would find his worth from degrading another? What kind of man would sneak into a back alley to buy a slave in secret? What kind of men were these, who would not buy their servants legitimately, but instead sought those stolen from another or those who had once been free but had been captured without regard for justice? She did not want to think about such things. One such man would soon be her owner. She felt the bile rise in her throat.

A tiny breeze played through a strand of Kwelik's hair that had loosened from her braid. It brushed over her cheek and then blew across her chin. The bruise there had faded considerably, she had been told. It left only a hint of yellow beneath her olive skin, evidence of an escape attempt a fortnight past. If only the slave trader had not turned when he did. A moment longer and she would have been free, never to face the moment that would soon be upon her. She had heard the river calling her, the sound of her mother's voice. But she had been wrong. And she paid dearly for the error.

"Sold!" The word cut through Kwelik and jolted her attention back to the auction. She looked up to see a man from the crowd grab the rope around Jim's neck and pull him off into the crowd. She wished she had not seen the blood vivid on his cheek where his new owner had already struck him.

Old Jim had been kind to her after she'd been caught trying to escape. When she'd returned to them, bruised and beaten, it was Jim who had wiped her face and shown her how to ease the pain in her ribs. He had helped her walk when she thought she'd faint with the pain. To fall behind would have meant her death. She prayed for him as his tall head was lost to her sight.

Now it was her turn. She shuddered, feeling the rope chafe her neck and wrists. She squeezed her eyes tight shut and then lifted her head to focus on the heavens. The words came before she could form a plea. *Nothing can separate you from the love of God. Remember.* Was it her father's voice or God's? Even the cruel ropes of slavery could not destroy God's love for her. Did she believe it? Kwelik took a deep breath and stepped onto the platform. Even this she would endure.

"Here we have a fine Indian squaw, gentlemen, brought in fresh from the wild frontier. Just like a wildflower, she is. What will you give me, gentlemen, for this lovely little flower?"

Kwelik tried to block Jennings's prattle from her mind. Soon this atrocity would be over . . . and a new one would begin.

"Come on, you'll be the envy of all your friends. Speak up now." Jennings continued to harangue the crowd.

"Five pounds!" From the corner of her eye, Kwelik saw the man who spoke. She would not turn her head to look.

"Come now, Skinny, this here's serious business," Jennings rebuffed the man. "An indentured costs that for just one year."

"Everyone knows you can't get them Injuns to work for ya," the man shot back. "She'll be running back to her people within a fortnight. Six pounds, and that's my last offer, and you're lucky to get it too."

Jennings laughed. "She ain't got no people. They were all killed by another bunch of savages."

Kwelik felt a knot forming in her throat. She would not break now. Not now. Not yet. She continued to hold her head high, refusing to look at the rabble at her feet. *Even this I will endure*, she repeated the words to herself.

"She's all alone now, just waiting for one of you fine gents to take her in and . . ." Jennings paused and flung a wicked grin at the crowd. "Look at the well-formed arms and good, strong teeth." He squeezed her arm and forced her mouth open as he spoke. "And not just a pretty face, but she's got nice, firm buttocks too." The men guffawed as Jennings slapped her on the rear. "Let's hear some good bidding now. This one's a good worker, and she's got other advantages over the blackies." He winked knowingly at the crowd.

Kwelik swallowed hard and clenched her teeth. She would endure even this. She must. *Oh, God, have mercy on me*. She dared not whisper the words aloud.

It was then that her father's voice washed through her, soothing, strong, cleansing. *Child, be not afraid of them that kill the body and after that have no more that they can do. But fear him, which after he hath killed hath power to cast into hell. Fear God only. Are not five sparrows sold for two farthings, and not one of them is forgotten before God? Even the very hairs of your head are numbered. Fear not therefore: ye are of more value than many sparrows.*

With a final glance to heaven, Kwelik lowered her head, her face bereft of fear.

~

Jonathan took another step forward. His breath caught in his throat. What was the matter with him? It was just her eyes. They were different, nothing more. He shook his head. She was an Indian girl—that was all—and a Delaware, by the looks of her. He was simply surprised to see an Indian so far from home.

He rubbed his hand over his face, fighting the chaos of emotions raging within him that one like her should endure such indignity. Who was she? How could she stand there like that, tied yet undefeated, humble yet not humiliated? Jonathan dropped his hand from his face and waited for the bidding to continue. Who would dare to buy this girl's life? Something constricted in his chest.

"I'll give you eight pounds for her, Jennings. And that be a fair price." Jonathan shifted his position to see the man who bid. The bidder's tongue darted out nervously to lick his fat lips, like a wolf preparing for the feast. Jonathan could almost see the man beginning to drool.

The girl trembled, or did she? At this distance Jonathan couldn't be sure.

He clenched his fists and released them again. How could the girl endure it? But she did. She remained like one impervious to the will of men. She looked like an Indian princess, except for those blue eyes. He had never seen such a face—confident, resolute, regal, yet obedient. To whom? Surely not to the wretched little man that held the end of her rope and leered into the crowd. No, to another he could not see.

Jonathan's brows came together in an outraged frown. Indian or not, it wasn't right. No woman should be subjected to the lecherous men who stood before him. Someone should stop this affront. He nearly stormed away, disgusted at the depths to which men could fall. But something stopped him. Maybe it was the clear blue of her eyes. Maybe it was the call of the man he wished he would become. Whatever it was, he stayed, watching the crowd warm to their bidding. What would happen to the girl?

"Nine pound and two pence," a man from the side of Jonathan's vision whined.

Jonathan's stomach knotted.

"Ten pounds!" A hand encrusted with gaudy rings raised to indicate the source of the bid.

"Ten pounds?" Jennings interjected. "Come on, men. Surely such a comely wench is worth more to you than that. Who will give me fifteen for her?" The man looked expectantly into the crowd.

The words were out before Jonathan knew what he was saying. "Forty pounds," he shouted. His bid fell into sudden silence.

EIGHT

Little Cloud clutched his spear more tightly, his palms sweaty despite the coolness of the night. A sharp wind bit at his back where there were no arrows, no bow, no musket. The air was cold, even for autumn, cold like death. *Whose?* he wondered. His own perhaps. He felt the tomahawk bump against his leg. A shiver raced up his back. Tonight everything would change. Tonight he would leave behind his childhood and become a man. The night's chill reached around his heart and squeezed. Soon the gods would come.

The memory of Long Brow's words earlier that day still goaded Little Cloud. "This hide is not soft enough," Long Brow had complained, throwing the skin at his feet.

Little Cloud stared up in anger and defiance.

"You are a worthless boy. Why do I keep you?"

Before he could respond, Taquachi, third son of Chief Tumaskan, had come around the side of the hut. Taquachi laughed as he stepped on the offending hide and ground it into the dirt. "The boy does not please you, Long Brow?" His words held a tone of mockery that Little Cloud had never dared to use.

Long Brow grunted.

The smile faded from Taquachi's face as it froze into a look of command. "Leave him to me."

As Little Cloud watched the chiseled features of the young warrior, he knew why the man was called the Frozen One.

Long Brow knew too. He nodded once before sullenly returning to his hut.

Taquachi put his hand on Little Cloud's shoulder and led him toward the edge of the village. "You are a strange boy, Tankawon," he said, his words like ice in Little Cloud's ear. "I see the fire that burns in you. Perhaps it is time you joined the war against the white man."

Little Cloud gulped and nodded, his excitement driving away the coldness of Taquachi's grip.

"Go tonight alone," the Frozen One said. "See if the gods will meet you and make you into a man. Then you will join us."

"The war band?" Longing hardened in Little Cloud's chest as he thought about the small group of warriors led by Taquachi. They were honored among the tribe, and they hated the white man above all. In that moment Little Cloud had seen the fulfillment of his dreams. So he went alone into the night to meet his destiny.

But destiny had not yet met him. Little Cloud sighed and gripped his spear in cold fingers, his eyes scanning the dark outlines of the forest trees. What form would the gods take tonight? The bear? The wolf? The great cat? His father would have said that God is none of these, but Little Cloud did not believe in that God anymore.

Gods, he thought bitterly. He hated them all. They were not friends but enemies. Even the Indian gods seemed distant, unreal, only a whispering in his imagination. Perhaps they too were a lie. Tonight he would find out.

The moon shone in a tiny sliver, spitting light through the leaves overhead. Little Cloud followed the curve of light with his eyes. Where were the gods of night?

A low growl sounded behind him. Little Cloud whirled toward it. Blood pounded in his ears. A lone wolf. The moment had come.

Every detail froze in Little Cloud's mind with eerie precision. Gray fur stood up on the wolf's back as he plastered his ears flat against his head. His teeth bared to show white fangs that gleamed in the scant moonlight. His eyes glowed with yellow fire.

Little Cloud gripped the spear and stood his ground.

The wolf lunged.

With a battle cry trembling on his lips, Little Cloud hurled the spear. It grazed the beast and clattered on the rocks behind him.

The weight of the wolf crushed him into the ground as the beast landed on top of him. He grabbed for his tomahawk. Fangs ripped into his arm. The smell of his own blood made Little Cloud wild. In a frenzied rage, he slashed at the beast. The wolf's blood mixed with his own, flowing hot over his chest.

Little Cloud felt teeth sink into his shoulder, barely missing his neck. A growl echoed in his ear. He grabbed the wolf's neck in one hand and thrust the tomahawk up into the beast's chest. With blind fury, he jerked the weapon through the animal's gut. Entrails spilled over him as the wolf crumpled, dead.

With grim elation, Little Cloud pushed the beast from him. Panting, he staggered to a standing position. The wolf's mouth still lay open in a vicious sneer. Its blood made a dark stain at Little Cloud's feet. He turned away and again faced the moon. *This god*, he thought, *is dead.*

The next day Little Cloud skinned the wolf, threw the pelt over his shoulders, and returned to the village. He left blood still crusted to his cheek as a seal of dark victory.

As he entered the village, Taquachi and the war band met him. "You have fulfilled the challenge," Taquachi called, gripping his arm in the greeting of equals. "Let all who hear know this: You will no longer be called Tankawon, but Waptumewi—White Wolf!"

A cheer broke out from the others in the war band. Taquachi gripped a bottle in his right hand and raised it high in the air. "Waptumewi, we celebrate your manhood!" He drank deeply from the bottle and handed it to White Wolf. "Drink, Waptumewi. It is brandy, the drink of warriors."

The new White Wolf nodded, his heart turning cold within him. Brandy. His father's warnings against the drink echoed through his mind. But his father was a fool, not a warrior. Without another thought, White Wolf put the bottle to his lips and drank. The strange taste burned a path of fire down his throat. The warmth drove away the chill of memory. He smiled without mirth, clutching the bottle tighter as he took another drink.

Waptumewi, he thought, rolling the name over in his mind, *slayer of gods*.

~

"Sold!" The word echoed in the silence, leaving Kwelik breathless. No one spoke as the man reached inside his shirt and pulled out a pouch filled with coins. Kwelik looked down at him, her eyes locking and holding his for a split second before he averted his gaze.

She watched the crowd part magically before the man as he strode to the platform to claim her, his slave. Kwelik held herself firmly, refusing to tremble. His coin bag hit the wood with an eerie smack. He reached for the rope around her neck and pulled it over her head. In one violent movement, he threw it away from her and led her through the crowd.

The silence echoed off the drab buildings and reverberated through Kwelik's mind. What nightmare awaited her now?

Only when they were out of sight did the crowd break into noisy discussion. Kwelik heard the sound, like the warbling of so many frogs.

She watched the broad shoulders in front of her, refusing to think of her future. The man's brown hair ruffled in the wind as he studied the buildings to their left and right. Who was he? He would not look at her as they walked, nor had he since that last glance as she stood on the platform. His grip on her wrist was firm but not cruel. *A strange man*, she decided. A strange man who would buy a slave in such a place and yet throw the rope from her neck as if such a thing offended him. And he had paid forty pounds for her. From the men's reactions, it must have been a high sum. That one fact both frightened her and tempted her curiosity.

At least he was not the fat man with the sallow yellow skin and the sweaty look of lust. She thanked God for that. But who was this man, and what would happen to her now? Despite herself, she shivered.

The man glanced at her briefly, avoiding her eyes. He almost seemed as frightened of her as she was of him. But that could not be so. The alley came to a T, and the man stopped, turned, and finally looked at her, his amber eyes at once stern and gentle.

"My name is Jonathan, Jonathan Grant. I did not plan . . . I mean, I did not intend . . ." He paused, as if wrestling with himself over his next words. Kwelik watched his callused fingers run through his hair once before he turned back to stare at the rough cobblestone at his feet.

"I never should have come to Philadelphia," he mumbled. "Now if I just knew how to get out of here." It was not what he had been about to say. He shrugged, as if to shake off an unwanted thought and started off in a new direction. "I believe this is the way. Ah yes, here is Elfreth's Alley." His countenance brightened.

Kwelik's eyes widened as she stared up at the three- and four-story brick buildings on either side of her. For the first time she could see the city clearly. The buildings towered above her, with no space between them. They seemed to glare at her with rectangular eyes that she knew were shuttered windows. Short stairways led to each door. Kwelik wished she could run up one of them and put her hand on the red brick wall. Would it be rough or smooth to her touch? Hot or cold? For a moment she closed her eyes and stretched out one hand, trying to imagine the feel of the brick. It would be smooth, she decided, and warm, like the ground in the middle of the village after it had been stomped down by a night of ceremonial dancing.

To her right two small trees grew up from the cobbled walk and tilted toward the center of the alley. They were the only reminders of home in a world that was less like the wilderness than Kwelik had ever dreamed. Even the horses, tied to round posts outside the doorways, seemed different from the ones she had known in her village. These were sadder, their necks more bent, their faces wearier.

A young boy darted from a shop to Kwelik's left, slamming the door behind him. She jumped at the sound, a small gasp escaping her lips.

Jonathan stopped and turned toward her. "It's not much like the frontier, is it?" He spoke with a longing that surprised her. "So very different."

Different. If only he knew. Nothing was like she had imagined it. Papa's sketches had not prepared her for any of it. Even the cobblestone was different from what she had thought it would be. Instead of round stones, these were more like rectangular pieces of broken rocks, each fitting with the ones next to it to shut out any infringement of nature. Where were the grass, the flowers, the butterflies?

"This alley," Jonathan continued, "was laid out to provide easier access to the mill and the blacksmith shop down there at the end." His voice sounded strange, as if he were trying to cover his discomfort with his words. "See there." He pointed to a building with a tall arched doorway. "Adam Clampffer, the hatter, lives there. And next to him William Will, the pewterer." He paused. "I wonder if you can understand anything I'm saying." He glanced at her intently for a moment before turning away. "Ah well, it doesn't matter. Look!" He waved his hand in the air. "This is where honest men make their homes, men who work with their hands and are proud to be living in this great land. A locksmith, a nailsmith, a privateer captain, a tailor, sailors, and bakers—they're all on this street. And I lived and worked among them before I went to the frontier." Jonathan pointed to several homes as he spoke. "And there in number 122, in the rooms of William Maugridge the carpenter, Ben Franklin regularly meets with his *junta*, or club." He smiled. "Of all the city, this is the grandest place."

Grand? The word mocked Kwelik. To her it seemed anything but grand. No, it was crowded, dark, and filthy, like a great chasm that blocked the light of the sun until even the two trees seemed to droop and wither. Kwelik stared down at her dirty feet and shuddered. If this was Papa's world, she understood better than ever why he left it.

Soon the man named Jonathan led her from the alley onto a main street crowded with every kind of people. Sunburned sailors, ragged apprentice boys, Englishmen with tall black hats, women wearing bright-colored dresses. Kwelik's head spun with the sight of them. So many, many people. The city was like Papa had described it, and yet so very different too. His quietly told stories had not prepared her for the frantic crush of bodies or for the incessant noise of man and beast. Kwelik cringed as one of the sailors brushed against her. The smell of his sweat sent a shiver of revulsion racing across her skin. How did a person even draw a breath in such a city?

Something rattled on the street behind her. Kwelik turned her head to see a large black contraption drawn by a single horse. Wheels jostled over the cobblestone street as a dark-skinned man urged the horse forward from his seat in the front of the box-like thing. Kwelik tilted her chin. *I know what that is*, she thought. The realization filled her with a sense of cruel irony. *It is a carriage. Why did I ever want to see a real one?* The question lodged as a lump in her throat.

Just as the sun began to dip into the west, Jonathan turned a final corner and stopped beneath a sign that read Red Fox Tavern. A breeze danced in off the water to make the sign creak above their heads. Kwelik glanced up. The little fox seemed to look at her with pity as she passed underneath. She had seen one like that before once when she was a girl. She did not think that the next one would be painted on a placard as a witness to her captivity. The door opened before her, sending the candlelight inside flickering across the walls in a wild dance of the wind.

As they turned toward the stairs, the fear that she had been fighting rose from the depths of Kwelik's heart.

NINE

Kwelik stood alone, her forehead resting on the single window pane in the tiny room. The man had retreated to the common room below almost as soon as he could push her through the door and lock it behind her. She drew a deep breath, then released it. Who was this Jonathan Grant? That moment when he turned, about to say something, that briefest glance he gave her said more than she could understand and yet less than she wanted to know. What kind of man would buy a slave in a back-alley black market? He did not seem like the others. That piercing look—it spoke of no subterfuge, no guile. Papa said you could tell a man by the mask in his eyes. What would Papa say of this man?

And when he threw the rope from her neck, she had almost begun to hope . . . but, no, such things were foolishness. She had no strength left for nonsense.

Kwelik sighed and glanced back at the room, its scrubbed floor worn smooth by many feet, its shabby curtains that did not cover the dirty window, and in the corner a single bed. She stopped there and averted her gaze. She would not think of such things. She turned toward the basin sitting on a small table against the opposite wall. Nobody had thought to fill it for the likes of a slave. Perhaps when the man came back, they would bring some water too. What she would give to be clean again—to be clean, and free, and laughing.

The thought stung her. She ran one finger down the cloudy pane, watching her skin smudge the dull surface. Somewhere out there people laughed and danced, wept and worked. At this moment she seemed capable of none of those things. What had happened to her? She had wished to come here, to Papa's world, but not like this, never like this. She'd wanted to come on her own terms, as an adventurer, not as a slave. She choked on the word, still unwilling to fully believe it. Her eyes stared blankly into the tiny alley behind the tavern as twilight threw gray shadows at peculiar angles, like a shaman's bizarre dance of mourning. She heard the yip of a dog as a small brown-and-white mongrel raced under the window.

Lapawin. The thought of him came unbidden to her mind. He would hate it here. He loved the meadows, the flowers, the splash of the stream upon a round stone. He loved it as much as she did. If only she could go back, could start again. She had not known what she had until she lost it. Lost it all. *All dead*. Even the menace of slavery could not drive the words from her mind. Even Lapawin was dead. He had given his life to save her and failed. The lump grew in her throat. *All dead*. She watched a wisp of smoke rise from a house two doors down. Whose spirit would follow the trail to heaven? She shook her head to rid herself of such thoughts.

"Nothing can separate me from the love of God which is in Christ Jesus my Lord." She gripped the threadbare curtain in one fist and spoke the words aloud. "Nothing. Not even this." Her throat closed.

A brisk rap on the door preceded its opening. Kwelik turned to see a woman pushing her way through the doorway. She had a bucket in one hand and rags in the other. Her head, full of graying red hair wrapped tightly in an old cotton cloth, bobbed up when she saw Kwelik.

"Well, I'll be," she muttered, stopping short and dropping the bucket by the bed. She wiped an arm across her forehead, cocked her head, and stared at Kwelik.

"Why you be either the oddest-looking savage or strangest-looking white woman I ever saw." Her thick Scottish brogue rolled over Kwelik like the lapping of water. "So which is it?" The woman chuckled and put one hand on her hip.

Kwelik stepped back and reached out behind her to steady herself with the wall.

The woman grinned again, showing rotted teeth. "Oh, there, there, lassie. No use getting fidgety now. You just startled me a bit.

Now what was I saying?" She scratched her head and wrinkled her nose in concentration. "Humph, can't remember."

She glanced good-naturedly back at Kwelik. "Well, where's me manners? I be Rosie McDonald, and who would you be, lassie?"

Kwelik watched as the woman stretched out a hand toward her. She stared oddly at the extended hand, remembering vaguely her father's teaching on the purpose of such a gesture. Slowly she offered her own hand as her eyes met Rosie's gaze. The frankness in the woman's pale blue eyes shattered Kwelik's defenses, and the agony of capture, sale, and slavery rose up, refusing to be quelled.

As her hand was engulfed in the warm, rough one, Kwelik felt tears gather behind her eyes. "I'm no lassie, ma'am." She squeezed out the words. "I'm only a slave."

Rosie laughed, a rich sound that rumbled in her belly before it erupted to flow through the room and break through Kwelik's despondency. "Well, you still be a lassie, miss. Unless you're hiding something under that there skirt of yours." The woman ducked her head as if to check for herself.

Kwelik could not help but smile at the woman's audacity. "No."

"Well, you be a lassie then." Rosie dropped her rags and slapped her hands together in a "that's that" fashion. "Me, I'm just indentured." She plopped onto the bed and patted the spot next to her. "Not so bad really. In two more years I'll be free." She pulled out a bottle of strong-smelling ointment and motioned to Kwelik. "Now you have some cuts I need to be attending to. Come now, show me where you need a dab o' me brew."

Kwelik wrinkled her nose.

"Won't hurt but for a second. Come on now."

Reluctantly Kwelik pulled aside the torn buckskin on her back and showed Rosie the wounds across her shoulders and upper arms.

"Oh, there're some bad ones back here." Rosie clucked her tongue and dabbed a cloth into her ointment. "So what might you be called, little lassie?"

Kwelik hesitated.

Rosie took Kwelik's hand in her own and squeezed it again. "It's all right, lassie. I'm here to help you. I see by your back that you been through some tough times here of late. Might be that you need someone to talk to."

Kwelik allowed a quavering smile to brush over her face.

"Now I know I'm not much to look at," Rosie continued. "Especially compared to yourself. But that ain't no reason to shun me now." She flashed a quick grin at Kwelik to soften her jibe as she picked up her jar of ointment. "Come now, lass, let's start with your name."

Kwelik felt herself drawn into the woman's warm gaze. "I'm called Kwelik. Owww."

"Aye, it'll hurt a bit, but this here brew's been used by me mum and her mum before her. No one's died of it yet, though many a brave gentleman's yowled from the sting of it." Rosie cackled and patted Kwelik's arm before smearing some more salve on the girl's back. "You're doing just fine, lassie. This'll heal you up in no time, mark me words." She paused to dip her fingers in the yellowish ointment. "What a strange name you have there, just about as strange as yourself."

Kwelik turned slightly to face the woman. "My name means sky. My mother was Delaware and my father English."

"Turn around there, lassie, while I tend to the cuts on your arms."

Kwelik gratefully pulled the buckskin down over her sticky back and turned her head to look at the long slice across her left shoulder. "That one was the result of not stirring the stew quickly enough," she murmured. The sight brought back unwanted memories. She had learned how to be silent and efficient, like an ant on the ground that no one noticed. Eventually it had saved her much pain.

Rosie gave her a swift look, responding with another low "humph." She cleared her throat. "Kwelik, sky. Aye, I like it." Her voice was a little too loud. "Like the color of your eyes. Beautiful they are, you know, like the color of summer." She smiled again and leaned over Kwelik's arm. Her foot knocked the pail at her feet, causing water to slosh over onto the floor.

"Bless me, now look what I've done." Rosie shook her head as she tossed a rag onto the spilled water. She looked back at Kwelik. "Aye, I think I like you. Half-breed, you say. Except for that black hair and olive skin, I would have never known. You ain't got no accent at all. Nothing like mine at least." Rosie chuckled and patted Kwelik's hand again.

"Papa taught me languages. They came much easier to me than to my mother."

"Ah," Rosie sighed, "the young—they always learn so quick. Me, I think me brogue will be with me to the day they roll me in the ground." She intentionally exaggerated the rolling *r*.

Kwelik giggled.

"Well, your papa must be an educated man."

"Ouch."

"Sorry, lassie. This is a bad one. Hold still now."

"Will it heal?"

"Aye, God willing, I'd say so. Seems God's looking out after you so far."

Kwelik gave the woman a scrutinizing look, her voice dropping to just above a whisper. "Papa was a missionary. He brought the message of God to my mother's people. He said that no matter what happened to me, God would be with me and take care of me." It felt good to finally talk about her father, to get it out, to remember.

"He be a wise man, then, and a brave one, to go out to those savages. Begging your pardon, lassie."

Kwelik smiled. "Papa would not have called himself that. And the 'savages,' as they're called, were the only ones who would accept his message. He would say that he only went where someone would listen."

Rosie's eyebrows raised as she squeezed Kwelik's hand in her bony one, encouraging her to continue.

Kwelik's eyes blurred as Rosie dabbed another cut above her elbow. "He came to my mother's village in 1715 with, as my mother laughingly called it, some wild story about the true God who was Creator of all they saw around them—the sky, the stars, the trees, the animals, even themselves. Yet this God was more personal than the Great Spirit, was closer than even the spirits of earth and wind. He spoke of God's Son dying so that people could be children of this almighty, yet loving, God. The chief did not believe, but in time my mother did, and many others with her."

Rosie did not raise her eyes as she spoke. "'Tis not such an odd message. Hold still, lassie."

It was Kwelik's turn to raise her eyebrows in disbelief. "Not odd? It was why Papa was driven from the church as a heretic."

"Seems to me 'tis naught but the same message that George Whitefield's been preaching up and down the colonies these past years. He says that we can experience God though Jesus Christ our Lord. Why, the colonies are ablaze with it."

"Ablaze with the same thing that Papa tried to preach?" Kwelik's voice stumbled over her bewilderment.

"Aye, and folks everywhere are turning from dry, impersonal religion and finding a Savior in Jesus Christ. 'Tis the way o' things." Rosie shrugged her shoulders and pierced Kwelik with a quick glance.

"It cannot be so."

"Aye, it is." Rosie stopped her ministrations and raised her head with a mighty grin. "Even I have found Him."

"Even you?" Kwelik smiled, an odd expression after these many weeks of captivity. "How Papa would have loved to know of it! He wept many nights in secret for his people. He didn't know that I heard him pleading with God to save his countrymen." She paused and shook her head. "And all the time God was doing just that." Wonder replaced the bewilderment in her voice.

"Where's your papa now, lassie?"

Kwelik's eyes clouded like a midsummer storm. "Dead, with an arrow in his chest. And here I am, sold into slavery to a man who could be either an angel or a devil, for all I know."

Rosie squeezed Kwelik's shoulders. "He's a man, lassie, and that means he's no angel. But Jonathan's no devil either."

"You know him?"

"Aye. He's an honest man and a fair one. He don't know our Lord, nor does he like to hear of Him. He thinks he can overcome every obstacle with his own power." Rosie waved her hand in the air and then leaned closer to Kwelik, her voice dropping. "But he'll learn." She winked at Kwelik.

"Don't worry, lassie. He'll do right by you. Ain't no more honorable man than Jonathan Grant." She gave one last dab to Kwelik's arm. "There, that be it. The cuts should be healing up fine now." Rosie stood and started for the door, oblivious to the fact that the bucket and rags still lay on the floor next to the bed. As her hand reached for the doorknob, she turned her head back toward Kwelik. "Just don't be getting in the way of his plans for that wretched frontier of his. Mark me words and remember 'em."

With that, she was gone, and with her the last of the day's sunshine. Kwelik dipped her hand into the bucket and let the water dribble through her fingers, like the loss of all her dreams. Had those dreams fled with her freedom, or were they hiding somewhere, on the wings of the butterfly, waiting to be discovered once more? Someday she would find them again. Someday God would show her that He had been answering her prayers all along, just like Papa's. Someday . . .

But not today.

TEN

The wind swirled into the tavern from an open window, teasing the curtains that lay in its path. It raced around Jonathan's table and then began a frenzied dance with the sputtering candlelight. Yet even the wild gyration of flame failed to advert Jonathan's attention from his thoughts. Finally the flame blew out, leaving a trail of wispy smoke floating just beyond fingers that beat out a rapid pattern on the rough-hewn wood. Still Jonathan ignored the smoke. Nor did he pay attention to the raucous laughter of the other guests sitting at tables near him. He scarcely smelled the sausage cooking in the kitchen or the pungent aroma of sour wine. He did not notice when twilight turned to night and a group of men thumped their mugs on the table to demand one last ale. No, for him the world had narrowed to encompass only one thought: What had he done?

He, Jonathan Grant, was a slave owner. The thought turned his stomach. Yet his father would have said slavery was a necessary evil, that there was no difference between buying your servants or hiring them. Some people were created to be servants and some to be masters. It was God's will, and who was Lord Grant to stand in the way of God's design? But Jonathan was not like his father. He would not be. He could not be.

The girl's face wavered before his mind's eye, her very image accusing him. He didn't want to think of her, of the way her blue eyes had held steady amid the storm of bidders, of how those same eyes saw through his defenses and somehow shamed him. She was only a slave, his slave. He winced at the thought. How had it happened? What had he been thinking? He must have been mesmerized by those strange blue eyes.

Jonathan held his head in his hands and stared at nothing.

Surely he had gone momentarily mad. The encounter with his uncle had thrown him, made him less of a man. Why else would he do such a thing as buy a slave? Yet it had seemed the right choice at the time, for at least that split second when he had spoken those fateful words, "forty pounds." Ah, the speaking had been so easy. He was a fool.

Jonathan reached out a hand to spin the tankard of ale in front of him. The amber liquid swirled, reflecting Jonathan's eyes as he watched the froth undulate and threaten to spill. He sighed. His life felt like that, swirling around, confused, almost tipping, but not quite. He would control it yet. He would break the bonds of his father's legacy and be the man his mother would be proud of. He would control his anger, his impulsive nature.

Jonathan clenched his fist and ran it along the table. No, he would not be defeated—not by his past, not by his brother, not by his uncle, and not by the words "forty pounds."

A familiar chuckle arrested Jonathan's attention. He raised his head to see Rosie working her way down the stairs.

"That be a fine lassie you got there, Jonathan," she called across the room.

Jonathan grimaced as Rosie wove through the tables toward him. With a knowing wink, she pulled out a chair and plopped beside him. "So what are you planning to do with her?"

The question jabbed him. He ran his fingers through his hair and tapped on the full glass before him. Long seconds ticked past before he attempted an answer. Finally the words pushed through his stiff lips. "I don't know, Rosie. I just don't know." He raised his eyes to meet hers.

Rosie shook her head. "What you be doing, Jonathan, buying a slave? It's not like you."

Jonathan dropped his gaze, no longer able to meet her searching eyes. She had known him too long. "I don't know that either," he mumbled. "I didn't come to Philadelphia to buy an Indian girl."

"A half-breed," Rosie interjected.

"What?" Jonathan looked up again.

Rosie gave him a deprecatory look. "Didn't the blue eyes tell you anything?"

The question held a double meaning for Jonathan. He chose to ignore the more probing one. "Ah, yes, of course. Half Indian, you say."

"Aye, and her name is Kwelik, not Indian Girl." Rosie quirked her mouth into a half-smile. "Lovely, don't you think?"

Jonathan glanced at her from the corner of his eye, refusing to read a deeper meaning into her words. "Humph. Well, I suppose she knows a little English then."

Rosie shrugged. "Maybe. There's a lot you don't know about the lass."

Jonathan rubbed his hands over his face. "What am I going to do with her, Rosie?"

"Well, that be a question worth considering." She leaned a little closer to Jonathan, her voice dropping. "How about you let her go free?"

Jonathan shook his head. "In a city like this? Where would she go? What would she do? No, that's not the answer either." He took a swig of the ale and wiped a forearm across his mouth. "Besides I paid forty pounds for her."

"Forty pounds?" Rosie sat back in her chair. "Why so much?"

Jonathan did not meet her gaze. "It was all I had. The last of the money I saved from working here in Philadelphia. Don't worry though. I've already paid Mr. White for my room and board."

Rosie continued to stare at him. "I ain't worried 'bout that, Jonathan."

Jonathan cleared his throat and spoke again, his voice louder this time. "I've been thinking I'll take her back to the frontier with me. She can teach me about Indian ways and how to survive in her land. She can show me how to find edible roots, how to cook certain types of bark, and how to recognize local medicinal plants. I need to know these things. That's why I bought her." He wondered if Rosie could see through his white lies.

She gave him a scrutinizing look. "Then you'll let her go?"

Jonathan did not answer.

Rosie continued to pierce him with her gaze. "You think on it.

Ain't no call for such a lass to be a slave. But you got a more urgent problem. What will you do with her tonight?"

Jonathan sighed. "She's a slave. I suppose I should tie her to my bedpost and make her sleep at my feet. But—"

Rosie was on her feet before Jonathan could finish his sentence. "I should think not, Jonathan!"

Jonathan could almost see the sparks of ire flying from the red in Rosie's hair. He chuckled. "If I didn't know better, I'd think you'd grown attached to the girl."

"Aye, and why shouldn't I, I'd like to know? With what the lassie's been through, she shouldn't have to suffer the likes of you as well. You remember that, Jonathan Grant." Rosie gave a curt nod of her head and sat back down.

"What are you talking about? I saved her with my bid."

Rosie's voice dropped to its normal level. "You didn't save her soon enough. The cuts on her back are as bad as I've seen after many a brawl. And the bruises. It hasn't been an easy time for the lass here of late. Like I said, you remember that and treat her right, or you'll have God to answer to, not just ol' Rosie."

"Now don't be flinging your threats around. You know what I think of that God of yours."

"You ain't even met that God of mine, as you call Him."

"And I don't care to. Ever since that Whitefield came through, you haven't been the same."

"I hope not!" Suddenly Rosie softened again and leaned over to pat Jonathan on the arm. "God's real, laddie. He ain't the same as what your father believed. You see Him in my own life. Give Him a chance in yours. Come with me Sunday to hear Rev. Tennent."

"I won't be around that long. We're leaving in a day or two."

"Your life will never be right 'til you find God. You'll never defeat those devils you've been fighting all your life. You remember my words, Jonathan. You remember 'em."

The intensity of her look shook him. He did not want to hear such things, let alone remember them. He was fine the way he was. He didn't need a God to make him into a man. The frontier was all he needed. This talk of God was woman's prattle. Religion was for fools and for those who used it as a cover for their own brutal arrogance. He would have no part of it. Jonathan turned the mug of ale around and took another gulp. The liquid burned its way into his stomach, as if attempting to erase the impact of Rosie's words.

Jonathan took a deep breath, his voice filling with an irritation that the drink didn't kill. "Enough. You want me to act honorably, but this talk won't solve the sleeping arrangement for tonight, will it? Do you have any other rooms with locks?"

Rosie shook her head. A look of disappointment flooded her face. "So you ain't gonna free her." She sighed, resignation lacing her tone. "We be all full for tonight. Most everyone's leaving tomorrow morning though."

"That doesn't help much." His voice turned harsh. "I won't be sleeping on a cot in the common room for the likes of any slave."

Rosie's eyebrows drew together in a frown. "She can come sleep with me. I'll bring in a cot. Won't be no trouble at all."

Jonathan barked out a rough laugh. "She's a slave. She'll run away before the sun peeks across the water." He waved his hands in frustration and then thumped his knuckles on the table. "No, I've got to keep an eye on her."

"Well, she can't sleep in the same room with you." Rosie's voice raised in annoyance. "Think, Jonathan!"

"I am thinking! She's a slave, I tell you!" Too late Jonathan realized he had shouted the statement. The few other people in the tavern turned to stare at him. He looked down to see that he was standing. Nervously he cleared his throat and sat back down. "I don't know, Rosie. I think I'm losing my mind. I'm sorry."

Rosie smiled and winked at him. "One would think you were the one with feelings for the girl, the way you're carrying on."

Jonathan gave her a fierce look, then grinned. "Stop badgering me, old woman, and tell me what to do."

Rosie laughed. "You don't want to hear my advice."

"You're probably right. You've been trying to get me a wife ever since we met. Back then only the best would do. Now I'll bet you'd be willing to settle for a half-breed slave."

Rosie leaned closer and tapped him on the chest. "Maybe the

slave is the best of all. Consider that." Rosie gave a quick nod of her head and sat back, her eyes sharp on Jonathan's reaction.

Jonathan pushed his chair back from the table. "I was wrong. It's you who've lost your mind."

Rosie cackled. "Aye, perhaps it's true. But I've been right about you before. I remember the first time you came through that door five years ago." She motioned with her hand. "All full of fight and fury, your head full of dreams of the wild frontier. I knew you'd make it out there someday, despite all the Injuns. You even doubted yourself, if you recall, but not old Rosie. I knew you'd survive and make a life for yourself. And you have. You have, Jonathan."

"Have I?" Jonathan shook his head, feeling the same doubts that he did five years ago.

"Aye, you have. You ain't dead, and you ain't quit. I believed in you then, and I believe in you still. You'll do the right thing. I know you will."

"I have to, Rosie, I have to. You know that."

Rosie leaned over and patted him on the shoulder. "I know it. Don't you worry, Jonathan. I'll take care of Kwelik." She gave him one last wink and was gone.

~

Jonathan returned to his room later that night to see that Rosie had put up a partition separating the room into two sections. The girl lay huddled in a blanket on a cot that Rosie must have brought her. She looked small, innocent, helpless. He didn't want to see her like that. The sight of her tugged at him, demanding that he protect her, help her. He fought down the impulse. She was only a slave. He repeated the words to himself, ignoring their implications.

Jonathan saw one eyelash flutter, but the girl did not open her eyes. Perhaps she was awake after all. He didn't know. He cleared his throat, willing his voice to be steady in the event she could hear him.

"I hope you're comfortable." No, that sounded weak. They were not the words he should use with a slave. He tried again. "Rosie will take care of your needs in the morning."

The girl still did not move. Her breathing remained steady, her face composed.

Jonathan made his voice stern. "You will obey her and not give her any trouble." He wondered if she could understand his words even if she were awake. He gave her what he hoped was an authoritative look, just in case she could see him through her black lashes. Then he escaped to his own bed.

One last thought pounded through Jonathan's mind before sleep invaded him: *Yes, he was indeed a fool.*

Eleven

Kwelik gripped the blanket beneath her chin and willed her breath to remain steady. She did not move as the man's footsteps carried him away from her. She listened as he threw himself onto the bed and removed his boots before lying down. But it was not until his deep, rhythmic breathing washed through the room that she allowed herself to succumb to her own weariness.

Just as her body relaxed into the deepest part of sleep, she felt it. A nudge on her shoulder. Her eyes flew open, but no one was there. The man's breath still came slow and steady, the only sound that dared to interrupt the night. The quietness weighed down upon her, but sleep was gone. She rubbed her hands over her face and drew a deep breath. It was as if God Himself had shaken her by the shoulder and told her to rise.

She allowed her eyes to wander out the window above her cot. The stars sparkled and winked, beckoning her, calling her to pour out her heart, her fears, before God in this, the darkest part of night before dawn dared to break. They were so beautiful, yet so distant, so cold. Was God out there among them, so far away, so untouchable?

Kwelik sat up on the cot and folded her arms across the windowsill. Slowly she laid her head on her arms, allowing her eyes to search the heavens above. Where was God now? Did he see her fears? Did he feel her pain, her sorrow? The wind whispered through a tiny crack where the window did not fit snugly to the sill. She listened to the sound, trying to discern its words. But it meant nothing. She sighed.

"Oh, my God, don't abandon me now. I am so alone. So afraid." She allowed the words to squeeze from her throat and slip quietly into the night air.

A single tear glistened on her lashes before it escaped to make a wet trail down her cheek. She let the words come silently, yet unchecked, boiling up from the depths of her being, with the memories of the girl she had once been and was no more. They swirled around her and took shape, dancing through her mind, encompassing her, like a song that must be sung, a song that searched through her until it found her soul.

"Oh, God, where are You now?" she whispered to the stars. "I knew You were with me when I walked among Your creation, in the fields, under the trees. I heard Your voice in the stream, in the rustle of the wind through the leaves above me. I saw the evidence of Your love in the bloom of a daisy, in the flight of an eagle. I watched a bear rumble into the forest, and I knew You were with me. But what about here—here where there are no bears, no eagles, no flowers? Here where the wind speaks of nothing, and the walls close in around me, threatening to choke me. Here where ropes bite into my flesh and tell me I am not free. What has happened to me? Are You with me here? Do You see my pain, my fear?" The tears were flowing freely now, dripping onto her arms as they made their descent to the windowsill. "God, I need You. Where have You gone?"

The silence wrapped its arms around her as she waited, and wept, and waited some more. Kwelik sniffled and wiped her hand across her eyes, drying them. "Even in this, my Lord, I must trust You. I don't know if I can. Help me. I feel so weak. Help me not to fail You." She raised her head. It was a strange request, not the one she had planned to ask. Yet in it His strength touched the depths of her need and gave the tiniest glimmer of hope.

As if in unison with her own spirit, dawn began to steal over the night, fading the cold, distant light of the stars. As the first birds began to sing of the morning, Kwelik settled back in her bed. *The birds*, she thought, and wondered. *Perhaps, just perhaps, God is here too.*

~

When the man arose the next morning, Kwelik was already awake. When he approached her, she sat up, blankets clutched to her chin, eyeing him warily.

He took a step back. "I hope you slept well." He put forth the words like a peace offering.

She did not respond but continued to regard him with scarcely veiled suspicion.

"Listen," he tried, "I've never had a slave before." *And never thought to either*, his eyes seemed to say. "I'm not the slave-owning type." He paused, as if waiting for some response from her. He received none.

Kwelik cocked her head and clutched the blanket more firmly in her fists.

Jonathan took a deep breath and started again. "Listen, Kwelik." He paused. "That is your name, isn't it?"

She made no move, just continued to look at him and wonder.

He averted his gaze and instead studied the tips of his boots as he scuffed one heel over the wood floor. "You can teach me where to find roots and medicinal herbs and show me how to prepare them and such. That's why I bought you."

Kwelik narrowed her eyes. His words were meaningless. They did not say what his face spoke of. They were no more than a mask, protecting him. But from what?

Jonathan pulled a chair from his side of the room and sat down. "To be honest," he said, "I need your help out there. I must succeed. You can help me. It won't be so bad. It'll be a good life compared to what any of those other men would have given you." He swallowed and ran his hand over his face, his eyes flashing briefly to hers. "If you don't cause trouble, we'll all be fine. You remember that."

Kwelik listened to his hurried words and remained silent. He was a strange man, she decided, trying to justify himself to her, who was nothing but a slave to him. Why did he struggle so with himself? She studied his face, how his eyebrows furrowed when he was trying to make a point, how his hair flopped disheveled over his forehead even after he reached up to put it in its place. *It is indicative of his whole personality*, she thought. *Always fighting himself. He was not a slave owner, and yet he bought a slave. He seems to be a gentle man, yet he tries to be harsh. It's as if he is trying desperately to become someone else. But who? Perhaps Rosie is right—he may be an honorable man. He did not force himself on me. And he has been kind in his own way. But what of him now, sitting there in that chair, trying to say one thing with words that mean something else?*

Jonathan continued to study his boots. "I'll be gone for the day. Rosie will bring you whatever you need. Do you understand?"

Kwelik nodded, her eyes not leaving his face.

Jonathan returned the chair to its place and headed for the door. He did not look back.

Before the door closed completely, it swung open again. Kwelik looked up. Was it him? Her heart gave one wild thump.

"Good morning to you, lassie." Rosie pushed through the doorway with a huge tray of porridge, fresh milk, and bread teetering on one hand. "Thought you might be hungry."

Kwelik smiled with a strange mixture of relief and disappointment as Rosie bustled in and set the tray on the cot. She eyed the delicious food, noting the steam that curled up from the bowl and the pat of butter still melting on the bread.

"Eat, lassie." Rosie waved her hand toward Kwelik. "You be a bit scraggly. Eat."

Kwelik felt her mouth watering, and with no further hesitation, she grabbed the bread and sank her teeth into the brown crust. She mumbled a quick "thank you" and took a gulp of creamy milk, savoring the taste, so different from anything she'd ever had before. She turned grateful eyes to Rosie, who immediately broke out in a low laugh.

"Ain't you a lovely lass. Look at you."

Kwelik put up her hand to feel her upper lip, wet now with milk. She smiled.

"Good, ain't it?" Rosie handed her a napkin. "Squeezed it fresh from the cow this morning."

Kwelik picked up the bowl and started spooning the porridge into her mouth. She felt it making a warm path down to her stomach.

Rosie grinned at her as she finished the last bit, then leaned over to take the empty bowl from her hands. "I got something special planned for you today, lassie." Her voice dropped to a conspiratorial tone. "But first you must promise that you won't run off now. Would take me a good eight years or more to make up for the forty pounds that Jonathan paid for you."

Kwelik reached over to squeeze Rosie's hand in assurance. "I promise."

Rosie shook her head and chuckled again. "For some reason I trust you. Come along then."

She took Kwelik's hand and led her through a narrow hallway to the kitchen downstairs. The doors swung open, giving Kwelik an unhindered view of the large washbasin sitting in the center of the room. Water filled it to just over halfway, with more water steaming on the stove. Kwelik walked over to the basin and touched the rim. "There were pictures of these in the books that Papa had. I've never seen a real one before."

Rosie stepped up beside her. "Well, you ain't only seeing one, but you're gonna take a bath in it too. Mr. White's gone today, and there ain't no guests left this morning to bother us." Rosie strode over to the stove, picked up the kettle, and poured more hot water into the bath. "We keep the basin here for important guests."

Kwelik watched the steam rise from the basin and form tiny droplets on Rosie's hair. She furrowed her brow. "But I'm not important."

Rosie straightened, the kettle tipping precariously in one hand. "What's that you're saying? You're a daughter of the most high God! That be the most important guest we ever had to grace this humble establishment." Rosie feigned an indignant look before walking back and setting the kettle on the floor next to the stove. "Besides, this be me day off. Now I usually go on down to the market, but I think I'd rather give you a bath today. You want a good bath, don't you?"

The steam that continued to curl up from the basin tempted Kwelik. Suddenly a smile broke over her face, like the sunshine after a storm. "Could I?" she whispered, wondering if she were truly awake or still in the midst of some impossible dream.

"O' course, lassie. That's what it's there for. Take off that thing." She pointed to the clothes Kwelik still wore. "And hop in." Rosie squeezed a piece of Kwelik's tattered buckskin between her fingers and shrugged. "Not much left of it anyway."

Kwelik hesitated.

Rosie patted her on the shoulder and laughed. "Oh, lassie, I've seen me share of skin in me day. A little more won't matter."

Kwelik nodded and pulled off her dress, running her fingers over the torn buckskin. "It was such a soft yellow color when I first made it." Her voice was low, husky, as if she were speaking from very far away. "Like the color of the moon when it rises huge and luminous on the night's horizon. I tanned it and sewed it together myself. I remember the first time I wore it. I was so proud. It was Papa's birthday, and he took me in his big bear arms and squeezed me tight. Then he told me I was beautiful, just like my mama. And I hugged him back just as fiercely. It seems so long ago now. Sometimes I think that it must have been some other girl. It's like a dream that floats on the mist, as if the sun of reality will burn it away at first light."

"Ah, lassie," Rosie sighed, "you speak just like a poem. You'll break ol' Rosie's heart." Rosie took the dress and set it to the side of the basin. "You must feel like this dress these days, all tattered and worn out. But it'll get better. You just slip in the water now and forget all about your troubles."

Kwelik touched the water with one toe, then gratefully allowed her body to sink below the surface until the water just lapped over the necklace at her throat. She ran her fingers along the leather strap, stopping at the piece of antler attached to the end.

"What's that you got there, lassie?" Rosie leaned over and peered at her neck. "'Tis a strange sort of necklace."

Kwelik held the piece of antler in the palm of her hand and lifted it for Rosie's inspection. "It's a reminder of God's faithfulness and love." She stopped there, somehow unwilling to explain further. Perhaps such things as God's love were still believable when she was surrounded by the luxury of warm water. The water told her that God had not forgotten her. It was such a wonderful feeling, the warmth stealing over her body and the tension of the last month oozing from her.

"Now you just lay back, and I'll wash you up good." Rosie grabbed a rag and knelt by the basin.

"Oh." Kwelik sat up abruptly, causing water to slosh onto the wood floor. "I can do it myself."

Rosie frowned. "No, you won't. You're a princess today, and don't you forget it. Besides," she softened her tone, "I don't want you breaking open your cuts, do I? No, you just relax and let ol' Rosie take care of you. There now."

Kwelik sighed with pleasure as she let the warm water caress her. She hadn't been bathed by another person since she was a very little girl when Mama had washed her in the Susquehanna. But it was never like this, with water so warm it tingled along her skin and brought a fine blush to her cheeks, and with Rosie scrubbing away all her cares, at least for a time. Good, honest Rosie. "You are a wonderful woman, Rosie," Kwelik murmured. "All full of God's love and grace."

Rosie blushed. "You ought not to say such things. You'll give old Rosie a swelled head."

Kwelik smiled and closed her eyes. For this one moment she would forget her predicament and listen instead to the soothing sound of Rosie's chatter mixing with the gentle lapping of water on the sides of the basin.

"You know, lassie," Rosie continued. "I ain't always been like you see me today. Aye, I was a bitter woman once, full of hate and anger. But God touched me. I never knew it could be like this, never knew He could change an old woman like me. And I ain't ever been the same since."

Kwelik opened her eyes again and looked at Rosie. "Tell me about that, please. How God touched you."

"Aye. I remember it like it was just yesterday, though it be four years ago now. The fall of '39. A warm day, it was, and the sky all full of the threat of rain. Hadn't been indentured long then. 'Twas me day off, just like today. I was wandering down Market Street, wondering how I was ever going to make it through the next six years. Aimless I was then, and angry at me fate, indentured at my old age with no husband to take care of me. Oh, a man asked me once a long time ago, but he got himself killed in a tavern brawl. So I was feeling bitter toward life and toward God for making me like I was."

Kwelik watched the emotions play across Rosie's face.

Rosie scrubbed at Kwelik's legs as she continued her story. "A cool breeze came up just then, and I saw a crowd gathered there on Market Street. There was folks everywhere, standing as still as the stars above them. And there was even folks leaning out the windows of the houses all around and lights glowing from nearly every upper story." Rosie looked up as if she could still see the lights.

"Well, I stopped and stood on me tiptoes to see what they might be doing. And there on the steps of the courthouse he stood." Rosie stopped her scrubbing for a moment, her eyes misting over with the memory. "A man of middle height, slender, fair, full of life, and with a squint that even I could see. *Bless me*, I thought, *it must be that George Whitefield that everyone's been talking about*. And, mark me words, that's who it was. And there beside him stood Rev. Tennent, who my papa had thought was just like God Himself.

"At first I kept listening 'cause I thought to myself, *This Whitefield character is good to look upon despite that squint*. Twenty-four years old he was, just a boy. But the way he could speak." Rosie shook her head. "Even now I don't know how he did it. No notes—he had not a one. Yet he spoke straight out with words even old Rosie could understand, with that clear, musical voice of his and his face all lit up as he talked. I still remember the first words I heard.

"'Father Abraham,' he shouted to the crowd that stretched away down Market Street and Second Street, 'whom have You in heaven? Any Episcopalians?'

"'No.'

"'Any Presbyterians?'

"When he said that, I started to listen real close 'cause me mum was a Presbyterian.

"'Any Independents or Seceders, New Sides or Old Sides, any Methodists?'

"'No! No! No!'

"'Whom have You there then, Father Abraham?'

"'We don't know those names here. All who are here are

Christians—believers in Christ, men who have overcome by the blood of the Lamb and the word of His testimony.'

"About that time I started to scoff to myself. *The man's a loon*, I tells myself. Then I sidled closer to the three girls who were giggling to my left. After that a man hollered out, loud as can be, 'You got bats in your belfry, Whitefield.' The three girls, they giggled some more. And I started to giggle with them.

"Then I tell you the truth, lassie, that Mr. Whitefield, he looks right through the crowd and pins me with his squinty eyes. I felt myself starting to quake right in me shoes. Then he says, clear as day, 'Remember the time will come, and perhaps very shortly, when we must all appear before the Judgment Seat of Christ!' And right then I knew he was talking to me. I'd never given no thought to no judgment before, but I was thinking of it then, and I was right scared.

"Suddenly I didn't hear Mr. Whitefield anymore, but I heard God Himself, speaking right in me head. 'Rosie McDonald,' He says, 'you'd better listen for once in your life 'cause this man's got the answers you've been looking for.'

"Well, I tell you, I almost wet me pantaloons right there. God was speaking to me. He knew me, Rosie McDonald, an indentured servant who never married and never made nothing of her life. I could hardly believe it. Then I started to listen to Mr. Whitefield real good.

"'The infinite ransom, even the precious blood of Christ,' he was saying. 'Remember, I beseech you, remember that you are fallen creatures, that you are by nature lost and estranged from God, and only by being born again as God's children can you know Him for yourself.'

"That Mr. Whitefield talked so loud and fast, and yet I could understand every word. Lean up, lassie, while I scrub your back. There you go.

"What was I telling you now?" Rosie rubbed her wrist against her forehead and frowned. "Aye, I remember. Mr. Whitefield, he was talking about Jesus. 'Accept Christ here,' he shouted and thumped his fist on his chest. 'Trust Christ alone for your salvation. It's not good enough to just be religious. You must experience the risen

Christ in your own life—not your mother's life, or your father's, or your minister's, but your own. He wants to save *you*.' Oh, lassie, how my heart pounded when he said that. Could hear it just like a drum in my ears, beating in time with Reverend Whitefield's words.

"'Some will stand before the judgment seat of Christ,' he said, 'and tell about all they've done. Those people will be thrown into hell. God forbid, brethren, that any such evil should befall you.'

"I tell you, lass, when I saw his expression of pain, I fell down on my knees and begged God for mercy and forgiveness in my own life. And, to my surprise, God forgave me."

Tears streamed down Rosie's cheeks. She wiped them on her sleeve and smiled at Kwelik. "I'm sorry, lassie. I'm losing control of myself."

Kwelik wrapped her wet arms around Rosie and squeezed her. "That was beautiful, just beautiful. God is amazing, isn't He? I only wish that Papa could have seen it for himself. I wish he could have seen the answer to his prayers." Kwelik stopped to wipe away the tear that had slipped from her own eye. "You know, Papa always said that you had to know God inside. He said it didn't matter how much you knew about Him. If you didn't know Him in the deepest part of your heart, it 'availeth you not at all.'"

"Aye, that be the truth, lassie. That be the truth."

TWELVE

~

Jonathan's neck itched. He was no longer used to clothes designed more for looks than practicality. His breeches pulled, his shoes felt too tight, and the ruffles on his shirt made him feel like a stuffed goose. He pulled at his collar and sighed. No sacrifice was too great if it helped his cause.

The building loomed in front of him. He took out his watch, checked it, and then clicked it shut again. Five o'clock. Late for the beginning of a meeting, but it was the time he had been told that the Assembly would gather. He would present his case, not allowing his uncle to speak for him. He must make them see the need to protect their frontier. They could not be so dimwitted, so short-sighted, as to allow the Indians and French to control the land. Surely they would not allow their own people to be destroyed by torch and tomahawk.

Jonathan dismounted his horse and strode toward the large oak door. The frontier was the future of this great land—they would have to see that. He would make them understand somehow, even if most of them were Quakers whose religious beliefs made them pacifists. Still they must protect their frontier. They must. With a deep breath, Jonathan gripped the doorknob and pushed open the door.

"Thank you for coming, gentlemen. I believe we have made much progress this day." The words slapped Jonathan in the face as he stepped through the doorway. What was this? He took a few steps into the room. With a look of disbelief, he watched a dozen men gather up their coats as if preparing to leave. It could not be so!

Jonathan hurried forward, the sound of his booted steps muted by the rug that covered the floor. Two lamps sputtered from each wall, casting yellow light over the circle of chairs that rimmed the rectangular chamber. The table around which the Assembly members had met was now pushed to one side against the far wall. As Jonathan had expected, the meeting room was starkly plain, in keeping with the Quakers' belief in simplicity. What he had not expected, however, was that the men would be leaving.

Jonathan searched the group, looking for one familiar, hated face. There it was. To one side of the room, Jonathan's uncle stood shaking hands with another man. Jonathan clenched his fists. He had been deceived. The meeting was over, not beginning. His uncle had lied to him yet again, and he had been blind enough to swallow the lie.

Jonathan felt his wrath rising beneath his collar. Firmly he quelled it. He strode forward to the middle of the gathering. "Pardon me," he said.

A few men flicked their gaze toward him and then looked away. Jonathan cleared his throat and raised his voice. "Pardon me, gentlemen. There is one more matter to discuss."

The men turned toward him, coats still in hand. "Sorry, lad," one interjected, "the meeting's over. You'll have to wait. No more business today."

Jonathan raised a hand and prepared to speak. Before he could formulate his thoughts into a sentence, his uncle stepped forward, an indiscernible look on his face. His next words cut off anything Jonathan had been about to say. "Ah, gentlemen, I apologize for my passionate, if impetuous, nephew." His uncle gave him a placating smile. "I'm sorry, Jonathan," he continued, "but you're too late. The Assembly has already decided on your request."

"Ah, yes."

Jonathan turned around to see the man who spoke. The short man grunted as he rose from his chair. Jonathan studied him, the buckles that shone on his shoes like two eyes, a cloak pulled tight over a thick abdomen, his double chin pressing to escape the confines of his fashionable collar, and a gaze that spoke eloquently of his disdain for the man who stood regarding him.

Jonathan reined in his temper and turned back toward the rest of the group. "And what, pray tell, did you decide?" His voice held his most arrogant tone.

The stout man stepped around to face Jonathan and then looked languidly toward Jonathan's uncle. "Archibald?"

Archibald nodded once.

The short man slid his eyes over Jonathan and coughed. "We do not have the resources at this time to send more men to defend your private home. If you cannot protect your land, you will simply have to move closer to civilization. That is sensible, is it not?"

Jonathan clenched his teeth and turned toward the others. "Surely this is not your final decision?"

The other men mumbled among themselves, and one by one they nodded their assent.

Jonathan gripped the back of a chair. "If you abandon your frontier," he continued, his voice even, "you abandon your future. Consider that."

The short man sniffed and lifted his chin to meet Jonathan's gaze. "Our future is here in Philadelphia. We need no other future." He waved his hand toward Jonathan as if dismissing a servant.

"At least hear me out, gentlemen. It can do no harm to hear my plea." Jonathan kept his voice calm, reasonable. The men began to take their seats again.

Suddenly his uncle cut in, arresting their movement. "There's nothing for you here, Johnny. Run back home." His voice was raised over the murmur of the other men. "These men have families waiting for them. Even now their wives are putting supper on their tables. They have no more time for your grand speeches on the grandeur of the wilderness or how our future rests on your success." His uncle chuckled. "No, our future is here, as you said, Joseph. And our business is completed for today. Come, gentlemen, you mustn't keep your wives waiting. You know how they worry." He winked at a thin, younger man who had just taken his chair again. "I know that your young Elizabeth will scarcely appreciate an unnecessary delay, Edward."

The thin man grinned.

"And what about Susannah, George? We mustn't have her sending a servant to discover your whereabouts again."

The men laughed as the man named George blushed.

"No," Archibald continued, "it's time to return to our homes. If the boy must speak, let him come back at the next meeting. On time perhaps." Jonathan's uncle let his words slide over the group.

The men had already begun to gather up their coats again and start toward the door.

"Wait!" Jonathan shouted.

No one turned. The first man, then the second, then the third walked out the door and headed for their homes.

Jonathan spun toward his uncle, still standing behind him. "If you and the Assembly won't help me, I will find my own militia, men who are not afraid to fight for a dream. I spent four years in this city. I will find men who will join me. Then where will your precious Assembly be?"

Jonathan pushed past the few remaining men and bolted out the door.

~

Rosie stood up and retrieved a comb from the kitchen counter. "Now for your hair." She knelt behind Kwelik and began to pull the comb through her matted tresses. "Beautiful hair you have," she said, "but you made a right mess of it. Such lovely long hair. Mine used to be thick like this but never so beautiful." Rosie plied the comb to Kwelik's hair until it fell straight and untangled to the floor. "Now we're all done in the bath, lassie. You hop out, and I'll check those cuts and bruises."

Kwelik stepped out of the washbasin, her wrinkled toes feeling strange against the rough wood floor.

"Wrap this blanket around you while I put more of me brew on your back." Rosie continued to chatter as she rubbed on the thick salve. "You're healing up fine. Scabs be gone in a few days, and you'll be as good as new. There." Rosie put the lid back on the jar of ointment.

"Thank you," Kwelik murmured, reaching for her clothes. "I feel wonderful."

"Aye, and you'll look wonderful too but not in those rags. They be worn right through. I brought a dress for you instead." Rosie walked over to the chair and held up a pale blue dress with lace around the wrists and collar. "It ain't too fancy, lassie, but it should do you nicely. Was left here by an indentured who got married. Her new husband bought the rest of her time, and she didn't think she would need this old thing anymore. Now step right in, and I'll button it up."

Kwelik stepped into the strange garment and stood still as Rosie worked at the buttons and hooks. She craned her head around to watch Rosie's quick fingers. "The color is very beautiful."

"Aye, and it matches your eyes. How does it feel?"

"It fits well." Kwelik frowned slightly. "All but the lace on the collar. It's very itchy."

Rosie chuckled. "I don't suppose you're used to such things, aye? Well, we'll just pull that right off there." In one deft movement, Rosie removed the lace, plucking away the loose strings until the collar lay smoothly on Kwelik's neck. "How's that?"

"Much better." Kwelik fingered the material. "It's very nice. What is it?"

"That be called cotton."

"It's much too fine for a slave, is it not?"

"But it's far too shabby for a princess," Rosie threw back. "No, I think it'll do just fine. Now we can finish your hair. I'll do it up nice for you. What do you think of that?"

Kwelik reached her hand back to feel her hair, unsure of what Rosie meant by "do it up." Her voice wavered as she spoke. "Oh, I can braid it."

"Nay, lassie. You're in the civilized world now. I got a ribbon for your hair. You turn around." In a few moments Rosie had wrought some kind of miracle, for Kwelik's hair was twined through the ribbon and somehow sat atop her head in a resemblance of the latest English fashion.

"There, you look lovely." Rosie grinned.

Kwelik put her hand to her hair again, feeling the silky ribbon. "Thank you, Rosie." Her voice stumbled, then stopped. She felt strange in different clothes with her hair pulled up in some kind of bow. Who was she? The beloved daughter of a missionary and a Delaware squaw, a wretched slave, or an English maiden? She didn't feel like any of them. She had known herself before, a girl full of dreams and wild schemes for adventure. She understood the girl that ran with Lapawin through the fields and dreamed of worlds beyond her own.

But who was this girl, dressed in this cloth called cotton, with no family or tribe, sold as a slave to a man who frightened and yet intrigued her? Rosie said she was the daughter of the most high God. That, at least, was something she was certain of. Perhaps she needed to know no more.

A tiny smile brushed her lips. For now, it was enough.

~

Moonlight glinted off burnished maple. A hand heavy with garish rings extended into the light to caress the wood. No lamp was lit to further illuminate the room. In the darkness Archibald narrowed his eyes. "Come," he spoke into the heavy silence.

Two men separated from the shadows and approached his desk. They did not speak.

"You have heard, I suppose, of our little problem." Archibald raised his head to search the darkness where their eyes must be.

One man nodded, opening his mouth as if to speak. A gold cap glimmered in the dim light.

Archibald waved his hand to cut off the man's speech. "He must not, of course, be allowed to succeed."

"The attack will be simple, sir." The man's voice grated through the night air.

"Simple?" Archibald turned his chair to face the window.

The second man cleared his throat. "We knows our job, sir."

Archibald turned back toward them. "Yes, of course. And no men will be foolish enough to join Jonathan's little quest, will they? A few well-placed words should convince them."

The men grinned. "Yes, sir, we'll make sure of it."

"Go then. Do what must be done. And don't leave any loose

ends." He paused to give his next words their full impact. "Jonathan must be convinced to return to England. Do you understand?"

The men nodded, grinned again, and then dissolved back into the night.

As the door closed with a quiet thud, another man disengaged himself from the shadows. Archibald looked up.

"That was well done, Archibald," Richard's voice rasped. "Perhaps you have a bit of my father's blood after all."

Archibald did not meet his nephew's gaze. "They will accomplish the task, milord."

"For your sake, I do hope so." Richard turned and paced to the window, his fingers lingering over the rich curtains as he spoke with words devoid of emotion. "It does seem a shame. Jonathan should not have run away from me. More's the pity." He turned back toward the desk.

Archibald adjusted his weight in the chair and swallowed hard. "He has always been too impulsive, milord." He tapped his fingers rapidly on the top of the desk, his next words coming in a rush. "Even now he attempts to defy you. If his plans succeed, all will be lost. We have worked for five years to find our little group of Indians and the Frenchman. The attacks are going well. It won't take much more to convince the king to grant you control over the Pennsylvania wilderness. We are so close . . ." His voice trailed off.

Richard took a step forward. "Do you think to instruct me, Archibald?" His voice grew sinister. "Do you forget that your exalted position here in the colonies is dependent on me and on my title? One word from me, and you will lose everything you have. I sent you here to keep an eye on that defiant brother of mine, to make sure he does not succeed in his little frontier quest." He paused. His voice lowered. "Is that small task too much for you?"

Archibald dropped his head. "No, milord. I am sorry."

"Yes, Uncle, you are always sorry." Richard changed his tone. "Nevertheless, all will not be lost, as you seem to fear. Jonathan's attempts to oppose me cannot but fail. He will soon return to England begging for my favor and forgiveness."

"But, milord," Archibald's voice quavered, "it's too late for that. He will never give up his foolish dreams. Let my men finish the job."

Richard strode back to the desk and leaned over it, his shadow growing long and menacing on the dark maple. "Silence, Archibald," he hissed. "Grant blood does not die so easily." He put his thumb under Archibald's chin, forcing his head up to expose bare neck. He ran his fingers along the skin covering Archibald's throat. "Or does it?" he whispered.

Archibald choked.

THIRTEEN

~

The afternoon sun shone hot and stifling on Jonathan's back as he turned down the road leading to the Red Fox Tavern. Failure. It tasted bitter in his mouth. He wiped the sweat from his forehead and tightened his grip on the reins. It was too warm for October, much too warm. As if sensing his master's irritation, the horse flicked its head. A bit of froth from its mouth flew into the humid air.

Failure. His words of last night echoed in his mind, taunting him. He had been so sure, so confident, as he flung his plan at his uncle: "I'll find my own men."

Jonathan ground his teeth in frustration and listened to the cadence of his stallion's hooves as they played a dissonant beat to the pounding of his thoughts. How could he have known that not even one man would be willing to join him on the frontier, no matter how well he knew them.

Jonathan shook his head and reined his horse to the side of the road to make room for two women taking an afternoon stroll. Their bonnets tilted this way and that as they engaged in animated conversation. Jonathan watched the oversized hats, garish in the newest Parisian shades of blue and yellow. He rarely saw such colors on the frontier.

"Easy, Samson," Jonathan whispered, leaning over to pat the horse's neck.

The stallion skittered away from the women and snorted. As they neared, a few stray comments floated past Jonathan's ears.

"Imagine," one woman was saying behind an uplifted hand, "his own nephew embarrassing him like that."

"It's unheard of," the other responded. "Joseph says the man's practically a savage himself. He even has an Indian mistress."

"No!"

"It's true."

As they drew abreast of Jonathan's horse, the two women coyly slid their eyes up to take note of the man on the proud bay stallion.

Jonathan nodded his head in formal acknowledgment and turned away from them, locking his eyes on the cobblestone street before him. The women raised their heads as they passed, as if irritated by his lack of admiration. When their footsteps faded behind him, Jonathan returned to his thoughts, purposely ignoring the import of their words.

He missed the wilderness. The city was choking him, defeating him. It bartered for his dreams without offering him anything in return. And now, his plan to recruit men had failed miserably. Jonathan frowned in disgust. He'd never seen such a reluctant bunch of men. He had listened to a myriad of meaningless excuses as each man pointedly avoided his searching gaze.

"Planning on getting me a wife here soon," one man had whined.

"Going back to England come the next ship," a sailor explained, his roughened face turned toward the dock.

Jonathan grunted as he recalled his personal favorite. "Sorry, got the gout. Can't make the trip."

Not one of his former friends could commit even a few months to come with him. It was unthinkable. What was wrong with this city? He had come to Philadelphia for a militia of armed men, and he would return with one young half-breed. And she was just a slave-girl, not at all what he needed to protect his home and his dream. Jonathan allowed a bitter smile to brush over his face. He had been outmaneuvered this time. He nodded his head, his eyes narrowing as he looked into his future. He had lost this battle, but he would not be defeated. Somehow he would find a way to succeed.

Samson threw his head back and snorted as a small boy darted from the shadows of an adjacent alley. Jonathan yanked back the reins. Too late. The boy crumbled into a heap at the horse's feet. With a shout Jonathan leapt from the saddle and knelt beside the huddled lump of ragtag cloth. Gently he turned the boy over and held him as

Samson blew warm breath into the child's face. The golden eyelashes fluttered and opened as the boy stared up at Jonathan.

"Are you hurt?"

"I-I don't think so," the boy stammered, attempting to rise to his feet.

Jonathan pulled him up and dusted off his clothes as he checked for any signs of injury.

"I bet old Samson here gave you quite a fright. He begs your pardon." Jonathan smiled.

The boy grinned and patted Samson's nose. "I'm all right. Oh . . ." His eyes widened. Furtively he reached inside his coat and pulled out a strange contraption made of silver. A look of relief washed over his face. "Oh, good. It didn't break. Oops." He shot a worried look at Jonathan.

Jonathan raised his hands in a gesture of innocence. "I didn't see a thing."

"Thanks, sir." The boy's face broke into another unabashed grin, showing two teeth missing in the front of his smile. "It's for Mr. Franklin. Very important. He must have it today."

Jonathan chuckled and patted the boy's shoulder. "You run along then and watch yourself. We don't want to keep Mr. Franklin waiting."

The boy scurried off, one hand holding tightly to the object inside his jacket. Jonathan watched him until he was safely out of sight before he vaulted back onto Samson and urged the horse to a trot. It had been a long time since he had been a boy like that, full of eager responsibility and innocent enthusiasm. Or maybe he had never been such a boy. Had he ever been innocent of the world's wiles? Or had his family stolen that bit of childhood from him too?

Jonathan sighed and shook his head. The city—it was getting to him, like a poison in his blood. It made him crazy with thoughts that he couldn't understand. It was time he went back home to the wilderness. High time.

~

The door to his room gave a quiet moan as Jonathan pushed it open and entered. He drew a sharp breath and stepped back. A strange woman sat on his chair, watching out the window as dusk fell over the city. Had he entered the wrong room?

Quickly he checked the door. No, this was his room. At least it was the room he had left that morning.

He cleared his throat and shut the door behind him. She did not turn around. "Pardon me, miss," he murmured.

At the sound of his voice, the woman turned. Jonathan was lost again in the sky-blue ocean of eyes that he had not been able to forget since he first saw them on the platform of a slave auction.

"Kwelik?" Her name welled up within him and escaped his lips in a husky whisper.

She rose to her feet, her dress falling gracefully around her slender frame. Slowly she turned to face him. Anything else he would have said caught in his throat as he regarded her. Silence twined its heavy fingers around him and held him motionless. Suddenly he heard nothing but the deafening beat of his own heart. His eyes locked with hers, and he knew that his were telling a story that he was not prepared to accept.

Kwelik took a step back.

Jonathan abruptly turned away. "I-I'm sorry, Kwelik. I don't know what I was thinking." He ran his hand through his hair and retreated to the far side of the room. "You look . . . different." His voice wavered and cracked, sounding a bit like the boy he had met on the road. Quickly he straightened the blanket on his bed and began to throw his possessions into it.

He took a deep breath, willing his mind to take control of the chaotic emotions raging within him. "Get yourself ready. We're going home," he muttered, trying to strip his voice of the feeling that threatened to betray him.

For a moment Kwelik did not move. Jonathan stopped and glanced back at her and then shook his head. She had no possessions to prepare. He turned back toward the bed and threw in his last change of clothes. "You're probably more ready than I to see the wilderness again." He sighed. "It will be a good sight. To go home." *Home*. He winced at the word. It was not her home, and yet it would be closer to it than this barren place. She would get used to it, to him.

Jonathan deliberately kept his back toward her. Yes, it would be good to see the trees, the streams, the homestead again. Perhaps then he would regain control over himself and stop acting the fool.

"You will be glad to get away from here?" He posed the statement as a question.

She did not answer.

He continued his nervous chatter, hoping to ease the tension between them. "And Nahum. You'll like Nahum. He was a slave once too." Why did he say that?

Jonathan folded the blanket and tied it with rope. "Come, it's getting late. Everything else is already on the horse." He stepped toward her, his last piece of rope in one hand. "Sorry about this, but it's necessary." In a deft movement he tied her wrists together, making sure that his fingers did not rest too long on her soft skin. For a brief flash, their eyes met. He swallowed hard. "Are you ready?"

Kwelik nodded and remained silent.

"Will you never speak?" Jonathan whispered the question under his breath, wishing that her words would somehow cover his discomfort.

She did not respond.

Jonathan rubbed his hands against his thighs and grabbed the bundle from his bed. Without another glance, he twisted her rope around his arm and strode toward the door.

"Rosie," he yelled into the hall, "bring Samson around to the front. We're leaving."

The sound of Rosie's smug "Aye" brought him back to his senses. Jonathan grimaced. He should have guessed her part in Kwelik's transformation.

FOURTEEN

Before Kwelik could compose her unsettled thoughts, she and Jonathan were in front of the tavern, the little red fox staring down at them with weathered eyes.

"Leaving so soon?" Rosie called, her hand resting idly on the horse's bridle. "Samson here was just getting to like me Scottish brogue."

Jonathan took a few steps toward the horse and threw his bundle behind the saddle. "It's time to go home. One more day in this bloody city, and I think I'll forget my own name."

Rosie chuckled and then turned her eyes to Kwelik, her gaze traveling down to the rope on Kwelik's wrists. "What's this?"

Jonathan mounted his horse. "She's a slave, Rosie."

Rosie looked up at him. "You remember me words, Jonathan Grant. Treat her right. Don't you forget."

He nodded his head once. "I remember. And don't think I don't know what you're trying to do by making her up like that. I won't soon forget your meddling."

Rosie gave him a wry grin. "I'm only helping you see what's already there." She lowered her voice. "Beautiful lass, ain't she?"

Jonathan grunted and turned away.

Rosie walked back to Kwelik and placed both hands on her shoulders. "It'll be all right, lassie. You just keep trusting in our Lord. He'll see you through." She wiped her hand across her nose. "Oh, lassie, I'll be missing you. Don't you give up now. Me prayers be with you." She hugged Kwelik quickly, then backed up, sniffling.

Kwelik felt the lump growing in her throat, belying any attempts to speak.

Rosie's mouth turned up in a watery smile. "Not a word, lassie, or you'll break my old heart for certain. You go on now."

Jonathan gave the rope a gentle tug as the horse started on its way. With one last look back, Kwelik stepped resolutely forward and followed him.

Once more the noise and bustle of the city sent shivers down her back. She lifted her head, wishing she could rise up on wings and fly away from it all, fly to a place where she could again find God and feel His touch. But the rough grip of the rope held her fast.

Strolling down the narrow street, walking in the opposite direction, two gentlemen approached, their hands clasped behind their backs as they engaged in animated conversation.

"It's nothing but pure enthusiasm, I tell you," said the older of the two men. "Men and women weeping and wailing. It's emotionalism, not religion."

The younger man shook his head. "I beg to differ, sir. It's a religious awakening that we are seeing here in the colonies. A great awakening. The emotionalism you speak of is no more than deep repentance, without which there can be no true religion at all."

Kwelik turned her head to watch the men more closely as the second man continued to press his point.

"Tell me, have you seen our Captain Hanabel of late?"

The older man frowned. "No, I haven't. Nor do I wish to. I have heard that he boards transport ships and offers a guinea to anyone who will tell him a new curse, just so that he can add it to his vocabulary." The man's scowl deepened. "He's a rogue and a blackguard. Why do you mention him?"

"He was indeed a blackguard," asserted the other man. "But he has heard the Reverend Whitefield preach and is said to have had a personal experience with God."

Kwelik watched the older man wave away the words with one hand. "Talk comes easily, my boy," he continued, "but truth is proven by time."

The younger man nodded his head in agreement and tipped his hat respectfully as he passed Kwelik. Then he turned back to his friend. "That may be so. But you should know this: Now Captain

Hanabel swears not at all. That, sir, is the power of a true religious awakening."

"Humph, a great awakening, you say?"

Their conversation was lost as they turned a corner and headed toward the river.

Kwelik drew a long breath and turned her head to the road in front of her. Perhaps Rosie was right. Perhaps Papa's beliefs of a personal God, of a God concerned with the individual lives of His children, really were sweeping the English colonies. But if that were so, those beliefs had not yet touched the man who rode beside her. Even now he sat with his back stiff in the saddle as if he had heard nothing of what the two men said.

Jonathan turned toward her and spoke over his shoulder. "We'll be stopping at the blacksmith shop to pick up a horse for you."

Kwelik looked up, startled. She had not expected to ride.

"She's a dark little mare," Jonathan continued. "A good mount, I've been told. I think you'll be pleased with her. Luckily I had bought her for Nahum before I saw you." Jonathan gave her strange look, as if his words had flustered him.

Within a few minutes they turned down an empty street and stopped in front of a short, wood-clad building with "Blacksmith" carved roughly over the wide double door.

Jonathan leapt from his horse and tied Kwelik to the hitching post. "You keep an eye on old Samson for me." He tried to make his voice light, but it faltered and left his words hanging awkwardly between them.

"Listen," he continued. "I'm only doing this for your own good. You must not try to escape. You would find it hard to survive in this town." He paused and tied Samson's reins beside the rope. "You will stay here and not move?" It was more of a question than a command. Kwelik nodded her head and stepped close to the horse.

"This shouldn't take long." Jonathan gave her one last look and then walked inside the shop.

Kwelik leaned against Samson and let his presence comfort her. The horse, at least, did not know the difference between a slave and a free person, a half-breed and an English lady.

Samson turned his head and gave her a playful nudge.

"You stop that now," she whispered, reaching up her tied hands to pat his neck. The horse's warm breath tickled her ear as he began to nibble her collar.

Suddenly Samson perked up his ears and swung his head toward the alley behind them.

"What's wrong, boy?" Kwelik dropped her hands and cocked her head to listen. Samson stamped his foot and gave a nervous nicker.

Through the sound of a hammer banging on an anvil, she heard it—the quiet shuffling of feet and low whispers. A pang of fear shot through her. She sidled closer to Samson.

"What have we here?" A rough voice flung the question at her from the other side of the horse. Before she could pull away, a man dressed in the tattered garb of a sailor stepped around Samson and grabbed her rope. "Look, lads," he called, "a fine bit of woman all trussed up and ready for the taking."

Two other men slipped from the alley to form a rough semicircle around her. "What shall we do with her, boys?" One of the men gave a mock shrug of concern and laughed.

The first man sauntered up to her and ran his fingers over her wrists and up her arms.

Kwelik shivered and attempted to pull away, but the bite of the rope stopped her.

"What's the matter? You don't like the looks of ol' Brody here?" The man grinned, revealing a gold cap on his front tooth.

Kwelik lifted her chin. "Leave me alone." She kept her voice steady.

"I don't think so, missy." The man gripped her arm and squeezed until she winced. "We need you to do us a little favor, see?" He stepped behind her and put his arm around her throat, wrenching her head back.

Kwelik squirmed and sank her teeth into his arm.

He did not loosen his grip. "Did you break your teeth, missy?" he scoffed.

A knife flicked from the hand of the second man. "Now you be a good little girl, and we won't harm you, at least not too much." His voice felt wet and lecherous in her ear.

The knife advanced toward her, its blade flashing cruelly from the thick fist of the man who held it.

"Jonathan, help!" The words sprang from her throat before she realized that she had shouted. Brody jerked her head back, violently cutting off her shriek.

"Much obliged, missy," he whispered. "That's just what we needed."

Before the chill of his words faded from her ear, Jonathan burst from the shop's door. He grabbed one of her assailants and flung him to the ground. Two more men leapt from the shadows to seize Jonathan. With a cry as savage as any Indian, Jonathan threw one man off his back and then pounded his fist into the face of the other. The second man howled and fell to the ground, blood spurting from his broken nose.

A shriek erupted from Kwelik's throat as the blood spattered across her skirt. With a move learned from the warriors of her tribe, she kicked the knife from the sailor's hand in front of her and then crashed her heel against the instep of the man who still held her tightly against him. He yowled in pain as the sound of breaking bone filled the air. His cry was cut off as she jammed her elbow into his midsection. With a startled "oomph," he dropped to the ground, his hands gripping his injured foot.

"Help. Someone help!" Kwelik's cry echoed hollowly off the surrounding buildings.

She turned toward the shop. She could see the blacksmith through the window. Kwelik shouted again.

Without looking at her, the smith turned and walked to the back of the building.

From the corner of her eye, she saw one of the men dart into the shop and disappear into the dark interior.

With a groan of frustration, Kwelik pulled against the rope, but the knot stayed tight. She backed against Samson and prepared herself for the next attacker, but they had seemingly forgotten her, so intent were they on Jonathan.

Jonathan grabbed another man, shoved him to the ground, then laid a punch into the stomach of another. Three men now lay, injured and helpless, at his feet. Jonathan turned toward the fourth. Kwelik could see the anger mixed with fear in the man's face as he shuffled just out of Jonathan's reach. His hair hung in dirty clumps over his eyes, obscuring his vision as badly as the cut that bled profusely from his forehead.

Jonathan took a step toward him, challenging him.

A glint of steel caught Kwelik's attention. She screamed a warning. "Jonathan, behind you!" Too late. The shovel split the air and crashed down on Jonathan's head.

He made no sound as he crumpled to the ground at Kwelik's feet.

She leaned over him, straining at her ropes, her face above the bloody gash on his temple. "Jonathan?" Her throat closed around his name.

He did not move.

A single tear squeezed from her eye to fall on his cheek.

FIFTEEN

Darkness swirled across Jonathan's vision and danced to the wicked cry of demons in the night. He flailed his arms in the nothingness and felt his heart rend at the sound of the scream. It came again. He tried to run toward it, but his feet refused his command. He turned. She was there. But so far away.

The blackness closed around her like fingers from hell. He watched, helpless, as the fingers tightened their grip. Her eyes burned with blue fire. She did not scream again, even as the darkness choked her, squeezing the life from her lithe body. Jonathan shouted as she was lost to his view. His voice died in the nothingness. She was gone. Gone.

A tremor ran through Jonathan's body. He was drenched in a cold sweat. Slowly his eyes cleared. She was there. He blinked. Was it still a dream? The bed felt damp beneath him. He closed his eyes tight and opened them again. She did not disappear. "You're here." He heard the words in his mind, though no sound reached his ears.

"Shhh," Kwelik whispered, wiping his brow with a cool rag.

"Where am I?" He scarcely recognized his own voice.

Kwelik removed the rag from his forehead. "Back at the Red Fox Tavern."

Jonathan lifted his head to sit up, but she pushed him back. A wave of nausea washed over him as his head descended to the pillow.

"You mustn't get up." Kwelik scowled at him. "The doctor said you got a very bad crack on your head and must rest for a few days. Do you understand?"

He felt himself smile as she spoke with the same tone of voice that he had used with her. "I understand. Are you all right?" His voice gained strength.

"Me?" Kwelik shrugged. "Just a couple of scratches."

"What happened?"

"After you were hit, some men came. Our attackers ran away. I think they thought you were dead."

Jonathan grimaced. "I thought I was too." His vision blurred, then cleared again.

Kwelik turned her face away and dipped the rag into a basin. She wrung it out then placed it again on Jonathan's brow.

He sighed. "Everything will be all right once I get back home. Can't stay here anymore. Got to go home."

"Those men might come back?" Kwelik's brow furrowed at the possibility.

"I don't know. Don't want to wait to find out. We've got to leave."

Kwelik shook her head. "Not for a couple of days."

Jonathan raised his hand to the bandage on the side of his head. Even that small movement caused his stomach to heave. "I suppose not."

"The doctor came and sewed it up last night. He says two days, maybe three." Kwelik turned away. She took a deep breath. "By the way, thank you for saving me."

He smiled. "Is that why you're still here?"

Kwelik frowned and shook her head. "What do you mean?"

Jonathan's voice became faint. "The blackness. I saw it. It took you away from me."

Kwelik placed her hand on his shoulder. "I'm here. I'm not going anywhere."

Jonathan's eyes met hers. "Thank you."

She smiled and tucked the blanket beneath his chin. "You must go to sleep now."

Jonathan nodded and closed his eyes. Their talk had wearied him beyond belief.

~

Kwelik looked at him there, half-asleep already, his breath coming deep and even. She felt her heart constrict. He was so much like her brother, with his head tilted that way, when Little Cloud was sick and wanted her to stay beside him so that he could hear the story of the great bear when he awoke. She allowed a tiny smile to peek from her lips. Jonathan had rushed out to save her though she was but a slave. He had fought valiantly too, until he was knocked unconscious. She leaned over him and brushed her fingers over the lock of hair that had fallen over his eyes. So much like Little Cloud, yet nothing like him.

At her touch, he roused slightly. "Sleep. Yes, I'm so tired," he muttered, turning his head on the pillow and allowing his eyes to close completely.

Had she not been leaning over him, she would have missed his next words. "Please," he whispered, "don't leave me." He reached out his hand to rest it on hers.

Kwelik did not remove her hand from his.

Sixteen

White Wolf caressed the long branch in his hand. He took his knife and notched one end. It would make a fine bow. He smiled and tested the flex of the wood. Perfect. The weapon would be finished before the sun reached its zenith. White Wolf glanced behind him to check the sinew that was still soaking in a copper kettle.

The sight caused familiar anger to tighten in his chest. Everywhere were reminders of the white man's influence, even as he made a weapon to kill them.

With a groan of frustration, he picked up the kettle and threw it into the trees. But he knew it wouldn't stay there. One of the women or a child would be attracted by the shiny exterior and soon trot back to the village with the offending pot under one arm. Before he finished smoothing the branch in his hand, it would be back, reminding him of the white man's invasion of his people's land and spirit. He could not escape it. How could he make enough bows to kill them all?

White Wolf let the branch drop and covered his face with his hands. Then he heard it—the thud of boots on the hard-packed earth. His eyes flew open as he searched for the source of the sound.

A *white man!* He felt a flash of fury flame across his chest and stomach. He rubbed his eyes as if to dispel the mirage. But the white man remained, striding through the village as confidently as if he could not feel the heat of White Wolf's hatred. The man stopped and glanced toward the area where the women were grinding corn. A smile quirked at the corner of his lips.

White Wolf's eyes narrowed. He pulled out his tomahawk and gripped it until his knuckles turned white. Rage exploded across his vision as he watched the man pat a child on the cheek before nodding to the mother. White Wolf took a step toward the man and stumbled over a young boy in his path.

"Waptumewi! Waptumewi, look!" the boy squealed, holding up a stick that had been carefully shaped to a point at one end. "It's my fire stick. Bang! Bang!"

White Wolf growled and shoved the child out of his way. "Go play with the babies. Get away from me."

The boy's face fell into a mask of disappointment. He slowly turned away, dragging his stick behind him. White Wolf placed the tomahawk carefully behind his back and continued his pursuit. The man would not see the weapon until it was too late to save his scalp. He could almost feel the triumph of seeing the man beg for his life before his eyes rolled wide in death. White Wolf savored the thought. Taquachi would be pleased.

The man stepped toward a wigwam and slowly turned, the same shadow of a smile brushing over his face. The look reminded White Wolf of the man who had led the attack on his Lenape village, killed his people, and captured his sister. The memory burst through his mind with all the hatred and fear that he had felt then. White Wolf embraced the bitterness of his memory and returned the man's smile with a cold stare.

The man put his hand toward the wigwam door and nodded casually at White Wolf. "*Bonjour, mon ami,*" he said, the smile suddenly absent.

French! White Wolf choked.

Quickly the man turned and ducked into the wigwam.

White Wolf rushed toward the wigwam. With one hand, he gripped the hide that covered its opening, ready to rip it away and follow.

But wait! This was Taquachi's wigwam. White Wolf stepped back and dropped the skin as if it had scalded him. Sudden coldness washed over his fury.

"*Bonjour, mon ami.*"

White Wolf caught his breath as the words echoed out to him through the hut's doorway. It was Taquachi's voice that had spoken the greeting! White Wolf watched his own hand tremble on the hide. His vision tunneled and blurred with confusion. *Taquachi speaking the white man's tongue? How can it be?* Betrayed! The knowledge stung him, mocking his loyalty to the older warrior.

White Wolf dropped his tomahawk and stumbled to the far side of the wigwam. His stomach heaved as he crumpled behind the back wall. How could Taquachi meet with the enemy? How could he call him *friend?*

White Wolf put his hands to his head as if he could somehow erase the sound of Taquachi's welcome. Surely the warrior had a reason for his cordiality. He hated the white men as much as White Wolf did. Even when others traded furs with the French, Taquachi scorned their presence. White Wolf had admired him for that, trusted him, followed him without reservation.

He leaned his head against the wall and tried to think. The dried mud mixed with grasses scratched his skin, but he didn't care. All that mattered was that a white man had come, and Taquachi had welcomed him. Somehow there must be an explanation. Perhaps Taquachi was only putting the white man at ease so he could more easily slit his throat. Surely the man would not leave the wigwam alive. Taquachi was only playing with the man, mocking him, luring him into a sense of security.

As White Wolf searched his mind for a plausible answer, the voices of the two men floated out to him through the cracks in the wigwam wall.

"You have news?" Taquachi continued in French. White Wolf could hear his eagerness. The tone of voice sickened him.

"News, indeed, bad and good," the Frenchman responded.

White Wolf heard Taquachi's low grunt as the man continued. "Do you remember the one we spoke of before? The one who came over the ocean, the Dawn Sea as you call it, to take your land?"

Taquachi's voice was firm as he answered, "I remember."

The Frenchman paused before continuing. "He returns to the frontier."

"What?"

"Are you surprised? You did nothing but burn his barn. A minor deterrent." The Frenchman's voice conveyed the weight of his scorn.

White Wolf leaned closer to the wall. Now it would come. The white man's death. He held his breath and listened for the telltale gasp of surprise followed by a low gurgle of blood. But the sound did not come.

"You said he would go back over the sea. He would not come to our land again." Taquachi's words were not fierce but petulant. White Wolf writhed as he realized that Taquachi would not make the other man pay for his contempt.

"He returns."

"What more do you want from me?" Taquachi's voice turned sullen. Silently White Wolf rose to his feet and searched for a crack large enough to see through. He found none.

"Even now he's on his way. You must not allow him to reach his homestead."

"Is he alone?"

White Wolf felt the weight of silence as the Frenchman paused. "He is alone."

"Then we will kill him."

A surge of anticipation rushed through White Wolf as he heard Taquachi's statement. This was the warrior he knew and followed.

"You must reach him while he's still on the trail," the Frenchman continued. "Otherwise you will fail as you did before. But the Englishman in Philadelphia does not wish him dead. Yet." The man paused, his voice lowering. "I say, do as you must. This man must not succeed."

"Then we will kill him," Taquachi repeated.

White Wolf felt his own soul echoing the promise. With that prospect, he forgot his former doubts. *White men are fools*, he thought, *betraying each other*. He pushed from his mind the dark faces of the Shawnee warriors who destroyed his village. He turned from the remembrance of how easily Taquachi had spoken the white man's tongue. None of that mattered now. The only thing that mattered was that a white man would die. White Wolf relished the thought.

The red man was noble and pure. All white men were to be

despised and hated. Whatever ancestry he shared with the white man was now gone, washed away in the ceremony that had made him part of this new tribe. Gone too was the boy who had turned his back on his sister, run away a coward, and left her in the hands of the white man. He was that boy no longer. Now he was a Shawanowi warrior.

White Wolf fingered the pelt around his shoulders. He had a new name, a new tribe, and a new life. The life of victory. He felt the thrill of war coursing through his blood—red, hot, and angry. This time he would not be afraid, he would not run, and he would not have to be ashamed. Many white men would die to pay for what had been done to him, his sister, and his village. His wigwam would be surrounded by a hundred scalps of his enemies. He would have to cut down a dozen trees to make poles to display them all. He leaned back against the wigwam wall and closed his eyes. No white man would escape the sharp edge of his revenge.

White Wolf's dreams merged suddenly with reality as he felt the cold edge of a knife at his throat. His eyes flew open and met the freezing gaze of Taquachi.

"What are you doing, Waptumewi, listening at my wall? Do we have a traitor in our midst?"

"Me?" White Wolf's rage returned at the accusation. "The Frenchman is in *your* wigwam! How can you greet the white man as a friend?" White Wolf's voice cracked on the last word, betraying his youth.

Taquachi laughed and lowered the blade. "You are a brave little man, Waptumewi. You will come with us tonight. Perhaps you will taste the white man's death at the end of your blade."

White Wolf's face hardened with eagerness. He quickly forgot his anger, his feelings of betrayal. All that mattered now, he reminded himself, was the spilling of the white man's blood. He retrieved his tomahawk from the dust and nodded. "Tonight."

White Wolf dropped his eyes from Taquachi's and ran his thumb lightly over the edge of his tomahawk. A thin red streak formed across his skin. Tonight it would be the white man's blood that would stain his hands and blade. Tonight the real battle would begin.

White Wolf lowered the weapon and faced the setting sun. For a moment his anger quieted, and he heard the whisper of his fear: *How much blood will it take to wash away your shame?*

He shoved the thought from his mind.

SEVENTEEN

From atop her horse, Kwelik watched the dying sunlight dance across the rolling surface of the Susquehanna River. She breathed deeply of the fresh scent of pine and autumn grasses. All around her yellow, orange, and red leaves glowed with their fall hues, until the forest seemed like some imagined palace built to house the sun's rays. A few boulders poked their heads from their leafy beds to show wrinkled faces marred by lichens. Kwelik smiled down at their gray frowns and remembered how she had once woven wild tales about the "rock men," as she called them. Her brother would always giggle with delight, his eyes brightening, as he listened to her stories. Then his mouth would form a small "o" as he reached out one finger to touch the rock's face. The memory caused Kwelik's throat to tighten with familiar grief. She lifted her eyes from the rocks and stared into the scattered pine trees that rose tall and straight beyond the maples.

Beneath her horse's hooves, fallen leaves crunched and crackled as if to herald the passing of the miles. Kwelik switched the reins to her right hand and patted her mare's neck with the left. It had been a long day for both of them. But the Allegheny Mountains still rose tall and majestic in the distance, seeming no closer than they had that morning. Though now the sun slipped behind the tallest ridge, crowning it with golden glory. Kwelik brushed a stray wisp of hair from her face and sighed as the breeze playfully tossed it back across her cheek.

This was the land she knew, the way it laughed and danced and beckoned her to revel in the glory and beauty of God's creation. There were no strange sounds of the city, no shouting, no clang of the smith's hammer, no ring of horse's hooves on cobblestone. Here nothing had changed. But everything was different.

They had left Philadelphia over a week ago. In that time the very nearness of God's creation should have soothed her, should have been a balm to her fear and pain. But the beauty of the wild fell on eyes that were no longer free, ears stopped by the dread of slavery, a heart that still wept for a village destroyed.

What will happen to me now, Lord? she prayed. *You have exchanged my dreams for this nightmare, my laughter for chains. How long will You be silent?*

Kwelik dropped her head and closed her eyes to listen. She heard the soft gurgle of the river, the rustling of branches overhead, the squawk of a blue jay in the distance. In them she searched for the voice of God but could not find it. Instead, forcing its way to the forefront of her consciousness was the steady crunch of horses' hooves on the leaf-covered ground—the sound of her enslavement.

Kwelik opened her eyes and studied the back of the man in front of her. His shoulders still slumped from unhealed injuries. Yet he had insisted that they leave as soon as he could sit upright. And she had not objected. She'd hoped that she would find peace again in the wilderness, that she would remember the girl she had once been, a girl full of dreams and ambitions, without fear. A girl whose faith never doubted, never questioned, always believed. But that girl had vanished. That life was lost, sold on a cheap wooden platform for a bag of coins that could be held in one hand. How innocently she had sat in the meadow weaving her grandiose dreams of adventure. Was it then that she had been free and happy? Had she ever been free?

Kwelik caught her breath and considered the thought. Had she truly known freedom there in the meadow with Lapawin? Or was she bound then too, bound by impatience and dreams that contained only the future and scorned the present? What did it mean to be free? Would she ever know?

Still she would trade that bondage for this. Her eyes traveled down to her wrists, unbound now by physical ropes, but still tied by the power of a promise. At the outset of this journey, the man had held a rope and asked her a single question: "Will you run away?" When she had answered "No," a bond stronger than rope held her. She meant to keep her promise. Her papa had always said that you become a slave to a lie once you tell it. She would not become more of a slave than she already was.

Jonathan interrupted her thoughts. "We'll make camp over that hill. I know the spot." He did not turn to look at her as he pointed to a gently rising knoll over a mile away.

Kwelik didn't answer. She knew the spot well, a place where rocks jutted out to form a rough shelter from unexpected storms. As a child, she had lived not far from there, before her people were forced to move further west by encroaching settlers and ill-conceived treaties.

Kwelik turned her head and listened again to the quiet tumble of the river, its laughter belying all that had happened to her. *River Laughing*. Her mother's name. The vision of a gentle face filled her mind with the same quiet persistence of the river as it wended its way through the land. Kwelik turned away from the water, but the heaviness of memory still clung around her. She knew what would come with the memory. But she wasn't ready. Not here. Not now. Maybe not ever. Silently she cried to God. *No, God! I cannot bear to remember, not now . . .* But memory came. Memory of her mother's death.

It seemed a lifetime ago, though in actuality it had only been a few short years. She remembered her mother lying thin and wasted on her bed. Death hung heavily in the air, permeating the darkness that grew thicker the closer Kwelik came to her mother's still form. Slowly River Laughing's eyes flickered open, blurred with pain and the last stages of fever. She reached out to grip Kwelik's hand.

"Do not grieve, little Kwelik," she whispered. "Soon I shall be in heaven with Jesus. How bad could that be?" Her laugh ended in a hacking cough.

With her free hand, Kwelik clutched the blanket. It was damp with her mother's sweat.

"Don't leave me, Mama. I need you." The sight of her mother blurred behind her own tears.

"Less than you think, child," was River Laughing's quiet answer. Her voice gained strength. "You need Jesus more. He's enough."

"No, Mama. Don't . . ."

"Shhh, child. All is well." She paused. "Take care of your

brother. He needs a steady hand." Her smile gave way to a look of gentle intensity as her hand traveled up to grip Kwelik's arm.

"Remember, Kwelik, don't be afraid. Never be afraid. You are not alone." A pale, shaking hand brushed over Kwelik's hair and dropped weakly to the blanket. "What a future He has for you, child. I can almost see it." Her eyes bored into Kwelik with a fervor that shook the young girl. "I wonder, are you brave enough to find it?"

River Laughing died that night, a slight smile still touching the corners of her mouth. Her death left the question ringing in Kwelik's ears: "Are you brave enough?"

Kwelik swallowed past the lump in her throat and tried to push away the memory. It should have comforted her, but it never did. And Kwelik knew why. Because she could not escape the question, the challenge of her mother's last words. They burned through her even now. "Are you brave enough?"

She was no longer sure.

~

Night fell quickly, too quickly as far as Jonathan was concerned. In the daylight he could forget, but not at night. In the darkness the truth haunted him, questioned him, demanded that he answer for actions he did not want to face. He had been full of desperate hope the last time he had passed this way. He had believed in himself. He had believed in his dreams of freedom on the frontier. But now he was returning, not as a man ready to conquer the future, but as a slave owner and a fool. He had once believed that the frontier had changed him, made him into a new man. But it was all a lie. His conduct with his uncle and the purchase of a slave proved that. What hope did he have of succeeding in the wilderness now?

Yet the frontier still called to him, beckoned him to try again, to fight, to win. If it hadn't been for his injuries and the girl who now rode behind him, he would press on through the night and not stop until he lay down on his own rough bed. But night demanded its due.

Silently Jonathan slipped from his horse and listened for the soft thud of the girl as she dropped to the ground behind him. He did not turn around. It was enough to know she was there.

They had developed a pattern since they left civilization behind. They rode in silence, not the silence of enmity, but of trust. At times he almost wished she would escape. Perhaps then some of the shame of his circumstances would ease. But now that he was used to her, he would miss her if she were gone, even though he had spoken but three sentences to her since that first day he had awakened from delirium. Now she had become a silent presence, as necessary to his surroundings as the mountains, trees, or sky.

The clatter of sticks behind him drew Jonathan from his thoughts. He turned to see that Kwelik had already gathered dead wood for a fire. Placing the wood carefully against a rock, she arranged the smaller pieces beneath the larger ones and piled the remaining sticks neatly to one side for later use. Silently she stepped back and glanced at him.

Without a word, he approached her and pulled a piece of flint from his pack. *It's odd*, he thought, *how much can be communicated without the clamor of many words*. All the women he knew in England had filled the air with their endless chatter. But this girl said more in her silence than they ever did with all their meaningless words.

Jonathan knelt down and started the fire, blowing gently on it until it caught into a rosy flame. He stood and brushed his hands against his pant legs. "You may get the water tonight," he said. He watched the emotions play over her face. Despite her promise, he had not let her out of his sight since they left Philadelphia.

Kwelik nodded once and faced him. "Yes, Jon—umm . . ." She paused, as if embarrassed by her own impertinence. She lowered her eyes to the ground and began again, "Yes, milord."

Jonathan cringed. It was his father's title and his brother's—the title of men who abused their authority, who hurt those weaker than themselves, who betrayed those who loved them. Is that how this Indian girl saw him, as a master and a brute? Jonathan swallowed hard. "Do not call me that." His voice cracked.

Kwelik's face revealed her confusion. "Milord?" This time her voice barely breathed the word.

Jonathan took a step toward her, unreasonable anger flaring up in a hot flash to his face.

Kwelik stepped back, one hand pressing against her chest as fear flickered through her eyes.

Jonathan read the look and despised himself. It was the same look his mother had often given to his father. He rubbed a hand over his face and sat on a nearby rock. "I'm not like him," he whispered to no one.

Kwelik did not move.

Slowly the heat receded from Jonathan's face. "Your people use only one name, do they not?" His voice sounded calm, reasonable. He surprised himself.

Kwelik nodded.

"Then so it shall be with us." Quickly Jonathan ran through all the names she could call him—Mr. Grant, sir, master. But none satisfied. All were but a reflection of his brother and his father. Only his first name truly belonged just to him. It was the name his mother had chosen. With sudden resolve he spoke again. "You will call me Jonathan. That is my name. You've used it before."

He watched a fine pink color rise to her face. She lowered her eyes again.

"Yes, Jonathan." Her voice was barely a whisper. She turned and hurried toward the river.

Jonathan watched her disappear behind a clump of brush before he turned back toward the fire. He would see whether or not she returned.

Soon the wild gyration of flame captured his attention. He stared into it, remembering his last day at the homestead. The fire had flared up this same way, its flames licking the dying embers. Now he was returning to his charred dreams, and nothing had changed, nothing except the addition of one small slave girl.

Sudden anger toward his uncle swept over him. If not for his opposition, all would have gone as planned. He would have muskets and militia men. And he would have never wandered into that back alley to find the girl.

Jonathan scowled and silently cursed his uncle. How dare the man think that he could manipulate him to return to England. If he ever went back, his brother would make him a mere puppet, without character or integrity. Never! He would never yield.

Jonathan's expression relaxed. Instead, he would be a man of honor. He would teach his neighbors to protect themselves against the Indians and the French. He would help men to stand on their own, make their own lives, and not be dependent on anyone else. He would never be like his brother, who gained power only by stealing it from others, who took a man's dignity, devoured it, and made men minions to his own will.

Jonathan sighed and poked the fire. His anger at his brother was pointless. Richard was half a world away and no longer impeded his life. And his uncle was not worth the energy it took to sustain his hostility. He was only angry with himself. Jonathan leaned his head against the rock behind him and closed his eyes.

The snap of a twig startled him. He looked up to see Kwelik standing silently before him, her slender form illuminated in the dull glow of firelight. She handed him a cup of water and knelt by the fire. He took the water and drank it in a single gulp, hoping to quench the heat of his thoughts.

"Who are you, Jonathan?" Kwelik's words jolted through him.

His eyes flew to her face, but nothing there betrayed the fact that she had broken her long silence. For a moment he doubted he had heard her. Perhaps it was only the echo of his own uncertainty.

Jonathan ran his fingers through his hair and slowly formed the answer he knew he must give, to himself and to her. "I don't know anymore. Maybe I never have."

Kwelik nodded as if she understood his words better than he did. Then she stared across the fire into the night, her voice floating through the darkness like some ghostly whisper. "You will never defeat the demons that pursue you unless you surrender to God."

Rosie's words came back to him. She had said the same. How did these women see through him? What did they know that he didn't?

Quietness again fell over them. Furtively Jonathan watched the girl. The fire's shadows flickered over her in a strange dance that seemed to beckon him to face the truth, a truth that he had denied ever since he escaped England.

Kwelik turned back to him. She seemed to see his pain, and softened. Her eyes met his, and he was shaken by the compassion he saw there.

"Look at the stars, Jonathan." Her voice reached out to him, held him, drew him from his fears. "See the outline of the trees against the sky. See how the firelight shimmers off the rocks around us, how the grass throws shadows across the earth. Smell the dampness of the night on the wind as it groans through the leaves and seeks for its home. Listen to the howl of the wolf speaking to the moon. Do you hear it? Do you know what it says?" She paused, her head cocked as if she were even now listening to the eerie call of the wild. "Listen, Jonathan. It cries for its Creator."

He poked a stick into the glowing embers before him. The coals flared, illuminating her eyes with a blue fire that he had seen only once before, and that time in a dream.

"You are the wolf, Jonathan." Her words flamed through him. "How long will you cry to the moon?"

EIGHTEEN

The rustle of leaves woke Kwelik from a dream too disturbing to remember. She turned over, her eyes searching the trees that lined the small clearing where she and Jonathan had stopped for the night. Her gaze traveled over the glowing ashes of their night's fire and then paused to study the two horses that stood sleeping a few yards away. The sound had not come from the horses. Had she heard it at all?

Kwelik frowned. The hairs on the back of her neck prickled with growing dread. Perhaps it was only the dream. She could still see scattered visions of Tankawon, her father, and a fire that burned, roared, and refused to die. Was her uneasiness caused only by the haunting memories of the attack on her village, or was it more than that? She rubbed her eyes and stared into the night sky. Black storm clouds, driven by the wind, gathered around the moon and shrouded its light. In the distance thunder rumbled across the heavens.

In the silence that followed, it came again—the sound of a branch snapping against a tree trunk. It was not a dream or a memory. A cat perhaps? Maybe a wolf? Kwelik sat up and pushed her hair behind her ears. A footstep. A man.

She held her breath, concentrating on the sound. Her stomach tightened. Not one man but several, walking lightly and lithely, moving closer, closer. Without a sound Kwelik pulled back her blanket and laid it beside her. Like a piece of the night, she silently drew her feet beneath her and rose.

The fire had smoldered to a dull red glow, casting no light to betray her movement. Only the moon peeking occasionally from between the dark clouds illuminated her surroundings. Carefully Kwelik stepped around the remains of the fire and knelt beside Jonathan. Her eyes again searched the darkness and found nothing.

Behind her a huge boulder, over seven feet in height, nestled into a hillside, forming the southern end of the clearing. The men would not come from the south, she knew, but from the trees that formed a dark curtain on the other three sides of them.

With her back toward the boulder, Kwelik laid her hand on Jonathan's shoulder and squeezed. Her free hand pressed against his lips as his eyes flew open. Another crack of a branch sounded beyond them in the blackness.

Jonathan struggled to a sitting position.

Kwelik leaned over and whispered in his ear, "They come from the north. Five, maybe six of them. A war band."

Jonathan nodded and picked up his gun as he rose to his feet. "Do you know what tribe?"

"Shhh!" Kwelik glared at him and listened again to the advancing footsteps, so quiet that had she not been trained by her mother, she would not have heard them. The pattern of their approach was not familiar. She would guess they were Shawanowi or maybe Huron. In either case they were a long way from home.

From the edge of the camp, the horses stamped the ground, straining against the ropes that bound them. Their restless movement covered any further sound of the approaching band.

Jonathan sidled toward the horses and put a calming hand on Samson's neck. Both horses quieted. Silently Jonathan pulled another musket from his saddle pack and motioned to Kwelik. Without a word she pointed west. The men had changed their direction.

Kwelik backed toward the large rock and faced into the night. Still she saw nothing, but she knew that danger was drawing nearer, waiting for the right moment to attack.

The moment came. An eerie war whoop keened through the air. Kwelik had heard it before—the battle cry of the Shawanowi. She shuddered. Was that how it had sounded before they attacked her village? Had her people trembled as she was trembling now?

Jonathan raised his musket and pointed it toward the sound. At once three burning arrows flew toward them. One bounced off the hard surface of the boulder and landed at Kwelik's feet. She kicked dirt over the flame and pressed herself against the rock. Soon the full attack would come.

Another arrow landed in the leaves in front of them and smoldered. Frantically Kwelik edged toward the eastern end of the clearing.

"Do not move!" Jonathan's voice cut through the night.

Kwelik halted and turned toward him, fear emanating from every pore in her body. "What do I do?" Her voice cracked.

"This." Jonathan shot into the western trees and quickly reloaded. With a searching look, he tossed the other musket to Kwelik and grimaced. "Don't run. Shoot."

Kwelik's mouth went dry as she touched the deadly fire stick. More arrows arched through the air, blazing a path against the stormy sky.

Jonathan's next shot blasted into the night. At the same moment an arrow thudded into Kwelik's mare. The horse screamed with a high, unearthly pitch that rose above the war cry of the Shawanowi. Chills of horror sped down Kwelik's back. She clutched the musket and raised it, watching how Jonathan held the deadly device. Her hand shook as she rested the gun against her shoulder. She felt a scream gather in her throat and die there.

Jonathan turned toward her. "Shoot it!"

Kwelik gripped the metal barrel and steadied it as one Indian burst from the trees. He shot a flaming arrow toward them. "Aaaaiiieee," he shouted. One of Jonathan's packs caught fire. A blast threw Kwelik into the rock as the gunpowder stored in the pack exploded. Bits of burnt cloth flew through the air to land at her feet.

Sweat beaded on Kwelik's face. She regained her footing and swung the gun toward the advancing Indian. Through the smoke she saw him running toward her, his tomahawk raised to the sky. Terror clutched her, choked her, blinded her, until she could see nothing but the edge of the weapon shining in the red glow of the firelight. She squeezed her eyes shut and pulled the trigger. The kick of the gun knocked her against the rock as her shot exploded into the air. The Indian spun and fell.

"No!" The word tore from Kwelik's lips. Horrified, she dropped the gun and shuddered. What had she done?

Kwelik rubbed her hands on her dress as if to erase the evil touch of the musket. She hated the feel of cotton now. Who had she become? A woman who shot at her own people, a woman who would take the life of another to save her own. Kwelik groaned, fell to her knees, and buried her face in her hands. That young brave could have been her brother, her uncle, her friend. How could she do it?

Kwelik choked on the smoke that still billowed from the burning pack. Despair welled up within her. *Let them come*, she thought. *Let them take my scalp with the tomahawk, pierce my soul with their arrows.*

Jonathan shouted something at her, but she paid him no heed. *Let them come.*

Another shot rang through the air as two more warriors emerged from the trees. Kwelik glanced at them and then raised her face to the heavens. She would not yet give up the fight. *Oh, God, forgive me.* The words rose from the depths of her heart to combat her despair. *Save us. Help us.*

The sound of Jonathan's angry shout echoed against the rock and through her trembling frame. She did not turn her eyes from the sky. *Oh, God, save us. Please save us. We need You. I need You.*

From the corner of her vision, Kwelik saw Jonathan look wildly at her as one of the Indians flung himself across the fire at him. Jonathan toppled to the ground and twisted his body, pulling the Indian beneath him. He slammed his fist into the man's face and yanked the tomahawk from his hand. With one fluid movement, he then sprang to his feet and watched the Indian rise. Cautiously they circled one another until the brave stood facing Kwelik. A flash of lightning lit the warrior's features.

"Taquachi!" She did not know if she spoke his name aloud.

He did not look at her but faced Jonathan and pulled a knife from his belt. The firelight flickered off the blade as he tossed it from his left to right hand. Still they circled.

Kwelik's eyes flashed to the shadowed outlines of the other braves who stood among the trees. She clenched her teeth, knowing that they would now hold their attack, waiting for their leader to make the first kill. Above them thunder again rumbled across the sky, bringing with it the first patterings of rain. Kwelik turned to watch the two men, circling, circling, each searching for a weakness in the other's stance.

Jonathan held the tomahawk in two hands, ready to fend off the imminent attack.

Taquachi crouched low, the knife moving from one hand to the other while he studied his opponent, his eyes as black as the surrounding night.

Kwelik held her breath, unable to watch the outcome of the fight. Like the other braves, she knew better than to interfere in a warrior's battle. A woman who did so would be killed without mercy. Therefore, she turned away, her hands raising to the storm-lashed sky. *Father, into Your hands I commit my spirit. But, please, save Jonathan.*

A crack of lightning split the clouds as the storm broke out in its full fury. Before the light died, a roar of thunder rolled over the clearing. The sky opened, pouring its rain in torrents onto the forest beneath. Kwelik shivered. Lightning again sizzled through the night, impacting the boulder behind her with a loud crack. A scream lodged in her throat as the sound jarred through her.

Still the two men circled, neither breaking his fierce stare.

Rain pelted Kwelik's face and hissed into the fire that was only now beginning to lessen. She did not bother wiping away the water as her eyes followed the movements of Jonathan and Taquachi.

Another rumble shook the sky above just as lightning cracked around them. Taquachi lunged. Kwelik screamed. Before the knife could find its mark, a lightning bolt split an oak near them. Sparks flew. Half the tree toppled toward the clearing. Taquachi shrieked as a fiery branch knocked him to the ground.

The howl of the other warriors echoed into the sudden silence. "*Kitanitowit-essop*," one brave called before he disappeared into the forest. Taquachi staggered to his feet and spun around, startled. "*Kitanitowit*," he whispered, his eyes wide. Quickly he turned and bolted back into the trees.

Kwelik watched in amazement as the leaves shifted over the place where he had fled. "They are afraid." Her voice softened with awe. "They say the Great Spirit moves. It is the hand of God."

Jonathan ignored her. Without a glance in Kwelik's direction, he reloaded his gun and fired at the retreating backs of the Indians. The shot echoed defiantly through the night as the last warrior melted into the trees.

Rivulets of water streamed down Kwelik's face and mixed with her tears. Gratitude flooded through her. "God saved us," she whispered. "He delivered us from the hands of our enemies." Her voice grew stronger. "He saved us, Jonathan."

"Silence, woman!" Jonathan spun on her with unconcealed fury.

Kwelik rocked back in surprise as he rushed toward her and pulled her to her feet. "What did you think you were doing?" His voice grated harsh and uncompromising in her ear.

At his words anger replaced her exuberance. "What is wrong with you?"

"I heard you speak that Indian's name. I heard you!" Jonathan's face twisted with the accusation as the rain plastered his hair against his forehead and soaked his buckskin shirt. "Did you tell them we were here? Was it because of you they attacked?"

"No!"

"Then why didn't you fight with me? What were you doing?" Jonathan shook her, his fingers digging into her arms.

"I was begging God to save us!" Kwelik's voice grew sharp with exasperation. She blinked rainwater from her eyes.

"By collapsing to your knees in terror?" Jonathan's hands continued to bite into her arms.

Frustration overcame Kwelik's sense of propriety. "By falling to my knees in prayer! You don't think that just you and I could have fought off that war band, do you?"

"If you would have helped." Jonathan let go of her suddenly.

Kwelik stumbled back against the rock. "Even they knew that God was against them tonight. That's why they retreated." She motioned toward the gun at her feet. "If we had only these horrid fire sticks to depend on, our scalps would now be hanging from their belts, and you know it." She kicked the dropped musket with her foot. It skittered a few inches and stopped.

Jonathan grabbed it and rubbed off the mud with his sleeve. He turned and shoved the offending weapon in her face. "This is the only thing that will save us out here," he shouted, "and don't you forget it."

Kwelik shook her head. "No. It's only God who can save, out here or anywhere."

"God!" Jonathan spat out the word. "God doesn't care anything about me or you either. Do you see a fancy church, or even a preacher?" He flung his arm out toward the trees.

Kwelik looked up at the sky and took a deep breath. "Yes," she answered, her voice quieting despite the raging of the storm around her. "I see a church with the sky for its ceiling, trees for its pillars, and boulders for its pews." She paused. "And I hear the preaching of the thunder and rain. Why won't you see the obvious?"

"Do you really believe that God saved us?" Jonathan's tone was scornful as he turned on her, challenging.

Kwelik saw his look of desperate fury and . . . She caught her breath. For a moment she saw hope glimmer in his eyes. She smiled. "Yes, Jonathan. I know He did."

Jonathan stared at her, incredulity masking his features. He stepped closer, his amber eyes burning, demanding a response. "How can you know that?"

"Because it's true. I asked Him to."

~

The war band huddled around the fire in Taquachi's wigwam. Firelight flickered off the faces of the braves, still covered with the eerie designs of their war paint. White Wolf brushed the dried mud from his breechcloth as he watched the shadows dance off the black eyes of his leader. The dark silence oppressed him, frustrated him, angered him. At last he could stand it no longer.

"Their scalps were ours," he muttered. "They could not escape." He slammed his fist against the ground. "Why did we retreat? Are we warriors or cowards?"

"Silence, Waptumewi." Taquachi stared at him across the fire, his voice cold and deadly.

White Wolf shivered and looked away. A hundred conflicting emotions raged within him. He had been so close. He had felt their very lives pulsating in his hands. All he had to do was squeeze. But then the woman had aimed the fire stick at him and shot. He could still feel the searing pain as the bullet grazed his shoulder. But he was only stunned for a moment. He could have fought on if they hadn't turned back. Yet Taquachi was a wise, well-seasoned warrior.

White Wolf groaned with frustration. He couldn't help but voice the question again. "Why did we turn back?"

This time Taquachi chuckled. "My brothers, if only all our people were so thirsty for the white man's blood." He leaned toward White Wolf. "Next time, Waptumewi, you will have scalps hanging from your belt. By the Great Spirit, I promise you." Taquachi thrust his hand across the fire and squeezed White Wolf's arm, bringing new blood to the torn flesh on the boy's shoulder. "Next time you will have more than a wound from a woman to prove you're a warrior."

The other men laughed.

White Wolf winced at the rebuke as Taquachi again sat back on the other side of the flame. He touched the raw flesh on his arm, covering his fingers with the new blood that oozed to the surface. The sight of blood had once sickened him, but no longer. Not since the night the hot blood of the wolf spewed over him, a baptism far stronger than the water baptism that his father had believed in. Now he reveled in the smell of blood—the sign of a warrior. He would never be afraid or ashamed again.

White Wolf smeared the blood down his arm and bare chest. *Little Cloud is dead*, he thought. *I am White Wolf, man of power and hate*.

Taquachi's next words interrupted White Wolf's thoughts. "Our brother Waptumewi asked a question that I will answer." He paused and pinned each man with an icy stare. "Tonight the spirits opposed us. In their anger they stood in the path to our enemies. The fire from the sky was a sign of their displeasure."

"What will we do?" asked Gray Bear, at forty summers the oldest of their group.

"We must appease the spirits before the dawn breaks," Taquachi answered.

"Spirits?" White Wolf could not help but scoff.

"Silence, young one." Taquachi waved away his objection. "If Gray Bear had not pulled you from the clearing, you would be lying dead beneath the tree split by the spirits' fire."

Gray Bear nodded his agreement.

White Wolf frowned and remained silent.

Taquachi leaned closer to the flames, his face illuminated by the flickering glow. Only his eyes remained black. White Wolf felt the chill in them. "Tonight we join in the blood bonding."

"It is forbidden!" Gray Bear's tone revealed his shock.

A hush fell over the group.

Taquachi was undaunted. "We are weak because we have forgotten the old ways. It is because we scorn the dark spirits that we now cower before our enemies. Well, I say, no longer. Are you with us or against us, Gray Bear?"

Gray Bear bowed his head. "I will follow you, Taquachi."

The others mumbled their agreement.

"My brothers," Taquachi continued, "tonight we join ourselves to the spirits and to one another. No one else must know of the bond we fulfill tonight—not even my father."

Gray Bear raised his head in apparent confusion. "But the *sachem* leads our people. He will support us."

Taquachi growled, "He is an old man and a fool. Soon I will lead the people. Do you question me, brother?"

White Wolf watched the exchange with curiosity, wondering at Gray Bear's troubled look as he answered the younger man. "As you say, Taquachi. I do not question you."

Taquachi nodded. "Then let us begin the ritual." He pulled out a knife and wooden cup.

White Wolf watched the firelight flicker wickedly off the blade. His stomach knotted as if in foreboding of the ceremony to come. His eyes met Taquachi's.

Taquachi smiled at him without amusement. "Are you truly ready to become a warrior, Waptumewi?"

White Wolf's eyes did not waver from Taquachi's. Slowly Taquachi raised the knife, still holding White Wolf in his dark gaze. He slashed the blade across his own palm and squeezed his fist. Blood dripped into the cup. Taquachi again opened his palm, took two fingers and smeared his blood across his cheeks. He passed the cup and knife to White Wolf. "Join me, Waptumewi." His voice was like the blackness of night.

White Wolf took the knife, his eyes again seeking Taquachi's. The look he saw there was questioning, mocking. White Wolf felt the old cowardice clawing within him. This time he would not run away. With resolve he gripped the sharp blade in one hand until he felt its wicked bite in his flesh. His own blood dropped into the cup, making a quiet splash as it mingled with Taquachi's.

Taquachi smiled while White Wolf handed the cup to the next man.

Moments later the cup, now full, returned to Taquachi's hand. He raised the vessel above the fire. The air pulsated with black intent. "Now, brothers, we hail the spirits of darkness. May it be our enemies' blood that we drink in the days to come." Taquachi lifted the cup to his lips and drank. As he lowered the cup, a look of dark elation spread over his face. "With this drink I bind myself to you, my brothers, and to the spirits who guide us."

White Wolf took the cup in his own hand. He did not hesitate. The blood tasted bitter, sweet, and hot. He stared into the dark liquid and spoke his oath. "I bind myself to my brothers and to the spirits who guide us." At that moment a part of him died.

PART TWO

The Gathering Storm

NINETEEN

Pennsylvania frontier, February 1744

Kwelik held her breath, not daring to move. Her eyes squinted into narrow slits as she looked into the brightness of the sun on new-fallen snow. *Come on, come on, just a little bit farther.* Silently she willed the small gray rabbit toward the snare she had set. It hopped closer, its pink nose twitching in the cold air.

From behind the cover of a cranberry bush, Kwelik tightened her grip on the rope. Branches scraped at her sides and arms. Their prickly fingers poked her skin. All around her snow draped softly over the forest landscape, dressing the trees in brilliant robes and giving the "rock men" tall hats of glittering ice. To her left a group of pine trees huddled together to make a wall of forest branches, glistening white and green in the winter sun. Beyond them a frozen stream shone like glass, reflecting shards of sunlight into her eyes. A cardinal twittered into the late morning air, as if scolding her for entering its private domain.

Slowly Kwelik reached up and pulled the deer hide closer around her throat. The day was cold despite the brightness of the winter sun. As she moved, the rabbit sat on its haunches and sniffed the air. Kwelik froze, her free hand still gripping the hide at her neck. After a moment the rabbit again dropped to four paws and inched closer to the bait. Kwelik's hand remained steady on the thin rope as she drew a quiet breath. *Come on. Just one more step.*

There! She pulled the rope with a sharp jerk, closing the snare around the rabbit's back legs. "Gotcha!" The triumphant cry burst from Kwelik's lips. She jumped to her feet and trotted toward her captured prey. At the sound of her voice, the cardinal fluttered into the sky. The sound of its beating wings echoed against the forest branches. Kwelik watched its rapid flight and then leaned over to retrieve her quarry. *This will make six rabbits today*, she thought, *an excellent hunt. Jonathan will be pleased.* This was the first time since they arrived at his homestead that he had allowed her to hunt alone. Every day he trusted her a little more, and somehow it seemed imperative that she repay that trust.

Kwelik gathered the rabbits she'd caught and stuffed them into her hunting pouch. Their furry bodies made a warm lump against her skin as she slung the pouch over her shoulder and started back toward the homestead. They would feast tonight. The thought made her smile.

Kwelik retraced her shallow footprints from earlier that morning and soon reached the homestead. As she stepped into the clearing, she raised one hand to shade her eyes and glanced around the place that had become her home. Built opposite the two cabins, the bare shell that would become Jonathan's new barn rose against the backdrop of snow-laden trees. Only a scant frame stood now, like a dark sketching against the white snow. In the center of the oblong clearing, a single birch tree splayed leafless branches from its whitened trunk, its shape nearly lost against the snowy background. And there beyond the tree were the cabins.

Kwelik dropped her hand from her eyes and then trotted across the clearing and up the two steps that led to Jonathan's cabin door. There she paused. Icicles melted from the eaves, the water making soft splashing sounds on the snow beneath. She turned, reached up, and broke a dripping icicle from the eave. She put it into her mouth, breaking off the tip with her teeth. The cool liquid trickled down her throat as the ice melted on her tongue.

Unwilling to enter the cabin just yet, Kwelik turned to her left and broke off another icicle. The ice felt pleasantly smooth against her fingers. Before her, Nahum's cabin sat at an angle to Jonathan's, and inside Kwelik could see Nahum bending over a piece of wood that he was carving into an arm for his rocking chair. She smiled and turned away, knowing enough, even after only two months, not to disturb Nahum when he was at his favorite work.

Kwelik's smile grew wider as she remembered the first time she had seen Nahum. As she and Jonathan had ridden into the clearing, the tall, lanky man bolted from his cabin, fire stick in hand. Then upon recognizing his friend, he cast the weapon aside, his broad grin flashing white across his dark face as he hurried out to meet them. After gripping Jonathan's arm in greeting, Nahum had looked up at her and removed his hat. Even now the memory of that small gesture of respect warmed Kwelik's heart.

She pulled the hunting bag from her shoulder and listened to the sounds of hammering that echoed from within Jonathan's cabin. Kwelik smiled, guessing that Jonathan was repairing the shelf that fell in the last storm. Despite the winter weather, he hadn't let up on his work since they arrived. First he made a small lean-to attached to his cabin for her. She appreciated that amount of privacy. Then whenever the weather cleared, he busied himself traveling from one homestead to another, giving away maps of the area that she had helped him to draw and teaching other men how to protect their families. Between his journeys, he also started the work on his barn. And when he couldn't get out because of the winter storms, he went to Nahum's cabin to help build the rough furniture that now adorned both of their homes. The man rarely rested.

Kwelik swallowed the last of the melting icicle and wiped her fingers on her buckskin skirt. The cotton dress that Rosie had given her hung inside, its material too flimsy for the job of snaring rabbits. She rubbed her hands over the soft deer hide. Jonathan had allowed her to make a new set of clothes from the first buck that he shot after they returned. It was more suited to life in the wilderness, he had said.

Now there was nothing left to do but go inside. With her full pouch in hand, Kwelik reached for the doorknob. Before her hand touched it, the door was flung open, and Jonathan burst out, almost running into her. For a startled moment, Kwelik's eyes caught his, and she saw the worry written there.

Jonathan drew a quick breath, an exclamation tumbling from his lips: "You came back!"

Kwelik frowned, confused by his statement. "Did you need me for something? Are you going somewhere?"

"No. Nowhere," he answered too quickly.

"Then why are you . . ." Kwelik paused and dropped her gaze, finally understanding the meaning behind his words. He was coming after her. He thought she had run away. She sighed. Why was trust so hard for him to give?

Kwelik lifted the bag between them, her voice heavy as she spoke. "Six rabbits today. I've never seen such a good day for hunting." Her words fell between them, seeming to splash on the snow like the melting icicles.

Jonathan stepped back. "Six?" He cleared his throat, his voice again calm and controlled. "You're a good hunter." He put his hands on his hips and gazed out over the clearing, his brows furrowing slightly as if he were turning an idea over in his mind. Then he spoke again. "This is the first winter here for Daniel and his family down the creek. I've been wondering how they're getting along. I haven't seen them for over a month." Jonathan pulled out three of the rabbits from the bag in her hand and tossed them onto the snow beside his cabin. All the time his eyes avoided hers. "Would you like to come with me to give them some rabbits and deliver one of the maps you've drawn?"

Kwelik caught her breath. "Today?"

Jonathan smiled, finally glancing at her again. "Yes, today. This is the first clear day we've had since we arrived from Philadelphia. Besides, I'd like to see how Daniel's coming along with that cellar I showed him how to build." Jonathan reached out to take the satchel of rabbits from her hand. "Come," his voice was gentle. "The mare is completely healed now from our encounter with that war band. You would enjoy the ride, would you not?"

Kwelik nodded, confused by his sudden friendliness. For the past two months, he had seemed to be almost avoiding her, leaving the cabin when she entered, his manner hurried and distracted. But today was different. She shrugged. Maybe it was just the weather or his way of making up for doubting her.

Before she could consider the thought further, Jonathan was already past her and getting the horses.

"I thought we could do without saddles today," he called as he came back leading the animals. "Come, I'll give you a lift up."

Kwelik descended the steps and laid her hand on the mare's woolly neck. Jonathan's hands felt warm on her waist as he helped her to mount. She lay flat on the horse's back and swung her leg over, arranging the slit in her skirt so that her leg did not show. Then she sat upright and gathered the reins in her hand while Jonathan mounted Samson. For a moment their eyes met again, and she smiled.

Tentatively Jonathan returned the smile.

Soon the clearing fell behind them as they wound through the snow-laced trees that grew beside the creek leading to Daniel's homestead. Beneath the top layer of ice, the stream's waters still flowed, carrying bits of dirt toward the Susquehanna River.

After the horses leapt the ice-covered creek, Jonathan turned toward her, his features more relaxed than she had ever seen them. "You will like Daniel and his family, I think," he said. "Good folks, even if they are religious. Amish, I believe. Mary, Daniel's wife, has even promised to give me some of her hand-woven cotton to make into a new shirt." Jonathan grimaced. "Though I don't see what's wrong with buckskin."

Kwelik nudged her mare alongside Samson. "My father told me that the Amish usually live close to one another. It's strange that this family has come here alone."

Jonathan shrugged his shoulders. "Strange or not, they moved here last spring. I'm sure if all goes well, more of their people will move out." Jonathan took a deep breath. "This land will be settled yet." His face darkened. "And it will be done without any ruler, or governor, or so-called Duke of the New World." With that cryptic comment, he turned back in his saddle and began whistling a tune that sounded to Kwelik like a battle song.

Unsure of Jonathan's shifting moods, Kwelik dropped behind him. Although she had settled into life at the homestead, this man who had purchased her with his bold "forty pounds" remained a mystery. Sometimes she could see memories burning in his eyes, memories that even his determination could not erase. She could sense that something haunted him, pursued him, though he tried to deny it. Yet today it seemed that he had put that out of his mind and was trying to be different. Didn't he know that only Christ could heal the past?

Kwelik sighed and watched Jonathan's broad shoulders sway with the horse's gait in front of her. What was it that smoldered within him and chased away his peace? Was it fury, or fear?

Jonathan looked at her over his shoulder, as if reading her thoughts. "My brother wants to rule this land. He thinks it is the key to future power." He paused.

Kwelik waited. Jonathan had never spoken of his family before.

Slowly he continued. "He doesn't see the beauty of the wilderness. All he cares about is control and power."

Kwelik's heart ached at the bitterness of his tone.

"Richard wasn't always that way. He used to be kind and quiet. But he changed after our father died, after he became Lord Grant in my father's stead."

Kwelik again urged her horse forward, her voice low and compassionate as she spoke. "It would be hard to see your own brother change like that. I think it would hurt very much."

Jonathan didn't answer.

"I'm sorry, Jonathan."

His eyes flickered over to hers. "Let's not think about such things today. Let's forget the past and just enjoy the day." He smiled.

Before long the trees spread to reveal a gently rolling hill with a cabin as big as Jonathan and Nahum's cabins combined. A long porch graced the front of the structure, and on it sat two chairs that Kwelik recognized as Nahum's handiwork. Open windows were cut on each side of the door to give Kwelik a peek into the cabin's homey interior.

Jonathan nudged his horse forward as he entered the clearing. "Daniel! Mary! Is anyone home?"

Before the call faded from the air, a middle-aged man stepped from the cabin's door. Strands of scraggly brown hair stuck out from beneath his hat, at odds with the thick beard that trailed down his chest. Behind him a heavy-set woman with pale skin and a round face hurried onto the porch and stopped short.

The man stepped down and came toward them. "Hello, Jonathan!" he called. "What brings you here on this fine day?" The warmth of his tone set Kwelik at ease. With one hand he tipped back his black hat, his plain, dark clothes rustling as he approached them.

"Kwelik here," Jonathan motioned over his shoulder toward her, "snared some extra rabbits, and I thought you might like a few." He handed the bag to Daniel and dismounted.

Daniel's brow furrowed. He looked down at the bag and then up at her. His long face wrinkled into stern lines as his voice lost its warmth. "Didn't know you had a savage living with you."

Kwelik's spine stiffened at the words.

Jonathan's features hardened. Without answering, he strode to Kwelik's side and lifted her from the mare. His amber eyes clouded as he put one arm around her shoulders, drawing her close to him.

His simple gesture spoke more to her than any words he could have said. She glanced up at him, hoping he would see her gratitude.

Jonathan's arm tightened around her as he turned back toward Daniel. "Did you say something, friend?"

Kwelik's heart beat with a strange emotion as she stood at Jonathan's side and felt his strong arm around her. As a slave, she had not expected him to stand beside her, let alone defend her. And now, as her heart thudded awkwardly in her chest, she wondered if it would have been better if he had not.

Daniel glanced from Jonathan's protecting arm to his face. "No, Jonathan. Forgive me. I meant no disrespect."

Jonathan nodded once, his eyes losing their annoyance.

"Thank you," Daniel muttered, his gaze again dropping to the hunting pouch as he pulled open the wide mouth. He put his hand into the bag and pulled out a rabbit. "Three rabbits!" he exclaimed. "And good-sized ones!" His voice held awe as he dropped the rabbit back into the bag. "God bless you, my friend! I'm sorry to say that we've had no meat for weeks. Here, Mary, take these inside." He handed the bag to his wife who still stood on the porch, warily watching the interaction.

Jonathan smiled, his voice holding only mild rebuke. "As I said, it was Kwelik who snared them."

Daniel's face reddened. He turned toward her. "Umm, thank you, Kwelik. Much obliged, we are." He wiped his hands on his shirt as he spoke.

Kwelik inclined her head, accepting his thanks.

As if satisfied with the outcome, Jonathan allowed his smile to widen into a friendly grin. "Come, Daniel, let's look at that cellar of yours." He squeezed Kwelik's shoulder, then dropped his arm and walked toward the older man.

Kwelik tilted her head, regarding him while he strode away from her. *He is a complex man*, she decided. *It will take more than a few months to understand him*. She sighed. *But one thing is certain. He is respected by those who know him, not because he demands their respect, but because* . . . Kwelik's brows drew together as she attempted to put words to her observations and failed. *Well, just because of the man he is.*

Daniel smoothed his beard with one hand. When Jonathan reached him, he pointed to the far side of the cabin. "Come around the back here. I think you'll be pleased with the construction I've done." He patted Jonathan on the back as the two men walked away, leaving Kwelik standing with the horses.

The sound of shuffling drew Kwelik's attention to a rough wooden cart that stood near the house. With its wheels sunken in the snow and its two poles for hitching buried, it looked as if it hadn't been moved all winter. Kwelik ducked her head and looked closer, searching for the source of the sound.

In a moment a young boy poked his head from around the side of the cart, his eyes wide as he regarded her. "You a real Injun?" he called. From the porch his mother shushed him, but the boy paid her no heed. "I ain't never seen a real Injun up close before." He craned his neck to get a better look.

Amused by his curiosity, Kwelik knelt in the snow and motioned for him to come nearer.

Cautiously the child stepped from behind the cart and approached her.

"Awk! Matthew, come back here!" Mary cried. As far as Kwelik could tell, the woman had not moved from the spot where she had stopped on the porch. Rather she seemed rooted in place, transfixed by the sight of a "savage" in her snow-covered yard.

The thought sent a surge of irritation through Kwelik. Firmly she dismissed the feeling, put on her most pleasant look, and then turned her eyes from Mary to the child.

The boy continued toward Kwelik until he stood within a foot of her, his eyes level with hers. "Yer kinda pretty," he whispered, as if surprised by the observation. Then his voice turned indignant. "You don't look so scary to me at all!"

Kwelik chuckled. Before she could respond to his words, Mary bustled toward her and grabbed the boy, hustling him back into the cabin. Without a word, she pushed a lock of dirty blonde hair behind one ear and followed him. She did not look back. Pale curtains fluttered in the window as she forcibly closed the door behind her.

Kwelik sighed and turned away, her gaze drawn back toward Jonathan. She studied his tall frame. His shoulders were thrown back with a confidence that contained no arrogance as he pointed to the side of the cabin. In a moment he dropped to his knees, grabbed a saw, and began working to cut a hole in the cabin's wall near the ground. Daniel knelt beside him, nodding as Jonathan continued the work. In a moment Jonathan paused, his voice drifting over to Kwelik.

"If you put the window here, which will be near the ceiling of the cellar, you'll always have two ways out. You won't be trapped if the cabin is set on fire." Jonathan wiped his forehead and then began sawing again.

"I hadn't thought of that." Daniel's voice rose above the grinding of the saw.

Kwelik stepped forward, her eyes steady on Jonathan as he worked.

"There." Jonathan removed the small section of wall and rubbed his hand along the rough edge of the hole. "You'll want to smooth this a bit and cover it against wild animals." He stood and faced Daniel. "You've done well, my friend. It's the best-looking cellar I've seen yet. You were made for life on the frontier."

Daniel laughed. "You flatter me, sir. Nevertheless, I'll take your words as kindness and as much needed encouragement."

Jonathan grinned at the other man, his quiet laughter erasing the look of uneasiness that so often marred his features. The sight brought a smile to Kwelik's lips. She had not expected to see him like this, relaxed and laughing. Nor had she expected him to be a man who worked to help others as vigorously as he pursued his own dreams. Rosie had been right about him. He *was* a good man and an honorable one.

Kwelik felt a strange warmth coursing through her as she watched Jonathan pick up the extra pieces of wood and set them on the woodpile. She liked this side of him, maybe too much. She sighed. She was only his slave after all—a piece of property without the right to likes or dislikes, feelings or hopes. A slave, and no more. She must never forget that.

The door slammed behind her. Kwelik turned to see the woman exit the cabin and hurry toward her, her head down. "K-Kwelik?" Mary said her name cautiously as she approached. With a trembling hand, she extended a cloth folded carefully into a thick rectangle. "Here's the material I promised Jonathan." She held it out further.

Kwelik smiled at her. "Thank you, Mary."

Mary's eyes widened with surprise. "You speak English."

Kwelik nodded, a chuckle rising in her throat. Firmly she quelled it, willing her voice to remain courteous. "Yes. I am only half Lenape, that is, Delaware Indian. I am very pleased to meet you and your family." She held out her hand in the gesture of greeting that she remembered from Rosie.

Mary stared at her extended hand and then quickly reached out to touch her fingers to Kwelik's.

Before Kwelik could say another word, the woman scuttled back inside, the door closing with a thud of finality.

In a moment Jonathan returned from the far side of the cabin. "Looks good, Daniel," he said, smiling at the man walking next to him.

Daniel put his hands on his hips. "I couldn't have done it without your help. The door's made of thick oak too, just as you suggested. It'll hold for several hours if Indians ever do set the cabin on fire."

Jonathan nodded his approval. "Let's hope it's an unnecessary precaution, my friend."

"Let's pray it is," Daniel added, "for I won't fight them."

Jonathan frowned and shook his head as he took Samson's reins from Kwelik's hand. "We've had this argument before. Religious beliefs or no, you've got to protect your family."

"God will protect us."

Jonathan opened his mouth to object, but Daniel cut him off. "No, my friend. No more words now. Let us part company in peace."

Air escaped Jonathan's lips in an exasperated sigh. "As you wish. But remember, I and my musket are just a few miles up the creek if you need us." Jonathan helped Kwelik onto her mare and then mounted Samson. With a final wave over his shoulder, he turned and entered the forest with Kwelik behind him.

After an hour of riding in silence, Jonathan pulled up on Samson's reins and stopped beside the creek. He slid from the horse's back, tossed the rectangle of cotton onto a nearby rock, and jammed his boot heel through the water's frozen covering. "We'll stop here for a moment to let the horses drink." He did not look up at her as he kicked at the ice until he had made a large hole.

Kwelik dismounted beside him.

Both horses dropped their muzzles to the water, their lips pushing away the chunks of ice as they drank. After a moment Samson lifted his head and shook it. His bridle jingled merrily in the crisp air.

"Oh, look!" Kwelik's voice was no more than a whisper as her hand touched Jonathan's forearm. Before her a small finch hopped across the path and flitted to a branch overhead, trilling its melody to the trees. She watched in breathless wonder as the tiny creature's chest swelled with sweet song.

It was a moment before she noticed that Jonathan was looking at her instead of the bird. She turned toward him, gratitude flooding through her. "Thank you for bringing me out here today. I had forgotten how peaceful, how lovely, the winter could be." She paused, her voice lowering. "You are a good man, Jonathan."

Jonathan turned toward her. Without a word he reached up

and brushed his fingers lightly over her cheek. His touch sent a quiver of some nameless emotion tingling through her. His eyes met hers for a long moment before a smile touched his lips. "Thank you," he whispered, his voice so low that she wondered if she had heard it at all.

Kwelik's gaze did not leave his face as something indescribable passed between them.

TWENTY

Kwelik rubbed the back of her hand across her forehead and sighed. Spring was coming early this year, bringing with it days that seemed too warm for March. Even the tiny violets she was now planting in front of the cabin seemed to droop in protest of the early heat. She leaned over to breathe in their gentle fragrance. They reminded her of her childhood. Sometimes, even now, when she closed her eyes and smelled the budding flowers, she could remember what it was like to be at home, safe, with Lapawin, Father, and her brother. Sometimes she could even remember her mother. When the trees stood tall and proud against the blue sky, when the breeze sighed through the leaves unhindered by human habitation, when squirrels chattered and darted to and fro, then she remembered. And, almost, she could forget that she was only a slave, could forget that her life was no longer her own, but belonged to the man who had bought her.

She sat back and leaned against the cabin wall. Only Jonathan seemed undaunted by the unusual spring heat. He worked across the clearing now, fashioning the walls of his new barn. He scarcely paused to wipe the sweat from his brow. Kwelik brushed the dirt from her hands and watched him pull another log across the clearing.

She always seemed to find herself looking for him and noticing all the little details that made him who he was—the way his hair flopped disheveled over his face when he and Nahum sawed through a tree trunk, how his eyes lit up as he saw it fall, and the sound of his laughter floating across the clearing when he had accomplished the day's goal. She had rarely seen a man so intent on achieving his dreams. He was like her father in that manner, so determined to overcome every obstacle that threatened his call. Only Jonathan thought his call was to conquer the frontier. If only he would embrace God's dreams and pursue them with such fervor. What a man of God he would be then!

Kwelik drew a sharp breath and squelched the thought. It was only another foolish fantasy. And where had all her hopes taken her so far? Nowhere but into slavery. She sighed.

Jonathan had rejected God, she reminded herself. Even as his heart cried out for his Creator, he would not accept Him. He scorned God's healing touch and thought he could find peace through his own work. He thought he could bury the past beneath the future, escape memory by drowning it in a dream. Sometimes she wondered if he was more a slave than she.

Yet she understood his desperation. She too had memories she longed to forget. Kwelik felt a sudden chill despite the heat.

"You all right there, Miss Kwelik?" She glanced up to see Nahum's tall, lanky form standing above her. His shadow shaded her from the sun. "You look all done in."

Kwelik smiled up at him, noticing the way his dark brown eyes crinkled at the edges. "Thank you, Nahum, but I'm fine. Just thinking, that's all."

He sat beside her and rubbed one finger across his broad nose. "I'm listening." A wide grin split his face.

Kwelik patted his arm and returned the smile. She didn't want to think about those memories, let alone talk about them. "It's nothing," she murmured, turning her attention back to Jonathan. "Look at him out there." She waved her hand in Jonathan's direction. "He won't quit until it's too dark to see whether it's a log he's cutting or his own leg." She grimaced.

Nahum chuckled. "You're fond of him, ain't you, Miss Kwelik?"

Kwelik jumped at the question and looked away. "Why do you say that?" Her mouth went dry.

Nahum smiled. "I got eyes in my old head, ain't I? He's a good man. You couldn't do no better."

"Nahum!" Kwelik glared at him, his comment causing a strange ache in her chest. "Not another word! I won't listen to any such prattle."

"I ain't said nothing but the truth," Nahum continued.

"You just keep those crazy thoughts to yourself." Kwelik turned away.

Nahum chuckled, then grew silent.

Satisfied that he'd dropped the subject, Kwelik turned back to him and asked, "Why do you stay here? Don't you have family somewhere?"

The grin faded from Nahum's face. "Jonathan's my family. The only one I've had for a good many years."

"But before you came out here," she continued, "where did you live? What was your life like then?"

"Wasn't a life worth remembering."

"Please, Nahum, tell me. Were you ever a slave?"

"That I was. Born on a plantation in Georgia and mostly worked the fields, 'cept for the time I helped to build Mr. Whitefield's new orphanage. He's that fancy travelin' preacher from England, you know."

"How did you become free?"

"Don't see why you'd care to know about such a thing. But since you ask, about six years ago I saved my master from an attack by the other slaves. They had some crazy idea of breaking free and sailing back to Africa. They even managed to find a boat. 'Bout twenty feet long, it was. Crazy." Nahum shook his head. "Only thing that stood between the master and them was me and ol' Bessie."

"Bessie?" Kwelik gave him a dubious look.

"A musket."

Kwelik cringed.

"Anyway, that preacher-man, Mr. Whitefield, urged the master to set me free. And free I am."

"I'm glad. Freedom is such a precious thing." She paused, her eyes taking on a faraway look. After a few moments, she sighed and refocused on Nahum. "I've heard of Mr. Whitefield before. I was told he was a great man of God. Do you know God, Nahum?"

Nahum's brow furrowed in confusion. "I don't rightly know. Can anyone know God?"

Kwelik leaned her head back against the wooden wall and smiled. "Sometimes I think that knowing Him is the only thing I'm sure of anymore." She watched a cloud float lazily across the sun before she stood up and rubbed her hand against her leg. "And if I only had my father's Bible, I could show you where it says so."

Nahum stood up beside her. "I got a book," he said. "My Aunt Nellie gave it to me before she died. Got it from her first mistress. Maybe it's a Bible." He looked at her wistfully.

"If only it were." Kwelik turned to go into the cabin.

"Wait. I'll bring it." Nahum jumped up with the alacrity of a man half his age and hurried into his cabin.

In a minute, he was back. "Here it is!" Nahum trotted across the grass with a large black book clutched in both hands. "It's a bit dusty." He handed the book to Kwelik. "Is it what you was talkin' about?" He leaned over and tapped the book's binding.

Kwelik brushed her hand across the leather cover and opened the book. "*The Holy Bible*." The words jumped out at her from the first page. "It is!" Her voice communicated her excitement. She flipped through the pages. "It's beautiful, Nahum. The words of life."

Nahum frowned. "I've kept it 'cause it's real pretty to look at sometimes. Makes me feel happy somehow." He took the book from her and studied the page that she had opened to. "But I'm sorry, Miss Kwelik, I don't know nothing 'bout no words of life."

Kwelik laughed. "Why it's right here. Read this." She pointed at the passage.

Nahum looked confused as his voice dropped to a shamed whisper. "I can't read it."

Kwelik took the book back and set it in her lap. "It says, 'But these are written, that you might believe that Jesus is the Christ, the Son of God; and that believing ye might have life through his name.'" She pointed at the verse. "See, here are the words."

Nahum watched her finger as she repeated the passage. "That's beautiful, Miss Kwelik. How I'm wishin' I could read like you."

"Would you like me to teach you how to read, Nahum?"

"Ain't I too old? Aunt Nellie could read a little, but I was never no good at it. She learned me the abc's and some of the sounds too. I got so I could read a couple words, but I never got no further than that."

"It's not so difficult." Kwelik's voice was soft, coaxing.

Nahum shook his head. "We ain't got no readers, Miss Kwelik."

"We've got all the readers we need right here in this book," she retorted. "There are some wonderful things written in here, and soon you'll be able to read them for yourself. How would you like that?"

"Oh, that would be more than I could imagine."

"None of that now, my friend." Kwelik patted his arm and handed him the book. "Come, we'll start with something simple." She flipped forward in the Bible and pointed to a word in bold, black print. "What's the first letter?"

"*N*?" Nahum glanced at her for approval.

"Good. Now sound out the word."

"N-N-Na," he stammered.

"That's a long *a*. Say, 'nay.'" Kwelik pointed to the letter.

"Nay."

"Very good." Kwelik nodded for him to continue. "Now what does the *h* sound like? Try to say the word."

Nahum's brow furrowed with concentration. "Nay-nay-h-h-hum." His eyes grew wide. "Nahum. Why, that's me!" He pushed the book back under Kwelik's nose. "That's my name! Written right there in the Bible."

Kwelik squeezed his arm and chuckled. "I told you there were wonderful things in that book."

~

Three weeks later Kwelik came upon Nahum with the Bible on his knees. His head was bent over the pages as he struggled to sound out the words. She stood quietly behind him and listened.

"That was very good," she said as he finished.

Nahum started at the sound of her voice. "I didn't see you there, Miss Kwelik."

"You're really coming along well. Read it again."

Nahum cleared his throat and began, "For ye have not re-re- . . . For ye have not re-ceived the spirit of bon . . . bondage again to fear; but ye have received the Spirit of a-adop-adoption, whereby we cry, Abba, Father."

Kwelik smiled. "Do you know what that means?"

He shook his head.

"Abba is the name a little boy calls his father."

"Like Pappy?"

Kwelik nodded.

Nahum looked skeptical. "You wouldn't be fooling an old man, would you now?"

Kwelik smiled. "No, indeed. God wants us to know Him like a little child knows his pappy."

Nahum laughed aloud. "Imagine me callin' God my pappy. I ain't never heard nothin' so crazy." He continued to laugh until tears ran down his cheeks.

Kwelik cocked her head to one side and studied his odd reaction.

"Oh, Miss Kwelik," Nahum sputtered, "my whole life's been worth the livin' if what you say is really so." He wiped his eyes and gave Kwelik a penetrating look. "I've gone my whole life without no pappy, and now you're tellin' me that God Himself wants to be my pappy." He shook his head. "Why, 'tis the most wondrous thing I ever heard."

Kwelik grinned up at him. "Yes, Nahum, He wants to be your father and your closest friend. He wants to be as close as your very own heart."

Nahum stood up and shook his head again. "God as my pappy," he muttered as he made his way back to his cabin. "Crazy idea. Wonder if it's so?"

~

She's coming! Archibald brushed back the velvet drapery and peered out the window. He held up one hand to block the sun's glare as he studied the road leading to his mansion. Was that a carriage? He caught his breath and looked again. Yes! Perhaps it was *her*. The thought tightened in his chest with indescribable longing. To see her again, to have her here in his own home—it was enough to make him forget how much he hated the colonies.

Archibald turned and poked at the fresh flowers that adorned a crystal vase near the window. He grimaced, wishing they were roses.

She may think these are no more than weeds, he thought. Quickly he took the vase and stuffed it behind the drapes. No, that was silly. Now it looked as if he had done nothing to prepare for her arrival. He pulled the flowers out again and set them on the table. Still they were shabby compared to her loveliness.

Archibald closed his eyes to imagine her as he had seen her last—a daring gown of rich red, golden hair swept atop her delicate head, curls just touching her white shoulders, her rich, cultured laugh ringing across the dance floor. The memory took his breath away. And she was coming here!

But she was not coming for him. The knowledge tore through Archibald and left him shaking. He pounded his fist against the window pane and groaned. She was coming for Jonathan. Jonathan! That miserable little frontiersman. How he hated him! Everything Archibald had ever wanted was first offered to that loathsome boy. It wasn't right! After all, his home was arguably the most beautiful in Philadelphia, and he was richer and more powerful than most men.

Archibald stepped back to admire his dim reflection in the window. He wasn't so bad looking either. So why didn't she want him? Archibald's eyes narrowed. If it weren't for Jonathan, she might. He paced up and down the room twice before stopping again at the window.

Why wouldn't Richard agree that Jonathan should die? Then his nephew would no longer be in the way, either with Elizabeth or on the frontier.

Even now that wretched boy was going ahead with his plans to help other frontiersmen protect their homes. From the report Archibald had received just that morning, Jonathan was arranging a signal for trouble, providing maps, and teaching the other men how to build their cabins to make them more easily defensible. He had even heard that Jonathan had a woman helping him. A half-breed. Probably that same one who spoiled his plans here in Philadelphia.

Archibald crossed his arms and frowned. Only with Jonathan subdued or out of the way could he be set free from his position in these accursed colonies. He might even be able to go home. But Richard demanded that he stay to keep an eye on Jonathan. If it weren't for Jonathan's stubbornness, he could have been back in England courting and winning *her*.

Archibald heard the door swing open behind him. He turned. "Elizabeth!" Her name came unbidden to his lips.

"Archibald." She spoke the word without emotion, one eyebrow lifting haughtily.

His heart stood still. She was even more lovely than he remembered, from the proud tilt of her chin to the dainty tip of her fashionable shoe. Archibald felt sweat break out on his forehead.

Elizabeth held out her hand, her fingers drooping elegantly down, awaiting his greeting.

Archibald raised her gloved hand to his lips. "My lady," he whispered, "welcome."

She turned back toward the door, dismissing his greeting. "Do come in, Richard. Your uncle awaits."

Richard strode through the door and slammed it behind him. "Well, Archibald," his voice boomed, "we have arrived at last. I trust that you have a full report for me."

"R-Richard!" Archibald stuttered in response. His eyes traveled up the younger man's tall frame. "I didn't know you would be here today too."

"Didn't you?" Richard's eyes narrowed as he regarded his uncle. "What did you expect, Archibald? That Elizabeth would come alone to your little estate?" He laughed, an unpleasant sound that echoed off the walls and died suddenly. "Not that it would matter."

Archibald winced at the jibe and turned toward Elizabeth. "Come, Lady Elizabeth," he cooed, "sit here by the fire."

She adjusted her dress and sat carefully on the edge of the overstuffed chair.

Archibald rubbed his hands together and leaned toward her. "Are you comfortable, my lady? Would you like some refreshment?" He wiped his brow with a linen handkerchief. "Something to take off the chill? Perhaps a touch of brandy—I mean, rum." Archibald looked disconcerted. He turned and grimaced at Richard.

Elizabeth waved him away. "Do get on with your business, Archibald," she commanded. "I did not travel all this way to listen to your prattle. Where is Jonathan? Why is he not here awaiting my arrival?"

Archibald cringed. "I'm sorry, my lady. I thought you knew. Didn't Richard tell you?" Suddenly he realized he was babbling again, and he quickly shut his mouth.

"Tell me what?" Elizabeth demanded.

Archibald glanced toward Richard and swallowed hard. "My lady," he stammered, "Jonathan is still living on the frontier. He does not yet know you've arrived or, indeed, that you were coming at all."

Smoothly Richard broke into the conversation. "We thought it best, Elizabeth, that you be a little surprise for him. Use your womanly charms to their full effect, so to speak." He patted her arm in a familiar fashion.

Archibald fumed.

"He will not be able to resist you," Richard continued. "Then we will all have what we want. Won't we, Uncle?" Richard looked pointedly at him until Archibald coughed and nodded his head in agreement.

Elizabeth smiled. "Yes, I practically had him eating out of my hand before you scared him away to these wretched colonies. We would have been betrothed before a fortnight."

"That will all be remedied now." Richard turned back toward Archibald. "You will send for the boy, Archibald. Have him come to my home in Boston. I have business there."

"Yes, I insist on going to Boston," Elizabeth agreed. "I am told it is more civilized than the rest of this heathen land. And you know that I work best among more elegant surroundings." She paused and glanced significantly at the flowers near the window. "Jonathan will soon be trailing me back to England, ready to do whatever I ask." She looked coolly at both men. "You may be assured of that."

With a nod toward Richard, Elizabeth stood and swept out of the room.

TWENTY-ONE

Jonathan drove the axe's head into a stump and turned to review his work. The barn stood yawning open before him, its doors swinging easily on wooden hinges. Except for a few details, it was finished now. Someday it would be piled high with the harvest. He could almost see it filled with grain, corn, and horses. He loved horses. If all went well, he could have a dozen of them. For now, though, he had barely cleared enough land to support the three of them and the two horses. The harvest this year would be small but sufficient.

Jonathan rubbed his hand over his face and looked out over the clearing—the tall birch sweeping the sky, with a pile of neatly cut wood for heat and cooking beneath it, and in the background their two little cabins tucked closely together, his with a tiny appendage extending out awkwardly to shelter the girl.

Strange how he always thought in terms of the three of them now. He had planned to free Kwelik after the winter, but here it was May already, and he still hadn't been able to bring himself to do it. He liked to see her working around the homestead, planting those little violets that she was so fond of or here lately studying that big black book of Nahum's. She was teaching Nahum to read, something he himself had never thought to do. So he couldn't free her yet, he told himself. Not until Nahum finished his lessons. Then maybe he'd keep his promise to Rosie and to himself. He would stop being a slave owner. Someday, he assured himself, he would free her. But not today.

Where was she now? Jonathan cast his eyes over the clearing. There! He saw her trudging up from the stream, a full bucket in each hand. Her hair shimmered in the sun and swung over her shoulder. Jonathan smiled. A sense of peace washed over him as he watched her set the buckets on the ground and wipe her forehead. Jonathan placed his axe against a tree stump and started toward her.

Before he could reach her, Nahum ran out of his cabin, waving the book over his head. "It's true!" Nahum's voice carried across the clearing. "I read it for myself." Jonathan watched Nahum set the book on a tree stump, grab Kwelik, and swing her around in a circle, laughing.

"Put me down, you crazy man!" she sputtered, then giggled.

Nahum released her and grabbed the buckets. "Come over here, Jonathan," he shouted. "I got something to read to you."

Nahum slipped the water inside Jonathan's cabin door and ran back to retrieve his book. "See, look what it says here." He pointed to the passage. Slowly he formed the words: "'Now the Lord is that Spirit: and where the Spirit of the Lord is, there is liberty. But we all, with open face beholding as in a glass the glory of the Lord, are changed into the same image from glory to glory, even as by the Spirit of the Lord.'"

Nahum looked up proudly from the text and thrust the book toward Kwelik. "It's right here in 2 Corinthians, jus' like you said. I'm bein' changed to be like God Hisself. That's jus' so wonderful, Miss Kwelik. Who woulda thought it? The Spirit of God livin' in me and makin' me a free man." Nahum shook his head. "'From glory to glory, by the Spirit of the Lord.' Well, I'll be."

Jonathan frowned as Kwelik nodded.

Nahum tapped his fingers on the book's pages, his voice dropping to a sudden whisper. "This book is really true, ain't it, Miss Kwelik?" he questioned. "God really means these things, don't He?"

Kwelik's eyes met Jonathan's for just a moment before she turned her attention back to Nahum. "Look around you. All nature testifies to God. Listen to the sweet melody of the stream splashing on the rocks. Look at the sky. Smell the delicate fragrance of the violets. They all stand witness to the God who loves us so much that He sent His only Son to suffer and die so that we would no longer be separated from Him."

Jonathan put his hands on his hips and turned away. How could Nahum listen to such nonsense? The wilderness was nothing more than unconquered land. If anything, it testified to his own strength in subduing it.

But Nahum believed Kwelik's words. "Can I hear it too? Can I hear nature testifyin' to God?" he whispered.

"I don't know. You have to listen with your heart. See here." Kwelik flipped through the pages of the book. "In Romans 1:20 it says, 'For the invisible things of him from the creation of the world are clearly seen, being understood by the things that are made, even his eternal power and Godhead.' You see, everything around us tells us that what God says in this book is true. Listen to the wind when it rustles through the leaves of the sycamore. You can hear the voices of nature praising God, their Creator. Then let the wind of His Spirit flow through you to make the same praise. Even the morning song of the bluebird, as it wakes to thank God for another day spent in His care, speaks of the wonderful grace of God." Kwelik paused and lowered her voice. "But you can't truly hear it unless you have faith in Christ, until you surrender your life to God."

That explains it, Jonathan thought. *I will never surrender to the God my father claimed to believe in. Never.*

Nahum's earnest voice pierced Jonathan's resolve. "I believe it, Miss Kwelik. And He can have this ol' life of mine if He wants it, though it ain't worth much."

"It was worth Christ's own life."

Jonathan glanced at Kwelik. The quiet, intimate quality of her voice disturbed him. She hadn't spoken to him that way since that night under the stars. Something changed after the savages had attacked them, something he still did not understand. Was it because he had rejected her God?

Jonathan shook his head to rid himself of such thoughts. Nahum was speaking again. "I never knew we could live like that, feelin' God with us all the time, knowin' He's there. I always thought I was free once my master let me go, but I ain't never known no freedom like the one you've given me, like the freedom of knowin' God."

"It's not I who gives freedom, but God Himself."

"I know it, Miss Kwelik. But who woulda thought it possible? There ain't no freedom like this!"

Jonathan felt his chest tighten at Nahum's words. Hadn't Nahum been free from the first time he'd met him? He'd never oppressed the older man, never belittled him, or treated him as anything less than an equal. So what was he talking about? How could he say that only now, after reading something in that book, he was truly free? Jonathan turned back and glared at Nahum, but the man ignored him, his attention now focused fully on Kwelik.

"Do you feel free, Miss Kwelik?" Nahum's voice turned gentle.

"Do I? I wonder." Kwelik eyes traveled to Jonathan's face and then looked away. "I remember the day my mother brought me into a field and showed me a wildflower. As I touched the velvety petals, she told me that the flower demonstrated how I must open myself to God, as it opened itself to the sun, and lay before Him all the beauty He created in me." Kwelik sighed. "I've been forgetting these things. It was difficult there in the city with the cobblestones, and buildings, and hard wood floors. But the birds still sang. They reminded me of the things I know in my heart. But still, I miss being free to roam the woods and follow the flight of the butterfly."

Jonathan cringed as he heard the longing in her voice. It was his fault that she was trapped here. Yet he couldn't let her go. Not now. Not yet.

"Well, why can't you go?" Nahum asked. "It's mighty nice of you to stay here with us and all, but it's not like you're our slave or anything."

"Not yours maybe," Kwelik answered, her eyes again meeting Jonathan's.

He caught his breath. The time had come. Jonathan swallowed hard and hoped to stop what he knew would come next.

"What?" Nahum sputtered. "My ol' befuddled mind thought you said you was a slave."

Kwelik looked up at him, startled. "I thought you knew."

Jonathan groaned as Nahum turned and pinned him with a look that shot to his very soul. "Is Miss Kwelik your slave, Jonathan?"

Judgment had come.

TWENTY-TWO

"Liar!" The word tore from Nahum's lips like a curse.

Jonathan swallowed hard and took a step back. A thousand memories flashed before his mind's eye—he and Nahum choosing this plot of land, working to build each other's cabins, laughing together over a joke, sharing their dreams and disappointments. Never before had Nahum turned on him with such fury.

"You told me she had nowhere else to turn. You said you was takin' care of her since her village was destroyed." Nahum's face turned red beneath the dark pigment.

"She doesn't . . . I am!" Jonathan heard his own voice shouting desperately at Nahum.

Nahum's next words cut him off. "I don't want to hear no more of your fine-soundin' lies. How can I believe anything you say now? You claimed to be my friend, 'like a brother,' you said." Nahum put his hands on his hips and glowered at Jonathan.

"I am your friend." Jonathan's voice sounded weary. "I knew you wouldn't understand."

"What's there to understand?" Nahum threw his hands in the air. "You bought yourself a slave and brung her here to flaunt her before me." His eyes narrowed. "Why did you do such a thing? To be remindin' me of my position? To say that I'm still a slave in your eyes?"

"No! You know that's not true."

"Then why?"

"Because . . ." Jonathan paused, groping for the right words. "I had to. Because . . ." He stopped again and looked at Kwelik, who stood fearfully beyond Nahum, her eyes wide. He sighed. "I don't know why. But it didn't have anything to do with you, Nahum."

Nahum took a deep breath and glanced back at Kwelik. "Look

at her." His voice grew softer. "How could you do it? This sort of thing might be jus' fine among your people, but you said you was different. I *thought* you was different." Nahum turned back toward Jonathan. His eyes misted as hurt slowly replaced his anger. "How could you?"

Jonathan felt his throat close at the disappointment in Nahum's voice. But this was crazy. All this fuss over a slave-girl. He had treated her well, with more kindness and respect than she would have received with any other master. Jonathan's mind traveled back over the group of men who had been poised to buy her. He remembered their slick voices and greedy eyes. He had saved her. He must remember that. "It's not that bad, Nahum," he heard himself explaining. "It would have been much worse for her if I hadn't bought her."

Nahum's voice turned hard again. "It could have been a lot better too. She shouldn't be no slave." Nahum reached out and grabbed him by the shoulder. "Let her go. Set her free."

Jonathan turned his head away, unable to meet Nahum's searching gaze. "I can't," he muttered. Suddenly he knew the words were true. He needed her. He couldn't let her go, at least not yet.

"You mean, you won't." Nahum released his grip as if Jonathan's mere presence had become loathsome. "You was supposed to be different."

The bitterness of Nahum's tone tore through Jonathan's soul.

"Stop!" Kwelik's voice filled with remorse as she stepped between them. "Stop it, both of you!"

Jonathan could see the tears shining in her eyes as she turned from him to Nahum. "You are like two hawks squabbling over a tiny mouse in the field." She put her hand on Nahum's sleeve. "You are as close to one another as brothers. I won't come between you."

Nahum shook his head. "But he lied to me, Miss Kwelik."

"And you will forgive him." Jonathan saw the intensity of her gaze and wondered at it.

"Not 'til he lets you go back to your folks."

A single tear escaped and trickled down Kwelik's cheek. Jonathan's heart constricted as she brushed it away. "I have no home anymore but this one." Her voice was gentle. "My village was burned. My people are dead."

Lines of compassion formed on Nahum's forehead as he looked down at her. His dark eyes moistened with tears. "I'm sorry, Miss Kwelik."

"Jonathan has done me no harm. Forgive him, Nahum."

Jonathan caught his breath as Nahum clenched his fists at his side and struggled to respond. Finally he raised his head to pierce Jonathan with another accusatory glance. "But he ain't got no right!"

"Yes, in this world he has every right."

"But we ain't of this world—you said so yourself."

Kwelik sighed. "No, but we are in it."

"You shouldn't be no slave. It ain't right." Nahum again turned his gaze fiercely on Jonathan.

Kwelik put her hand on his arm. "Enough, Nahum. I will stay." She turned, her eyes catching and holding Jonathan's. "Only God can free me now."

Her words cut to his heart.

~

Elizabeth turned her head away from the carriage window and shuddered gracefully. "What a terrible land," she commented. "How do you stand it here, Archibald?"

Archibald breathed a sigh that he hoped sounded eloquent. "It is difficult, my lady."

Richard leaned over and pinned him with a look of disdain. "Come now, Uncle," he scoffed. "I've heard this land has made you into quite an important man."

Elizabeth shivered. "I don't believe this land could make a man into anything but a savage, red or white."

Archibald turned his back on Richard. "And such is the case with our dear Jonathan, I'm afraid."

"Silence, Archibald!" Richard thundered. "With Elizabeth's guidance he will be everything I want and more."

Elizabeth smiled.

Archibald cleared his throat and promptly changed the subject. "Tell me, how could you ever leave England, my lady?"

"Oh." Elizabeth put her hand to her forehead. "England is quite a different place than it was when I was younger, Archibald. Madness abounds."

"Madness?" Archibald frowned.

"Madness, indeed." Elizabeth's hand fluttered to her chest. "There's truly no other word for it. Between that Rev. Whitefield and the Wesleys, England has been turned upside down. Why, I can scarcely go to a party anymore without hearing the most outlandish religious talk."

Archibald drew a sharp breath. "Who would dare such a thing?"

Elizabeth leaned forward and tapped his knee. "Sometimes even the most elegant people. It's a madness, I tell you." She shook her head. "Religion used to be a private affair, as it should be. But no longer." She lowered her voice and leaned toward Archibald, her tone becoming conspiratorial. "I even overheard Susannah, my own sister, talking at the Earl of Bath's latest gathering. 'It's been the most wonderful experience, knowing Christ and being assured that He saves me,' she said, just as plain as that. And she was speaking to the earl himself!" Elizabeth gave a quick nod of her head. "I just shuddered in horror. Imagine speaking of knowing God that way. It's shameful."

Richard's harsh laugh broke through the conversation. "Don't fret, Elizabeth. Soon we will all be above such madness, as you call it. Now that France has officially declared war with England, Jonathan will have even more reason to obey our summons." He turned his eyes to Archibald. "You have dispatched the letter, have you not?"

Archibald shifted in his seat and nodded. "I have, milord. And, as you directed, I offered him the militia he requested."

"Militia from Massachusetts?"

"Yes, milord. I told him that I had already spoken to the colonial government in Boston. He will find out too late that there's no such militia."

Richard nodded. "Very well. We will soon discover how well you have carried out my orders."

Archibald cleared his throat. "He will come, milord, I assure you."

Richard's tone turned dry. "Please, Archibald, do spare me your assurances."

"Oh, look there, ahead." Elizabeth pointed a gloved finger toward the road. "What are they doing?"

Archibald leaned out the window to study a group of people walking on the dirt road before them. He pulled his head back in. "Why, I believe they're singing."

"Singing?" Elizabeth turned up her nose. "It sounds like some new hymn by that Wesley fellow."

Archibald poked his head out the window again. "You there, get out of our way. And stop that caterwauling. Do you hear me?"

Apparently they didn't hear. As the carriage drew abreast of the group, a man at the front called out and waved, "God be with you, brothers."

Archibald sneered and turned away. *Ignorant fools!*

"Beastly commoners." Elizabeth echoed his thoughts as she put her lace handkerchief up to her nose.

Unaware of the hostile response, the group continued to sing. A phrase floated through the carriage: ". . . Jesus, born to set Thy people free. From our fears and sins release us. Let us find our rest in Thee."

Archibald rolled his eyes to the ceiling. "Free?" he mocked. "Such people don't deserve to be free." His voice turned hard as he pulled down the window shade and faced Elizabeth. "I believe you're right, my lady. The whole world has gone mad."

Twenty-Three

Pennsylvania frontier, June 1744

Black clouds billowed in from the northeast, spattering a few drops of rain over the clearing. From inside his cabin, Jonathan rested his hand against the window and looked outside. The full fury of the storm would hit in the night.

The birch, again covered with green after the short winter, now swayed and rustled in the growing wind, its leaves fluttering like hundreds of wings. Beyond the tree the new barn stood tall and complete against the dark backdrop of the untamed forest. Everything appeared perfect, just as he had once imagined it. So why did the same uneasiness still haunt him? Why did he not feel satisfied even now?

Jonathan sighed and shifted his position, his eyes automatically searching for Kwelik. He spotted her near the clothesline that hung between the two cabins. Unaware of his perusal, Kwelik flipped her braid over her shoulder and waved toward the edge of the clearing. Jonathan followed the direction of her gaze to see Nahum, who was just coming in from a long day of plowing the western field. Nahum smiled back at her and headed for the barn as Kwelik continued to skin two rabbits for the night's meal.

Jonathan tapped his fingers against the window's frame and scowled. *There they are again*, he thought, *laughing as usual*. He shook his head. Ever since that day when Nahum discovered that Kwelik was a slave, he'd been protecting her, acting as if he were her own father. Jonathan considered turning away from the window but didn't.

Their closeness intrigued him, awakened in him a longing that he couldn't understand. They seemed to enjoy a deeper fellowship than even he and Nahum had. Jonathan rubbed his hand across his forehead and sighed. His feelings had been so contradictory here of late. He couldn't understand it. Here in his own home, why did he feel like the outsider?

Yet when he tried to join them, Nahum just glared at him, and Kwelik turned quiet, though she served him as well as ever. Even now the cabin was swept spotless, the horses were watered, his clothes were clean, and she kept them well fed with quail, rabbits, and fish. He should have been happy with the arrangement, but he wasn't. And he knew why. It was because he knew he was missing something, something that Kwelik and Nahum shared. In his more sentimental days, he would have called it joy. He didn't know what to call it now.

Jonathan watched Nahum pull the barn door shut behind him and stride toward Kwelik. She put one finger to her lips and motioned for him to come quietly. As Nahum reached her side, Kwelik pointed to a small squirrel chattering at a butterfly that flitted over its head. Jonathan watched Nahum crouch down to coax the little animal into his hand. Even from this distance, he could see Kwelik's gentle smile as the squirrel took a few steps forward, cocked its head, then skittered back into the trees. Nahum shrugged and grimaced.

Jonathan saw Kwelik pat Nahum on the shoulder and laugh. He could almost hear her voice assuring him that the squirrel would come next time. Nahum's wide grin was his only response.

Jonathan shook his head again. With Kwelik, Nahum was like a new man. Jonathan had never seen him so happy. What was it about the girl that put the older man at ease, that made him stop and consider a squirrel and still laugh at a butterfly even after a full day in the field? Jonathan sighed and looked up at the sky. It would be dark soon. Why didn't they come in?

Nahum grabbed an armful of wood and carried it to the side of the cabin. Kwelik picked up the two rabbits and followed him. The sound of her light laughter drifted over to Jonathan, causing his heart to constrict with a longing that was becoming all too familiar.

Suddenly he could stand it no longer. He snatched the bolt of material that Mary had given him from a nearby table and stormed outside. "Kwelik, come in here," he called. He watched her turn, her smile dissolving into a look of submission. He clutched the material tighter in his hand. "I have work for you."

A look of confused indignation crossed Nahum's face as Jonathan approached them. Kwelik turned toward Nahum and shook her head almost imperceptibly. "No, Nahum," she whispered.

Nahum nodded once, his face taking on a look of stony acquiescence. "Go on." He waved his hand toward Jonathan. "I'll cook the rabbits and bring them in when they're ready."

Jonathan gripped Kwelik's arm and pulled her after him into the cabin. His bed nestled behind a new partition on the far wall, leaving the rest of the room open for the single table and three chairs that occupied the left side of the cabin. Two sets of clothing hung from nails above his bed, though only the collars of his shirts showed above the slender partition. But no pictures hung on the rough wood walls. No trinkets lined his shelves. Not even a single reminder of his past life graced any corner of Jonathan's cabin. Everything was stark, plain, in obstinate contrast to the elegance of his ancestral home. On the right wall, near the opening that led to Kwelik's room, a small fire smoldered in the rock fireplace and threw scant shadows onto the bare rafters above him.

Jonathan glanced at the oil lamp that hung near the door and then stepped past it. Tonight he was in the mood for fire. With that thought, he blinked into the dimming light and threw a few pieces of wood into the fireplace. He fanned the flames with one hand and turned back to Kwelik. "Here," he said, pulling the material from under his arm and tossing it toward her. "I want a shirt made from this."

A look of distress crossed Kwelik's face as the material landed at her feet. Gingerly she picked it up and handed it back to him. "I'm sorry, Jonathan. In my village we used thin pieces of leather to tie together our clothing. Like my skirt here and my tunic." She showed him the seam, held together by a looping piece of hide tied at both ends. "I don't know how to sew." Firelight flickered off her features, showing her concern.

Jonathan frowned. "All women know how to sew."

She turned her hands up in a gesture of helplessness. "Not among my people."

Jonathan could no longer contain his exasperation. "What good are you then?"

His tone caused Kwelik to cringe. "I don't know." Her voice choked on the words as her eyes sought his, melting his anger.

"Sit down, Kwelik."

Instead, she drew closer to him and put her hand gently on his arm. "What's wrong, Jonathan?" Her words cut through the last of his anger, leaving him defenseless.

"Don't." Jonathan's voice filled with anguish. He strode back to the fire and stared into it. Silence hung awkwardly between them.

After a few moments, he ran his fingers through his hair and turned to meet Kwelik's questioning gaze. "Why don't you run away? Why do you stay here?" His voice cracked over the words.

Kwelik lowered her eyes. "What do you mean?"

Jonathan felt all the confusion of the last few months well up within him, refusing to be quelled. "It's because of Nahum, isn't it?" The words tumbled from his lips and fell between them, accusing, desperate, demanding a response.

She looked up at him, startled. "Nahum?" She searched his face, her gaze seeking the source of his frustration.

Jonathan felt himself drawn into the liquid depths of her eyes.

Quickly Kwelik looked away. "No, not for Nahum." Her voice was so quiet now that he could scarcely hear it. "For you."

Jonathan's heart beat faster. "What?" His voice caught in his throat.

Kwelik drew back. "I promised; don't you remember?" The explanation spilled from her lips too quickly.

Jonathan wondered at it. "Promises don't mean much."

"Maybe not to others, but they do to God. I won't break faith with Him or with you either."

"Does this God mean so much to you that you would give up your freedom for Him?" Jonathan studied her features as she looked up at him earnestly—the high cheekbones, the deep blue eyes, the soft lips curving now into a smile. He looked away.

"He means that much and more, Jonathan," she answered. "I would give Him my very life."

Jonathan shook his head. "Even after He's allowed you to be a slave? I can't understand you."

"Oh, Jonathan, God cares for you too. He loves you like a father loves his son."

They were the wrong words. Jonathan pulled back from her as he heard them. "Ha! That I understand. He'll love me as long as I do what He wants, as long as He feels like it. But when something goes wrong, beware, for someone's going to pay." His voice dropped to just above a whisper, carrying all the bitterness pent up within him. "That's the kind of fatherly love I know."

"Oh no, not like that." Kwelik wrung her hands and leaned closer to him. "He hurt you, didn't he?"

Jonathan dropped his gaze, unable to speak the words. Finally he squeezed the admission from between his tightened lips: "And my mother too."

"Oh, Jonathan," Kwelik breathed, "I'm so sorry that your father was like that. But surely there's something good you remember about your childhood? Weren't there happy times too?"

"Not many."

"Tell me about the good times. Please."

Jonathan looked at her, noticing the pleading in her eyes. He softened. "I was happy once, a long time ago."

"Tell me," she coaxed.

"There's nothing to tell."

"Please, Jonathan, forget your anger and your hurt for a moment." Kwelik drew closer to him.

Jonathan felt his heart thumping in his chest. Couldn't she see the turmoil she caused within him? Perhaps memory was safer after all. He glanced toward her. "It was a long time ago."

She nodded.

Jonathan's eyes grew hazy as he remembered. "I was just a boy then, racing through a lush pasture, whistling for Sir Charles,

Mother's old gelding. It was spring, and I could smell the scent of fresh grass and wildflowers. Sir Charles trotted toward me, nickering his welcome. I climbed atop his chestnut back and urged him to run, until his hooves made shallow divots in Father's perfect green grass." Jonathan smiled at the memory. "I remember looking back to watch the great clumps of dirt fly behind me in all directions. *Father will be angry*, I thought. But at that moment I didn't care, because just for that breath of time, I was free—free of my father, his heritage, and everything it meant to be the son of Lord Grant.

"After a time I slipped off the gelding's back, raced across the field, crawled under a fence, and climbed our old apple tree. I remember picking two apples, one for Sir Charles and one for me. Then I sat out of sight at the far end of the pasture and munched the fruit until there was nothing left but a thin core." Jonathan strode over to the stone fireplace and rested his hand against the mantel.

"Go on," Kwelik whispered. "What happened next?"

"Eventually I grew tired and trotted back inside. Richard was there, as if he had been waiting for me." Jonathan paused and refocused on Kwelik. "You see, when Richard was young, he never liked the outdoors. He was always happier with his books, and later with his paints and canvases. I can still see him there, mired in the latest books that Mother had contrived to get sent from London." Jonathan paused, fighting to quell the anger that always rose in him when he thought of his brother.

"When I burst through the door, Richard looked up, smiled, and patted the place next to him. Then I curled up beside him while he read to me of knights and kings and daring adventures . . . until I became restless and dashed outside again to play." Jonathan stared blankly into the fireplace. His voice again lowered to a whisper.

"That was the last happy moment I remember. The next day my father died in a riding accident. And Richard became Lord Grant, in more than just the title. He turned into my father—cold, haughty, and ruthless. It was as if Richard had died instead of my father." Jonathan paused, his voice tightening with old pain, old betrayal. "I thought we'd all be free. No more beatings, no more cruelty, no more bruises livid on my mother's face. But instead within a week Richard banished Mother, sent her away before I could even say good-bye. I never saw her again."

He sighed. "So you see, I lost the brother I had once loved and the mother I had always wished to protect. Then there was nothing left for me but memories to mock my childhood hopes." He grew silent, his eyes focused on a distant place, a distant time.

"I'm sorry, Jonathan," Kwelik whispered again, her eyes seeking his. "It always ends bitterly, doesn't it?" She laid her hand on his arm. "But God can heal all that. He can set you free again, freer than you ever were when riding Sir Charles."

Pain laced his voice as he looked down into Kwelik's soft gaze. "He'll just snap His fingers, and I'll be free? Like He's set you free?" he scoffed.

Kwelik was silent.

"Answer me." Jonathan hoped that she would not hear the desperation in his voice.

Kwelik dropped her hand and turned away. "Why must we argue? Let go of your anger, Jonathan. God says, 'If the Son therefore shall make you free, ye shall be free indeed.'"

A bitter smile spread over Jonathan's face. "If only it were so simple."

Kwelik turned back toward him. "It is." Compassion welled up in her eyes as she regarded him. It took his breath away.

Jonathan took a step toward her and groaned. "Kwelik," her name caught in his throat, "don't look at me that way."

"Jonathan?" Her eyes mirrored his own confusion.

He leaned toward her. Her nearness jolted him.

"Don't you understand?" Jonathan's voice sounded deep and husky. With one finger, he tilted her chin back to look into her face and felt himself drawn into the flashing depths of her eyes. He saw them soften, then grow wide.

Jonathan put his hand on her shoulder and drew her close until he could feel her heart hammering to the beat of his own. Kwelik's lips parted as her breath came in erratic spurts. She swayed toward him, her body brushing his.

Softly, like the touch of a butterfly, one of her hands fluttered up to touch his chest. "Jonathan," she breathed, "wait."

Her voice washed over him, drawing him closer. She was so beautiful, so gentle, so pure. And she was his.

Before he could think of the consequences, Jonathan's lips came down to capture hers.

TWENTY-FOUR

The door slammed behind Kwelik as she fled Jonathan's cabin. His kiss still burned on her lips like an unfulfilled promise. She drew a ragged breath and headed for the forest. She had to get away, to quiet the wild thumping of her heart, to silence the throb of longing that clamored within.

The door swung open again.

"Kwelik! Come back."

Kwelik did not turn around. She didn't dare.

From the corner of her eye, she saw Nahum step from his cabin. He called after her, his words lost in the sudden roar of thunder. She could feel Nahum watching her, questioning.

She must not turn back. If she did, she would be lost, lost in a flurry of emotions that she must deny, must forget.

As Kwelik raced through the trees, the water began to come down in torrents, the wind whipping the saplings and bushes around her. Rain spattered her face and drenched her dress, but she didn't care.

"Kwelik!" Jonathan's shout grew distant, though the sound of his voice still shot to her soul. Her eyes blurred as her heart answered the cry. *Jonathan . . .*

But no! She pressed her hands against her ears even as she ran. She would not go back. She could not. She must run, escape, flee the temptation of his arms, his voice, his kiss.

Kwelik continued her frantic pace, weaving though the trees and bushes until all sounds of Jonathan's call faded in the distance. A creek cut across her path, its turbulent waters swelling with the storm's downpour. Kwelik scarcely glanced at it as she plunged through the stream, not caring that the cold waters splashed up to soak her wet legs.

As she crossed the creek, her pace slowed, her breath coming in uneven sobs from her throat. A tall oak loomed in her path. Already she had put at least a mile between herself and Jonathan. Was it enough, she wondered, to still the painful yearning that had swept through her like a storm? Could she ever run far enough?

Kwelik stopped and leaned against the oak, listening as its branches swayed and cracked overhead. Now her heart raced as much from her exertion as from the touch of Jonathan's lips.

She drew a shuddering breath and noticed a small meadow to her right, unsheltered from the storm. Slowly she pushed herself away from the tree and stumbled into the meadow. A few steps took her to the center where she knelt in the wet grass, allowing the water to stream down her face unhindered. Thunder rumbled overhead as lightning illuminated the sky. At the edge of the meadow, a tree cracked, sending a branch whirling into the night. She listened to the moaning of the forest as the storm raged through it. It was like the groan of her own soul. And her own yearning was the storm.

Kwelik gripped the grass in both hands and pulled. The blades tore in her hands, leaving flecks of green over her skin. What had happened to her? And how had it happened? She could still feel Jonathan's lips on hers. Even the rain couldn't wash away the heady feeling of his mouth warm and demanding, his arms encircling her and drawing her close, the feel of his hand on her chin, her hair. She trembled even now to remember it.

She could still hear her own words explaining why she stayed at the homestead. *I promised; don't you remember?* But that was a lie. She knew that now. More than a promise held her to Jonathan. Much more. How had she allowed her feelings to become entrapped by him, a heathen white man? How did her heart become wrapped around his? She was only a slave to him, something to be used and discarded. Why else had he thought he could kiss her? And in that brief moment she had responded with all that was in her heart. Oh, the shame of it!

Rain pelted at Kwelik's back until she shivered under the intensity of the storm. It raged outside and within until she could no longer detect the distinction.

Kwelik groaned. What was she going to do? She had been avoiding the truth for months, denying it. But now it was inescapable. The moment he kissed her, she knew. She loved Jonathan. How could she be such a fool?

Kwelik's thoughts swirled around her in a frenzied dance. She couldn't face Jonathan again. Not now. Maybe not ever. Her only hope was to run as far and fast as she could and never come back. She must forget him, forget the promise, forget the feel of his lips on hers. Only then could she escape and be free at last.

Free. Kwelik's throat closed over the word, knowing it, too, was a lie. How could she be free with a broken promise haunting her steps, with the memory of a love despised, with the knowledge that she had run away before Jonathan had come to know his Savior? How could she find her own freedom while condemning him to live as a slave to sin and death? If she didn't go back, he would believe that everything she had ever said to him was untrue.

Kwelik rocked back and forth on the wet ground, her hands gripping her sodden skirt as the truth ripped through her. To gain her freedom, she would have to go back to slavery. The thought was impossible. How could she go back, speak to him of Christ, of God's love, while all the time knowing that she loved him—she who was no more than a piece of property to him?

Tears streamed down Kwelik's cheeks as she raised her face to the heavens. "How can I go back, God?" she cried. "How can I?" Her voice grew louder and mixed with the pounding rain. "Mother, I have your answer. I am not brave enough. I am not." The last word ended in a sob.

Kwelik lowered her head, her voice softening. "Oh, God, help me."

Long moments passed before Kwelik stood and allowed the rain to whip the tears from her eyes. Ah, the taste of the storm—it permeated the air and tingled along her nerves like some ancient cry of angels. All around her the hand of God swept with power and fury, lighting the darkness and cleansing the earth. If only He would cleanse her too, cleanse her of this impossible love, allow her to fulfill her promise without fear.

Kwelik raised her arms and let the wind tear at her, whipping her hair around her face in the unbridled dance of the tempest. At the same moment, lightning flashed across the sky, outlining black clouds driven by the gale. Kwelik shut her eyes and allowed the storm to roar around her, the wildness like a balm to the wounds within. Somewhere out there in the vast expanse of wilderness, the storm raged unhindered by human woes, and for a moment she wished she were part of its wildness, its freedom—the freedom to dance with the wind beneath the mighty hand of God, unfettered by impossible feelings, by promises, by fear.

But perhaps freedom was only that, a promise made to the wind and no more. Could she ever be free?

She must find out. Somehow she must obey God's call and go back. The thought sent a shiver racing through her.

Kwelik bowed her head as the worst part of the storm passed overhead. Slowly the wind died from a howl to a whisper. The rain began to fall softly, like teardrops from heaven. Kwelik pressed her hands against her cheeks and listened to the gentle patter. Did the wind weep for her?

She rose and turned toward the oak tree. One branch, split and smoldering, dangled precariously above the wet grass. She walked over to it and reached up to touch the rough bark. The branch swayed and cracked. The storm had done its pruning, but the tree still stood. Would she too be left standing after God's will was done?

Kwelik glanced up the path that would take her back to Jonathan. At that moment the branch crashed to the ground behind her—the echo of her fears.

She caught her breath and gripped her necklace in one hand until the antler bit into her skin. "I must go back," she whispered. "I must."

Kwelik paused, her eyes searching the dark sky. "But not today, God. I can't face him yet." The wind caught her words and tossed them to the ground. "Please, Lord, just not today."

~

Jonathan stared into the black forest where Kwelik had disappeared two days before. He could scarcely believe she was gone. He had done little else but watch for her since she fled. He could still see the look in her eyes the moment before he had kissed her. Had he been wrong?

"She's not back?" Nahum's question split the air.

Jonathan shook his head, one hand still resting on the door frame.

Nahum glared at him and tightened his coat around his shoulders. "Well, I'm goin' after her."

Jonathan turned on him. "No." His voice felt heavy with remorse.

"Maybe she was hurt in the storm," Nahum cried. "We've got to bring her back."

Jonathan laid a restraining hand on Nahum's arm. "It's too late tonight. She'll come back if she chooses."

Nahum studied him, then nodded, his voice filling with sudden wonder. "You're letting her go free then?"

Jonathan did not look at him as he answered. "No."

Nahum growled and threw a pheasant that he had cooked onto the nearby table. "Then you can eat alone. You know where to find me if you change your mind." Nahum trudged to his own cabin and slammed the door shut behind him.

Jonathan saw a candle flickering from the window in Nahum's cabin. He sighed. Both would wait out their vigil alone.

For hours Jonathan continued to stare into the darkness, wondering where Kwelik had gone. Had she found her people? Had they welcomed her? Would she still return, or had he driven her away forever? The questions spun around him, mocking him. He turned from the window, his gaze falling on the pheasant that Nahum had left. The thought of food sickened him. He closed his eyes. In the blackness her image came back to him, her eyes like liquid sky, drawing him into their depths. He could still feel her softness in his arms, the sweetness of her lips, the quiet drawing of her breath as she gazed up at him.

But he had frightened her. He should not have done it. Even though she was his slave, she was not chattel to use any way he wished. He didn't want her to be that.

What did he want? He didn't know. But he knew it was something more, something closer, something deeper. Jonathan turned toward the fireplace. The embers had long since grown cold. Perhaps all was lost now. She had flown, had become part of the storm, like a dream that's swallowed up in the night and never returns. He groaned. What would he do without her?

A knock sounded at the door. Jonathan's heart leapt in his chest. With a trembling hand he reached toward the handle. "Kwelik?" His breath stopped.

"Mr. Grant?" The face of a small boy from the neighboring homestead looked up at him from the darkness. The boy wiped a pudgy hand across his eyes, brushing away a lock of light brown hair plastered to his forehead.

Jonathan took a deep breath and regained his composure. "What are you doing here, Matthew? It's late, and this is no night for travel." His eyes flickered out over the darkness. She was out there, somewhere. Jonathan shook his head and returned his attention to the boy.

Perspiration beaded on the child's anxious face. "Mr. Grant, we need help! Injuns . . . attacking . . . farm . . . help," the boy sputtered.

"Slow down." With one hand Jonathan drew the boy inside and knelt on one knee before him, his eyes now level with the child's. "What are you saying? Have Indians attacked your pa?"

"No." The word squeezed out from the boy's teeth. "The Hanleys down the creek from us. We saw smoke rising from their farm this morning. Papa went to check." Matthew shivered, then continued. "Oh, Mr. Grant, the Hanleys' homestead was burned right to the ground! Nothing was left. Wasn't no trace of the Hanleys either. They're gone."

Jonathan rose, pulled out a chair, and nudged Matthew into it. "Go on."

"Father's sure we'll be next. Tonight maybe. You've gotta come. Quick!"

"Your father sent you to me?"

The boy looked down, ashamed. Slowly he shook his head. "He doesn't know I've come."

Jonathan hesitated.

Matthew raised his head again, his eyes pleading. "Please come," he begged. "I know Father refused to listen to you about fighting the Injuns. That's 'cause we're Amish. But he did finish the cellar just like you said."

Jonathan looked down at the boy's earnest face and softened. With a final glance into the darkness, he nodded. "I will come."

A smile flashed across Matthew's face as he jumped from the chair, took hold of Jonathan's arm, and tugged. "Hurry," he muttered.

Jonathan disengaged the child's fingers from his shirt and opened the cabin door. "This way." He motioned toward the barn. "We'll ride."

Matthew's eyes grew wide. "Me too?"

Jonathan grinned. "Yes, you too. Come on."

Jonathan told Nahum where he was going and then went to the barn. The smell of damp hay assaulted his senses as he threw open the door. He grimaced. He'd have to fix that leak before another rain. Tomorrow maybe he'd get to it while Kwelik spread out the hay—*Kwelik*. Her name lodged in his chest. She was gone. Gone! Jonathan clenched his fists. How long would it take for him to accept that fact? How long before he stopped expecting to see her across the clearing? How long would it take to forget?

Jonathan grabbed his saddle and tossed it onto Samson's back. He tightened the cinch and then worked the bit into the horse's mouth. Within seconds he sat atop the stallion and pulled the boy up after him. He reined the animal toward the trail and galloped away with the boy's arms squeezing tightly around his waist. The image of Kwelik came unwanted to his memory. That last day on the trail, she had to ride behind him like this boy did, but her touch had been softer, like the breath of the wind and no more.

Jonathan shook his head to rid himself of such thoughts. Daniel's family needed him now. He must focus on a plan. If the Indians were routed at Daniel's farm, the whole valley would be safe, at least for a time. He must convince the man to fight.

Jonathan kept his mind trained on the problem until the cabin came into view. As he approached, he saw Daniel throw open the cabin door. The man's burly frame filled the opening, making a dark silhouette against the candle-lit interior. Though it was now the middle of the night, Jonathan noticed no signs of sleep in the straight set of the man's shoulders nor in the well-lighted cabin behind him.

Jonathan slowed Samson and waved. "Is everyone safe?"

"Is that you, Jonathan?" Daniel stepped onto the small porch and raised the lantern that he held in one hand. "We can't find Matthew."

Jonathan nudged the horse into the light cast by Daniel's lantern. "He's here with me." He turned and helped Matthew slide from the horse's back before again addressing the father. "I heard of the attack on the Hanleys' homestead. The boy says you figure you'll be next."

Daniel scowled at Matthew and then peered up at Jonathan as Samson drew abreast of the cabin. "Aye, I believe so." He pulled off his hat and scratched his forehead with the same hand. "But we can't use your help, Jonathan. You'd best go back and protect your own place."

"No." Jonathan swung off his horse. "We'll beat them back here. Cut off the attack before they can go further up the creek."

Daniel frowned and turned toward his boy. "Why did you bring him, son?"

Matthew hung his head and scuffed his bare feet over the dirt. "To help us, Father."

"The Lord will help us, child."

"But, Father—"

"Silence, Matthew." Daniel turned back to Jonathan. "I'm obliged to you for coming all this way, Jonathan, but you may as well get back on that horse of yours and go back home. We don't need you here."

Jonathan pulled his musket from the back of the saddle. "How do you plan to protect yourself and your family?"

"The good Lord will protect us or not, as He sees fit. Go along now, friend. You know we won't fight."

Jonathan grabbed Samson's reins just as Mary bustled from the cabin, a rag in her hands. "Jonathan, is that you out there in the dark?" she called.

Jonathan smiled. "It is."

The woman glanced at her husband. "Haven't you invited him in for a drop of cider?"

"He's got to go on back now, Mary."

"Now, Daniel, don't go running him off. No one's going to get any sleep tonight anyway." She took Jonathan by the arm. "Come on in and have a bit of cider before you go."

"Mary!" Daniel's voice crackled with exasperation.

Mary only chuckled. "Show some hospitality, Daniel. Could be that we're entertaining angels unaware, you know." She gave Jonathan's arm a gentle tug. "Perhaps we won't see any Indians tonight at all. It will be light in a few hours, and besides everything's a bit damp."

She pulled Jonathan into the cabin behind her, with Matthew tagging along at his heels.

"It's not wet enough to stop a fire," Daniel called after them as he tied Samson to the hitching post.

Mary ignored her husband and smiled up at Jonathan. "Come on in, my boy. Sit here by the hearth." She paused beside a large black dog lying before the fire. "Move over, Bear," she whispered, tapping the dog with her foot until it scooted a few inches to the right.

Matthew plopped down on the floor next to Jonathan and looked up at him with adoring eyes. "Bear is my dog," he stated proudly. "Do you like him?"

Jonathan smiled and leaned down to pet the dog's massive head. "He's a fine dog." Behind him Daniel stepped into the room and closed the door. Jonathan could hear him muttering his disapproval as he wiped his feet on the rag rug.

Matthew wrapped his arms around his knees and grinned. "Bear will protect us from them Injuns too. You'll see."

As if to echo his master's confidence, the dog raised its head and growled.

Jonathan's head snapped up. Silence fell over the room. Another low growl echoed from the dog's throat.

"Is it . . . them?" Matthew's voice cracked.

Daniel strode to the window, pulled back the curtain, and peered outside. "They've come." His voice was flat.

TWENTY-FIVE

~

Jonathan joined Daniel at the window. In the scant moonlight he could see the shadowy figures of four Indians crouching low near the bake oven. He reached for his gun.

Daniel put his hand out and gripped the barrel. "No, Jonathan. We will not shoot them."

"But, Father!" Matthew cried behind them.

Jonathan too felt disbelief. He had thought that Daniel would change his mind. Maybe he would yet. "Surely you want your family saved?"

"Not that way." Daniel took the musket gently from Jonathan's grip.

"Are you mad?" Jonathan could not keep the desperation from his voice.

"You know it is not our way. It's never right to take the life of another, even to save our own." His eyes pierced Jonathan's. "We will not shoot the Indians. Do I have your word?" His voice never wavered.

For a moment Jonathan stared into the firm face of the man before him. Nothing flickered in the man's gaze. No fear. No doubt. No indecision. Slowly Jonathan nodded.

Daniel handed the musket back to him. "You may still be able to escape out the back if you go alone."

Jonathan shook his head. "You've got to let me help you." A glow from outside the window betrayed the fact that the Indians had already set fire to the barn.

Daniel pushed Jonathan toward the back of the cabin. "There's nothing for you to do here."

Jonathan glanced out the window to see a torch flying toward the roof. He heard the thatch burst into flame. In moments smoke filled the cabin as the fire began to lick through the ceiling.

"God help us," Daniel muttered. "I'm sorry, Jonathan, it's too late to run."

Mary screamed.

"Quickly, into the cellar." Jonathan heard his own voice shouting. "Mary, get the boy and hurry."

She grabbed Matthew and headed for the cellar.

"Bear!" Matthew shrieked, breaking his mother's grasp and lunging toward the dog.

Jonathan grabbed the animal and pushed it and Matthew toward the cellar door. "Go!"

Daniel hurried through the door after his son as the curtains caught fire behind him.

Jonathan dropped the dog down the cellar steps and entered himself, pulling the thick door shut behind him. The heavy wooden brace thudded into place across the opening as he latched the door against the growing flames. Then Jonathan turned to see the family huddled at the far end of the cellar.

Daniel's voice rose above the sobs of his wife. "Father in heaven, we pray Thee deliver us from the hands of our enemies. But more than that, Father, keep us faithful to Thy precepts. May our trust in Thee not falter, even in this darkest hour. Amen."

Jonathan scowled and turned away.

Daniel had already lit a small candle to send shadowy light flickering across the bare earthen walls. Three wooden barrels filled with Mary's cider lined the right wall, spanning the entire length of the cellar. Above the barrels a short shelf held a dozen pickling jars, most of which now stood cleaned and empty after the winter.

Jonathan laid his hand against the heavy door. It was not warm yet, but it soon would be as the fire outside it raged hotter, beating its flames against the wood. Jonathan sighed, his eyes raising to the single narrow window near the cellar's ceiling. Daniel had built this room just as Jonathan had instructed him. And yet he doubted it would be enough to save them now. How could Daniel not see that?

How could the man insist that they trust in some invisible God to save them?

Jonathan ran his fingers through his hair. His gaze fell to Mary's frightened face as she slouched on the bench against the back wall. Daniel put one hand on Mary's trembling head and leaned over her. "The door is thick," Jonathan heard him say. "It will hold for several hours."

"What will we do then, Daniel? Burn or face the tomahawk?" she cried.

At the sound of her terror, Jonathan could contain his frustration no longer. He whirled toward Daniel, his voice tense. "This is madness! Why imprison ourselves in this cellar when we can fight?"

"No! God will save us. And if not, we will burn."

Jonathan could hear the ugly crackle of the fire above them. A piece of furniture crashed to the floor.

Mary groaned, tears wetting her eyes as she clutched Matthew to her breast.

Jonathan could not bear the sound of her moaning. He stepped up to the tiny window near the ceiling and looked outside. The Indians stood guard, watching, waiting for the flames to drive them to the ends of their tomahawks. Jonathan turned from the sight and sat with his back toward Mary and the boy. He should never have come to this crazy family led by a man who was willing to die for a belief.

Soon minutes turned to hours. Sweat began to pour down Jonathan's face. The heat was nearly unbearable now. He rose and glanced again out the window. The flames had died down so that darkness now covered the clearing, masking any signs of a waiting war band. The Indians could have retreated, but without proof, escape wasn't worth the risk. If only the dawn would come. The door could not hold forever.

He was right. Jonathan heard Daniel's cry as flames licked around the door's weakened frame.

Daniel grabbed a blanket and began beating back the fire. "The door's giving way. Jonathan, help me!"

Jonathan pulled open a barrel of cider and threw the liquid onto the flames. The fire sputtered for a moment and then continued to burn.

Mary's scream again rent the air as she stumbled toward the flames and attempted to beat them with the rag in her hand. Her efforts only fanned the fire.

Jonathan pulled Mary back from the door and pushed her toward the far wall. "We can't stay much longer, Daniel. Will you fight now?"

"It's nearly dawn," Daniel shouted back over the roar of the encroaching flames. "The light will show us if our enemies have left. But even if they remain, I will not kill them, Jonathan."

Jonathan grimaced and continued to help Daniel fight the fire. Soot covered his face, mixed with his sweat, and ran down his cheeks like black tears.

"The light, the light!" Matthew squealed, pointing toward the window.

Daniel straightened and turned toward Mary. "Check the window, Mary. See if the Indians still wait."

Mary stood on her tiptoes and peered into the dawn. "They're gone!" she cried. "I don't see them anywhere."

"Thank the Lord," Daniel muttered.

Flames burst from beneath the door. Jonathan leapt backwards and fell, his legs just missing the fire's searing bite.

"Hurry, crawl out the window," Daniel yelled, reaching down one hand to haul Jonathan to his feet.

Jonathan helped to hoist Matthew, then Mary, then the dog out the window before turning to Daniel. "You're next."

For a moment Daniel's eyes met Jonathan's in a look of hope and sympathy. "I hope you understand, my friend. It had to be this way."

Jonathan did not answer as he helped Daniel through the window and pulled himself up after him.

"God has saved us, Mary!" Daniel's voice filled with awe despite his house crumbling behind them.

Flying ash sputtered in the morning air and died at Jonathan's feet. He turned away as Daniel hugged his wife and son.

"God is faithful. He has spared our lives. If the dawn hadn't come, we would have been lost. But God rescued us from the lions' den just as surely as he rescued my namesake so long ago. Glory be to God." Daniel turned toward Jonathan, his hand extended.

Before Jonathan could accept the gesture, Matthew shouted and pointed west. "Look!"

Jonathan's eyes followed the direction of the boy's finger. *No!* He felt anguish twist in the pit of his stomach. Before his gaze, smoke curled up, black and ominous, darkening the sky above his homestead.

~

Kwelik woke to the howl of a lone wolf in the distance. Low, eerie, mournful, the sound reverberated through her until she heard nothing else.

Jonathan! His image swept through her mind with sudden longing. Another howl echoed through the night, closer this time. Kwelik sat up and listened to the wolf's cry. *Too late, too late*, it seemed to say. A chill crept over her.

"It's only been two days," she answered aloud. "How can it be too late?"

The low moan of the breeze rustled through the trees as if to echo the sense of condemnation that suddenly hung over her. *Too late.*

Kwelik groaned and rubbed her hands over her face. Had she failed Jonathan, failed God, by not going back immediately?

"I need more time. Just one more day." Her voice echoed hollowly against the wide trunk of the oak tree under which she had taken shelter. She lay back in her leafy bed and squeezed her eyes shut.

Too late. The words came again, and with them, guilt. She rolled up on her elbows and glanced into the night sky, her eyes following a line of stars until they ended in the brightest.

With trembling resolve, Kwelik rose to her feet and poked at the remains of the evening's fire. The wood crumbled into gray ash and spewed a final spark onto the damp ground. She brushed dirt over the embers and scattered the leaves she had gathered for her bed.

Urgency screamed through her. She swayed against the oak. She must go back.

Kwelik stumbled to the swollen creek and splashed water over her face and arms. The coldness pierced through her apprehension. With a deep breath, she turned to the path that would take her back to Jonathan, back to slavery, back to everything she feared in herself. One last time she looked up into the dark sky. "How can this be Your will, God?" she whispered.

As if in answer, the call of the wolf again echoed through the night.

Kwelik shivered and wrapped her arms around her shoulders. She must go back. Now. Just as dawn threatened to break over the horizon, she turned and headed toward the homestead.

When she approached the clearing, she saw it—smoke blackening the morning sky like shadows from hell, so like the remnants of destruction she had seen before. Memories flashed through her mind—her father's blood staining the ground, the black ash of her village, a knife playing at Tankawon's neck, and death, so much death, trails of death to heaven.

"No!" The word tore from Kwelik's lips as she raced toward the homestead. She pressed her hand to her chest to still the thump of dread that beat in her ears.

Kwelik came to a stop at the edge of the clearing. A sick feeling rose in her stomach. "Oh no," she moaned. The earth spun beneath her. "Oh, Jonathan!" She choked on his name.

The acrid smell of smoke assaulted Kwelik's senses. Before her the barn smoldered in gray ash. An eerie silence hung over the clearing, except for the wicked whisper of dying flame as it consumed the last of Jonathan's hopes, and hers.

With a muffled cry, Kwelik stumbled toward Jonathan's cabin just as its roof collapsed into the embers of the dying inferno. She fell to her knees before the devastation, tears blurring her sight. "Oh, God, oh, God, why didn't I come back sooner? Why did I let fear keep me away?"

The clothes she'd hung to dry before she fled still burned like unholy effigies, left to remind her of her guilt. "Oh, Jonathan, I have failed you. Now it's too late. Too late." Kwelik's head dropped into her hands.

A low moan sounded from the far side of the clearing. "Kwelik?" a voice rasped.

"Jonathan?" Kwelik jumped to her feet and turned. "Nahum! Oh no!"

Nahum lay on his side, an arrow protruding from between his shoulder blades. Blood dripped from his mouth.

Kwelik ran toward him. "No, not again. Not again," she whispered. "Oh, Nahum." Tears splashed from her eyes onto his cheek as she cradled his head in her lap.

Nahum's eyes rolled open.

"Miss Kwelik." His voice was weak. "I knew you would come back." His hand reached toward her face, then fell back. "Don't weep."

"Nahum, hang on. I'll find help somehow. Where's Jonathan?" Cold fear clutched her as the question whispered from her lips.

A crooked smile brushed over his face and then faded. "He's all right. He's gone."

"Then I'll find him. We'll get you help."

Nahum closed his eyes. "No. It's too late."

Too late. The words wailed through her.

"I go to my final freedom. I go a free man. Be free, Miss Kwelik." Nahum choked on his own blood, his voice dying.

Kwelik clutched his shirt and leaned over him. "No, Nahum. No." Her plea ended in a sob.

The sudden hiss of a torch at the edge of the clearing roused her attention. They were not alone. Kwelik lifted her head to see the form of a tall brave, his face malevolent with streaks of war paint. Her hair fell over her face, masking her features. She trembled as the light from his torch cast evil shadows across him as he regarded her.

Kwelik sprang to her feet. A scream gathered in her throat. Before it could escape, the silence was broken by a war cry that echoed through her like the laughter of devils.

The brave lunged across the clearing toward her.

"Run!" Nahum whispered hoarsely.

Kwelik turned to flee, but the brave was already upon her. His fingers clawed at her back and dug into her flesh. She struggled free, her tunic tearing in the man's hand. His ragged cry sounded in her ear.

Kwelik's breath stopped in her throat as her feet took flight. Her heart hammered in rhythm. She could hear the thud of the brave's footsteps just behind her. She dared not turn. The earth flew beneath her feet. He was closing in. Her eyes blurred with terror as she sped toward the trees. A few more steps and she might be able to lose herself in the forest.

Too late! The words shrieked in her mind just as the brave's body crashed into her from behind. She felt his hot breath on her neck as she hit the ground. Her necklace was ripped from around her throat. A mixture of blood and dust filled her mouth, cutting off her scream. Fingers like steel dug into her shoulder and turned her. Now death would come. Why did she ever come back? Kwelik saw the glint of the tomahawk above her as a hand grabbed her hair and forced her head up to accept the wicked bite of the blade.

With cold precision, the weapon descended, and Kwelik focused on the face of her killer.

TWENTY-SIX

"Kwelik?" The tomahawk clattered to the ground. The sound reverberated in her ears, chasing away her terror.

"Tankawon!" She pressed her hand to her chest, hoping to quiet her heart's rapid beating. "Tankawon, is it really you?"

With a choked cry, he pulled her into his embrace. "Kwelik, my sister, Kwelik." His voice sounded rough in her ears. "I have found you."

After a moment Kwelik pulled back and looked into the unfamiliar eyes that belonged to her brother. He had grown into a man, a warrior who wielded his weapon as skillfully as if he had killed a hundred men. The thought lodged in her mind and brought a flush of confusion to her cheeks. "What are you doing here, Brother?" she questioned. "Do you know what you have done?"

White Wolf leaned away from her and frowned. "You should not be here."

Kwelik's expression grew grave as she traced the lines of paint on his face. Her eyes caught his. "Are *you* part of the madness, Tankawon, and the killing?"

White Wolf straightened his shoulders. "I am a warrior. I am called White Wolf now."

"A warrior." Kwelik dropped her hand. "You are the ones attacking the innocent families in the valley. Oh, my brother, I would not have believed it."

White Wolf scowled. "What is innocence? They take our land, burn our villages, kill our people."

"These people did not burn our village or kill our people. Nahum has been like a father to me. Now he lies with an arrow in his chest. I cannot bear to think you've killed him."

White Wolf scowled. "I did not kill him, but I would have."

"Why?"

White Wolf's eyes pierced hers, his anger shooting to her soul. "I do it for you."

"For me?"

White Wolf nodded, his eyes challenging her to disagree.

Kwelik took his hand in hers, choosing for the moment to ignore the import of his words. For now it was enough that they were together. "It is good to see you again, Little Brother. I've missed you much." She smiled faintly.

White Wolf's anger dissolved before her eyes. His grip loosened as he turned and yelled to the others, "The gods are good, my brothers. See who they have brought us."

"The gods?" Kwelik questioned, her breath catching in her throat.

White Wolf ignored her.

Kwelik struggled to her feet, her mind spinning, as the war band approached. Her eyes skimmed their faces, then stopped. She took a step back. "Taquachi . . ."

Taquachi gave her a mocking grin. "Kwelik, my betrothed. Are you pleased to see me?"

Foreboding shot through her at the sound of his voice.

"I have waited long for you." Taquachi's tone dropped to an intimate whisper.

Kwelik felt an uneasy tightening in her chest. "No, Taquachi," she breathed.

He grinned and turned toward her brother. "White Wolf, bring your sister."

White Wolf turned toward her, an awkward smile playing on his lips. "I have four scalps hanging from my wigwam door," he boasted. "You will live with me and my wife."

"Your wife?" Kwelik put a hand on his forearm, her eyes searching his face. "Oh, Tankawon."

He growled, "I am a man now. No longer a child."

She raised her hand gently to his cheek. "What has happened to you?"

"Stop that." He batted her hand away. "We must go."

"Go?" Kwelik whispered. "I can't go. I'm needed here."

Taquachi's eyes slid over Kwelik and then returned to White Wolf. "Come, and bring the white woman." He laughed as Kwelik winced at his words.

White Wolf gripped her arm and leaned toward her. "Come." His voice sounded anxious.

Kwelik shook free of White Wolf's grasp. "No, we must help Nahum. He's my friend. Help me."

White Wolf turned toward Taquachi.

Taquachi's eyes narrowed. "The dark one dies; leave him." His voice was cold.

"No, Tanka . . . White Wolf, please," Kwelik begged, running to Nahum. She ignored the shout of her brother behind her.

Without a backward glance, Kwelik knelt beside Nahum, taking his limp hand in hers. "Nahum, can you hear me?"

His eyes rolled in her direction but remained unfocused. His hand tightened briefly on hers as he mumbled a few words.

Kwelik leaned over him. "What? I can't understand."

"Your brother?" The words were garbled but intelligible.

Kwelik nodded. "Yes, Nahum."

He closed his eyes and turned his head away.

Realization dawned over her. "No!" She squeezed his hand and turned his head back toward her. "No, it's not like that. I didn't bring them here. I promise."

A hand gripped her shoulder as White Wolf pulled her away from Nahum. "He is nothing but a white man's slave." White Wolf spat out the words. "Do not waste your tears on him."

"Please, White Wolf."

"Someone comes." Taquachi's low statement cut off her plea. He motioned the others toward the forest. "Back to the village. Now."

As one, the braves lifted their heads. A final war cry echoed from their throats before they melted into the woods.

Tears streamed down Kwelik's face as White Wolf pulled her roughly after him. "No," she cried, her hand reaching back toward the burning homestead. "I must go back."

"Silence the woman," Taquachi shouted.

White Wolf tightened his grip on her wrist and glared at her. "Do not embarrass me."

Kwelik swallowed hard and stumbled behind her brother. She glanced over her shoulder one last time before the trees blocked her vision of the clearing. Anguish rose in her throat, choking her.

"Jonathan . . ." His name escaped her lips in a sob.

Kwelik glanced down at White Wolf's hand encircling her arm. It reminded her of a shackle.

~

The shriek of the Indian warriors echoed through the trees around Jonathan. He tightened his grip on the reins and urged Samson to a faster gallop. Smoke, like black fingers beckoning, still rose thick and ugly from his homestead. Jonathan ground his teeth at the sight. He must get there before it was too late.

Samson skidded into the clearing as Jonathan pulled back on the reins.

"No!" The denial burst from his lips when he saw the burning remnants of the cabins and barn. Nothing was left untouched by fire. Jonathan's heart hammered in his throat. He leapt from his horse and raced to the charred shell of his cabin.

The door squeaked on its hinges and then crumbled into the warm ashes beneath it. Jonathan reached down and rubbed the ash between his fingers. If only he'd come earlier.

He turned his back on the decimated cabin and surveyed the clearing. The barn was no more than a heap of smoldering rubble. Nahum's cabin still burned, the source of the smoke that now blackened the sky. But where was Nahum? Jonathan had expected to see him standing belligerently before his cabin, with Bessie still smoking in his hand.

"Nahum?" Jonathan's voice echoed eerily over the clearing, his call met only by the distant cry of a robin.

He hurried to Nahum's cabin. Nothing met his gaze, except the flames that licked quietly up the charred walls. Fear whispered through the emptiness. Jonathan could feel dread stalking him like a wolf on the hunt. His eyes searched the clearing until he spotted a huddled mass on the eastern side.

"Nahum!" Jonathan ran toward him. Anguish clutched his heart as he saw the arrow protruding from Nahum's back and blood staining the grass beside him.

Jonathan fell to his knees beside Nahum. "Hold on, my friend. Hold on," he whispered, taking the older man into his arms. His own words sounded feeble and hollow. He knew it was too late. Death hung in the air as thickly as the smoke from the fire's burning.

Nahum's hand reached up to weakly squeeze Jonathan's shirt. "Kwelik . . . Indians." Nahum choked out the words, his eyes flickering to Jonathan's before they fell shut again. "Her brother."

"What? What did you say?" Jonathan felt his heart stop within him. He wiped the blood from Nahum's mouth, his fingers trembling at the clamminess of the man's skin.

Nahum's eyes opened to pierce Jonathan's one last time. "Jonathan." His voice was so low that Jonathan had to lean over to hear him. "I forgive you."

Nahum's features grew blank, his eyes glazing over in death.

"No!" Jonathan's shout echoed against the sky as his hands spasmodically clutched Nahum's bloody shirt. "No, Nahum, no." Rare tears blurred his eyes.

Jonathan gripped Nahum's dead body to his chest and rocked back and forth. How could this happen? His arm brushed the arrow in Nahum's back. He gripped it in one hand and pulled. The shaft came loose, releasing another gush of blood over Jonathan's arm. He took the offending weapon and cast it into the trees. The arrow clattered through the leaves and landed upright between two rocks, its tip pointing toward heaven like a memorial to the life it had taken.

Jonathan turned back to Nahum. Gently he wiped the blood from his friend's mouth and pressed his eyelids down to cover his lifeless eyes. "I'll find whoever did this to you, my friend," he whispered, his voice cracking with grief. "Your death won't go unavenged."

Jonathan's thoughts spun in a flurry of anguish and confusion until they settled on a single remembrance. Nahum had said something about Kwelik. Had she come back?

Jonathan laid Nahum's body gently on the ground and stood. Beyond him the grass lay torn and flattened, the sign of a struggle. Jonathan stepped toward the area, his eyes catching an object that glinted white against the dirt. He leaned over to pick it up—a severed thin leather strap with a tiny bit of antler on it. Kwelik's necklace.

Jonathan gripped the strap in his hand as realization washed over him. She was here. She came back!

She came back, the thought twisted through him, *at the same time as the attacking Indians*. The small bit of hope that had surged through him was suddenly replaced by suspicion. Jonathan put his head in his hands and groaned. Had Kwelik brought the Indians? Had she found them and brought them back to destroy him? There was no other answer. Coldness spread through him.

He remembered her talk of trust, of promises, of a God who loved him and called to him. "You will never defeat the demons that pursue you unless you surrender to God," she had said. How could she then bring demons herself, lead them to him?

Jonathan gazed over the smoldering remains of his dreams. His eyes settled on the tilled area in front of his cabin. There she used to plant little violets and exclaim over them joyfully when they bloomed. He sighed. They were all dead now.

And there beneath the birch he could almost see her teaching Nahum to read, smiling as the older man struggled to pronounce a word. Even now he could hear her laughing as she discovered a nest of robin's eggs or humming a song as she washed their clothes at the creek. He could still see her look of earnest longing as she told him about her God.

It seemed that it was all a lie. The knowledge tore his heart in two. He groaned in agony.

Jonathan gripped the piece of antler in his hand until the end pierced his skin. He then slipped it into his pocket as a reminder of the deceitfulness of women and of God.

"Kwelik, Kwelik," he cried to no one, his voice echoing oddly in the clearing. "Was it all a lie?" His voice grew soft with grief. "How could you betray me like this? How could you?"

The words dissolved into cold silence. Never had he felt so utterly alone.

PART THREE

Kitanitowit-essop

(The Great Spirit Moves)

TWENTY-SEVEN

Boston, January 1745

Jonathan put his hands on his hips and stared at the tall brick mansion, an ornate, commanding structure built six years before. It was Richard's colonial home, designed exactly to the specifications that their father had written up before his unexpected death. Jonathan shook his head.

Once he had vowed he would never set foot in this house. Yet here he stood, prepared to toss away his convictions based on a promise made by his uncle, a man he had learned to distrust. Still that promise was the only thing he had left on which to hang his dreams.

The afternoon sun glared off the mansion's windows, spitting light back into Jonathan's face. New ivy climbed up the impressive walls, making dark, intricate patterns on the red brick. *Like a web of deceit*, he thought.

Men in cravats and breeches hustled down the cobbled street, going about their business. Ladies strolled leisurely, and dirty-faced apprentices scampered in and out of doorways. Carriages rolled along the narrow road beside the Charles River as seamen called loudly to one another from their boats. Everywhere the life of the city hummed and hurried and continued on its way, unaware that a man stood in its midst, his dreams held together by the most tenuous of hopes.

During those endless weeks following the destruction of his homestead, Jonathan had found that he no longer had the heart to pursue his dreams alone. He tried trapping for a few months. Yet that too left him empty. Then he returned to Philadelphia, working as a shipwright as he had done before he ever went to the frontier. There the letter had reached him. The letter from his uncle. It had tracked him down like a hound from hell, nipping at the heels of his consciousness until he obeyed its summons.

Jonathan pulled out the letter from his coat pocket, his eyes again scanning the words.

> *Dear Jonathan,*
>
> *I have secured a regiment of militia men from Massachusetts to fight the Indians and French. Due to the war with France, this group is free to go southward with you and fight on the Pennsylvania frontier. But you must come to Boston and lead the men yourself. I will be awaiting you at the Grant manor in Boston. Do not delay!*
>
> *Archibald*

So, despite everything he had sworn to himself, everything he had promised Nahum, here he was, standing before the elegant home that belonged to Richard. Jonathan frowned, wondering how and why his uncle had secured the much-needed men. *If* he had done so at all.

"Master Jonathan?" A feeble voice quavered from the entrance of the mansion. "Would that be you?"

Jonathan's eyes squinted into the descending sunlight. "Tobias?"

The old servant hurried down thc steps toward him. "Yes, Master Jonathan. We's been waiting long for you." The man caught Jonathan in his frail arms and squeezed him. "Surc is good to lay eyes on you again." He grinned.

Jonathan returned the embrace. "What are you doing here in the colonies, Tobias?"

"Why, I come to serve your brother, as I've done since your father's death."

"My brother?" Jonathan pinned the servant with a look of startled anger. "My brother is here?"

Tobias dropped his gaze. "I thought you knew."

Jonathan's eyes scanned the windows in front of him. "I did not even know Richard was in the colonies. I never would have come if I had known *he* was here." Jonathan narrowed his eyes.

Tobias scuffed his buckled shoe over the cobbled walkway. "I'm sorry, Master Jonathan. But won't you come in now? They've seen you standing out here."

Jonathan studied the massive brick structure that suddenly symbolized not only his brother's betrayal but also his vile presence. "He's here." Jonathan's words came quietly. "I can't believe it. That sneaking, conniving . . ." He stopped. His voice raised as he again addressed the servant. "No, I'll be going. You may tell my uncle," he paused, his teeth clenching over the next words, "and my brother that they need not expect me—militia or no."

Tobias's expression flickered between fear and determination. "No, you can't go," he sputtered. "You must come right in."

Jonathan shook his head. "I won't see him."

Desperation came into Tobias's voice. "Oh, Master Jonathan, what have I ever done to you that you should do such a thing to me?"

Jonathan put a gentle hand on the man's quivering arm. "What are you talking about? You know that you were my only friend back in England once Mother was sent away."

"I often thought it was so." Tobias nodded, his gaze seeking Jonathan's, then dropping. "So why are you doing this to me now?"

"Doing what?" Jonathan's voice raised in exasperation.

"Why, sending me back to my master, your brother, to tell him that I've failed to bring you in to him. You know what will happen to old Tobias then."

"I see." Jonathan sighed, remembering many times when his father had beaten servants in situations such as this. With cold certainty, he knew that Richard would now do the same. "For you, Tobias, I will see Uncle Archibald but not my brother. Do you hear me?"

A look of relief washed over the old man's face.

Jonathan changed the subject, hoping to delay the imminent confrontation with his uncle. "How long have you been here with Richard?"

Tobias squinted his eyes as he calculated the time. "Been in Boston six or seven months now."

His emphasis on the city raised Jonathan's suspicions. Tobias never lied, but he had hidden the truth on occasion to protect the family. Jonathan stepped closer. "Were you somewhere else before you came to Boston?"

Tobias licked his lips and turned away.

"How long have you been in the colonies, Tobias?"

"Tobias!" Archibald's harsh reprimand sounded from the doorway.

Tobias scuttled back into the house as Archibald strode down the steps to meet his nephew.

Jonathan grimaced and crossed his arms. "Hello, Uncle. I've come for my militia." His voice held the driest of tones, the question to Tobias forgotten.

"Jonathan, my boy, it is so good to see you." Archibald's hand extended toward him. A weak smile washed over his flabby face.

Jonathan ignored the gesture. "I don't remember such friendliness from you before. Has something changed? Something, or someone perhaps, that caused you to send for me?" He raised one eyebrow as he regarded his uncle. "What are we doing here in Boston, Uncle? Where is my promised militia?"

"Now, now, no need to get into a huff. We'll discuss the militia later. But for now, suffice it to say that I needed you here." Archibald swept his hand toward the house.

"Needed me?"

"I have someone who wants to speak with you."

"Richard." Jonathan stated it without emotion.

Archibald's eyes narrowed. "Tobias told you?"

"I won't see him, Uncle. You can tell him that for me."

"It appears you won't have a choice, Jonathan." The low, cultured voice jarred Jonathan. *Richard!*

He turned to see his brother's tall frame filling the doorway. Richard's dark hair lay hidden beneath a fashionable wig. His clothes were immaculately tailored, from the shiny buckles of his boots to the stunning white cravat tied perfectly at his neck. He was the very image of their father. Jonathan felt his blood run cold, then hot again. "I have nothing to say to you." He squeezed the statement through tight lips. Deliberately, he turned his back and began to walk away.

"Perhaps not now," came Richard's calm response. When Jonathan didn't answer, he continued, "There's nothing left for you here in the colonies. You need me, Johnny. You can't make it alone."

"Oh no?" Jonathan tossed the words over his shoulder and kept walking.

"I know about the Indian woman."

The statement stopped Jonathan in his tracks.

"Ah, so now I have your attention." His brother's voice was mocking now. "You cared for her, didn't you, foolish boy? But where is she now? She was just a savage after all."

Jonathan turned back around. Fury clouded his vision. He clenched his teeth. "How do you know about her?"

Richard smiled. "Well, it seems that we have something to talk about after all."

Jonathan scowled. "Tell me how you know about her!"

Richard chuckled as he ignored the command. "That is information best shared over a cup of tea. It is about that time, is it not, Archibald?"

Jonathan's uncle nodded and called to Tobias. "Tobias, we will be having tea now." He paused, a tiny grimace contorting the corner of his mouth. "All of us."

Richard's hand descended like a vise on Jonathan's arm. "Come, Brother." By sheer force he propelled Jonathan into the house. "There's someone here I think you'll want to see."

Jonathan scowled. "Who?"

His brother laughed. "A real woman."

Richard guided him into the finely furnished parlor and pushed him into an overstuffed chair. "Now, Jonathan, the tea will be brought in shortly. But before our guest arrives, there are a few things we should discuss."

"How do you know about Kwelik?"

"Is that her name? Ah, you speak it with such passion." Richard's voice grew hard even as he continued to smile. "But I think you will soon forget about your little Indian maiden."

Jonathan felt his stomach roil with frustration. *What does he know about her? And how did he find out? Perhaps Kwelik tried to find me. Perhaps she did not betray me after all.* Jonathan frowned and squashed the thought. Then he slipped his hand in his pocket and fingered the piece of antler he kept there.

Richard's voice dropped. "Surely you don't think that I haven't kept track of you, you and your pathetic little homestead out in the wilds. I have my contacts, you know."

"What contacts?"

Richard waved away the question with one hand before leaning closer to Jonathan. "That you do not need to know. But let us talk of something else. I know that you've had trouble both on the frontier and in Philadelphia. You've been attacked."

"Yes," Jonathan answered warily.

"I want to help."

"Help?" Scorn flew through Jonathan's mind at the thought. "You have not helped anyone but yourself since Father died. Or perhaps you wish to help me like you helped our mother?"

A rare look of pain crossed Richard's face. "I had to send her away." His normally confident voice stumbled and grew weak.

"Why?"

Richard avoided the question, his voice growing strained. "How was I to know she would die of the fever?"

Jonathan felt no pity. "You may as well have pulled out a pistol and killed her yourself."

"You don't know what you're saying. Mother was mad. You know that."

"I know nothing of the sort."

"You know she went to hear that Wesley character speak in the fields. She came home with some crazy notions and started to speak like a mad woman. Surely you remember that."

Jonathan's anger turned cold and twisted like a knife within him. "I'll tell you what I remember." His voice rang with suppressed fury. "I remember the day you banished her. I was just seventeen then, too young to fight you, but old enough to despise you for what you'd done. She never did anything but love you. And you killed her for it."

Richard looked as if he had been struck.

"Let me tell you more," Jonathan continued. "What you call

madness was simply the glow of some newfound happiness. She came in the door that day, her shawl wrapped tightly around her shoulders. I had never seen her so beautiful, so assured, so regal in her gentleness and trust. I was proud that she was my mother. But you couldn't stand that, could you?"

Richard shook his head, his gaze evasive. "I couldn't stand her madness."

"You are just like Father with your lies and your arrogance. Tell me, was it madness that made her hold her head high for once in her life?" Jonathan paused, the vision of his mother passing before his eyes. Her look of confidence and faith reminded him of something, of someone more recent. He closed his eyes and saw a face looking to heaven from the platform of a slave auction. Abruptly he opened his eyes. Older memories were safer.

"You hated her new assurance, didn't you? It was something you couldn't control." Jonathan felt a surge of emancipation as he expressed the pent-up anger. "I remember how you derided her for her 'enthusiasm.' You spat the word out as if you would scald her by it. Then you labeled her a 'Methodist' and cursed her." He paused, his voice growing deadly. "And that is not all I remember."

Richard remained silent, as if paralyzed.

"I saw you do it, Richard. You thought I had left the room, but I turned back. I saw you hit her!" All of Jonathan's fury, his suppressed fear, his childhood hurt was contained in that one painful sentence. It echoed through the room like a jury's verdict, condemning and irrevocable.

Richard blanched.

Jonathan's voice dropped to a strained whisper. "How could you do it? How could you be just like our father? Don't you remember our dreams, our promises, the plans we made even as Mother's cries reverberated from the next room, and we were too young, too weak, to help her? But you betrayed our mother and me and everyone who ever loved you."

"Such a sad story."

Jonathan whirled around at the sound of a feminine voice

behind him. "Elizabeth!" Her name escaped his lips in a whisper, his anger giving way to confusion.

"Jonathan?" Her voice, soft and sultry, caressed him as she approached, her gown sweeping elegantly over the wooden floor. She was more beautiful than he remembered.

Jonathan caught his breath as his emotions swayed between the dichotomy of the memory of his mother and the vision of Elizabeth. He looked from her to Richard and then back again. "What are you doing here?"

She glided over to him and placed her hand gently on his. Her hazel eyes beseeched him. "I'm so glad you've come. I've been waiting for you."

Jonathan felt his voice sticking in his throat. "I didn't know you were here."

Her sensual laugh floated through the room. "I am your surprise." She leaned closer to him. "I've come all the way from England for you."

Jonathan could feel her breath warm and inviting on his cheek. He stood and stepped away, his heart still thudding from the encounter with his brother. "I'm sorry you came so far, Elizabeth. Had I known you planned to come, I would have told you not to bother."

"Jonathan!"

He spoke before she had a chance to continue. "Now if you will excuse me, I must go. Good day, gentlemen." The word slipped from his lips with only a touch of mockery. "Elizabeth." He nodded cordially in her direction.

She pouted prettily. "When will you be back?"

"I'm not coming back." Jonathan felt a sense of release as he spoke the words.

"But, Jonathan!" Elizabeth flew to his side, her hands entangling his arm. She gazed into his eyes. "Surely you will be here for my ball."

"What ball?" Jonathan regretted the words as soon as he spoke them.

"Why, to introduce me into Boston society." Elizabeth fluttered her eyelashes in coy appeal.

That look had once caused his heart to race, but now nothing seemed to affect him. Instead, he felt dead inside, as if his soul had suddenly stopped living while his body went on with its daily functions.

Elizabeth tightened her grip on his arm. "Please, Jonathan. You left England without so much as bidding me adieu. I thought we meant more to each other than that." A look of reproach flitted across her features. "And here you are running off again. How can you be so cruel?"

Cruel. The word touched a raw nerve in Jonathan. It was a term that had identified his father and now embodied Richard. But it didn't apply to himself. Did it? Jonathan shivered. Perhaps he *had* been unfair to Elizabeth. He was a fool when it came to understanding women. His failure with Kwelik proved that. Besides, what did it matter if he stayed or went? He had nothing to hurry off to but emptiness. He would not be like his father, like his brother. He would not be cruel. "I'll stay until the ball, then, but no longer," he heard himself saying.

Beside him Elizabeth smiled. The look reminded him of a cat that had a bird squirming between its paws.

Jonathan grimaced. Perhaps he was the bird.

~

Music and polite laughter swirled around Jonathan like the chattering of a thousand seagulls. He pressed his fingers against his temples and stepped into the bright lights of the ballroom. Oil lamps and candles flickered against every wall, throwing dusty shadows into the corners as silent reminders of night. A hundred people, it seemed, crowded in tight groups along the walls while couples dressed in colorful finery swirled across the dance floor.

Jonathan wiped his hand over his face to clear his thoughts. What was he doing in this social melee that Elizabeth called a ball? Why was he wearing these foolish clothes? Buckles winked, silver and shiny, from his shoes as coattails gently slapped the back of his thighs. He hated the feel of it. But at least he was not wearing one of those ridiculous wigs so unsuited for colonial life. The neat black ribbon at his neck caught up his own brown hair. Surely Elizabeth would frown upon him for that, but he didn't care. He had come, despite the urge to escape to the local tavern and forget her wooing.

"Don't be such a beast, Jonathan." Elizabeth put her hand lightly on his arm and laughed. "Are you going to wear that unpleasant frown all evening?"

Jonathan deepened the look. "At least while I'm trussed up in this ridiculous costume."

"Come now, you look wonderful. Surely you know that horrid buckskin would have made you the laughingstock of all Boston." Her laughter faded as she tapped him on the chest. "And I with you."

Jonathan grunted.

Elizabeth twined her arm around his and smiled up at him. "Now do try to be cordial to the guests," she whispered. "Please, for my sake." She pursed her delicately painted lips and waited for his response.

Jonathan sighed, wondering if it was all a game. Yet he smiled down at her, hating himself.

"Why, here's the young Mr. Adams now." Elizabeth's voice lilted past Jonathan's ears. "Come, Jonathan, meet the son of the wealthiest brewer in the colonies."

Jonathan nodded toward the man without seeing him and began to disentangle Elizabeth's hand from his arm.

"Oh, there's Lady Huntington," she cried, tactfully removing her hand before Jonathan could do so. "Excuse me for a moment, Jonathan, Mr. Adams." Elizabeth turned a charming smile on both men before whisking over to meet the elegant older woman who had just arrived. "Lady Huntington, how delightful that you could come." Elizabeth's greeting carried gracefully across the room.

Taking the opportunity, Jonathan turned and headed toward the balcony.

"I imagine the sight of one sunset on the frontier is more breathtaking than a thousand society balls." The words were spoken quietly behind Jonathan.

He turned back to the brewer's son and regarded him. The man was of middle height, about his own age, with an understanding smile playing around his mouth. Jonathan returned the smile. "That's just what I was thinking. How did you know, Mr. Adams?"

"You can call me Sam." The smile broke into a quiet laugh, so different from the empty sounds around him. "And to answer your question, I read it as plain as print on your face."

Jonathan grinned and gripped the hand of the other man. "I'm Jonathan. And you're the first man I've met here in Boston who understands. Come," he motioned toward the balcony, "take some fresh air with me. This is my favorite spot in the house."

Sam nodded as Jonathan pushed open the balcony doors. "Ah, it faces west. You can almost see the mountains from here."

"You are an observant man, Sam." Jonathan gripped the rail and breathed deeply.

Sam stepped up beside him, his voice lowering. "A man always loves the window that faces toward home."

The smile faded from Jonathan's face. "*Home* is a tricky word, my friend."

"Sometimes."

Silence fell between them as they stared into the western sky.

Sam cleared his throat. "Tell me, Jonathan, have you heard the young Reverend Whitefield speak here in the colonies?"

Jonathan shook his head, glad for the change of subject. "Haven't heard him myself. He causes quite an uproar wherever he goes, I've been told."

Sam chuckled. "Sometimes an uproar is just what people need to break old habits of bondage and embrace new ones of liberty."

Jonathan raised his eyebrows. "He speaks of such things, of liberty and bondage?"

"Of such things and more." Sam paused. "I heard him when he came to Harvard a few years back. I've never been the same since. He made me see these colonies and my life from a new perspective." Sam turned toward Jonathan. "He's back here in Boston, you know."

"Now?"

"Indeed. He's speaking Friday at Dr. Coleman's meetinghouse."

"Samuel!" Both men whirled as a loud voice called from inside the ballroom. "Samuel Adams, come in here a moment. We have a question of law for you."

Sam sighed. "Excuse me, Jonathan." He patted Jonathan on the arm in a friendly gesture of equals. "Think about it. Friday."

When he had gone, Jonathan turned back to the railing. Loneliness surrounded him like a cloak. Despair whispered through his mind. Did the wilderness call out to him even now? Once his dreams and ambitions had been as clear as stars in the sky, but now they seemed no more than phantoms from the distant past, memories of something beautiful, something lost. He sighed. What had happened to him? There was no passion left anymore, no desire, no hope, no conviction. Nothing but this awful sense of emptiness and resignation. The dream was dead. He had lost it, lost everything to a woman who still held his heart even though she had betrayed him.

Jonathan leaned his hands against the wooden railing and groaned. Maybe he should just go back to England. What did it matter now? What did anything matter?

At that moment the moon peeked out from behind a cloud. Jonathan stared into the glowing orb. "*You are the wolf, Jonathan.*" Kwelik's words came back to him as clearly as if she had just spoken them in his ear. Anguish shot through him.

"Kwelik," he whispered hoarsely to the wind, "what have you done to me?" Jonathan's head came down on his arms.

"What did you say?" Elizabeth's voice cut through him.

He raised his head. "It's nothing."

She looked at him suspiciously and then rubbed her hand lightly up his arm. "Come back inside, Jonathan. Dance with me."

He looked down at her, her image replacing that of another. Without another word, Jonathan followed her back into the ballroom.

TWENTY-EIGHT

The birds were silent, the butterflies dead, the flowers withered and gone. Stark branches swept the winter sky, bleak despite the noonday sun. Kwelik sighed, her voice echoing hollowly against the day's stillness.

Even the snow did not brighten her spirit as it once had. She used to love the way it sparkled in the winter's sunlight, how it melted in her hand, the freezing softness of it. But now it seemed only an unyielding, cruel backdrop to her new life in the village. Was it just because it kept her from Jonathan, kept her from going back as she knew she must?

Kwelik reached down and grabbed a fistful of the white ice. Slowly it trailed through her fingers and fell gently to the ground. She had promised herself that after the first thaw, she would try to to find the homestead again, to find Jonathan. If she could.

When she first arrived at the village, and for many months thereafter, Taquachi's ever-watchful war band had kept her from leaving. Then with the onset of winter, they relaxed their vigil, knowing that she could not go far in the freezing snow. But in the spring maybe, just maybe, she would be free to obey at last God's command to face Jonathan again.

Kwelik brushed her cold-numbed hand against her thigh and turned back to the grinding rock. Purposely she ignored the low chatter of the other women who now worked inside various wigwams. She closed her ears to the rough laughter of the men as they gathered in the longhouse situated at the far end of the village. She turned away from the tendrils of smoke that rose from the center of each building, indicating the warm fire within. She didn't want to see the hides curing in the morning air, nor the trampled snow that lined the center of the village, nor the large kettle of boiling deer meat that bubbled near the chief's hut. None of that could comfort her now. She sighed. No matter how many months she lived in the village, she never felt a part of its life, never felt as if she truly belonged. *That's because I don't belong here*, she thought. *I belong with Jonathan. If only I had not waited to return to him.*

Kwelik gripped a smaller stone in her numbed fingers, its heavy smoothness cold against her skin. Nothing was simple anymore. Nothing was like it should be. A shiver raced through her. She pulled the bear skin more tightly around her shoulders.

An ear of corn lay brown and dry in the hollow of the rock before her. She pushed the stone against the hardened kernels as if by her effort she could crush the doubt and despair that haunted her. The corn resisted, then gave way beneath the onslaught. She gripped the stone harder, grinding one kernel into a fine powder. The grating sound of rock against rock filled her ears until she heard nothing else.

Another bit of corn cracked beneath the pressure of the stone. Kwelik picked up the broken kernel and held it in her palm. She turned the pieces over with one finger. *This is me*, she thought, the image flooding through her mind unbidden, *like dust in the hand of destiny*. She had found Papa's world, and it made her a slave. Then she returned to village life, and still she was not free. Kwelik's eyes searched the pale winter sky. *Is life no more than bondage, Lord?* A cloud passed across the sun's path, blocking the dismal light.

"Am I no more than a bit of powder in the wind?" Kwelik's voice broke the silence, then faded. She tossed the broken kernel into the breeze. The wind caught the remnants and threw them to the snow. They shone dark against the blinding whiteness. *Like my prayers*, she thought, *withering half-formed, without strength, and falling unheeded to the ground*.

Behind her a wigwam door rustled in the breeze, beckoning her into its warm interior. Kwelik kept her back to it. She needed the crisp air to clear her head, needed the time alone to think, to remember, to understand why she felt the way she did.

Kwelik shook her head and attacked the corn again. She should be happy here, but she wasn't. Nothing was right. Nothing made sense anymore. What had happened to her?

The wind picked up a dead leaf and twirled it through the air until it landed at her feet. She picked it up and studied the brown surface before her eyes traveled up to the bare branches of the tree from which it came. Stark, bleak, and desolate, it reflected the feelings of her heart. She watched the way the branches reached for the sky and swayed in the breeze without breaking. In spring they would be covered with bright green leaves, the sign of new life, new hope. Soon spring would come. *Perhaps it will come for me too—someday.*

Kwelik grimaced and looked up into the gray sky. "I know," she whispered. "Not today. Never today."

"*Manito-dasin!*"

Kwelik whirled around to see Snow Bird, White Wolf's wife, hurrying toward her.

"No, no! No work." The young woman snatched the grinding stone from Kwelik's hand.

"What are you doing, Chilili?" Kwelik frowned as she noticed the fear in Snow Bird's deep brown eyes.

"You must not work here." The words were spoken in haste as Snow Bird dropped her gaze.

Kwelik put her hands on her hips and stared at her brother's small wife. "Why not? I'm not hurting anything."

Snow Bird shook her head violently and clutched the stone to her chest. "*Manito-dasin* not work," she mumbled.

"*Manito-dasin*? Spirit daughter? I'm not a spirit daughter. What are you talking about, Chilili?"

The woman glanced up at Kwelik and then shoved the stone beneath her own fur cloak. "Waptumewi told me who you are." Her delicate chin quivered as she chewed her lower lip.

Kwelik furrowed her brow. "Who I am? I am the same person that I've been for the past six months. I am Kwelik."

"Yes, Kwelik." Chilili nodded vigorously. "Daughter of sky god. Waptumewi told me so just now. He said the sky god looks out from your eyes." She wagged a trembling finger in Kwelik's direction, gaining courage. "Why did you come to stay with us? To bring us disaster? To close the sky and make the sun stop shining?"

"It's winter, Chilili." Kwelik couldn't keep the annoyance from her voice. Still Snow Bird was young yet. She had only fourteen summers, fewer even than White Wolf. Who knew what fantasies filled her silly head? Kwelik continued, her voice gentler this time, "I have nothing to do with the sun shining or not. Only God has control over such things. I don't know what my brother told you, but you must stop thinking such foolishness."

Snow Bird bowed down, her face in the snow at Kwelik's feet. "Forgive me, *Manito-dasin*."

"Get up!" Kwelik grabbed the woman's arm and yanked her to her feet. "I am not *Manito-dasin!* Do you hear me?"

White Wolf staggered from the wigwam behind them. "Chilili, what have you done?" He stumbled closer and swiped a hand over his red eyes.

Kwelik rushed toward him. "White Wolf!"

He barely glanced in her direction. "Stupid woman," he slurred. "I told you not to say anything."

Kwelik took him by one shoulder and shook him. "What did you tell her?" She pointed toward Snow Bird, still trembling from her husband's harsh words.

White Wolf laughed. The sound grated in Kwelik's ears. "She asks too many questions. She wonders why you are different, strange. So I told her you are the daughter of the Great Spirit. What did you want me to tell her?"

Kwelik glared at him. "The truth."

"Isn't it? That's what Papa used to say. 'Sons and daughters of God.'" White Wolf mimicked their father's intonation. "Don't you believe him anymore?"

Kwelik bristled beneath his insulting tone. "That's not what he meant, and you know it."

"I don't care what he meant!" White Wolf's humor quickly turned to anger. "You will be whoever I say you are."

"I am Kwelik!" She hated the sound of desperation in her voice.

"What is Kwelik?" he scoffed in response. "Nothing but a slave.

Should I have told her that?" White Wolf spat on the snow and fixed his blurry eyes on hers. "Now you are *Manito-dasin*. You will be treated with respect because of me." He thumped his chest for emphasis.

Kwelik bit her lower lip and remained silent.

He stepped closer. "Do not argue with me."

His breath smelled of brandy. Kwelik wrinkled her nose at the pungent aroma. Her eyes flashed with sudden comprehension and fury. For months she had quelled her suspicions about her brother's drinking, but now the truth could not be ignored. "How could you drink the poison water from the French? They killed our people, burned our village!"

A ridiculous smile spread over White Wolf's face. "It is the drink of warriors, Sister."

"It is the drink of fools." Kwelik pressed her hands against her temples and shut her eyes. *This is not happening. Oh, God, tell me this is not happening.*

White Wolf's words broke through her thoughts. "It wasn't the French who killed our people. It was the white man's God."

Kwelik groaned. This was the conversation she had dreaded ever since her brother had found her. Thus far she had avoided it. "How can you say that? I thought you believed in God."

"I believe in the power of the tomahawk. I believe in the spilling of the white man's blood. I believe in hate. Those are the things that matter now."

"No! Don't say such things." Kwelik trembled as she spoke, wishing she could erase her brother's words from her mind.

He leaned close to her. His hand gripped the bear skin that covered her. His breath blew sour in her face. "Listen and understand, Sister. The white man's God is a lie. Father was a fool."

Tears streamed down Kwelik's face. She didn't bother wiping them away. *Oh, God,* she prayed, *tell me this isn't happening. Tell me that it's a dream, a terrible, horrible dream.* She looked at the hard features of the young man before her, his eyes narrow with anger, his jaw clenched, his chin thrust forward in belligerence. Was this her brother? The one she had teased and cuddled and taught to fish? The one for whom she had given up her freedom? She had tried to tell herself that he had just grown up. But there was more to it than that, so much more.

Kwelik spoke again, her voice low and quiet. "Oh, Tankawon, White Wolf. All these months I've remembered the destruction of our people, our village. Their deaths have haunted me, but I clung to one thing, that you, my brother, were alive." The bitter truth washed through her, knotting in her stomach until she could deny it no longer. "But you aren't. You died there too."

"Yes." White Wolf's voice rang harsh and hateful against the winter landscape. "Little Cloud died with the rest of our village, and White Wolf was born."

"What about Jesus? What about everything our family believed in? What about your faith?"

His eyes narrowed with fury. "Do you know what I remember, Sister? I will tell you. I remember that our clan believed in this Jesus and were slaughtered. Father's faith did not save him from the arrow's deadly bite."

"But it saved his soul. He's with God now for all eternity."

"What do I care about eternity? I refuse to spend it with the white man's God."

"He's not the white man's God." Kwelik heard her voice rise with the futility of her argument. "He's Papa's God, Mother's God, and my God. He was your God too."

"Not anymore."

"Oh, Tankawon." Kwelik put all the agony of her soul into the plea.

"I am White Wolf!" he shrieked as he gripped her and shook her by the shoulders, then shoved her to the ground at his feet. He stood above her, his eyes dull and angry. "Why would you believe in a God who made you a slave?" he demanded. "Such a God is either cruel or powerless."

Kwelik turned her head away, unable to bear her brother's words. "He is still God, White Wolf, whether you acknowledge it or not. He is God whether I am a slave or a spirit daughter. And one day every knee will bow before Him. Every tongue shall confess to God." She paused, her hands pressing into the icy ground. "Even yours."

White Wolf leaned over her, his voice cold and heartless in her ear. "Never!"

"Enough, Waptumewi." Taquachi's voice echoed sternly from the longhouse door. "Your talk gets you nowhere. Words are for women, action for warriors." He flipped his knife over in his hand and shoved it into his belt.

White Wolf straightened. "We will talk later, Sister." He turned toward his wife, his hand digging into the flesh of her arm. "Come, woman."

Snow Bird stumbled and fell as White Wolf pushed her toward their home.

"Get back in the wigwam, you little fool."

The woman cringed away from him.

White Wolf shot Kwelik a final glance. "See what you have done." His words echoed in her ears as he ducked through the wigwam door. From there he continued to harangue his wife in loud, surly tones.

Kwelik buried her face in her hands and tried to stem the flow of her tears. She heard a step behind her. She sniffed and turned her head.

Taquachi towered above her. His black eyes pierced hers.

Kwelik wiped her hand over her face to dry the tears. "I-I'm sorry for disturbing you. I'll go back in now." She held her breath, hoping Taquachi would accept her words and return to the longhouse.

Instead, he smiled down on her, extended his arm, and gripped her by the elbow. "Come, Kwelik, we must talk." His voice was oddly gentle as he pulled her to her feet.

Kwelik's face brushed his chest as she rose. He smelled of fire and sweat. Even now flecks of gray ash clung to his skin and adorned his hair, which was pulled back in a thick braid. Kwelik shuddered, noting the confidence of his grip, the power and arrogance that defined him. It repulsed her.

Taquachi's hand moved to her shoulder, denying her escape. She swallowed as he drew her to his side. "Let's walk," he murmured in her ear, nodding toward the forest. "I have something you will like to see."

Without another word, Taquachi guided her through the trees, his hand firm on her arm. Snow decorated the branches around them, but Kwelik scarcely noticed it until a clump fell with a soft thud as she passed. Within moments the angry voice of White Wolf grew distant, the sound swallowed by a silence that was broken only by the quiet rumble of water beyond them.

"Here we are." Taquachi's voice split the air.

Kwelik stepped from the covering of trees to a place where water tumbled down a small cliff and made a gentle splash in the crystal pond below. She caught her breath at the splendor of the scene. Water droplets froze midair as she watched, making tiny snowflakes that swirled in the wind and settled in a heap to one side of the waterfall. Beyond it tall trees rose skyward, their tops dark against the winter sky. Kwelik reveled in the rainbow of colors as bits of frozen moisture danced around her, lit by a single ray from the setting sun. She allowed the water to kiss her cheek and dampen her lashes. "It's beautiful," she whispered. Her voice held her awe.

"I knew you would like it." Taquachi's confidence spoiled the beauty.

Kwelik turned toward him, his silhouette black and foreboding against the pristine beauty of the scene.

"Come, stand here." Taquachi motioned to the spot next to him.

Reluctantly she joined him on a rock that jutted out over the water.

"See there?" He pointed to a place downstream where the water swirled into a tiny inlet before escaping to tumble over rocks below. "I swam there as a boy."

Kwelik glanced quickly at him. It was hard to imagine him as a child.

His eyes grew narrow and fierce. "That is where I made my first vow that I, not my brother, would someday rule the tribe. And there," he jabbed his finger toward the top of the waterfall, "is where I decided the white men must die." Taquachi's eyes captured and held hers. "There is where I declared my war on the white man's God."

Kwelik drew a sharp breath. All the loveliness of the scene suddenly vanished.

Taquachi stepped closer. "And soon, my love, I will have all that I want."

Kwelik stepped away from him, her voice wary. "What do you mean?"

He smiled. "We will be married when the first flower of spring breaks through the ground and blooms. It will be a sign of the gods' favor on our union."

Kwelik's breath stopped in her throat. "No, Taquachi." She pressed her back against the wet rock behind her. "I cannot marry you."

Taquachi dismissed her objection with a flick of his fingers. "I did not ask your permission. It will be as I say."

"I cannot."

"You will reconsider."

Kwelik felt dread rise in her throat, choking her. "How will marrying me make a difference?" The words echoed, rushed and desperate, against the rocks surrounding them. "I'm a half-breed, remember."

"You are daughter of the sky god."

"Surely you don't believe that nonsense."

Taquachi's laugh sent a chill of horror through her. "No, but the tribe will. And they will follow me if the *Manito-dasin* is my wife."

Sick understanding washed over her. "What about the shaman? What about your father, the chief?"

"The shaman will assist you, and my father is old and of no account."

Kwelik pulled the bear skin tightly around her as if it could ward off his plan. "Please, Taquachi, I cannot be this *Manito-dasin*. You know that I believe in Christ, not any sky god."

"We will see."

Kwelik's heart quaked at the assurance of his tone. "No, Taquachi," she pleaded, "surely there is someone else you wish to marry. Blackhair would love to be your wife. You saw how her eyes followed you at the harvest ceremony. Or Elkfoot or Waterflower." Kwelik fumbled through her mind for additional names.

"No, I want none but you." Taquachi leaned over her, his breath warm on her cheek. "Soon you will forget this Christ of yours, and you will serve me well as wife. You will see."

Kwelik took another step away from him.

Taquachi reached out, his fingers gripping her wrist. "You will not get away so easily." He pulled her close to him, drawing her to his chest.

Revulsion shot through her as he brushed her hair back with his hand. His eyes searched hers, mocking her. "Fear becomes you, my love." He chuckled low in her ear. "Remember, Kwelik, you will be mine. One way or another."

TWENTY-NINE

~

Archibald stood on the balcony and placed his hands on the railing just as Jonathan had done. In the distance carriages creaked along cobbled streets as tall lanterns reflected off the rippling surface of the Charles River. A small barge skimmed down the river, hauling its cargo toward the bay. Archibald took a deep breath. The air was saltier here than in Philadelphia.

Below him a couple walked arm in arm along the river's bank. The sight of them caused a knot to form in his stomach. The moon shone brightly, glaring on the whiteness of new-fallen snow. Tonight the sky was clear, the clouds driven away by a wind that pierced through a man's soul.

Archibald sighed and looked into the dark sky. He could see every winter constellation he had learned as a boy. But the stars were different here, different from at home. If it weren't for Jonathan, he'd be there now. He felt hatred twist in his chest. Jonathan! How he would like to see him dead and out of the way at last.

Archibald gripped the wooden railing until his knuckles turned white. What did the boy see when he gazed into the night? What did he hear when he listened to the darkness? What did he know that had allowed him to thwart all of Archibald's hopes? And what did Richard know? Jonathan was right about one thing. Richard had changed after his father's death, changed enough to send that Irish mother of theirs away. Archibald ground his teeth in frustration. Secrets. Harlan's sons were full of secrets, secrets that bound them together and drove them apart, secrets that left Archibald caught in a web he could only wonder about. He sighed.

A man stepped from the darkened ballroom behind him. Archibald heard the rustle of velvet curtains but did not turn. He knew the sound. He coughed. "Good evening, milord." His voice echoed against the silence of the night.

"Jonathan is mine, Uncle, just as I told you he would be." Richard did not come into the moonlight as he spoke.

Archibald turned and stared into the shadows. "I would not be so sure. He has slipped from your fingers before."

Richard's chuckle was low and calculating. "Not this time. I have watched him. I've seen how he dances with Elizabeth, how he accepts her advances, how he looks into the western sky with eyes dulled by despair. He is a man whose dreams have died. And I am the one who killed them." Richard smiled. "He will go back to England without so much as a whimper."

"Do not be fooled, milord." Archibald shook his head and reached toward the shadowy figure.

"Careful, Archibald."

He dropped his hand and again turned toward the night sky. "Jonathan is a man of passion. He will not easily abandon his dreams. Methinks he is still a hindrance to our plans."

"I tell you, his dreams are dead, and with them his power to defy me any longer. Have you not seen it in his eyes, in the set of his shoulders, in the very tilt of his chin?"

"I have seen something." Archibald cleared his throat. "Do you know what has caused his apathy?" His voice sounded strained as he spoke. "Surely not Elizabeth, not seeing you again."

"I believe the destruction of his homestead, the death of his friend."

Archibald gasped. "What news is this, milord? I had not heard. Have you been in contact with our French ally?"

Richard grabbed the hair at the nape of Archibald's neck and pulled. "Silence, you fool! Will you shout your knowledge to all with ears? I should take your tongue for that." He tipped Archibald's head back until the stars blurred through the older man's tears of pain. "The English are, as you know, at war with France."

As his nephew loosened his grip, Archibald whimpered, "Forgive me, milord."

"You are lucky that I still need you." Richard dropped his hand

and stepped beside Archibald for a moment as the moon slipped behind a cloud.

"Yes, Nephew. Do not forget my work when you come into power."

Eyes as cold as death slid over Archibald. "Of course not. You will be my chief tax collector."

Archibald licked his lips. He could almost feel the coins running through his hands now.

"Make no mistake, soon I will rule the Pennsylvania wilderness and beyond." He paused, a slow smile spreading across his shadowed face. "In the name of King George II, of course."

"Of course, milord."

"And I will squeeze the very lifeblood from these commoners until they obey me." Richard made a fist in the darkness. "George may be their king, but I will be their ruler."

At his words Archibald felt the first chill of the coming storm.

~

"Shut up!" White Wolf's fist slammed into his wife's delicate chin before she could duck away from the blow. He raised his hand again. "Stop that sniveling, or I'll stop it for you."

Snow Bird gulped spasmodically and pressed the back of her hand against her mouth, trying to quell her sobs.

"That's better." White Wolf's voice quieted as he turned from her and pulled aside the pelt that covered the wigwam's doorway. From where he stood, he could just see his sister and Taquachi disappearing into the trees that would lead them to Taquachi's waterfall.

White Wolf's lips stretched into a cold smirk. Now Kwelik would see that her God had no power, that He was no more than a delusion concocted in the white man's dreams. Taquachi would show her. He would make her see the truth. *Truth*—the word spun through White Wolf's mind in a flurry of drunken confusion. Truth was a tomahawk, a bow, a gun. Truth was war. And God was a lie.

"What are you looking at?" Snow Bird's hand brushed lightly, fearfully, across his shoulder. The touch startled him.

He spun toward her, noticing the ugly swelling that had already begun on her cheek. Her eyes searched the forest and then sought his. "He's gone, husband." She frowned. "Why do you let him speak to you like that?"

White Wolf's anger at Kwelik, at God, and at himself erupted at the question. Without thought, his hand smacked hard against Snow Bird's mouth, driving her to the ground. "Little fool," he spat out, leaning unsteadily over her. "You will learn to keep your mouth shut."

Snow Bird trembled. "Please, White Wolf," she muttered, her voice sputtering and stalling into silence.

White Wolf glared at her. His vision blurred and doubled as he wiped his hand roughly across his mouth. "Leave me alone." He turned away and grabbed a bottle from beneath the woven platform that formed their bed. The slender neck felt cool in his hand as he tipped the bottle and swallowed more of the burning liquid. It did not quench his anger. He liked brandy better, but the man had brought rum instead. Next time he wanted the brandy. Maybe Gray Bear had some. He would check.

White Wolf took a step toward the door and stumbled over his wife. He pressed the bottle to his lips again and sucked it dry. "Empty." The word released his fury. He spun and threw the bottle to the ground near Snow Bird's head. The glass shattered and sprayed over her. She screamed as shards of glass cut into her arm and face.

White Wolf frowned and tried to focus on the woman. Her figure swam before his eyes. "Quiet!" His voice slurred. With one hand, he reached over and gripped her by the tunic, yanking her to her feet. "You disgust me." He spat the words in her face. "I thought you would be strong, a worthy mate for a warrior. I was wrong." White Wolf growled low in his throat and cast Snow Bird onto the bed.

She screamed again, her arms flailing as she hit the furs.

White Wolf leaned over her. "My sister has more strength in her sleep than you do awake. She would be a fit wife for a warrior."

Snow Bird buried her head in the bedding to muffle her cry. Her terror goaded him.

"Get up!"

She did not move.

White Wolf stared at her slender shoulders, jerking in time with her tears. He turned away, disgusted, and stormed out of the wigwam.

"White Wolf." He heard her call his name, her voice choking through her sobs.

He scowled and staggered toward the longhouse. He would not go back, at least not until he found some brandy to sustain him. Brandy. That's what he needed now. Then he would feel right again—strong, assured, and powerful.

White Wolf staggered toward the far end of the village, the sounds of tribal life raking across his nerves—families laughing together in their wigwams as wisps of black smoke escaped from the center of each home, women grinding dried corn for the evening meal, men sharpening their stone knives, children giggling over a cornhusk doll. And in the midst of it all, one familiar voice rose above the other sounds: "Get away from me, Taquachi!"

White Wolf whirled around to see Kwelik racing toward him, her face flushed with a mixture of fury and fear. Taquachi's laugh rang out behind her. She pressed her hands to her ears.

White Wolf reached out to grab her as she passed.

Kwelik paused, her blue eyes flashing with anger and accusation. "How can you follow that man, Brother?" Her voice filled with pain. "How could you do this to me?"

In that moment a vision crystallized in his foggy mind—Kwelik, an arrow protruding sharply from her calf, as she urged him to run, to save himself. And he had run, had left her in the hands of the enemy. She had saved him, loved him, laid down her life in exchange for his. White Wolf focused again on the face before him.

Kwelik's eyes filled with tears.

He knew she could smell the fresh rum on his breath. He dropped his head and winced.

"My brother, what have you done?"

Her words, soft now with disappointment, bit through him, shredding his defenses. He saw Taquachi's mocking face emerge from the trees behind her. Had he been wrong to go along with Taquachi's plans? Doubt shimmered through White Wolf's mind as he reached out to touch his sister's face.

A tear slipped down her cheek. She pushed his hand away. "It's too late for your excuses, White Wolf. Too late."

His breath stopped in his throat. What had happened? How had he failed her? Had he betrayed her love? White Wolf dropped his hand and turned away, unable to bear his confused thoughts. He had longed to be a warrior. And so he was. But what else had he become?

He stared into Kwelik's eyes, drowning in the aching depths of them. *Too late*. The words rang through him.

And he knew they were true.

THIRTY

The dim, wavering sunlight shone through the open door at Dr. Coleman's meetinghouse. Archibald slipped through and found a seat near the back. Long icicles scattered pinpoints of light through the large window pane to his left as he searched the front of the room. Rows of narrow benches, filled to overflowing with men and a few women, lined the wooden floor of the meetinghouse. Archibald craned his neck to get a better view.

There! Several seats up and to the left, Jonathan sat next to that young Adams fellow. Archibald let out his breath. He would be well hidden in the back of the room. Jonathan must not suspect that he had followed him here.

Archibald kicked the bench in front of him and settled into his seat. What was that fool boy doing at a religious gathering like this one? Had he become one of those accursed New Lights, those who sought a personal experience with God? They were mad, all of them. Archibald scowled and crossed his arms. He would wait and see, hear what that heretic Whitefield had to say. Then perhaps he would know why Jonathan had come here, and in knowing, he would find a way to best him.

Archibald's face darkened into a scowl. If only he could rid himself of Jonathan. Since the boy had come to Boston, Elizabeth had eyes for no one else. It sickened him to see her pining over that coarse woodsman just because he was young and handsome and because his brother was wealthy.

Why, he was wealthy too, and much more sophisticated than Jonathan. Elizabeth should look at him. But she didn't. Even this morning as they sat around the breakfast table sipping tea, Elizabeth had spoken of nothing but Jonathan. It was as if Archibald didn't exist at all.

A man in a long overcoat pushed past Archibald and took a seat further down the bench. Archibald turned his head to survey the room. The whitewashed walls were bare of coverings, their drab appearance broken only by a window on each side and several unlit wall lanterns. Archibald dropped his gaze to where Jonathan sat. The boy hadn't moved, despite the people who were crammed together on every side. There was scarcely an open space even in the aisles.

Another man crushed into Archibald's shoulder from the right. "Pardon me, sir," the man muttered, tipping his hat in Archibald's direction as he removed it and set it on his lap.

Archibald turned to glare at him, noting the weak chin and watery green eyes. He raised his own chin a notch until he was looking down on the man. *Probably a Scotsman*, he sneered, *a typical follower of wild-eyed heretics like this Whitefield*. Archibald pretended to flick a bit of dust from his coat before he turned pointedly away from the stranger.

The man grinned. "Ever heard the reverend speak before?"

"No," he answered curtly, cutting off any further conversation.

The man swallowed and turned away.

Through the window behind him, Archibald noticed a crowd of people gathering outside in carriages and wagons. *Commoners*, he thought. The sky was darkening. A storm was nearly upon them. He would see how many people remained once it became uncomfortable. When the heavens poured out their fury, the peasants would scatter like chaff in the wind. He at least was under the roof with a clear view of the slender young man at the front. *Is that Whitefield?* he wondered.

He craned his neck to see over the woman in front of him. *What an unimpressive fellow*, Archibald thought. The man was not particularly tall, nor commanding, nor even especially handsome. Indeed, he was little more than a youth.

The crowd grew quiet as the man spoke. "Brothers, many of you have come today from long distances despite the weather, the cold, the threat of the storm. You have come to hear a word of hope, a message that will save you from a storm far greater than the one that now brews around us." He paused, his fist clenching, then opening again to point to the sky. "I speak of the storm of God's judgment."

Archibald scoffed at the words. He would not be judged by God. Judgment was for the rabble, the heathen savages, perhaps even the French, but certainly not for an English nobleman like himself. Archibald raised his chin a bit further in defiance of the man's words.

"Do not think your riches will save you," Whitefield continued, as if reading his thoughts. His eyes seemed to pierce Archibald's as if he were the only one in the crowded room, the only one in the world.

The preacher's voice softened, yet remained loud and commanding. "I too once feared God's judgment. For God showed me that I must be born again or be damned! I learned that a man may go to church, say prayers, receive the sacrament, and yet not be a Christian . . ."

What is this? Archibald leaned forward in his seat. *Not a Christian?* Every civilized Englishman was a Christian! Everyone knew that. At least he, Archibald, was certainly a Christian. After all, he attended church, when convenient, and had even donated for the new building in Philadelphia.

Whitefield's voice broke through his indignation. "Holding Henry Scougal's book in my hand, I thus addressed the God of heaven and earth: 'Lord, if I am not a Christian, or if not a real one, for Jesus Christ's sake show me what Christianity is, that I may not be damned at last!' God soon showed me, for in reading a few lines further that 'true Christianity is a union of the soul with God, and Christ formed within us,' a ray of divine light was instantaneously darted into my soul, and from that moment, and not till then, did I know I must become a new creature. I must be born again."

Archibald sat back, a haughty smile brushing his lips. *Too bad the new creature still had that disfiguring squint,* he scoffed. *Born again, indeed! What is this rubbish?*

"God was pleased to remove the heavy load of sin," Whitefield continued, "of always grasping after power and pleasure. He enabled me to lay hold of His dear Son by a living faith, and by giving me the Spirit of adoption, to seal me, even to the day of everlasting redemption." He paused and stepped to the edge of the platform. A broad smile lit his face. "O! With what joy—joy unspeakable—even joy that was full of and big with glory, was my soul filled when the weight of sin went off, and an abiding sense of the love of God broke in upon my disconsolate soul! My joys were like a spring tide and overflowed the banks. I was born anew!"

Born anew. This time the words blazed through Archibald like a burning flame, hot and searing. *Born anew.* Archibald pressed his handkerchief to his forehead and dabbed away the thin line of sweat that had formed there. Surely he would not succumb to the madness! Yet . . .

His thoughts stilled; his breath quickened. What if it were true? He could hardly believe he was considering such a thing. But, oh, the possibility! Then he wouldn't be a Grant any longer. He wouldn't be the older, less powerful henchman of Richard. It wouldn't matter then that Richard had gained the title of Lord Grant. Maybe he could be born again as someone that Elizabeth would respect, would admire, would perhaps even marry. But this was insanity. The strange heat of the room was confusing his senses. How could a man be born anew? It was crazy, mad.

Archibald's thoughts spun around the concept, whirling, questioning. Soon he realized that Whitefield had been speaking for some time but had now stopped. The crowd seemed to wait in breathless silence, broken only by an occasional half-suppressed sob. Whitefield's eyes searched the assembly, pausing on this one, then that, his gaze quiet and beseeching.

"Tell us, how can we be born anew?" someone shouted. Archibald caught his breath. Was it his own voice that was echoing in his ears? He clamped his lips shut. A chill raced through him. Had he too gone mad?

Archibald stared at Whitefield. He could see the joy that exuded from the man even now—a joy that required no earthly power, no wealth, no property. He shook his head and pressed his hands to his ears, but he could not shut out the voice of the man on the platform.

"Would you have peace with God, sir?"

Archibald held his breath. Whitefield was looking directly at him again, intense and questioning.

"Away then to God through Jesus Christ, who has purchased peace; the Lord Jesus has shed His heart's blood for this. He died for this; He rose again for this; He ascended into the highest heaven and is now interceding at the right hand of God. Beg of God to give you faith; and if the Lord give you that, you will by it receive Christ, with His righteousness, and His all."

Archibald frowned at the response. *Righteousness?* Did he want Christ's righteousness? What would that mean? God knew things that no man ever saw. Was faith worth the cost?

He rubbed his hand over his fleshy face. What difference did this man's words make? Even if he did go to God, he would still be in bondage to a tyrannical nephew, would still be stuck in this miserable land with England far across the sea, would still be scorned by the beautiful Elizabeth. He was a fool for even considering such prattle.

After all, who was George Whitefield? Just a youth, a lowly preacher, a one-time member of the despised Holy Club formed by those accursed Wesley brothers. Whitefield sometimes even spoke in meadows and fields. No self-respecting minister would so humiliate himself. Surely his words were just the dreams of an idealistic boy. Weren't they?

As if in answer to his thoughts, Whitefield began speaking again. "Those who live godly in Christ may not so much be said to live, as Christ to live in them. They are led by the Spirit as a child is led by the hand of its father." A smile broke over Whitefield's face. "Brethren, it is unutterable. They hear, know, and obey His voice. Being born again in God, they habitually live unto and daily walk with God."

Archibald's brow furrowed in doubt. Could it be true? To know God like that? To feel His protection, His love in such an intimate and personal way? The man must be mad to imply such things, nay, to even believe them. Yet . . .

Whitefield pointed out the window. "See that emblem of human life?" His voice cut through Archibald as a cloud passed over the sun, causing darkness to fall over the gathering. "The shadow passed for a moment and concealed the brightness of heaven from our view; but it is gone." Cold sunlight flickered again through the window. "And where will you be, my hearers, when your lives have passed away like that dark cloud? Oh, my dear friends!" He paused, his eyes beseeching again, as if he could see into the darkness of Archibald's soul.

Archibald felt himself quaking. Was it fear or hope?

"In a few days we shall all meet at the Judgment Seat of Christ. We shall form part of that vast assemblage that will gather before His throne. Stop being false and hollow Christians. Let not the fires of eternity be kindled against you!"

As his words died, lightning flashed across the sky. A cry went up from the listeners around Archibald.

"See there!" Whitefield's voice boomed over them. "It is a glance from the angry eye of Jehovah! Hark!" He raised his finger in a listening attitude as thunder broke in a tremendous crash. "It is the voice of the Almighty as He passes by in His anger!" As the sound faded, Whitefield covered his face with his hands and fell to his knees.

Archibald looked down at his own hands and saw that they were trembling. A trickle of sweat ran down his face despite the winter air. Others around him groaned. A shriek resounded from a wagon near the door and then resolved into quiet sobs.

As the storm passed, the sun burst forth, throwing across the heavens a magnificent arching rainbow. Rising and pointing to the colorful arch, Whitefield cried out, "Look upon the rainbow, and praise Him who made it. It compasseth the heavens about with glory, and the hands of the Most High have bended it. It is the banner of Christ's love, uniting us to Him and to one another that we might be one nation under Almighty God." His voice grew quiet, then silent. His glance swept the crowd and again seemed to rest on Archibald. "It is time to throw yourself on the mercy of God, to surrender all your sins, your ambitions, your hearts to him. Tarry not, my friend."

His quiet pleading crushed Archibald's defenses. Suddenly his whole life seemed a worthless pursuit of the wind, a running after earthly power and wealth that would someday mean nothing. Even now his former aspirations seemed to pale before his vision and become meaningless. How had he been so blind? Was it too late?

"Your own righteousness will not save you," came Whitefield's answer. "Surrender to Christ's love. He will not leave you bereft. He will free you." The last words were spoken so softly that Archibald had to strain to hear them over the weeping of those around him.

Freedom? Hope whispered through Archibald's soul. Freedom from the pointless pursuits of a lifetime, from anger, hate, and sin? What would it be like not to be afraid anymore? Tears filled his eyes. Could he truly be free? Oh, if only it were so! Madness or no, it was worth the attempt.

Along with the hundreds of people around him, Archibald fell to his knees, his head bent before God. "Oh, God, have mercy on me. Save me. Set me free," he whispered, his voice lost to all but himself and the One who listened. He could manage no more words. But it was enough.

Whitefield's last words washed over him, gentle, joyful, and encouraging. "Now, brethren, put on therefore, as the elect of God, holy and beloved, bowels of compassion, meekness, longsuffering, humbleness of mind, forgiving one another, if any man have a quarrel against any; as God for Christ's sake, hath forgiven you, so also do you."

Forgive. The word came like a balm to Archibald's heart. That's how he would start his new life. God had changed him. He had looked down on his miserable state and shown him a way out, a path that he would never have dreamed existed. And now everything would have to change. He would have to change. And that change would start with Jonathan. He could not continue in ignorance and hate any longer.

He had been set free by the God of the universe, by the blood of Jesus Christ. A verse from Scripture came to him, one he had memorized as a youth. It had meant nothing to him then, like the babbling of senseless songbirds. But now it burst joyfully from his memory and danced around him in rhythm with the beat of his heart. "If the Son therefore shall make you free, ye shall be free indeed." Free, indeed.

THIRTY-ONE

Forgive! The word exploded in Jonathan's mind in one angry burst of denial. Forgive his uncle, forgive Kwelik, forgive his brother? Never! He refused to accept a God who would demand such a thing.

Despite the spectacle of the storm, the conviction of the preacher, and the quiet prayers of those around him, Jonathan crossed his arms and remained silent. He could almost feel God watching him, imploring, questioning, waiting. Jonathan closed his eyes and remembered the frontier, the way black smoke curled from the homestead, how the cabins crumbled to ashes, and Nahum. His thoughts stopped and refused to go further. Nahum accepted this Christ, and it had won him no more than death.

Jonathan opened his eyes and stared straight ahead. He would see no more than the back of the man in front of him. For he knew that if he turned, he would see the eyes of God, and they would appear like blue fire.

With relief Jonathan realized that Whitefield had finished speaking and had entered the crowd to gently encourage this one, pray with another, and answer the questions of several. Within minutes the listeners began milling around the room, greeting one another, some pushing toward the door and others toward the front where a makeshift altar had been constructed.

The bench scraped beneath Jonathan as he rose to his feet. Sam turned toward him, a smile on his face. "Well, friend, will you come and take some refreshment with me?" Sam clapped his hand on Jonathan's shoulder. "We will discuss our ideas of God and this new land over ale at the Royal Exchange Tavern."

"The Royal Exchange?"

"Best tavern in the city, my friend. Most of the members of the

General Court frequent the place, but don't worry," he winked at Jonathan, "I have a special table reserved by the fire. An advantage of being the brewer's son." He guided Jonathan out the door as he spoke.

Jonathan stepped into the crisp winter air and drew a deep breath before pushing through the crowd that still lingered outside the meetinghouse door. Determinedly he looked away from their joy-infused faces. He would not think about that man's message even for a moment. He would not surrender. He was not a wolf crying out for his Creator, as Kwelik had said. He was a man, a man who didn't need God, a man who could carve out his own life without leaning on any religious lies.

Jonathan grimaced, the reality of his life rising up in his mind to deny his assertions. He sighed as his gaze fell to the icy path before him. The rain had made myriad dents in the dirty snow, making the ground appear like a woman's washboard. Jonathan kicked a pile of snow with his booted toe and then followed Sam down the narrow street. Pressed close together on each side of him, fat brick buildings rose toward the gray sky. Jonathan frowned, longing for the homey warmth of a log cabin.

In a moment Sam slowed, drawing up beside him as he matched his stride to Jonathan's. Jonathan glanced over at him, noticing Sam's intent gaze.

"You look like a haunted man, my friend." Sam's voice was gentle. "But come, the tavern is not far. Then we'll talk."

Jonathan was relieved when the tavern loomed large and cheerful against the white backdrop of the city street. The warmth of the room reached out to embrace them as they opened the door and stamped the ice from their boots. A tiny flurry of snow swirled across the floor and melted beneath a stool before the door slammed shut behind them.

"May I take your coats, gentlemen?" A heavyset woman slid her tray onto a nearby table and bustled toward them.

Sam shook the snow from his coat and handed it to her. "Thank you, Sally." He turned and smiled at Jonathan. "Come." He motioned to a table near the fireplace.

Jonathan winced. He didn't want to see the flickering flames. He clenched his fist and sat with his back to the fire.

Sam glanced at Jonathan before calling over his shoulder. "Two mugs of ale, Sally."

"Your father's, of course, Mr. Adams?" the woman responded.

Sam grinned. "Of course." He turned back, his eyes searching Jonathan's. "What did you think of Whitefield?"

Jonathan cleared his throat. "He is a man of power and persuasion."

Sam leaned back his chair. "Ah, but you are not yet persuaded, are you, my friend?"

"Perhaps not yet."

Sam nodded. "Then let us speak of things on which we both agree. Thank you, Sally." Sam smiled kindly upon the older woman as she set two mugs on the table in front of them.

"Are ye talking 'bout liberty again, Mr. Adams?"

"What else is worthy of words?"

She chuckled and turned to Jonathan. "Mr. Adams here is one for fine speeches, he is. Ever since he gave his fancy talk at Harvard, we ain't heard of nothing else but liberty and the rights of free men." She rolled her eyes to the ceiling. "As if us poor working folk had time to consider such things."

"Thank you for the kind words, Sally." Sam's lips bent into a wry smile. "Would you not agree that liberty is a worthy mistress for rich and poor alike? What do you say, Jonathan? Methinks she is worth far more than riches, more than even life itself."

Jonathan studied the faraway look in his friend's eyes. "A noble thought. But is she not a fickle mistress to all but the most powerful of men?"

"True liberty makes no distinction between wealth and poverty."

Jonathan sighed. "What is true liberty?"

Sam's gaze became intense. "I believe it is the freedom to live the life that God intended for us, as individuals and as a people. It's the freedom to worship Him without restraint, the freedom to live lives of piety and virtue, the freedom to pursue our hopes without being enslaved to government or aristocracy."

"The freedom to do whatever we wish?"

Sam chuckled. "Only within the boundaries of morality and virtue, my friend. Real liberty is found in obedience to God. It is in the will of the Almighty alone that we are free."

Similar words, spoken softly and with conviction, whispered through Jonathan's memory. *You will never be free until you surrender to God.* He pushed the thought from his mind, turning from the personal implications of Sam's words.

"This is a land worthy of such liberty." Jonathan leaned forward in his chair and tapped the tabletop in front of him. "You should see the frontier, my friend—trees that brush a sky that's bluer than sapphire, mountains rising up white with snow, majestic and unconquerable, storms that rip across the wilderness with unleashed fury, and silent sunsets glowing gold and red like a painter's canvas splashed with all the colors of creation."

A silence fell between them, broken at last by Sam's quiet question. "What are you doing here in the city, Jonathan?"

Jonathan did not answer.

Sam shook his head. "I'm sorry I mentioned it. Let's talk of other things. When will you return to the frontier?"

"I don't know. I came to Boston to get a militia to help defend the frontier."

"Yes?"

Jonathan grimaced. "But whenever I inquire, my uncle who promised the help avoids the subject. He mumbles about delays and upcoming meetings and conflicting orders."

"So there is no militia."

Jonathan looked up. "I don't think so."

Sam nodded. "Still you must plan to return to the frontier sometime?"

Jonathan sighed. "I don't know. My brother would have me marry and return to England. Sometimes I think he's right. Maybe there is no life for me here anymore."

Sam studied Jonathan for a long moment before he spoke. "I don't believe you will go back to England. At least not now."

Jonathan eyed his friend. "What makes you so certain?"

Sam laughed. "Because this new land has betrothed you to it, as it has me. We are men called by God to a new destiny, a new world of opportunity and hope and a liberty that no land has yet seen—the freedom of uniting with one heart to the Almighty God. That, my friend, is freedom, for a nation and for us. For the right to freedom is a gift of the Almighty, of that I am sure." He paused, his voice growing quiet with longing. "Oh, that I might live to see such a day!"

"And I," muttered Jonathan.

"Tell me, my friend, what do you think about Whitefield's dream of 'one nation under God?'"

Jonathan rubbed his hand over his face as he considered his answer. "I think it is a grand dream." He frowned and shook his head. A vision of his brother crossed his mind. If Richard gained the power he sought in the colonies, if he controlled any part of the wilderness, no one would be free again.

Finally Jonathan's thoughts crystallized into a single question. "Tell me this, Sam—how will we be one nation under God if we continue to suckle from the vile breast of the mother country? England has no piety, no virtue, no morality approved by God."

Sam's brows drew together as he considered Jonathan's words. "You may be right about that. You just may be right." Sam put a hand around his mug and stared into the amber liquid. "We may have to wean ourselves from England one day." He looked up suddenly and winked at Jonathan. "But that is a thought best kept to ourselves, is it not?"

Jonathan nodded his agreement. "It is indeed."

Sam opened his mouth to speak again, but Jonathan cut off his words with a quick wave of his hand. "Listen." Jonathan pressed one finger to his lips.

Sam fell silent as voices drifted over from a secluded table beyond them. "A mad scheme, that's what I say," a deep-timbred voice proclaimed. "Governor Shirley is a fool for listening to that Bradstreet. Why should we attack Louisbourg, war or no? The fort is at least 500 or 600 miles northeast of us—too far away to threaten the Massachusetts colony, even if it is at the mouth of the Saint Lawrence Gulf."

"I didn't hear you raising any objections in the meeting," a querulous second voice inserted.

"That's Dr. Sheffield of our General Court," Sam whispered before Jonathan could shush him again.

"I didn't need to," the first voice responded. "I did not believe the idea would be approved."

"What difference does it make?" Sheffield whined. "Only volunteers will go. And we'll have plenty of those. It will be a diversion for the common farmers and give the wealthy an opportunity for a little adventure."

Jonathan held his breath. What was this? An attack on Fort Louisbourg—the idea was intriguing. Would such a thing be possible? He felt a glimmer of hope crystallize in his mind as he considered the thought.

"Have you been to Cape Breton Island?" the deep voice questioned. "It's cold, foggy, and miserable in the spring. It will not be much of a holiday for those who agree to go. They will never succeed in taking the French fort."

Sam nodded his agreement in silence.

"Ah, but what glory if they do!" The peevish voice sharpened with excitement. "It would be quite a blow to the French and a boon to the colonies. With God's help they may succeed!"

"Perhaps, with God's help."

Sam caught Jonathan's eyes as the men rose from their chairs, threw some coins on the counter, and headed for the door.

Before Sam could utter a word, Jonathan spoke. "What would you think if I joined those troops?"

Sam frowned. "What? Which troops?"

"The troops going to Louisbourg to fight for this land of liberty. What if I volunteered, Sam?" Jonathan's voice grew thoughtful.

"On the word of those two babblers?"

"Perhaps it is the answer I have been searching for." Jonathan placed his mug on the table and stood. "Like the men said, it would be an adventure. Besides, you were right. I cannot go back to England. Yet the frontier holds too much pain. But Louisbourg . . ." His voice trailed off, then grew strong again. "Maybe all I need is a good fight—something to stir my blood again, to remind me what it means to be a free man."

"It is not the fight itself that makes a man free," Sam responded cryptically. "It is what he fights for."

Jonathan frowned. "But it would at least give me a reason to get away from here, and from her."

Sam shrugged his shoulders in confusion. "From whom, Jonathan?"

Jonathan glared at his friend, annoyed. "From Elizabeth, the woman my brother has brought from England to entice me to return."

"You do not wish to marry the lady? Is she ill-mannered, of poor appearance, of quarrelsome temper?"

"None of those things." Jonathan grew quiet.

Sam nodded. "I see. There's someone else, isn't there?"

~

Dark foreboding hung over the village like an invisible mist, twining black fingers around trees and wigwams until it clutched Kwelik's heart. The winter sun hid its face behind angry clouds, as if afraid to hear the hollow cry of the wind. Kwelik gripped her satchel of wood close to her chest and shivered. The village was quiet today, almost eerie in its silence.

In large pots outside several wigwams, bark boiled untended for the evening meal. A few animal bones lay scattered and dried around the edge of the village, a cruel reminder of days when food was plentiful, days that now faded from memory and took on the form of lost dreams.

Kwelik dropped the sticks and hugged her fur close around her body. The acrid smell of burning wood taunted her senses, bringing to mind memories she wished to forget.

The warriors had left the village two days before—a hunting party, they said, but Kwelik knew better. Even the children knew, as they huddled in their huts, refusing to play, unable to laugh.

Ever since England and France had declared war on each other, bloody scalps had replaced deerskins outside every warrior's wigwam.

With the tribe's loyalty pledged to France, Taquachi had used every opportunity to take the men into battle. Often they did not return for days, even weeks. And the women, children, and old men went hungry. For three moons now, they had not seen meat other than field mice and an occasional rabbit to share among them. Kwelik sighed. This time the men had promised to come home with food, but promises meant little these days.

Kwelik was startled from her thoughts by a cry of victory sounding through the trees. The warriors had returned. She took a step forward as the men strode proudly down the path leading to the village. Within moments children burst from a dozen wigwams and ran helter-skelter toward the returning war band.

Kwelik grimaced. No deer, no bear, not even a bird to feed them. "Didn't you bring food?" The words were out before she could stop them.

Taquachi glared at her as White Wolf stepped forward, a canvas sack in his hand. "We took dry squash and corn from the white man. Enough for the whole village."

"Squash? Corn?" Kwelik shook her head in disgust and began to turn away.

"And a child." White Wolf's statement cut through her.

Kwelik caught her breath. "A child?" *Oh no, Lord.* Her eyes searched the war band until she spotted Gray Bear holding his prisoner, a white girl of ten or eleven years. Kwelik closed her eyes, a rush of old memories assaulting her—a father dead, a home burned, a life enslaved and cast aside without meaning. Her life. And now this child's. Kwelik opened her eyes to take a closer look at the girl. She had hair the color of autumn leaves just before they fall from the trees. Despite the trail's dust, red highlights shone in the scant winter sun, matching the fierce fire in the child's eyes.

She twisted and kicked at Gray Bear, her shriek of raw fury tearing the air. Taquachi laughed at her ineffectual rage. The girl glared at him and then sank her teeth into Gray Bear's hand.

The older warrior howled and turned to his leader. "Take the child yourself, Taquachi. I won't have her."

The smile froze on Taquachi's face. "She will replace the daughter you lost last summer."

Gray Bear shook his head and shoved the child toward the younger man. "She is a devil child. I say burn her. Red Cliff and I will not take her."

Compassion stirred in Kwelik at the look of confused anger on the girl's face. She understood none of what was being said around her, only that her life was held in the hands of the enemy and was despised. Kwelik knew the feeling.

Taquachi's hand dug into the girl's arm as he turned toward the villagers. "I bring you five scalps and one white child to replace our brothers who have died!" Taquachi's free hand grabbed the girl's hair, pulling back her head until she held still.

Gaining courage from Taquachi's words and manner, the villagers approached the girl, pinching and poking her as they watched for her response. One small boy yanked at the braid trailing down her back, causing the girl to again erupt in fury, kicking, spitting, and shrieking her contempt.

"Enough!" Kwelik stepped forward, suppressing a look of satisfaction as the girl's fist caught Taquachi on the chin. Perhaps the child could defend herself after all. Still there was something pitiful about the girl, like a cub caught in a trap from which it knows it cannot escape.

From behind them, an old woman dressed in a tattered deerskin robe pulled the cover from her wigwam door and stepped outside. Snakeskin curled around her graying hair. Kwelik frowned as the villagers parted to allow Sayewis to pass. Taquachi's mother rarely left the wigwam. Her appearance now boded ill for the child.

Sayewis tottered over to the girl and stopped inches from her face. She leaned over to study her through narrowed eyes. Kwelik could see the girl tremble under the scrutiny. After a moment the woman spat, then turned away and walked awkwardly back to her hut.

Sayewis's assessment angered the girl. She writhed in Taquachi's arms and jammed her foot into his shin. He groaned and loosened his grip, allowing her to jerk free. A guttural sound echoed from Taquachi's throat as he pulled out his tomahawk and followed.

Kwelik reached out and caught the girl in her arms, aware of Taquachi's blade, dark and menacing, behind her. She leaned over and whispered in English in the girl's ear, "Silence, child. I won't let them harm you. But you must be still."

"No!" The girl squirmed and wrenched one arm free to flail wildly in the air.

"Look!" Kwelik spun the child in her arms to face the approaching tomahawk.

The girl ceased her fight, her eyes widening as she stared at Taquachi's weapon.

"Since no one wants the girl, we will burn her tonight." Taquachi's voice rang triumphantly over the village. "Let the white child die as our brothers have died."

A shout echoed from the throats of the surrounding warriors.

"No!" Kwelik's cry rose above the voices of the others. She faced Taquachi, her hand firm on the girl's shoulder. "I want her. I will take her as my own."

"You?" Taquachi stepped toward her, his voice low and mocking. "But you have no husband."

Her eyes flickered up to meet his, then looked away, beseeching the women of the village. "I choose the child."

"What right have you?" called one warrior.

Taquachi raised his tomahawk to the sky. "I say she dies!"

"Taquachi, please."

He lowered his voice, his eyes gripping hers with cold intent. "You know the price, *Manito-dasin*."

Kwelik gasped. *Oh, God, no*. Her hand fumbled to the necklace that was no longer there, her gaze dropping to the girl before her—so young, so afraid, so alone. Kwelik's eyes blurred with unshed tears.

She took a deep breath and raised her chin. She could not let the girl die, could not allow the flames to destroy such a young life. So now she must pay the price.

Kwelik clenched her fist and willed her voice to remain steady. "I will marry you, Taquachi, at the summer solstice."

THIRTY-TWO

~

Jonathan rushed into the mansion and slammed the oak door behind him. His boots clicked on the tile floor. He ignored the parlor to his right and dashed up the curved staircase two steps at a time. For a moment he paused at the wide doors to the ballroom at the top of the stairs. It was empty now, devoid of the lilting music of violins and the accompanying laughter of noblemen. Empty and barren. *Just like me*. Jonathan scowled and turned away. Soon he would find a way to be filled again, filled not with music and laughter but at least with a purpose.

Above him a glittering chandelier turned in the breeze from a nearby window. Jonathan grimaced as he continued down the hallway. Long white walls lined with oil lamps led to the open doors of the library beyond. He slowed, his footsteps now muffled by the oriental rug that covered the wooden floor of the mansion's upper story.

Jonathan's eyes flickered to the library. Even from down the hall he could see the stone fireplace that dominated the room, a fireplace that was a replica of the one in England. Above it hung a portrait of his father. Though he could not see it clearly from this distance, Jonathan could feel the cold painted eyes looking at him, scorning him.

"My dear Jonathan!"

The silky voice washed over him. He turned to see Elizabeth ascending the stairs behind him. Her gloved hand extended toward him.

Jonathan hesitated then stepped toward her, taking her hand in his own.

Her perfectly formed fingers tightened around his as she drew close to him. "How do you like my new gown? Marie just finished it today." She smiled up at him.

Jonathan dropped her hand and looked down at the blue velvet affair, noticing the fine lace that covered the arms and bodice before his gaze traveled to the daring plunge of the garment's neckline. He glanced away. "It looks expensive."

Elizabeth frowned. "You are such a bore, Jonathan. Well, if you are not going to compliment my dress, at least you could come to the library and sit with me by the fire."

He grimaced. The library with its dominating portrait was the last place he wished to go. Yet he followed her.

As Jonathan stepped through the library door, his eyes lifted to lock on the image of his father. Shadows danced over the figure from the fire in the grate. Jonathan shivered, noticing how the painting's lifeless eyes seemed to follow him as he walked across the room.

Bookshelves filled with old, well-dusted tomes lined three walls and gave the room a feeling of solemnity. Two chairs and a long couch sat along the wall next to the fireplace. And before them, a small table held a blackened oil lamp. Other than that, no furniture dared to detract from the commanding presence of the fireplace and the portrait above it.

Elizabeth pulled a chair closer to the fire and sat. Her lashes lowered coyly. "So, my love, how soon can you come back to England with me?" Her words cut through Jonathan's senses.

England. The word sent a chill of abhorrence through him. He rubbed his foot over the carpeted floor. "I never said I would return to England."

Elizabeth rose, her hips subtly swinging as she approached him. "Oh, Jonathan, don't toy with me. You know that everyone plans for us to marry." She reached up to touch his chest, her fingers lingering lightly there. Her gaze fluttered to his. "I will make you very happy."

Jonathan frowned and turned away. Again his eyes caught those in the portrait. Now they seemed to be mocking him. He drew a deep breath. "I am thinking about going on a trip."

"A trip?"

"There is a French fort on the coast far north of us. I'm considering going with our troops to capture it. They are taking volunteers."

Jonathan heard Elizabeth's sharp intake of breath. "No! You can't go."

"Why not?"

"Because, well, because . . ." her usually calm demeanor wavered, "you must come back with me to England!" She pursed her lips, regaining composure. "Please don't disappoint me again."

Jonathan looked down at her, wondering if she really did care for him or if it was all a pretty act. And did he care for her? The question echoed through the emptiness inside him. He sighed and took her hand in his, his voice growing gentle. "Elizabeth, listen to me. I belong here in the colonies. Maybe going to Louisbourg will be my chance to prove that to myself. There's nothing for me in England."

Tears welled in Elizabeth's eyes. Her lower lip quivered delicately. "Wouldn't I be enough for you?" She turned her head away.

Jonathan let go of her hand. He walked to the window, deliberately turning his back on the painting above the fireplace. He reached out to touch the lavish drapes and twirled the drapery cord in his fingers. Why did everything have to be so difficult? Why did Elizabeth have to cry and make him out to be the villain? Why did he want to continue pursuing his dream of freedom when it was forever escaping him? Jonathan rubbed his hand over his face. Maybe going to Louisbourg was a silly idea after all.

"What's going on in here?" Richard's voice echoed from the doorway.

Jonathan spun around to see his brother striding into the room. He glanced at Richard's arrogant face, his expression so like the one above the fireplace despite the difference in features. Where their father's nose was arched, Richard's was straight and thin. Their father's face was square. Richard's was long. Their father's chin fell into the folds of his neck, but Richard's protruded to a sharp point. Yet for all their differences, Richard's face mirrored the cold conceit of their father.

Richard turned his haughty eyes to Jonathan before his gaze fell to Elizabeth's troubled face. "Why are you crying?"

Elizabeth turned her hazel eyes, watery with tears, up at Richard. "He—he says he doesn't wish to go back to England with me. He wants to go attack some French fort instead." She lifted her chin as she spoke.

Richard's jaw tightened.

"Oh, why did you ever bring me to these accursed colonies?" With those words Elizabeth clutched her skirts and stormed from the room.

Richard turned toward Jonathan. His voice hardened. "What is this foolishness? What did you say to Elizabeth?"

Jonathan did not turn as he spoke. "Only that I was thinking of fighting the French at Louisbourg."

"I have already made plans for you to marry Elizabeth and return to England."

Richard's supercilious tone angered Jonathan. He spun back around. "You do not rule me, Brother. I make my own plans."

Richard's face twisted into a sneer. "You will return to England on the next ship."

Jonathan felt his face flush with fury. "I will not."

He saw Richard's fists clench at his sides. "Listen, Brother, I have been patient with you long enough. Now it's time you get out of my way and go back where you belong. You have no business here in the colonies. You will oppose me no longer."

Jonathan's eyes narrowed. "Ah, so it comes back to your little plan to gain control of the wilderness, does it? I hoped you had given that up."

"Father would have succeeded in such a plan had he lived. And so will I."

Jonathan laughed, a cold sound that reminded him too much of his father. The comparison spurred his anger. "You go back to England, Richard. We colonists don't want you here. We can protect ourselves, and a victory at Louisbourg will prove it."

"You will obey me!"

"Never!" Jonathan's voice rose. "You may have the title Lord Grant, but you are not my father. So stop trying to be."

Richard's clenched fists slammed into the rock mantel. "I'm more like Father than you will ever be!"

"I hope so."

Richard closed the distance between them in a rush. His hand lifted as if to slap Jonathan. Then he stopped. "Enough of this. I *am* Lord Grant now. You will do as I say!" His words rang against the stone fireplace.

In that moment Jonathan saw his brother's weakness, his fear, and he despised him for it. "You are a fool, Richard. Look at what you've become." He shook his head in disgust. "Now I *am* going to Louisbourg, if for no other reason than to defy you and to prove that neither I nor my fellow colonists will ever be dependent on a man like you."

As Jonathan's words faded from the air, Richard stepped toward him, his face red with fury. For a moment both men stared at one another, neither breaking his fierce gaze. Finally Richard spoke. "So be it." His words fell like icicles into the silence. "You will regret this day, Jonathan. No one defies Lord Grant."

With that he turned and strode from the room.

~

Taquachi's eyes narrowed, and his lips tightened into a cold smile as he regarded Kwelik. "As you wish then, *Manito-dasin*. The girl is yours. Let the ceremony begin."

Kwelik felt her heart constrict as her breath came in short gasps. But it was too late, too late to turn back, to deny the words her lips had just spoken, too late to save herself from Taquachi's schemes. Kwelik's soul writhed beneath the agony of her decision, her mind tumbling over one final cry: *Oh, God, what have I done?*

As Taquachi's voice faded from the air, villagers scattered to their respective wigwams, returning with sticks, branches, and clubs in hand. They formed two lines in front of the child, one line facing the other and ending at the deep stream that flowed beside the village.

A young boy pounded his stick against the ground. "Run! Run!" he shrieked.

The girl stared down the imposing line of villagers and then glanced frantically at Kwelik. "Are—are they gonna kill me?" she stuttered, her voice choking in sudden fear.

Kwelik's eyes sought and held those below her, the child's terror and her own mixing until they became indistinguishable. A family dead, a home burned, a life enslaved, dreams withered and blackened beneath the torch. But this child would have a chance to live, to one day be free. It was not too late for her.

Kwelik squeezed the girl's shoulder in reassurance. "You must run the gauntlet. It will hurt only a little. It is the way of these people, my people." She paused, kneeling before the girl, her eyes looking deeply into the wide green ones before her. "Now you must be brave. You must be strong. Run between the lines as fast as you can. Run to the stream. Go!" Kwelik gave the child a gentle shove.

Clubs and sticks rained down on the girl as she sprinted between the lines. In accordance with the traditions of the adoption ceremony, each villager struck at her twice. Yet she did not cry out. Only once did she stumble as a stick hit the base of her neck, pushing her forward. Still she ran on, her hands raised to deflect the worst of the blows.

Kwelik smiled at the girl's courage as she jogged around the lines to meet her at the other end. In a moment the ceremonial beating would be over.

The girl stumbled again as she passed the last villager. She fell headlong, her knees scraping the ground. Quickly Kwelik leaned over and helped her to her feet. "Well done, child," she murmured.

As one, the women threw down their weapons and approached the girl. With nimble fingers, they set aside their bear skin robes and gently reached out to hold the child's arms and hands as they led her into the water.

The girl twisted in their arms, her eyes searching for Kwelik. Kwelik nodded her assurance and followed them into the water, taking the place beside the girl.

Within seconds the freezing water had numbed Kwelik's lower half. The stream swirled around her waist, knocking chunks of ice into her hips. Bumps rose on her skin in response to the bitter cold.

All around her, tall sycamores rose to the sky, providing a stark canopy for the women beneath. On the shore the men and children stood quietly, watching, waiting, their eyes emotionless as the ceremony continued. The water flowed sluggishly over brown rocks, swooping past the partially melted snow on the stream's banks. And beyond them, the village huts stood like dark shadows, waiting as silently as the villagers on the shore. Kwelik clenched her lips over chattering teeth and leaned over the girl. "You must go under the water."

The girl's head jerked up. "N-n-no! T-t-too cold." Her jaw trembled as she spoke.

Kwelik gripped the child's shoulder. "Don't make this difficult. Do it quickly, and it will be over."

The girl made a face and wrenched free. "Y-y-you'll drown me."

Exasperation replaced Kwelik's compassion. "Listen," she said, "if I wanted to drown you, I would have done so already. Now do what you're told."

"It is too late to change your mind, my love," Taquachi called mockingly from the stream's bank. "Perhaps we should marry this night. Why wait for the summer solstice?"

Kwelik turned, her voice hard. "The solstice, Taquachi, and not a day sooner."

Taquachi laughed. "I await the day. Then you will be mine forever." His words descended on Kwelik like blackest night.

"W-w-what did he say?" the girl whispered.

Kwelik shook her head, fighting back cold tears. "It is nothing. You must go under. Hurry."

The child clutched her thin arms around her shoulders, her skin pale and pimply beneath her fingers.

"No hurt you," muttered several other women as they motioned for the girl to duck under the water.

"Come, it will be over soon." Kwelik mustered a smile as the women's hands reached out to plunge the child under the icy water.

Sputtering, she returned to the surface, her face wrinkled in a furious frown. "I hate you! Get away from me." Her declaration ended in a cough. "I want out."

Kwelik rubbed her hands against the girl's arms. "I know you are cold, but you must wait just a few minutes more. Listen, I will translate for you if you are quiet."

Chief Tumaskan spoke from the shore, his voice booming over the assembly as the women huddled around Kwelik and the girl. "Today your white blood has been washed away. Today you are adopted into a great family. You will be called Wakon."

The girl scowled and glared up at Kwelik. "My name is Annie," she whispered fiercely.

"Shhh, not now," Kwelik answered.

The women drew closer, oblivious to Annie's anger and to Kwelik's despair. Gently they turned the girl in their arms, taking scraps of deerskin to wash her skin. Kwelik could see Annie stiffen under their touch.

Before they could finish the ritual, Sayewis burst from her wigwam and hurried toward them. "Wash the white skin from her!" Taquachi's mother screeched as she threw her tattered deerskin robe aside and scooped a handful of gravel and sand from the water's edge. "Clean the evil blood from among us." She plunged toward Annie and raked the sand across the girl's skin.

"Stop." Kwelik reached out her hand to arrest the woman's movements.

"You must wash away the white filth," shrieked Sayewis. "I will do it."

Kwelik did not loosen her grip on the woman's arm. "No, Sayewis. She is mine. You have no place here."

Sayewis glared and backed away, muttering.

"The ceremony is complete," Kwelik shouted.

The women nodded, mumbling to themselves as they withdrew from the cold waters.

"Come, child." Kwelik placed her hand gently under Annie's elbow and guided her from the water. She kept her gaze deliberately turned from Taquachi as they climbed the stream's bank and headed toward the village. Kwelik did not pause as she led the girl past the longhouse, past the stew pots, and past the deer hides curing between huts.

Without a word Annie matched her pace. Kwelik could almost

feel the rapid thudding of the girl's heart. What would the child think of being adopted into the tribe that killed her family? With that thought, Kwelik pulled aside the hide covering her wigwam door and stepped inside the home she shared with her brother and his wife. Then she drew Annie in after her.

A small fire burned in the hut's center, giving cheery warmth to the small room. Light flickered off the mud walls and illuminated a few ears of dried corn that hung from hooks on the ceiling. Platform beds covered with furs lined the walls and took up half the space of the enclosure. She sighed. Everything about the wigwam would be foreign to the girl. Everything would be a harsh reminder of what she had lost.

Kwelik turned, her voice gentle as she spoke. "Take off those wet things and bundle up in this." She placed a rough bear skin over Annie's shoulders and threw a handful of wood on the fire. "You will be warm soon." She smiled at the girl.

Annie's face did not lose its trembling scowl. "I thought they were gonna kill me."

The smile faded from Kwelik's face. "They would have, but now you are part of the tribe. You are safe."

"I ain't gonna be no Indian."

Kwelik's voice grew quiet. "Sometimes we have no choice as to what we are. Now." She pulled a basket from under the bed and rummaged through the old deerskin dresses and leggings stored there. "Put these on. We will make you something new later."

Annie crossed her arms, her brows furrowed in obstinacy. "I don't wanna be no Indian."

Kwelik turned, arms akimbo, and stared at the child. "No, I don't suppose you do, but you must pretend if you want Taquachi to leave you alone."

"Oh." Annie bit her lip, as if struggling between rebellion and logic. "Was he that tall, angry man?"

"Yes."

The girl shuddered. "Is he your husband?"

A chill raced across Kwelik's nerves. "No."

Annie nodded. "I'm glad. He's a very bad man."

"Yes, he is. But do not let him hear you say that." Kwelik turned, her eyes piercing those of the girl. "In fact, don't let him hear you speak English at all. You must learn the Algonquian tongue. I will help you. We must only speak English when we are alone. Do you understand?"

Annie was quiet for several minutes before she answered. "You're a nice lady. I guess I'll do what you say."

Kwelik smiled. "Thank you. I am called Kwelik. It means 'sky.'"

"Kwelik." The girl rolled the name on her tongue. "Kwelik," she repeated. "That's a nice name. What does Wakon mean?"

Kwelik paused, not wanting to answer, but the girl's frank gaze demanded it. "It means 'Evil Snake.'"

Tears filled Annie's eyes. "I'm not evil. I'm not a snake."

Kwelik marveled at the first sign of the girl's weakness.

"It's not fair. They killed my family and dragged me here. I wish they woulda killed me too." Wet eyes searched Kwelik's. "Why didn't they?"

"Shhh." Kwelik sat next to the child and put her arm lightly around her shoulders. "God has spared your life for a reason, just as He once spared mine. You see, we're not so different, Annie. My family is dead too."

Annie squinted her eyes and looked up at Kwelik. "You seemed much more important out there." She nodded toward the village center. "I thought you must be their leader or goddess or something."

Kwelik's smile was sad. "No, I am neither of those things."

"At least you stood up to that bad man."

"Did I?"

Annie's forehead wrinkled as she steadily regarded Kwelik. She ran her arm across her face, drying her momentary tears. Her voice filled with wonder and confusion. "I think you're just as much a prisoner here as I am. Aren't you?"

Kwelik felt her throat close around her own sudden tears. "Yes, I am." The words were like a death sentence in her ears.

THIRTY-THREE

Off the Coast of Nova Scotia, March 1745

"Stay in the hold, men! She's not blown over yet," Major Pomeroy shouted above the howling wind as Jonathan and the other men huddled below deck. The tiny schooner tipped precariously, then righted itself, bobbing like a broken matchstick in the tempest. The ship shuddered and moaned as the hatch clanged into place above the hold.

"This is no mild spring squall," someone muttered to Jonathan's left.

Major Pomeroy turned his head, his hand seeking the support of a bulkhead as he spoke again. "She's a northeaster, boys. We'll have to wait her out. There's food for those who can stomach it." He motioned toward a barrel on the far side of the room.

"Will the *KatyAnn* hold against the storm?" a young farm boy questioned.

"She'll hold. She's been through worse than this." An old sailor patted the ship's side as he spoke, his feet steady even as the boat continued its giddy dance with the wind and waves. "Ain't you been on the sea before?"

The boy clutched the straw around him, his face green with nausea. "No, and I hope never to be again. I wish that French privateer had captured us two days ago. Better a prisoner than this."

The seaman chuckled. "Land lover."

The boy glared at him and then quickly turned again to vomit into the small bucket next to him. The smell of bile quickly replaced that of damp straw and moldy timber.

Jonathan pressed his back into a space between the wall and a crate to keep from being pitched across the hold as the schooner jolted and dipped. On the planks before him, a bit of salt pork and hard bread rocked on a piece of burlap. He stared at the pork until the vision swam before his eyes. Food. Just the thought sickened him.

He kicked the cloth away, his mind whirling with the wild undulation of the boat. What was he doing here? Why had he chosen to be buried alive in the belly of this ship? Now his reasons for volunteering for this mission seemed vague, unconvincing. He had told his brother he was going to Louisbourg to spite him, yet the real reason was something deeper, something even he did not fully understand. Wasn't he really hoping that somehow the battle would prove him different from his father and his brother? They would never lower themselves to the rank of a common soldier.

The boat again lunged and shuddered beneath him. Jonathan groaned and closed his eyes. Why did fate mock him, making their little fleet of fishing sloops and trading schooners brave the storm's fury while they waited for the ice fields to break up around Louisbourg? Jonathan thought of the frontier, the wild openness of the forests and mountains. Such a contrast to the dark, cramped quarters that surrounded him now. Yet here he was, grasping at another dissolving dream, hoping that this time he would defy those demons of his past.

He shook his head at his own impulsiveness—or was it desperation? Seeing Richard again reminded him of the fear he could not face. If Richard could change to be so much like their father, perhaps it could happen to him as well. If only he knew why his brother had turned on them. If only he could prove to himself that he was a different type of man—a colonist, a frontiersman, a soldier. But would his efforts ever be enough to set him free?

His eyes traveled to the young farmer still clutching his small bucket. The boy had come to prove himself a man in his father's eyes. And the merchant in the far corner was simply bored and desired a little adventure to brag about to his children. Jonathan's gaze fell upon each of his shipmates in turn. Most were here for no other reason than because they were restless and wanted to prove themselves men of valor. The thought of military victory held for them all a mystique, a seductive promise that somehow they would find in battle what was lacking in their lives.

The creak of the ship sounded eerily like the cry of a hundred devils. A sudden crash of waves overhead drowned the low moaning from the seasick soldiers.

Jonathan's soul echoed the sound. He shivered, feeling hot and cold at once, as the ship danced beneath him. Shadows swayed in the dim flickering of a couple of lanterns that swung wildly from nails above. Soon even those would go out, leaving them in blackness and fear.

As if to confirm his thoughts, the boat rose on a huge swell, only to come crashing down again, leaving Jonathan's stomach suspended in his throat. One lantern sputtered and went out. Above him the mast cracked beneath the storm's fury. The sound reverberated through his nerves. The ropes that held the ship's gear snapped, sending their supplies bumping across the deck.

A wave surged across the ship. Water splashed through a plank overhead, wetting Jonathan's face like spittle from an angry foe. A final drop squeezed through, landed between his feet, then snaked a crazy path through the straw that would become his bedding.

Jonathan groaned again. It wasn't supposed to be like this. The fight, the bursting of cannons overhead, the smell of gun powder, the victory at Louisbourg—those things were supposed to set him free from his brother, his memories, and his despair. But here in this damp, cluttered hold of the schooner, despair hung around him like a tangible thing, skittering in and out like the occasional rat that scurried across the floor and disappeared behind a barrel of muskets.

Jonathan's head came down into his hands as his eyes searched his companions' faces in the wavering darkness. Men who had begun full of hope and dreams of adventure had since turned bleak and haggard after a dozen days of fighting the sea, the storm, and their bodies. Did he look the same?

Archibald had warned him against this trip. Now as the ship creaked and groaned around him, and the chill of the winter air bit into his bones, he wished he had taken his uncle's advice. *You're only running away again*, Archibald had said.

Jonathan sighed. Perhaps his uncle was right after all. Perhaps no matter how far he ran, his fears would stalk him still, hunting him down, stealing his life.

Major Pomeroy fumbled to secure the hatch above him before he turned back to his men. Jonathan noticed the tinges of gray around his mouth as he spoke. "Take heart, men. If we can make it through the night, a dozen provincial warships will escort all of our transports to Canso."

A moan of longing swept through the men at the thought of their feet on solid ground, land that did not pitch and sway and toss them about like rag dolls in the wind.

"I'd just as soon die tonight than spend another day in this wretched casket," one man mumbled as he clutched a bucket in trembling hands.

"Tomorrow?" another voice quavered from the darkness. "Will we land tomorrow?"

Major Pomeroy lowered his seasick eyes. "Perhaps."

"Perhaps?" quailed the farm boy. "When do the warships arrive?"

Major Pomeroy turned and stumbled a few steps toward his cabin before answering. "They are scheduled for the end of the week. Maybe they will be early."

"The end of the week?" The man who spoke staggered to his feet and retched in the corner. He lifted his head and wiped a shaking arm across his mouth. "They will be escorting a boat of dead men by then."

Several others murmured their agreement.

"Fine soldiers we'll make." The old seaman spat, crossing his arms and holding his footing despite the wild swaying of the ship.

"Aw, shut up, Harrison," another shot back, the end of his comment lost in a crash of waves on the deck above.

"Quiet, men!" Major Pomeroy reeled toward his room like a drunken man. "We'll live to fight the French yet, if only we can survive the night." He shook his head, his once-proud shoulders rounded with resignation. "I have no other words for you. Only God can help us now."

Jonathan groaned. *God!* Would he never escape such prattle?

They were doomed indeed if only God could save them. Jonathan would trust his fate to the winds before hoping in the God that had watched with blind eyes as his homestead burned, as Nahum died . . . as unmerciful blows rained down from his father's fists.

Jonathan felt his stomach tighten and heave. He frowned, his eyes piercing the dark shadows around him. He caught his breath.

There across the floor a man watched him with unblinking eyes. The same dark face that he had seen a dozen times now leered out from behind the bulkhead. Jonathan's gaze traveled from the coarse bare feet to the man's dirty hair stringing down over black eyes. He felt a shiver of dread race through him. It seemed that those eyes had not left him since they embarked from Boston. When he worked the rigging on the deck, stood in line for the day's meal, lay down on his hard little pallet of straw, the eyes were there, hidden in the shadows. Wherever he went, the man was near, watching, waiting. For what? Jonathan did not want to know. He turned his head away, suddenly afraid of the deep, fathomless eyes that never closed, the eyes like death itself, whispering in their black silence, saying that one day the waiting would end.

~

The door, massive and impenetrable, loomed before Archibald like the great gate of heaven. He clutched his hat in one hand, twisting the brim beneath sweat-drenched fingers. A lantern swung eerily in the night's mist, casting black shadows over the stonework before him. Somewhere in the distance a cat screamed. Archibald shivered at the sound. *Go home. Go back, you fool.* The sharp tongue of shame whipped through his mind. He bit his lip. What was he doing here? The voice was right. It was not too late to turn back, to forget his mission at the house of a stranger, to retreat to the comfort of the Grant mansion and become once again the man he had always been.

The thought chilled him. He could not go back. God had saved him. Now he must save Jonathan.

Archibald groaned. If it hadn't been for his hate, for his insistence that Jonathan must die, then perhaps the boy would not be in this danger now. If only he had not planted the idea in Richard's mind. And now he must somehow try to make amends for that past sin.

Apprehension clawed at Archibald's throat as his hand raised to the level of the door's knocker. Rejection or no, Jonathan's life swung above a precipice, and he was the only one who knew to throw out a rope. He drew a quick breath and rapped his knuckles unsteadily on the door. Before he could change his mind, the door creaked open to reveal a short man dressed in evening finery.

Archibald swallowed hard, his hat still clutched in desperate fingers. "May I speak with Reverend Whitefield, please. I know the hour is late." His voice sounded high and uncertain in his ears.

"Reverend Whitefield does not receive visitors after dark, sir. You may return tomorrow in daylight when respectable people come calling." The man inclined his head and began to close the door.

Archibald's hand flew out to stop it. "Please, sir. I must speak with him tonight."

"Who is it, Thomas?" a voice called from the stairs.

"A man."

A light laugh wafted from the direction of the voice. "Does he have a name, Thomas?"

Archibald pushed the door open further. "The name's Grant, Archibald Grant."

"Ah, just the man I have been expecting. I will be right down," came the voice.

Archibald's jaw slackened with surprise. Had he been mistaken for another? Or had the preacher somehow discovered his sin?

Thomas squinted and looked him over, his brown eyes traveling cautiously up and down Archibald's frame. Then Thomas nodded once and motioned for Archibald to enter. "Welcome to my home. Please step into the parlor."

"Thank you, s-sir," Archibald stammered as he followed the man into a cozy room to the left of the entrance.

"I suppose Reverend Whitefield will be with you shortly."

Archibald nodded, words forsaking him. As the man left the room, silence wrapped its accusing fingers around Archibald's heart. *You do not belong here*, it seemed to say. Above him a portrait of someone's ancestor glared down as if condemning him for his audacity. He could almost hear the thoughts that screamed from the painted gray eyes. *Unworthy*, they said. *Fool*.

Archibald dropped his gaze and allowed it to travel to a small table that sat between two high-backed chairs by the fire. A book lay open on the polished surface. Archibald took a step toward it. A Bible. He rubbed his hand across his eyes. If he glanced at the text, would it accuse or comfort him? He drew a trembling breath and stared at the open pages, yellowed with age, with shadows of firelight flickering warmly over them, beckoning him. Archibald turned away. He had not lived his life by God's precepts. But that life of sin and hate was over now. Or was it? He wished he knew.

Archibald sighed. All his life he had believed he was somebody, but now he knew the truth. He was nothing but a fat, selfish, little man. He had no credentials to place before George Whitefield. The thought of the preacher's possible disdain took his breath away. Yet here he stood with nothing to offer the man but the desperation of his request. He was nothing, nobody. The realization frightened him more than anything he had ever faced in his life.

No wonder Elizabeth had never looked at him. No wonder she wouldn't respond to his advances. Now he understood. And yet since he had thrown himself on the mercy of God, Elizabeth hadn't looked the same to him either. Her beauty had palled beneath the sharpness of her tongue. Her brilliant wit had seemed harsh and unmerciful. Still he would marry her if he could.

A quick step behind him drew his attention. He turned. "Reverend," he whispered.

A smile beamed from Whitefield's face as his hand extended in a gesture of unconditional welcome.

Archibald felt his own face lift in response. Somehow Whitefield seemed younger and slighter of build than he remembered. It made the man warmer, less intimidating.

Whitefield gripped Archibald's hand in his own firm grasp. "Grant, of the Pennsylvania Assembly, if I am not mistaken." His eyes twinkled merrily in the firelight. "What can I do for you tonight?"

"Help." The word stuck in a throat that was suddenly dry. Archibald swallowed and tried again. "Reverend, I'm so sorry to bother you. But . . ." His voice quit.

Whitefield chuckled and motioned toward a chair. "Come now, friend. Take a seat by the fire." He sat down himself and allowed one hand to linger lovingly over the open Bible. "Perhaps God's Word can illuminate your trouble. Tell me what you came to say."

Archibald lowered himself into the chair, his eyes averted from the Scripture. "I-I came to tell you how much you've helped me and to ask for help again."

Whitefield nodded, his face settling into solemn attentiveness. "Go on."

Archibald shook his head. "Reverend, I have no right to ask. I have not been a good man. I have done terrible things, terrible. Things no one knows about. Things no one would suspect. If you knew . . ."

Whitefield raised one hand to stop the flow of Archibald's words. "Have you confessed your sin to God, Brother?"

Archibald dropped his gaze. "Yes, I've told Him everything."

"And have you repented?"

"I have."

"And do you trust in the blood of Christ that washes away all sin?"

"I do." Hope swelled within Archibald as he spoke the words.

"Then I do not need to hear more. God has forgiven you and cleansed you. Listen to this." Whitefield picked up the Bible and read a verse from the open page. "'There is therefore now no condemnation to them which are in Christ Jesus, who walk not after the flesh, but after the Spirit.' Romans 8:1." He again smiled at Archibald. "You are free, friend. Go and sin no more."

"But . . ." The objection sputtered from Archibald's lips. He took a deep breath, steeling himself against the next admission. "Another man's life is in danger because of me, because of what I've done, because of who I've been." *Unworthy, unworthy, unworthy,* his fear howled. "Perhaps it is too late even now."

Whitefield's face tensed as he leaned forward in his chair. "With God all things are possible. Trust Him. Now how can I help you to set things right?"

The quiet words drew Archibald from his misery. "If I could just get a message to William Pepperrell at Louisbourg. I know he is a great friend of yours. Can you reach him? Can you send a message for me?"

"That is a thing easily done. I can send a message now if you wish, though it will take some time to get there." Archibald nodded as Whitefield twisted in his chair and called to the man in the adjoining room. "Thomas, can you come in here, please? And bring ink and parchment."

Thomas brought the materials, glared once at Archibald, and abruptly left the room.

Whitefield twirled the feather pen in his fingers and dipped it into the inkwell. "Now how shall the message read?"

A glimmer of hope flickered through Archibald. "Tell him, please, that a contract has been taken out on the life of one of his men, a soldier named Jonathan Grant. Another member of his company will kill him before the battle is over. Perhaps Pepperrell can change Jonathan's unit, keep an eye on him, somehow save him. Jonathan must not die!" Archibald's voice raised into a crescendo of panic.

Whitefield wrote quickly and then put a gentle hand on Archibald's arm. "There, I have written it. Do you have any further information?"

Archibald shook his head. "No. If only I had known sooner, maybe I could have stopped it. I should have expected it. If only I'd been a different man all along." The words sputtered from Archibald's lips in a desperate whisper. "Jonathan must live. If he dies, I will be to blame. And I won't escape judgment after all."

"Now, now, my friend. We will do all we can to right the wrong you have done. The rest is up to God. With all the chaos of siege and battle, you know that God must intervene if this Jonathan is to be saved." Whitefield placed the Bible in Archibald's lap, his finger tapping the cover. "But remember this: Nothing can separate you from the love of Christ."

Archibald swallowed hard and nodded. "The message will go out tonight?"

Without answering, Whitefield stood up and walked into the

next room, his voice traveling back into the parlor. "Thomas, this message must be dispatched to William Pepperrell at Louisbourg at once. Can you send it?"

"Tonight?" Thomas's voice wavered between doubt and concern.

Whitefield's answer came immediately. "Yes. Godspeed, my friend."

Archibald heard the door slam as Thomas left with the message. Now perhaps he would dare to hope. Archibald bowed his head with gratitude as Whitefield reentered the room. "Thank you, Reverend." The words escaped in a sigh.

Whitefield returned to his chair, his eyes intent upon Archibald. "Our work is not yet complete, Brother. We must now go to the One who can protect your Jonathan even better than Pepperrell."

Archibald's head shot up. "You know Jonathan's commander as well?"

Whitefield smiled. "No. I was speaking of God."

"Oh." Archibald's voice lowered with awe.

"Shall we go to Him together and beseech Him on behalf of this Jonathan?"

Archibald nodded his assent.

"Father in heaven," Whitefield began as Archibald quickly bowed his head. Simply, without assumption or pretense, Whitefield and then, more timidly, Archibald put Jonathan's life in the hands of Him who had created it. And suddenly Archibald's shame and fear fled before the presence of the One who knew him and loved him anyway.

As their prayer came to a close, Archibald's head lifted with a dazzling smile. "He hears me, doesn't He?" he whispered. "God has forgotten my sin."

Whitefield chuckled in response.

Archibald wiped a trace of moisture from his eye. Jonathan was in God's hands now, and so was he. Nothing else mattered.

THIRTY-FOUR

~

Louisbourg, May 1745

Tendrils of gray mist swirled around Jonathan's feet as he watched the great citadel of Fort Louisbourg soar high and proud against the red and gold of the evening sky. Like a tall sentinel, the Fort's towers rose above the fog, as if by their very grandeur they could guard France's possessions in the new world. Jonathan wondered, if he looked hard enough, could he see the outlines of French soldiers as they waited with their cannons and muskets ready?

A neck of land enclosed Louisbourg harbor on the south and west, and on this peninsula the fortified town stood, with its walls rising high so that Jonathan could only get a glimpse of the peaked roofs within. The city, defended on the land approach by huge earthworks with a great stone bastion in the center, nestled against the Fort's towers, like a child clinging to his mother's skirts. Inside, Jonathan knew, over 2,000 people watched and waited for the English to advance.

Jonathan clenched his fists. This fort, more than any other, was the visible symbol of the power and might of France in the new world. Even its public buildings were faithful reflections of the king's buildings in France, marked as they were with fleurs-de-lis, which stamped the town with the mark of royal ownership. Jonathan narrowed his eyes. If only they could capture it, they would prove beyond doubt that the English colonists didn't need men like Richard. They would prove that they didn't even need England.

Jonathan stepped beside a stunted oak tree and placed his hand on the rough bark. Louisbourg was not a typical pioneer town. There were few farmers and no fur traders. Instead, it was filled with merchants, fishermen, sea captains, and royal officials—men who were highly trained and very ambitious. They would not give up their city without a formidable fight.

Jonathan turned toward the mainland. Directly opposite the narrow entrance to the harbor stood the Grand Battery. He could barely see the huge stone structure through the fog, but he knew that it housed twenty-eight heavy thirty-six-pound cannons, ready to fire at any enemy ship that dared to enter the bay.

Jonathan shook his head. How would a bunch of ragtag colonials ever breach its defenses? They were only 4,000 inexperienced New England volunteers aided by a small fleet from the British navy. Their ammunition was low, their food supply short, their men untrained and undisciplined. It would take a miracle to succeed. But succeed they must.

From out of the fog, William Vaughn approached Jonathan and laid a hand on his shoulder. "What do you think, Jonathan? Those scoundrel French dogs know that we've landed to the west of them. The Fort will be harder to take now." Vaughn dropped his hand and placed it on his hip. "And look there. Our warships can't enter the harbor until we silence the guns of the Grand Battery. Its cannons could easily sink our incoming ships." Jonathan studied the Battery's walls as the man continued. "The land defenses will require formal siege operations of considerable magnitude before they can be breached. Yes, I'm afraid we have a long road ahead of us, my friend."

Jonathan nodded, loath to speak and affirm the absurdity of their mission.

"We've set up the main camp about a mile and a half west of here. Come."

"Are we out of range of the enemy's artillery?" Jonathan questioned.

"Yes, but barely. Don't worry, you will not die tonight."

Jonathan smiled, his face bitter. "No, I will fight the French. Fighting is all I've ever done." His voice dropped. "It's all I know how to do."

Vaughn nodded his sympathy. "We may yet be victorious. God willing."

Silence fell between them.

Jonathan turned toward him. "God can be a fickle ally, my friend." As he spoke, his eyes glanced into the descending darkness.

There in the fog beyond them, his face dark despite the illumination of the fire, a man stood watching, waiting. For a moment Jonathan's eyes locked with his. Then the night stepped between them and swallowed the black figure. But he had been there. Again. Still.

~

"I don't care!" Kwelik heard Annie's defiant shriek from across the village. She turned to see the girl standing outside the family wigwam with her face painted black, the usual form of discipline for disobedient children. Kwelik shook her head. It was the fifth time in the last three months that Annie had angered Snow Bird enough to receive this punishment.

Several village children gathered around the girl, taunting her with their chant. "Wakon is a bad girl. Wakon is a black snake."

Kwelik sighed as Annie crossed her arms and scowled, too angry to give in to their jeers. How would she ever train this child to obey the rules, to avoid stirring the anger of others? Kwelik shook her head. She had shown Annie how the turtle survived by being still, by withdrawing silently into its shell. Yet the girl remained much more like a wildcat cub than a turtle. Always she struck out at her enemies with her young claws extended. Why wouldn't she learn?

A boy lifted his arm and pushed Annie into the wigwam wall. Annie turned her head away, her face twisted with fury. Then Kwelik waited for the inevitable. The child knew that tribal rules would not allow her to retaliate during her time of punishment. And yet when had she ever listened to the rules?

Kwelik set her basket on the ground just as a pained howl burst from the boy's mouth. "Wakon is evil," he sniveled, holding the foot that Annie had slyly smashed with her own. A look of innocent pleasure passed over the girl's black face.

"Enough." Kwelik strode up to the children and shooed them away, keeping her face stern as she turned to Annie. "Still the wildcat, aren't you? Well, what happened this time?"

Annie made a face. "Just something I said. It was the truth too."

Kwelik grimaced. "It's always something you say. What was it now?"

"I said I saw a stranger coming to the village. She called me a liar." Annie's voice raised an octave. "And I didn't eat none of Chilili's maple sugar candy either."

Kwelik ignored the last sentence. "Is that all you said?"

Annie rubbed her foot across the ground and lowered her eyes. "No."

"What else?"

Her head shot up with a belligerent scowl. "I said the stranger was going to pluck her eyes out and put them in his soup."

"And you wonder why Chilili makes you stand outside." Kwelik raised her eyebrows. "They should have named you Fire Tongue."

"Well, they should have named Snow Bird Ostrich Head then, 'cause she's a silly bird with her head in the sand."

Kwelik suppressed her urge to smile at the girl's remark. Sometimes her words came too close to a hidden truth. "They don't even know what an ostrich is here. And you wouldn't either except for our lessons together." Kwelik poked Annie in the arm and sighed. Annie was really managing the language quite well. Too well sometimes. "Why must you continue to provoke Chilili?"

Annie echoed Kwelik's sigh, a sound too old for her years. "I know, I know: 'Love your enemies. Pray for those who persecute you.'"

"That's right."

Annie flashed a quick grin in Kwelik's direction. "But it doesn't say what I have to pray for, does it?"

This time the smile escaped Kwelik's lips. "Come, let's wash off that black paint. Eventually you will learn to hold that tongue of yours." She placed her hand on Annie's shoulder. "Tell me, what kind of stranger did you see?"

Annie's brow furrowed in momentary concentration. "An Englishman, in his twenties, I'd guess."

Kwelik did not hear the end of the sentence. "An Englishman?"

Her breath stopped as a vision of amber eyes and wind-tossed hair quivered through her mind. But, no, she should not hope.

Kwelik cleared her throat, willing her voice to remain steady. "Did you notice anything else about the man?"

The spring breeze picked up a lock of Annie's red-brown hair and tossed it across her cheek before she answered. "There he is now. Look." She raised her hand and pointed to the trees. "I told you so, Chilili," she screeched, wrinkling her face and sticking out her tongue as Snow Bird ducked from the wigwam.

Kwelik did not bother to scold her. Instead, she stared at the place where Annie pointed. Slowly a white man with his Lenape Indian interpreter emerged from the sycamores. Kwelik held her breath. Then she let it out again. The man was simply a stranger, as Annie had said. Yet kindness seemed to emanate from his features, his stride. Kwelik studied him more carefully, noting his closed collar and black hat. A preacher? Her heart beat faster. One like Papa? If only it were true. Maybe this man could tell her how to be free. She hurried toward him, stopping only when her way became blocked by women and children who poured from their wigwams to see this newest anomaly of a man.

The man and his guide halted as the villagers parted to allow Chief Tumaskan through. Tumaskan nodded his head once and stared at the Englishman.

The Lenape Indian stepped forward. "Greetings, brothers. This white man is called David Brainerd. He has come to tell you good news about his God, about one called Jesus Christ."

Brainerd smiled at the group. Kwelik noted that he looked too thin, almost sickly. Was he really here to tell her people about Jesus? Taquachi had threatened her when she had tried to speak about Christ, but perhaps now they would hear and believe, as her mother's village had done. Hope soared through her. Perhaps this was the answer to her prayer, and God had not forgotten her after all.

Kwelik listened as Brainerd began to speak, with his companion interpreting quickly after him. "God," Brainerd flung his hand toward the sky, "has made a way for us to know Him. I've come to tell you what has happened in a land far from here. Many villages along the Susquehanna," he gestured toward the river, "have received the good news of God's message. The Great Spirit became man and died for your sins."

Kwelik clutched her hands in front of her, eager for the villagers to hear the message of Christ. Surely this was her answer, her rescue. She could almost hear the voices of the people—Chilili, Tumaskan, Waptumewi—lifted in song to the true God. Surely then she would be saved from Taquachi's hand.

A scream of fury erupted from the longhouse door. Kwelik whirled. A low gasp escaped her lips as she saw Taquachi, his face dark with evil intent. "Stop your lies, white man!" He pulled out his tomahawk and plunged toward the stranger. His eyes flashed with black hatred. "We will not listen to stories of your God."

Before the interpreter could intervene, Taquachi had reached Brainerd. He grabbed the preacher's hair and pulled his head back, exposing his white throat to the blade. At the sight of the tomahawk, the interpreter backed away, fear painted vividly across his face.

"No!" The word burst from Kwelik's lips.

Taquachi glanced in her direction, his eyes dark and fathomless. He smiled, his voice shouting above the murmuring of the crowd. "A sacrifice for the *Manito-dasin*."

"No." The plea again groaned from Kwelik's throat as she pushed past the woman in front of her.

Taquachi leaned over the stranger until his face was inches from the pale one beneath him. "Listen to me," he whispered in broken English. "We spit on the white man's God. We spit on the white man." Spittle dropped from his lips to the preacher's face. The man dared not wipe it away. "Now you die." Taquachi's blade pressed into Brainerd's throat until a thin line of blood appeared.

"Stop!" Kwelik stumbled forward, her hand outstretched.

"Silence, *dasin*." Sayewis's wrinkled face loomed before her as clawlike fingers gripped her arm. Glittering black eyes bored into her own. "Do not interfere."

Kwelik pulled away and toppled over a young brave in her effort to reach Taquachi before the tomahawk breathed its sentence of death. She could see the preacher's blood beneath the blade—blood so much like Papa's, so red, so thick, so pure. A man of God, a missionary like Papa. "Oh, Father," Kwelik gasped.

From behind hands shoved into her back. She tumbled to the ground. Sayewis's fingers gripped her shoulder as the woman's knee pressed into her back. "You will not interfere, I tell you," she hissed.

Kwelik shoved Sayewis from her and struggled to her feet, her eyes never leaving Taquachi's blade. *Not again, Lord, please, not again.*

"No, son." Chief Tumaskan's voice cut through the silence of Kwelik's prayer. "Do not anger the white God. Shed no blood of the innocent man."

Taquachi did not loosen his grip. "He is English. He is not innocent."

Tumaskan shook his head. "He has no weapon."

Kwelik stopped. Her vision blurred.

Taquachi glared for a moment longer into the face of David Brainerd. Then he dropped his tomahawk. When Taquachi moved away, the interpreter again inched closer to Brainerd.

Tumaskan turned to the preacher, his voice quiet but stern. "You must go. We have our own gods and do not want to hear of yours. Go quickly before my son changes his mind."

Kwelik watched a drop of blood trickle down Brainerd's neck as he waited for interpretation, then bowed to the chief. "I am sorry. Perhaps we will speak another time, if my God allows."

Tumaskan inclined his head. "Perhaps."

David Brainerd and his interpreter left the village without looking back. Kwelik stood and watched them disappear as they had come, her momentary hope plummeting within her. *No, wait,* her heart cried, but she could not make her lips echo the sound. *Tell them the message. Tell them about Jesus.* For several minutes she did not move. She stared into the trees as the others around her returned to their work. A tear of hopelessness traveled down her cheek. With a muffled cry, she turned and ran into the wigwam.

White Wolf's new musket and powder horn hung inside the wigwam door. Kwelik closed her eyes to the sight. Her foot knocked a bark bucket, causing it to skitter across the dirt floor. A brass kettle hung over the fire. The smell of the deer stew bubbling within it turned Kwelik's stomach. She threw herself onto the bed platform, not caring that she spilled the baskets stacked beneath. What did it matter? What did anything matter now?

Her eyes flitted over the clay pots with pointed bottoms that sat propped between stones in the fire's ashes. Then her gaze locked on an ear of dry corn hanging from the rafters above her—ripped from its natural home and sucked of all life. She felt that way too. And all for the pleasure of others who did not care, did not understand.

A groan of agony tore from her lips. How could her father have cared for people such as these? Why had he left the English world to come and preach in the wilderness? "Savages," they were called, and now Kwelik understood why. The Shawnee in this village were terrible people—the men drunkards, the women afraid and powerless.

She sighed. But sometimes when she saw Chilili's timid smile or heard a baby gurgling his joy or saw the chief silent and thoughtful as he studied the evening sky, then her heart would fill with compassion and understanding. Then she knew why her father had loved these people, why he had given his life to them, to God.

Kwelik pressed her hands into her eyes, wishing to erase the vision of Taquachi's blade at the preacher's throat. *Oh, God, what am I doing here? Why haven't You rescued me? Why haven't You set me free from this nightmare that never ends? Do You still see me, remember me? How can You want me to marry that man?*

"*Manito-dasin!*" Snow Bird burst into the wigwam in a flurry of excitement. "Look what I have made for your wedding." She held up a new tunic, lavishly decorated with beads and feathers. "Look." She caressed a feather that had been positioned to fall over the wearer's heart. "It is the tail feather from a hawk. It will give your union endurance and pride." Snow Bird smiled.

Kwelik could not make her face echo the smile. "Didn't you see what happened, Chilili? Taquachi almost killed a man for coming to tell us about Jesus."

Sudden fear streaked across Snow Bird's face. "Hush! You must not speak that name! Taquachi will hear, and I will be punished with you. Speak only of the tunic. I worked hard on it. Tell me you are pleased with my work." Snow Bird's voice softened.

"It's lovely." Kwelik's voice sounded flat and weary. "Thank you." She took the garment and set it blindly on the bed next to her.

"What is wrong with you?" Snow Bird flopped down beside her, a frown marring her pretty features.

Kwelik did not answer.

Snow Bird clucked her tongue. "You are the envy of every woman in the tribe. Taquachi is handsome and brave. He will make you a good husband. If you do not make him angry, you will not need to be afraid."

Kwelik closed her eyes. Fear and dread were all she knew anymore. Snow Bird did not understand. No one did. No one but God, and He was silent.

Outside, Kwelik heard the thump of the ceremonial drums, followed by the crackle of a new bonfire. She glanced out the flap that swung in the breeze over the wigwam door. Darkness met her gaze. Had so much time passed since she had entered the wigwam? Or had the night descended with a rush, swallowing the day's light and her ray of hope in unmerciful black jaws?

Snow Bird clapped her hands and took Kwelik by the arm. "Come, the village celebrates."

Kwelik shook her head.

Snow Bird bit her lip. "Come. Taquachi expects you. He will be angry if I do not bring you."

Wearily, Kwelik wiped the lingering tears from her eyes and stood. "I will come if I must."

Women and braves, their faces painted red and black, danced in a circle around the fire, chanting, beating on drums, and shaking rattles made from turtle shells. Shadows flickered over darkened faces as they passed before the fire. Kwelik drew a breath, allowing the fine gray smoke to burn her eyes and throat. Chief Tumaskan sat cross-legged on the far side of the fire, his rasping voice leading the rhythmic chant. A spark, glowing yellow with heat, spun into the night sky and landed at Kwelik's feet. It burned for a moment and died, as if it had never lived. Kwelik's chest tightened. She drew back as Snow Bird laughed and pulled Annie into the dance.

"Like this," Snow Bird giggled, showing the girl how to step. "Foot in front, then back, kick, step to the side."

Kwelik watched listlessly as Annie glanced in her direction and then followed Snow Bird's lead. Taquachi and White Wolf swung toward her, red serpents painted vividly on their blackened cheeks. She lowered her gaze. What had happened to them, to her brother, to her? Everything had changed. With one swift attack, her life had been mauled and destroyed. And soon she would face the worst desecration of all.

As if reading her thoughts, Taquachi came around the circle again, his hand reaching out to pull her into the dance. He leaned over her, his voice soft and intimate in her ear. "The summer solstice approaches, my love." He caressed her arm with his thumb, flames dancing wickedly in his shadowed eyes. "I look forward to our wedding night."

Horror and revulsion screamed through her.

"*Danna witchee natchepung. Danna witchee natchepung,*" the villagers chanted, their words like a funeral dirge in her soul.

Kwelik's head spun as she whirled around the bonfire, her hand clutched in Taquachi's. Orange flames blazed against the black sky like a fire from the deepest pit of hell. Where was God now?

THIRTY-FIVE

The day dripped with a relentless fog, smothering all hint of sunlight in its gray cloak. After a day of futile scouting, Jonathan and a dozen others trudged back toward the main camp.

Jonathan sighed as he glanced at the man next to him. Dressed in the red coat of the British army, William Vaughn's stout frame showed no signs of tiring. His shoulders were still thrust back, his chin lifted. Jonathan shook his head. How did the man do it? A less persistent commander would have given up the search hours before. But Vaughn insisted on scouting one more hill, searching one more abandoned farm, discovering one more burnt warehouse where naval supplies could be hidden. Yet for all their scouting, they still had found nothing of value.

Jonathan dropped his head, more from discouragement than weariness. His vision blurred on the path before him. One step was the same as the next and the one before it. Nothing but wet mist and dismal sloshing through muddy countryside. Nothing but a shirt clinging damply to his bent back, his musket slick and cold in his hand.

"Look there!" Vaughn halted the small company and pointed through the trees toward the huge stone structure on the hill to their left. "The Grand Battery seems suspiciously silent, don't you think?"

Jonathan groaned. "It's been a long day already, Commander. Let's go back to camp."

Vaughn placed a hand on Jonathan's shoulder. "Do not give up yet, my boy. We may still see success today, God willing. Now look up there to the Battery and tell me what you see."

Jonathan wiped his hand across his face and focused on the Battery some two hundred yards up the hill. "I don't see anything."

"Exactly."

"Where are the French?"

Vaughn squinted his eyes. "Let's find out. You there." He called to the Indian who had guided their party. "You go check that building. See if any men are about."

The Indian frowned and shook his head. "I no go."

Vaughn pulled out a silver flask from beneath his coat. He winked at Jonathan. "I never touch this stuff myself, preferring rum as I do. But the savages sure seem to have a taste for it." He turned back to their Indian guide. "If you go, I'll give you this." He lifted the container up to eye level.

The Indian snatched the flask from his hand and sniffed the opening.

Vaughn grabbed it back. "It's brandy," he growled. "Some of the best. And it's yours if you do what I ask. Now go."

The Indian contemplated the flask for a moment, then nodded. "I go."

Before Vaughn could reply, the Indian dissolved into the fog. A minute later a dark figure reappeared on the hill. It sneaked up to the Battery and climbed in through an embrasure. Jonathan squinted to focus on the dark hole through which cannons were fired.

With breathless anticipation, the company waited to see what would happen. No one moved as the seconds passed in silence. Still there was no musket fire. No shouts. No shriek of pain from the lone brave.

Before they could break the silence, the Indian poked his head back through the embrasure. "No men here," he shouted. "Empty. Come." His one arm waved wildly, beckoning them to join him.

The group rushed up the hill and past the Indian who now stood smiling at the Battery's door. Jonathan looked around. Tall stone walls echoed the emptiness. Wooden crates, tipped over with the haste of the French departure, littered the floor. Cannon balls stood stacked neatly against the walls, waiting their chance to blast over the water. But not one Frenchman had stayed to fight for the Battery. Jonathan rubbed his hand over his eyes. Was it true? Had the French really abandoned their post? It was impossible. He would call it a miracle if he believed in such things. But he didn't.

Vaughn stepped beside him. "I guess they didn't believe they had the manpower to hold out against us. They must have pulled the men from here to help defend the Fort. Hmm." He shook his head. "This was a risky move. And I promise it will be one that will cost them later." Vaughn smiled.

Jonathan did not return the smile as his eyes traveled to the huge cannons pointed over the bay. He grimaced. "Looks like the French took time to spike the cannons before they left." Stout tempered-steel spikes poked out of the touch holes where they had been hammered in as far as they could go and then broken off flush with the top of the cannon's barrel. "If we're going to make use of this place, we'll have to punch out those spikes or drill new holes to light the cannons."

Vaughn nodded, then laughed. "Still this is a grand day, is it not? Once we get those cannons operational, we'll have the heavy siege guns we need. Ah, yes, the French will rue this day, my friend." He clapped Jonathan on the shoulder. "I told you we shouldn't go back to camp just yet, didn't I?"

Around them murmurings of astonishment echoed from the lips of their companions as the men continued to search the room. "Not a Frenchie left," one called.

"Ran off like scared rabbits, they did," added another.

"It's the hand of God, I tell you," proclaimed an older volunteer.

Jonathan watched Vaughn step to the middle of the room, his arms upraised. "They're gone indeed, men! The Battery's ours." He tore off his red coat and handed it to a soldier. "Nail this to the flagpole," he ordered. "They'll see it at the main camp. And how I wish I could see Pepperrell's face when he catches sight of it!" Vaughn chuckled, then turned back to his men. "Give thanks to God, boys." His voice rang confidently against the cold walls. "He is our fortress and our deliverer. Never forget that it was He who gave us this Battery today. Now let us pray that He might also allow us to take Fort Louisbourg."

Heads bowed throughout the Battery as Vaughn's prayer boomed over the group. "God of our Fathers, we are humble before You, grateful for Your help this day. You have not treated us as our sins deserve, but You have been merciful to Your servants. You are faithful even when we are not . . ."

Jonathan sank into a corner, his head tilting to rest against the stone wall. He was weary, weary of words that hunted his soul, weary of running, only to find that God had come ahead of him, and he had not escaped after all.

After a few minutes, the prayer ended, and the celebration began. Flasks of rum slipped from beneath several tunics as the men saluted their success.

"French dogs!" someone shouted.

"The Battery today, the Fort tomorrow," another called.

Jonathan shook his head, unable to share in their enthusiasm. Already he was tired of the fight. His heart remained elsewhere. His thoughts continued to return to a place and time that he wished to forget. He heard footsteps approaching him. He opened his eyes to see Vaughn standing above him.

"Good work today, lad," the man said. "But now the real work begins. Despite the celebration," Vaughn grimaced and motioned toward the others, "we have not won the victory yet. Come, we must get back to camp and haul the provisions and ammunition ashore in the darkness of the night."

Jonathan nodded and rose to his feet. "I'll meet you at the ship." Without a backward glance, he left the Battery. As he headed back to camp, his eyes scanned the peninsula that jutted out from the great marsh on which the French had built their Fort. Except for the harbor entrance, the coast was rugged and rocky, lashed for days on end by the heavy surf. With the fog, the ice packs of spring not fully melted, and the possibility of French warships arriving, the night's task would not be an easy one.

Hours later, with myriad crates and over a dozen small cannons hauled ashore, Jonathan struggled under the final load. Darkness penetrated to his soul as he slipped over surf-drenched rocks. Water soaked to his hips. Mud oozed into his boots, sliding between his toes. The soggy rope slipped in his hand. He gripped it more firmly and strained to pull the cannon across the slush. A stone beneath him turned, and he stumbled, groaning as the cannon sank further into the mud.

"Not again," Jonathan muttered as he dropped the rope and sloshed through the muddy water toward the back of the cannon. Joining the other men, he put his shoulder into the cold iron of the cannon's bulk and pushed.

The grunts of his companions echoed around him as they fought to free the cannon from the sludge. No one spoke. Only the sounds of their struggle pierced the night, mixing with the persistent pounding of the surf against the rocky coast. Finally the cannon broke free and slid forward a few inches.

Eventually, the cannon was pulled ashore, and Jonathan crumpled exhausted onto the damp ground. He rolled over on the few pine branches that he gathered for his bed and pulled the wet blanket over him. Others slept in huts made of wood and turf, but not Jonathan. He was a frontiersman, a man who knew how to brave the elements, how to survive on his own. He must never forget that.

Jonathan clenched his jaw as he stared up at the moon peeking in and out from behind the encroaching mist. He gripped his blanket in his fist. He was a frontiersman. He would forge his dream with his own two hands. He didn't need Richard. He didn't need his Grant heritage. He didn't need the fluff and finery of aristocracy. All he needed was himself.

As Jonathan closed his eyes, words whispered through him, quiet, gentle, and piercing. *How long will you cry to the moon?*

THIRTY-SIX

Jonathan's Homestead, June 1745

Gray ash. Cold. Wind-tossed. Dead. The last faded remnants of a time that had been devoured by torch and tomahawk, a time that had breathed for a moment, then died, its promise undiscovered, unfulfilled.

Kwelik stumbled into the clearing, horror rising in her throat at the sight of the charred birch in its center. The tree stood, blackened and gnarled, reaching stark fingers into a dismal sky. Once it had been green, vibrant, alive. But no longer. There she and Nahum had sat, him sounding out words as she held his black Bible. There Jonathan had leaned his back against the trunk, his head tilted to gaze into the night sky. There a squirrel had darted in and out, chattering its gossip to the wind. There a butterfly had once flown free.

Kwelik looked away, her eyes scanning the abandoned ashes of Jonathan's dream. Nothing was left. Nothing. Jonathan's homestead had vanished, except for the cinders, black markers of dead hope. Kwelik turned toward the burnt remnants of Jonathan's cabin and fell to her knees, tears stinging her eyes.

She had come to find Jonathan one last time, to talk to him, to somehow explain her absence, before it was too late, before the summer solstice claimed her life. All day she had consoled herself with the thought of seeing Jonathan again, believing he would be there still, waiting, wondering why she had not kept her promise, wondering why she had fled at his kiss. But the explanations died on her lips. It was too late. Forever too late. He was gone.

"Oh, Jonathan, where are you?" Kwelik's whispered plea echoed hollowly through the clearing. Silence answered her words. Tears dropped from her eyes and made dark craters in the ash below. Only the stone chimney stood, broken and forlorn, like a monument to a life that could have been. A charred timber sat precariously propped against another, its black hull moaning in the breeze. Kwelik dropped her head. No grass had grown, no wildflowers, no hint of the tiny violets that had once adorned the site.

"Oh, Lord," she whispered, her voice squeezing past her tears, "what has become of Jonathan, of me?" She closed her eyes. "Vaguely I remember a meadow, a wolfhound, and a village filled with laughter. I remember a man with dark skin who smiled over your promises. I remember another man whose soul cried to the moon like the wolf. But that was a long time ago, a lifetime it seems. I was happy then, wasn't I? Or was that some other girl? I have forgotten now." Kwelik's voice trailed off and died with her memories. She sighed. "Take care of Jonathan, my Lord. Do not forget him. As I cannot."

Kwelik pressed her hand into the cinders, imprinting her sorrow in the dust. "Good-bye, Jonathan, my love," she whispered, her voice scarcely audible in her own ears. "May God find you wherever you've gone."

The sharp crack of a branch snapping against another ended Kwelik's prayer. She stood quickly, wiping her ash-stained hand across one cheek. "Who's there?" A gasp escaped her lips as a figure emerged from the trees. "Taquachi! What are you doing here?"

He was upon her before she could back away, his breath hot in her face, the smell of liquor rank as he answered, "What are *you* doing here, *Manito-dasin?* You are far from the village. Did you think you could escape me?"

Kwelik pressed her hand to her chest.

Taquachi moved forward, strange, wild, uncontrolled.

Kwelik took a step backward. "What is wrong with you? I was not running away. I would have come back tomorrow."

"Liar!"

Before she could duck, the back of Taquachi's hand smashed into her face. Her lip split under his knuckles. She spun to the ground. Blood oozed in her mouth. She put her hand to her face and stared up at him.

His eyes blazed with fury.

"Get away from me!" Kwelik flung the words at him in desperate defense.

He stepped closer. "You cannot run away from me here, *Manito-dasin*. And there is no one to hear your scream."

Kwelik's stomach turned at his nearness. "Are you drunk?"

"Drunk!" Taquachi leaned over her, his words slurred, yet fierce. "You think to question me? You who sit like a fool, weeping for a white man. Who was he to you?"

Kwelik swallowed hard. "I told you. I was his slave."

Taquachi laughed. The sound froze with bitterness and disbelief. "Were you his lover too?"

"No!"

Taquachi did not hear. "Will I be receiving used goods on my wedding night?" He leered at her through bloodshot eyes. "Did you crawl to him, this master of yours? Did you beg him for mercy? Did you give yourself to him for a glance of his favor?"

"No!" The denial burst from Kwelik's lips in a futile shriek. "None of that is true."

"Well, *Manito-dasin*, you will beg me. You will crawl to me." Taquachi grabbed her tunic and pulled her to feet. "But you will not receive mercy." He flung her to the ground. His foot slammed into her stomach with all the force of his anger.

"Taquachi, stop." The words gasped from her throat and were lost in another slam from his fist.

"Beg, woman!" he shouted. "Show me you have forgotten the white man."

The bitter taste of blood filled Kwelik's mouth so she could not speak, could not beg. Taquachi kicked her again. She heard the cracking of a rib. Pain burst through her side. Blood gushed unhindered from above her right eye, blinding her.

"Have you forgotten the white man, you half-breed whore?"

Kwelik curled on one side and groaned as Taquachi's fist pummeled her again. *So this is how it will end*, she thought, *as it should have ended before when the French lieutenant captured me*, *when he too drove his fist into my face and cast me into a pit*. Taquachi's foot drove into her back. *Now the end will come. It must. There is nothing left to live for.*

"Stop it!" A high-pitched scream echoed vaguely in Kwelik's ears. *Annie?* She could not make her lips form the word. From the corner of her vision, blurred with blood and pain, she saw a small figure fling herself at Taquachi.

"No!" Kwelik cried from between swollen lips as Taquachi grabbed the child and threw her to the ground. The girl's head struck a boulder with a sick thud as she fell.

Annie. She must save the child. But she could not move, could not stop the wild throb of pain, the dizziness that spun its black web through her mind. Kwelik closed her eyes. The child. Perhaps she needed to live after all, for Annie's sake. But it was too hard, too difficult a task.

"Your little friend cannot save you, *Manito-dasin*." Kwelik heard Taquachi's voice from a distance, too far away to identify, to comprehend. "You will learn to respect me." His foot connected with her jaw again. A light blazed across her vision.

Now the end had come. And she welcomed it.

~

A blast rocked the air and filled the sky with gray smoke. Jonathan held his breath. A cannonball whistled toward him from the wall of Fort Louisbourg's west gate. "Incoming!" He shouted the warning above the battle's din and gripped his gun more tightly. Another blast crashed through the morning.

"Cover!" The command sounded from behind Jonathan as the ball landed near the small group of colonists poised to attack the gate.

"We're hit!" screamed one of his companions.

Jonathan dove into the trench behind him. He covered his head against the imminent blast. No explosion occurred. Breathlessly he waited. Nothing. Jonathan frowned, peeking between his forearm and musket to see the cannonball rocking innocently in the small crater it had made. Silence descended over the group.

"Is she live?" Captain Sherburne's voice echoed strangely through the morning air.

Jonathan rose to his feet, his gun still clutched in one hand. "I'd say she's another dud, sir. Our siege is finally taking its toll," he called back as he strode toward the ball and tapped it with one foot.

A farmer-turned-soldier stepped beside him. "I'll bet she ain't even got no ammo in her."

Jonathan rubbed his hand across his forehead and studied the failed missile. "There's a crack. See here." He pointed to a tiny fracture along one side. "Let's pry her open and see what the French are shooting at us now." With the edge of his bayonet, Jonathan worked at the encasement until a small hole opened, spilling the contents of the ball.

The farmer laughed and shouted their findings to the captain. "Full of sand and dirt, she is. No powder at all." He shook his head and sat next to Jonathan. "The Frenchies are getting mighty desperate since we captured the *Vigilant*. After seven long weeks of siege, they're running out of ammo and food too, unless I miss my guess. Won't be long now."

Jonathan nodded as Captain Sherburne knelt beside them and spoke. "Stay alert, men. Today may be our victory."

Victory. Jonathan tossed his musket into his other hand as a surge of anticipation washed through him. Soon he would know whether victory would free him from his past, whether battle would purge from him memories too painful to recall.

An English cannon fired at the gate from behind them. The deafening shot rang in Jonathan's ears.

"There she goes, men. Pray for a hit," cried the captain as the ball plunged into the wall and exploded. Stones crumbled upon one another, breaching the Fort's defenses. A shout rose from the men.

"Attack!"

Jonathan and the others surged forward, muskets ready, bayonets shining in the dim sunlight. In a moment they reached the wall and scrambled up the shattered stones. Before them a cobbled walkway stretched between two lines of buildings and traveled toward the center of the Fort. And on this walkway, a dozen French soldiers stood ready to fight. Jonathan drew a deep breath. The time for battle had come.

"We fight you in the strength of Christ," one sailor shouted as he rushed farther in to engage the enemy. The name formed a cold lump in Jonathan's chest. Christ would lend him no strength.

Smoke from a dozen muskets darkened the air as more English troops pushed forward, their weapons clashing against the enemies'. Shouts rang against the Fort's walls. A cannonball landed and exploded near them. Its fire scorched a dozen men.

"Tell our men to cease their fire," shrieked the captain.

Jonathan turned to the left of the broken gate. There beside a great heap of rubble, a French soldier stood, his bayonet pointed directly at Jonathan.

Jonathan raised his musket and fired. The shot ricocheted off a rock, missing its mark. He gripped the gun, readying his own bayonet for hand-to-hand combat. For a moment each man studied the other. Then the Frenchman charged. Jonathan fended off the blow. With a quick jab, he caught the soldier's arm with his blade, forcing the man backward.

Jonathan thrust his blade toward the French soldier again. The man fell back.

"Pepperrell's here!" a tall Englishman yelled.

"To victory, men!" Jonathan heard his captain's cry from the wall above him. A musket fired. A Frenchman fell. A blade flashed through the air. Jonathan ducked and jabbed with his own, stepping back into an open space between two buildings.

"*Chien Anglais*," spat the Frenchman.

Jonathan did not answer as he parried another bayonet blow and lured the man farther from his companions. The shouts of the other men grew dim.

Jonathan continued to back away, his musket held with both hands as he wielded the bayonet. From the corner of his vision, he saw another English colonist enter the alleyway.

Jonathan's gaze fixed on the French soldier. He lowered his weapon. The Frenchman relaxed. Jonathan lunged. His bayonet sank into the man's side.

The Frenchman fell to his knees. Surprise crossed his face as a red stain spread over his jacket.

"Who is the dog, now?" Jonathan muttered as he pulled the blade from the man's side. He spun back as a second Frenchman dashed toward him from an open doorway. The butt of the enemy's musket caught him on the shoulder. Jonathan stumbled, then righted himself.

Where was that other Englishman? Why hadn't he come to help? Was he perhaps afraid of the fight? He lashed out with his bayonet and then, with a sharp jerk, ducked away from another blow.

The smell of gunpowder filled the air. He could taste the smoke in his mouth. The sharp crash of metal against stone reverberated in his ears as his attacker's bayonet missed him and struck the wall.

"Reinforcements from the main camp!" the captain shouted. Jonathan could scarcely hear him.

At the sound a Frenchman called the others to retreat. The man in front of Jonathan took a final swing. He grabbed his wounded companion and fell back, bayonet extended. Jonathan gripped his musket to follow as the two Frenchmen disappeared behind a wall.

Behind him Jonathan could feel the presence of the other Englishman. "Press on, friend. The fight is ours." Jonathan called his encouragement over his shoulder as he wiped a hand across his brow. He turned to the other colonist. His words died in his ears. "You?" His breath stopped in his throat.

The man, his face dark despite the light, stared back at him, as he had done for countless days past. It was the face familiar in shadows, always watching, always waiting. But now the waiting had ended.

"Who are you?" Jonathan demanded.

The man raised his musket and pointed it, his face devoid of expression. "The fight is mine, you mean. I am your executioner." His voice was low and calculating, like the sound of a nightmare's wings.

"What are you doing?" Jonathan choked on the question.

The man smiled. "Killing you, Jonathan Grant." He cocked his gun. "I've saved this shot just for you."

Jonathan took a step back. "What have I done to you?"

The man laughed. The sound echoed cold and eerie off the surrounding stonework. "I'm to be paid a goodly sum to make sure you fall dead within the Fort's walls. And now here we are. Look around you, Grant. These are the walls of your tomb."

Jonathan crouched lower, his face dark with new fury. "Do not be so sure." As he spoke, he swung his musket around to catch the man's gun. Both weapons clattered to the ground and skittered out of reach. Jonathan leapt.

A cry of anger burst from the man's lips. He swung his fist, impacting Jonathan's jaw.

With one hand Jonathan reached out to grab the man's collar. He kicked his enemy's feet from beneath him. As one, the two men landed with a hard thump on the ground, rolling together over broken stone and cement.

"You will not kill me so easily," Jonathan gritted through clenched teeth as he pulled the man to his feet and slammed him against the wall. "Perhaps you should be the one to die." Jonathan reached for his gun. The man's leg swung out to trip him. Jonathan fell, rolling to fend off the imminent blow.

Jonathan again staggered to his feet, ready to lunge toward his attacker. Before he could move, the man plunged a knife into Jonathan's leg. Pain exploded across Jonathan's vision as the handle protruded from his thigh. He shouted and fell to his knees, his eyes clearing for a moment to see the man standing above him, his bayonet pointed and raised.

"Now, Grant, *you* die." Jonathan saw the man's knuckles whiten on the butt of the musket. "And I am a rich man."

A ray of sunlight reflected into Jonathan's eyes as the bayonet descended toward him like a specter of judgment.

And Jonathan knew the sentence was death.

Thirty-Seven

Kwelik's hand lay limp and pale in White Wolf's grasp, as it had for so many days that they seemed to stretch into eternity. Silently he sat, not daring to hope, not surrendering to prayer.

Kwelik groaned. Her eyes fluttered open to stare at nothing, to see nothing. "No! Stop." The words were muttered incoherently from her dry lips. She tossed on the bed, sweat covering her brow. White Wolf rocked back and forth on his seat, his eyes never leaving her face as he listened to her mumbled cry. They were the only words she ever spoke, repeating them over and over until she dropped again into a fitful sleep.

White Wolf pressed her fevered hand against his cheek and closed his eyes. What had happened to her? He remembered the day clearly when Taquachi had carried her into the village, a broken and bleeding shell of the sister he had known. Her arm had flopped awkwardly in the air, a trail of blood marring her skin. He had been sure she was dead. He remembered how his heart had turned cold within him, and it had not warmed since. Taquachi had laid her gently on her bed, his eyes filled with concern. But he'd offered no explanation, no words of assurance, no story of wild animal or rescue. Only silence, even after White Wolf questioned him.

"Oh, Skye, Skye," he whispered. "Come back to me. Please come back."

Kwelik moaned again, her head thrashing wildly against the furs.

"Move away, Waptumewi." Annie stepped to Kwelik's side with childlike efficiency and pressed a cold rag to her head. "Shhh," she whispered, her voice like the gurgle of a stream over stone. "It's over now. Everything's okay. You're home."

White Wolf noticed how tenderly Annie tended Kwelik, as if his sister were the girl's very life. Despite her own injury, she had hovered near Kwelik day and night, only leaving her side to wash bandages and mix new ointment.

Annie leaned over his sister, her hand gently brushing back the damp hair on Kwelik's forehead. Kwelik quieted under the touch. "You're safe now. Safe," Annie assured her. "No one will hurt you anymore." She turned flashing green eyes to White Wolf, her gaze suddenly fierce. "And you'd better make sure that's true, Waptumewi!" Annie put up one hand to adjust the bandage around her own head. "You keep that devil-man away from her. Do you hear me?" She snapped the command from between pursed lips.

White Wolf frowned. "What devil-man? What are you talking about?"

Annie stepped toward him, her face furrowed with the intensity of her demand. "You know who. That Taquachi. I told you before. He's the one who did it to her. If I see him come anywhere near her, I'll pick up that musket and blast him right between the eyes. Bang!" She raised her arms to imitate the action. "And don't think I won't either!"

White Wolf's frown deepened into a scowl. "He only wants to know how she's doing. She's going to marry him, you know."

"That's a lie!" Annie's voice erupted in a fierce whisper.

"It is not."

"Ain't no liars gonna be in heaven, Waptumewi."

White Wolf stepped toward her. "I never said I wanted to go to heaven. But I'm telling you the truth. Ask anyone."

Annie pushed out her lower lip in defiance. "She'd never agree to marry that—that monster!"

White Wolf's eyes narrowed at the epithet. "Didn't you know? She did it for you."

"For me?" Annie's voice turned hoarse.

"Why do you think they didn't kill you that first day when you came here clawing Gray Bear like a wildcat cub? You would have burned that very night if Kwelik hadn't saved you."

Annie grew silent as she walked over to the still figure on the bed and took Kwelik's hand in her own. White Wolf saw a tear slip from her eye and roll unhindered down her cheek. She turned back to him, lifting one hand to brush away the wetness. "I-I didn't know," she stuttered. "I hope it ain't true."

White Wolf scowled. Her sudden change in attitude irritated him. "It's not such a tragedy." He bit out the words. "Taquachi is the finest brave in the tribe."

"Fine? Brave?" The adjectives sputtered from Annie's lips with scorn. "He ain't nothing but a worm, a snake, a . . ." She paused as if searching for a more scathing term. Her hand flailed wildly in Kwelik's direction. "Look at what he's done to your sister."

White Wolf shook his head. "He didn't do that, Wakon."

Annie's face grew fierce. "You weren't there. You don't know. I saw it." Her voice rose to a subdued screech.

White Wolf felt his face begin to burn with fury. The girl was crazy, shouting insane things, just as she had done that day when she came stumbling out of the woods after Taquachi and Kwelik. Taquachi would never intentionally hurt his sister. He cared about her. He had said as much, hadn't he? Suddenly White Wolf couldn't remember. The thought frightened him, and his fear angered him all the more.

"I saw it all," Annie continued. "He hit her and kicked her until she just lay there like she was dead. That's when he got scared."

White Wolf's thoughts swirled in desperate rejection. It was not true. It could not be true. He flailed out with his words, scarcely hearing them himself: "She must have deserved it. She must have done something. He was only protecting her."

"Protecting her! What kind of fool are you? Use them two eyes in your head, will ya! Look at her."

White Wolf averted his eyes from the bed. He could not look at his sister lying there like that and believe that Taquachi—his friend, his leader, his mentor—had done such a thing. He took a deep breath and lowered his voice, willing himself to remain calm. "You are only a baby. You do not understand these things."

Annie's eyes narrowed. "This is what I understand, Waptumewi. I understand that your sister nearly died. And he," her hand flicked contemptuously toward the longhouse, "did it. How many times do I hafta say it? He's a devil, I tell you."

White Wolf crossed his arms, his face furrowing into a deeper scowl. "She shouldn't have left the village."

Annie dismissed his words with a snort of exasperation. "He shouldn't have beat her half to death. Taquachi is a coward."

Through the open doorway, White Wolf noticed that the villagers had stopped their work to listen, surprised at the heated outburst from the sickroom.

Annie pointed toward them. "See what you've done. They watch and whisper. I've heard them asking why you can't help your sister." She strode to the door and pulled the flap shut, securing it with leather ties. Then she turned back to him, her face stern with youthful judgment. "And do you know why, Waptumewi?"

He took a step back and did not answer.

"I'll tell you. You can't help her because you ain't no fancy warrior like you make out. You ain't even a man. You're nothing but a sad little puppet of a boy. I can see the strings from here." She paused to take a breath. "And do you know who's pulling them? That monster! 'Come here, Waptumewi. Carry this, Waptumewi. Do this. Do that.'" Annie mocked Taquachi's tone. "If I was Kwclik," she pointed to the pale figure on the bed, "if I was her, I'd be ashamed to call you brother."

White Wolf felt his fury explode at her words. "You go too far, Wakon," he shouted, his voice rising despite the invalid. With a quick movement, White Wolf pulled back his hand to slap Annie in the face. His fist tightened in anger as he saw her chin rise for the blow.

"Go ahead," she whispered, her words like fire in his ears. "You ain't no different than he is."

White Wolf lowered his hand, his anger fleeing like a bad dream at dawn. He shook his head, reaching up to rub a hand over his forehead, still wet with the heat of his fury. What had happened to him? Sometimes he didn't recognize himself anymore.

White Wolf drew a quick breath and closed his eyes, unable to bear the accusation in Annie's face. Suddenly he knew that she was right, for at that moment he recognized the monster within.

Then the moment passed.

~

A musket fired from above. Its blast echoed across the alley. Before Jonathan could blink, the bayonet clattered to the ground at his feet.

His assassin drew a sharp breath as his hands clutched his stomach. He gasped and toppled facedown. His blood spilled over the stonework and stained Jonathan's pants and shirt.

Jonathan pushed the man's body from him and rose unsteadily to his feet. His gaze searched above him where the shot had sounded. His eyes met those of William Pepperrell, whose musket still smoked in his hand. For a long moment Pepperrell regarded him, then touched one hand to his hat in silent salute before jumping from the wall to again engage the Frenchmen.

Jonathan stared at the vacated spot for a moment longer before turning to the man dying at his feet. He kicked the musket away from the man's reach and leaned over him. "I guess it isn't my day to die." The words fell harsh and dry into the air. Jonathan sucked in his breath and pulled the knife from his leg. With one quick movement, he threw it toward the wall, listening to the metal clatter against stone and dirt as it fell.

The man's eyes rolled open, as if only now hearing Jonathan's statement. "Maybe not today," he choked, his hand falling limply over his chest. "But someone will get that money. You're still a dead man, Grant." Blood gurgled up from the man's throat, silencing his words.

Jonathan turned away as the man's life seeped out in a red pool. He sighed. Perhaps the man was right. What life did Jonathan have now? A living death and no more. Yet the man could not see the future. He was only a paid assassin. No one was less honorable, no one more despicable, except the man who had hired him. Jonathan looked away.

A memory of men attacking him outside the blacksmith shop in Philadelphia came to his mind. He could hear again Kwelik's scream rending the air. Were the attackers simply street ruffians, as he had assumed, or something more? And from another time, he saw an Indian coming out of the fire, his tomahawk upraised in the feral night. A random attack or a planned maneuver? His vision glazed at the question. Death had stalked him for some time now, but always he had escaped it. Next time the blade might fall, for the price still stood on his life. A price paid by whom?

Jonathan's eyes narrowed with anger and suspicion. Had it been Richard, or Archibald? Both men had warned him against this trip to Louisbourg. But only Archibald had been there in Philadelphia. And in Jonathan's mind, either man was despicable enough to want him dead. One of them was the enemy. Jonathan frowned. But which?

He picked up his musket and dug the butt into the ground. Again he had been betrayed. But this time he would discover the reason. He would face them both. If they truly wanted him dead, then they would have to do it themselves. Or at least try.

Jonathan clenched his teeth. After the battle he would return to Boston, alive, in defiance of both his brother and his uncle. And he would continue to live, despite Richard, despite Archibald, despite every betrayal he had ever endured, despite Kwelik's lie, and despite the worthlessness of his life. He would survive.

Jonathan knelt to reload his musket. The French still needed to be defeated, the Fort captured, victory won. He ripped a sleeve from his shirt and wrapped it tightly around his leg to staunch the flow of blood. Then he rose awkwardly to his feet and stumbled a few steps forward.

Before he could meet the enemy, a cry of victory erupted from dozens of throats around him. The sound echoed against the stone walls and ricocheted off the battlements.

"We've won!" Captain Sherburne's deep voice boomed over the company.

Jonathan's grip loosened on his musket. He raised one hand to shield his eyes as he looked up to the Fort's flag. There, swinging innocently in the breeze, fluttered the white flag of surrender. Jonathan dropped his head. The battle had ended without him.

"The Fort is ours!" yelled a group of colonists as they thumped one another on the back, laughing. A great cheer surged from the soldiers. But Jonathan's voice was dead.

He waited for a rush of excitement, the elation of victory. Nothing came. Nothing but the emptiness, the same dreaded emptiness that had haunted him since Kwelik had betrayed him and Nahum had died. Or maybe it had been there even before then, even as long as he could remember. He closed his eyes, his musket hanging limply from one hand. Nothing had changed. Nothing.

Jonathan dropped to his knees and groaned.

~

Darkness danced in black flames, swirling, lunging, twisting. Kwelik spun in the turbulence, her mind whirling through a hundred nightmarish images of death. Pain became a ghoulish specter, mocking her with silent laughter as it spat its fire, touching now her head, her arm, her chest, her back—always near, always out of reach, never weary of the game.

She fought off another attack and fell, her arms flailing in the blackness—down, down, down to the very pit of terror, as the wind whispered its dark threats in her ears. She screamed. Silence smothered the sound. Someone laughed. She turned. Jonathan!

He reached out to her through an endless fog, his face pale, an arrow protruding from his chest. No! Kwelik raced toward him as he disintegrated into the mist, blackness swallowing his image.

The laugh came again. She whirled to meet it. There he stood, his arm resting on the mantel of his stone fireplace. Yellow flames licked the wood and reflected off amber eyes. She ran to his embrace. His arms enclosed her—tighter, tighter, squeezing the breath from her very soul. She tipped her head back. Amber eyes turned black, menacing. Taquachi!

Kwelik screamed again and struggled in Taquachi's grasp, his hands becoming the talons of a hundred demons. As she fought, her eyes caught a figure standing silently in the shadows, waiting for her call. She flung her arm toward it. "Help me! Jesus! Help!" Her plea dissolved in silence.

The figure stepped from the darkness, His strength dispelling the demons that held her. She fell to her knees, her face at His feet. A sob racked her frame. "Jesus." She whispered His name.

Gently He lifted her, His brown eyes searching hers. She clung to Him, her body trembling, her soul bruised by fear. For a moment more He looked at her, questioning, until she met His gaze. Then she heard it—two words spoken in the silence without making a sound: "Follow Me."

Flames burst around her as Kwelik stepped forward and placed her hand in His.

THIRTY-EIGHT

~

Boston, July 1745

Jonathan sprinted up the wide staircase, ignoring Tobias's flustered cries. His hand shook with pent-up fury as he reached the library door and gripped the knob. His jaw tightened with determination. Now was the time for answers. Now was the time for retribution.

Jonathan lifted his chin and thrust open the door before him. There across the room his uncle stood with a book in one hand.

Archibald turned, his features slackening with shock. "You're alive!" The startled exclamation echoed in Jonathan's ears and spurred his anger.

Jonathan slammed the library door behind him and crossed the room in two strides. "Are you surprised, Uncle?" He grabbed Archibald by the throat and threw him against the wall.

A pained "oomph" jarred from the older man's lips. A lamp tottered and fell from a shelf above them, spilling oil and glass across the hardwood floor. Jonathan ignored the mess, his eyes not shifting from Archibald's fleshy face. "The man sent to kill me is dead." He clenched his jaw, his face inches from his uncle's. "So, yes, I'm alive. And your surprise only confirms your guilt."

Archibald drew a gasping breath as his hand pulled ineffectually at the fingers that enclosed his throat. "No. Wait . . ." His voice sputtered and then choked into silence as Jonathan tightened his grip.

"Quiet, Uncle." He leaned closer. Fury clouded his vision. "It's too late for your pleas. Pepperrell saved me from your assassin's blade."

"Pepperrell?" A look of wonder crossed Archibald's face.

Jonathan did not stop to question it. "Why did you do it?" Jonathan's eyes narrowed as he studied his uncle's small eyes, wide now with fear. "I should have seen it before. You've always hated me, haven't you? But how did you get Richard to agree to the plan?"

Archibald closed his eyes. His lower lip trembled as he attempted to speak again. "I'm sorry."

Jonathan laughed, a cold sound that reminded him of his brother and his father. He shivered, dismissing the thought. "Sorry? Another lie. I didn't come to listen to your feeble apologies. I came for some answers." Jonathan's hand loosened from Archibald's neck. He pushed his uncle away from him. Then he walked over to an open window and rested his hand against the gilded frame.

Jonathan sighed, his voice low as he spoke again. "Ever since I can remember, this family has known nothing but betrayal, cruelty, and deceit. First it was my father, then Richard. And you. I've tried running, fighting, pursuing my dreams, but somehow I never seem to escape the long arm of hate and deception." He lifted his hand and tapped his fingers against the open window pane. Then he stopped and focused on the blurred smudges made by his touch. "Tell me this, Uncle. How can a man so hate his own flesh and blood that he would hire an assassin? What kind of devils did our ancestors spawn?" He asked the questions without turning, listening as his uncle shuffled his feet and came no closer. Silence enveloped them, broken only by Archibald's harsh breathing.

"Are you going to answer my question?"

"I-I don't know," Archibald stammered.

Jonathan nodded once, his heart hammering with suppressed rancor as he strode to the door. "Beware, Uncle." His voice echoed harsh and unyielding against the library walls. "I will not forget your treachery." He threw the threat over his shoulder, not pausing to witness the effect of his words.

Archibald stumbled after him. "Wait. Come back."

Jonathan continued toward the stairs, deaf to the plea.

"Please, I beg you." Archibald's words rang with remorse.

Jonathan stopped. His uncle had never begged before. Slowly he turned, surprised to see the look of humble repentance on Archibald's face. One arm was raised toward him in a gesture of pleading. Jonathan frowned. "What is this? You, begging?"

Archibald dropped his arm, his eyes not daring to meet Jonathan's. "The Grant family is all that you say. It always has been. But there is a way to be free."

Despite himself, Jonathan felt his heart beat faster. "Free?"

Archibald nodded. "I have come to know God and to follow Him—weak follower though I am."

Jonathan's eyes narrowed further. He had trusted one of God's followers before. "Words come cheaply, Uncle."

Archibald continued. "You must believe me."

"Why should I?" Jonathan took a step toward him. "You've always been a liar and a cheat. You've never cared for anyone but yourself."

Archibald closed his eyes as if the accusation had struck him harder than a physical blow.

Jonathan continued. "All your life you've run after power and prestige, no matter the cost. But what has it gotten you?" Jonathan paused, his gaze pinning Archibald as he continued, "You're still nothing but a lying, manipulating, little excuse for a man. You say you know God, but you see, Uncle, I know the truth about you. You knew what my father was and what my brother now is. But you supported them. You spread their lies. You covered up their abuse. All so you could hang onto the coattails of their power. So now I will not be fooled by your little act."

Shame reddened Archibald's features. "Yes, I know what I've been. I know what I've done," he murmured, lifting his eyes in quiet appeal. "And I ask your forgiveness for that."

"Forgiveness?" The word erupted from Jonathan's lips. "I will never forgive you."

Archibald dropped his head again. "I can't change the man I was in the past. I can only refrain from repeating my mistakes. I'm a new man now."

His gentle tone irritated Jonathan. "That's a convenient excuse. But enough lies." He closed the distance between them and gripped Archibald's clean lapel, crumpling it in his fist. He leaned over until his breath blew hot in his uncle's face. "Just tell me why you sent the assassin. Was it your idea or Richard's?" Jonathan released him with sudden force.

Archibald stumbled backward into the library, tripping over a chair in his path. The chair tipped, sending him sprawling onto the carpet. His legs entangled with those of the chair. "Please, Jonathan," he sputtered, pushing the chair from him. Archibald regained his feet, setting the offending piece of furniture carefully to one side. Jonathan watched the Adam's apple bob in Archibald's neck as he swallowed hard, misery covering his face. "If you will not listen to me about God, at least hear this: You must not let Richard find you here."

"Why not? Was it him who wanted me dead? Or was it you?"

Archibald remained silent, his face contorted with anguish.

Jonathan rushed toward him, ready to strangle the answers from his throat.

Archibald stepped quickly behind the couch. "You must leave here. You are in more danger than you know. Richard will—"

Jonathan scoffed. "Are you threatening me again?"

Archibald shook his head. "Please. Go back to the frontier, Jonathan, or go to England before it's too late. I cannot stop the plot against you. I tried, but I couldn't." The defeat in his voice subdued Jonathan's anger.

Jonathan turned his back, unwilling to waste more time on his simpering uncle. Without a backward glance, he headed toward the stairs. His foot reached the top step just as Archibald's voice trembled again in his ears. "One thing, Jonathan, before you go."

Jonathan spun around, unable to believe that Archibald would dare to speak again. "What is it?"

"I wish to ask for Elizabeth's hand."

Jonathan clenched his fists. "Are you asking my permission?"

"I am, humbly." Archibald folded his hands in front of him and waited for his nephew's response.

"Why?"

"If she goes back to England unwed, she will be shamed before all of our acquaintances. I couldn't bear to have that happen. But you are the one she cares for. She came to the colonies for you. But if you will not marry her, then I will."

Rage and revenge burst through Jonathan's mind. It was all he could do not to rush down the hall and slam Archibald into the wall again. Blood rushed in Jonathan's ears as his words grew soft and deadly. "I will not stand by and watch Elizabeth marry a snake like you."

"Please," his uncle stammered. "You have not asked to marry her. And you know that Richard plans to make a more profitable match for himself. Elizabeth is a fine woman, worthy of a good marriage. Surely you cannot object to her security."

"Security? With you?" An image of money passing from Archibald's hands to the assassin's crossed Jonathan's mind. "I curse you! You with your smooth words of God and your lying tongue. No woman deserves to be bound to you. May you die alone and miserable. May your life be haunted by loneliness and pain." *Like mine is.* The thought whispered unbidden through Jonathan's mind.

Archibald stepped from the library's doorway, his hand reaching toward Jonathan again. "Have mercy, Jonathan."

"Mercy? For you, never! You will not have Elizabeth, even if I have to marry her first." After Jonathan had spoken, his words echoed in his ears with cold finality. Marry Elizabeth? Did he really want to do that? He rubbed his hand over his face.

Marry Elizabeth? He turned the idea over in his mind again. What did it matter now anyway? He would never dare to love again, to care enough to expose himself to the pain of a woman's treachery. Perhaps marriage to Elizabeth was the only way to rescue her, and him—a way he should have taken long ago. But instead he'd followed an impossible dream, a dream that he had lost, and yet it haunted him still. Perhaps marriage would purge it from his soul and save Elizabeth from Archibald at the same time. Maybe it was the only escape for both of them.

Jonathan turned back toward his uncle. "Do you hear me? I'll take Elizabeth as my wife before I'll allow her to fall into your hands."

Jonathan heard a low gasp behind him. He turned at the sound. A chill of foreboding clutched his chest.

Elizabeth emerged from the shadows, a smile of triumph on her face.

THIRTY-NINE

Amber eyes met hazel in a moment of tense silence. Before either could speak, the sound of a bell shimmered through the air. Jonathan breathed a sigh of relief, turning to listen as Tobias hurried toward the outer door.

Elizabeth stepped forward, determined to hold Jonathan's attention. She wrapped her arm through his, her chin tilting up at him as she spoke. "Perhaps it is our first well-wisher, my love."

Her smile froze in Jonathan's soul. He did not answer.

Within moments Tobias trotted up the stairs, his eyes seeking Jonathan's. "A man to see you, Master Jonathan." He bobbed his head. "A Mr. Samuel Adams. Shall I tell him to call at another time?"

Jonathan shook his head, thankful for the interruption. "I will come down immediately, Tobias. Show him to the parlor."

Moments later Jonathan strode into the parlor, his hand extended in glad welcome. "Sam, my friend. How good it is to see you again."

Sam turned, his easy smile dispelling the heat of the last few minutes. "And you, Jonathan. I trust that the mission at Louisbourg was all that you had hoped."

Jonathan's smile faded, his answer guarded. "It was a good victory."

Sam nodded as he gripped Jonathan's hand in his own. "I see. It was not the same as conquering the frontier, I take it."

The truth of the statement penetrated Jonathan's defenses. He studied his friend, a grimace breaking over his face. "You never cease to amaze me. Again you are right."

"Will you return to the Pennsylvanian frontier?"

Jonathan dropped his gaze and wandered over to the fireplace, his eyes dwelling on the dead ashes in the grate. "There is nothing left for me there." The words became a stark admission in his heart. What would it mean to him to never see the frontier again, never feel its wind on his face, never hear the cry of the cougar nor the gentle thump of his axe in a tree?

Sam must have noticed his sorrow, for he laid a hand quietly on Jonathan's arm and drew him away from the mantel. "Perhaps I have an answer for you, my friend. Come, sit here while I tell you of it." Sam waved to a chair opposite the one he had taken. "A group of settlers has come to me, wanting to travel to the new territory that has opened west of the Susquehanna. They're New Sides."

Jonathan turned. "New Sides?"

"Surely you've heard the term. They're also called New Lights."

Jonathan frowned. "Don't tell me they are another group of wild-eyed religious zealots." His voice turned dry with the accusation.

Sam laughed. "Ah, you have guessed correctly. While you were at Louisbourg, the Presbyterians split into two synods. The New Side has emphasized faith built on a relationship with God, as they learned from Whitefield, Tennent, and others. But the Old Side wants nothing to do with them, even going so far as excluding them from the Philadelphia synod. So the New Sides have formed their own synod in New York. Now a small group of New Sides, tired of the bickering, wishes to find a new life on the frontier. A life of piety and peace."

"On the frontier?" Jonathan scowled over the thought. He had found anything but peace there.

"They are people who want to start again much as you did."

Jonathan shook his head. "What does that have to do with me?"

"They need a guide, Jonathan—someone who knows how to survive out there, how to scrape a living from the wilderness and protect against the savages. They need *you*."

Jonathan stood and turned away. To go to the frontier again—his heart filled with longing at the idea. Yet he had found nothing but death and betrayal there. How could he think of returning now? "I don't know."

"Take them, Jonathan. Do not deny them their chance." Sam's gaze focused on him with intensity. "You need these people as much as they need you."

Jonathan remained silent, considering his friend's words.

"They've found some land near an abandoned trading post along the West Branch of the Susquehanna. They tell me a man named Ned McCoy used to run the place."

"I know of it."

"Then why do you hesitate?"

For a long moment, Jonathan avoided the question. He placed one hand on each hip and studied the rug under his feet. The silence grew longer. Finally he spoke. "I'm thinking of marrying Elizabeth."

He heard Sam's quick intake of breath. "The woman from England? But what of your dreams, your hopes, your longing for the frontier?"

Jonathan turned, his voice dull with despair. "The dreams are dead."

"And the longing too?"

Jonathan's voice dropped to a whisper. "No, never the longing."

"Then it will eat you alive, my friend." Sam stepped closer, his hand resting on Jonathan's shoulder. "Your dream is not dead. It is only taking a new form. Take the New Sides to their home. Help them to gain *their* dreams, and just perhaps, in doing so, you will rediscover your own."

Jonathan closed his eyes. What if Sam's words were true? What if he could find his dreams again, resurrect his life? New hope whispered through him, then gained strength. Maybe he could start again, build a new life from the ashes of the old. His blood began to rush again, as it hadn't since his homestead had burned to the ground.

The image of Elizabeth flooded his mind, her with her dainty airs and aristocratic breeding. Jonathan groaned. She would never agree to life on the frontier. She was as unsuited to the wilderness as he was to the life his brother had once tried to force on him. But now had his impulsive words bound him to her? He was sure that she would believe they did, and his honor demanded that he yield.

Jonathan turned toward Sam again, his face filled with regret. "I'm sorry, Sam," he murmured. "I just can't do it."

Sam's eyes shone with his disappointment. "Wait a day to decide, Jonathan. Come meet the settlers tomorrow at noon."

Jonathan sighed. "I will come. But know that I cannot change my mind." He paused, his hand resting on Sam's arm. "If only I could."

Jonathan showed Sam to the door, waving as his friend descended the steps and disappeared around the corner.

"What was that about?" Jonathan spun around as Elizabeth's sharp query sliced through him. He frowned.

Noticing his displeasure, Elizabeth quickly changed her tactics. She leaned into him, her voice soft and alluring as she reached up one hand to lightly massage his chest. Her lips puckered into a seductive pout. "Do not frown at me, my love." She brushed her leg against his. "Come, let us talk about our wedding."

Sam's words grew distant in Jonathan's mind as he gazed down at her full mouth and lowered lashes. A tendril of blonde hair curled over her white neck and traveled down her chest. Longing washed over him. But not for her. For Kwelik. Jonathan drew a deep breath and spoke. "He wants me to take some settlers to their land in western Pennsylvania."

"Jonathan!" Elizabeth's brows furrowed with anger. "We are to be married! Then we will go back to England." Her voice softened. "Silly Jonathan. All your crazy notions are behind us now. You don't need the wilderness for happiness. You have me."

Jonathan's fingers gently squeezed her shoulders. "Perhaps you would like the frontier." Jonathan knew the words were a lie even as he spoke them. "We could make a life together there."

Her gaze turned icy. "With the savages? I think not! We'll have no wealth, no power, no society there. We'd be nothing, nobody." She flicked her fingers in disdain.

Jonathan's heart turned heavy within him. "The new world is not like the old. Here respect is not bequeathed with a family name. It is earned with hard work and integrity. Respect is cut out of the wilderness and tamed. It's a dream pursued and won."

"I will be your dreams. We'll make dreams together back in England." Her voice turned beguiling as she leaned closer to him, her fingers dancing on his chest. Her head tilted up to him, beckoning. "I will make you happier than you've ever dreamed." Her sweet perfume surrounded him, weaving its heady spell through his mind.

He smiled down on her. "Maybe you're right."

She raised her arms, her hands twining behind his neck as her perfect teeth flashed in an alluring smile. "Of course I am." She brushed her fingers lightly across his skin. "I always am." She laughed and tilted her head back further for his kiss. "You know, I told them you would come back alive."

"What?" The smile dropped from Jonathan's face as he disentangled her arms from around him. For the first time in their acquaintance, Jonathan saw obvious distress on her face.

Her eyes grew wide, feigning innocence. "Why, I meant—I said I knew you wouldn't be killed in battle, that's all," she stammered.

Jonathan dug his fingers into the flesh of her arms. "That is not what you said." He released her and backed away from her. "What do you know?"

She staggered, then regained her footing. "Nothing!" Her voice filled with tears. "I don't know anything." Fear and guilt streaked through her smoky eyes.

Jonathan knew she was lying. The knowledge choked him. She was part of it, part of Archibald's plan, and Richard's. His blood turned cold. He had been a fool to think that he must protect her. She was one of them! "You knew about the assassin, didn't you?" Jonathan's voice was hard.

"It wasn't my fault, Jonathan. I told him to wait. I knew you'd come back to me."

Jonathan flung his arm toward the door. "Get out. Now, I say!"

"But we're to be married," she shrieked.

"Not anymore. You're nothing but a beautiful, beguiling serpent! I'll never marry you now."

Elizabeth's eyes narrowed as she backed toward the door. "You are a fool, Jonathan. You always were. You will pay for what you've done to me." Elizabeth slipped out the parlor door and stumbled down the hall.

Jonathan followed, his voice rising over hers. "You have no power to hurt me, Elizabeth."

Her brittle laugh echoed down the hallway. "Not me, you fool. *He'll* make you pay."

"Who?"

Nothing but another disembodied laugh wafted through the corridor in response.

~

Archibald stood gazing blankly out the library window as Elizabeth followed Jonathan downstairs. It was Sam Adams at the door, he assumed. The man had stopped in several times during the last weeks to see if Jonathan had returned from Louisbourg. And now Jonathan had come back, alive and furious.

In the distance Archibald watched the last rays of sunlight ripple and dance across the surface of Boston's harbor, glinting like a sea of polished sapphire. A merchant ship lolled lazily in the blue waves, its tall masts raking the azure sky. His eyes followed a puff of white cloud as the breeze molded it with unseen fingers. The scene played a dissonant chord to Archibald's emotions as the cloud dissolved into wispy pieces.

From far above the city, a seagull glided and dipped, plunging suddenly toward the water for its afternoon meal. Archibald took a deep breath, the smell of the sea filling his lungs. The gull did what was necessary to survive, and so must he. And yet did God perhaps demand something more?

Archibald sighed. God had answered his prayer to save Jonathan's life. And now Jonathan blamed him for the assassination attempt. He leaned his forehead against the glass. It was ironic. Six months ago, before he had heard Whitefield, Jonathan would have been right to accuse him. But now as he tried to make amends for his past sins, those very sins came back to condemn him. How could he make Jonathan see the truth before Richard discovered the boy's whereabouts and finished the job left undone at Louisbourg?

Archibald groaned. It was another impossible situation, and again he found himself in the middle of it. He had told Jonathan that he was free. But was he? This time he needed to make a stand. This time he had to do what was right before he was sucked deeper into Richard's plans, before he again became mired in treachery and sin. If only he could get Richard to forget the frontier, forget Jonathan, and go back to England. What was that man hiding anyway? What secrets tied him to his pursuit of Jonathan? What had changed him into the man of hate he now was?

Archibald felt the air thickening around him and fear stirred through his chest. A shadow moved over the wall. Archibald did not turn as he addressed the shadowy figure. "Your plan is doomed, milord. We should return to England in peace."

The voice lowered with disbelief. "Doomed, Archibald?"

He gripped the window sill and stared at the afternoon sky. "The Lord is against it. It will fail."

A laugh, low and frightening, echoed through the room. "What is this talk of the Lord?" Richard stepped behind him, out of sight, yet so close that Archibald could feel the hot breath on his neck. "I am lord here. Do not forget it."

Archibald remained silent for a long moment before changing the subject. "How did you know I was here?"

"You cannot hide from me, Archibald."

"I know." Archibald's voice was barely above a whisper as he listened to the footsteps pacing across the floor behind him.

Then Richard stopped. "Ah, perhaps you are simply discouraged. The plan is not doomed, even though Louisbourg did not succeed. I know how it bolstered the confidence of these brash colonials. Yet they will find that they still need a frontier governor, someone to protect them, to represent them," his voice turned cold, "to tax them." Archibald could feel Richard's stony smile at his back. "And the king knows that I am that man."

Archibald still did not dare to turn and confront Richard face to face. "They will never submit to a frontier ruler now. They know they can defend themselves." He shook his head. "King George won't listen either. Even the French are angry. We should abandon the plan and return to England in peace. The frontier is lost to us." Archibald glanced over his shoulder.

"Perhaps." Richard rubbed his hand over his chin. "But I am not finished yet, despite your portent of doom."

Archibald sucked in his breath. "What will you do?"

Richard chuckled again. "You will see."

Archibald felt the fingers of burgeoning horror claw at his chest. "No, Nephew, give up the plan. It's too late."

Richard again stepped behind Archibald, his voice soft and threatening. "It's never too late."

Archibald took a deep breath, steeling himself for what he must do, and turned around. "I can no longer be a part of this. I, at least, am going back to England." He watched Richard turn slowly toward him.

"To England? Why the sudden urge for the motherland, Archibald?" Richard leaned closer.

Archibald felt his heart hammering in his chest. Sweat broke out on his brow. "Let Jonathan live his own life. Forget him. Come back with me."

Richard's voice raised in scarcely suppressed anger. "Go back? Allow Jonathan to defy me? With every breath that boy takes, he spurns me. I will not rest until Jonathan pays for daring to mock Lord Grant."

Archibald dropped his head and remained silent. Fear clutched him, stealing his breath, his words of entreaty. He turned back to the window, knowing that he could not stand against a man with the title Lord Grant. He never could.

"I own you, Uncle." Richard's voice washed over him like winter sleet.

"Yes." Archibald whispered the concession through trembling lips, hating himself for his weakness. Despite all he thought he believed, he was still afraid to die, afraid of the man who stood behind him, afraid to lose everything that he had gained. And those fears wrapped thick fingers around him until his breath came in short gasps, stopping his objections.

Archibald lowered his head and started toward the door. It had gone too far. He had been involved for too long to think he could escape now. He didn't have the power to save Jonathan anymore. Only God could rescue him. *Oh, Father in heaven . . .*

Richard's voice smothered the prayer. "I will rule Jonathan's precious frontier. I will prove that I am a man of power, that I am Harlan Grant's son!"

Archibald did not turn as Elizabeth hurried into the room. "Milord, he knows," she gasped. "Jonathan's here. And he knows that . . ."

Before she could finish her statement, Richard stepped closer, his words slicing through Archibald like a knife. "Remember, Uncle, your life belongs to me. Just as it belonged to my father."

Archibald closed his eyes, unable to deny the accusation.

FORTY

Jonathan stared at the place Elizabeth had just vacated. *Betrayed. Again*. Slowly his fury melted, leaving only emptiness in its place. He could hear Elizabeth's footsteps on the staircase. The floor creaked above him as she reached the top and scurried down the long hallway toward the library. Then the sounds stopped.

A light breeze whistled down the parlor's chimney and stirred the dead ashes in the grate. Jonathan turned his head to watch the tiny, gray flecks rise and then settle back into place. He walked to the fireplace and pushed his toe into the cold cinders. He removed his foot and watched the powder cling to the shiny surface of his boot. *Like the ashes of betrayal*, he thought. *Why can't I shake them free?*

He leaned over and wiped away the cinders with one hand. The ash felt gritty against his skin. With a grimace he straightened and turned toward the window. Pale streaks of dying sunlight lit the sky as evening approached. Jonathan stopped to light the oil lamp that sat on the mantel. The flame flickered up, casting a yellow glow over the room. He stepped to the window, his eyes raising to the trees that swayed in the wind. Then his gaze dropped to the cobbled walkway. His fingers tapped the sill. How long had it been since he had stood out there, looking up at the massive structure of the mansion for the first time? Months? Years? He sighed. He should have stayed on the frontier. There at least he knew who the enemy was.

A voice spoke from the doorway. "You couldn't just go back to England, could you, Johnny?"

Jonathan glanced up to see his brother's reflection in the pane. He did not turn as he answered. "I'm going back to the frontier, back where I belong."

Richard's voice grew taut. "You will not stand between me and my plans to control the wilderness."

Jonathan frowned as he focused on his brother's reflection. "Those aren't your plans, but Father's. He was the one who planned to come to the new world and rule it. He built this house for that purpose."

The oil lamp flickered, casting shadows over Richard's image. His features wavered in the glass. He took a step forward. "The frontier is mine! I am every bit the man Father was. I *am* Lord Grant!" The title rang fiercely, clearly through the parlor. Richard raised his arm. Silver glinted from his hand.

Jonathan heard the unmistakable sound of a cocking gun. His breath froze in his throat. He turned. His eyes traveled from Richard's face to the pistol in his hand. "You sent the assassin, didn't you?"

"You spurned me. You had to die." Richard paused, his voice growing low. "But you even defied me in Louisbourg. You never do what I want." He pointed the gun toward Jonathan.

"Richard, no." Jonathan held his breath. Fingers of alarm squeezed his stomach.

"This time I will make sure the ball doesn't miss." Richard's face flushed as he spoke.

Archibald and Elizabeth rushed into the room. Richard turned slightly. His pistol trembled.

"No, Nephew. Stop!"

Jonathan dared not move as Archibald crossed the room to stand beside him.

Archibald laid his hand on Jonathan's shoulder, his eyes on Richard. "You must stop this madness, milord."

Richard did not lower the gun. "That title will never mean anything unless Jonathan is dead." His gaze flickered to Archibald's face and then returned to Jonathan.

Jonathan's eyes locked with Richard's. He studied Richard's face, a face he had once loved because it was so different from their father's. Behind him the oil lamp's flame sputtered and grew stronger, casting new light onto Richard's features. Jonathan drew a quiet breath. There beneath the hardness, beneath the anger, he saw something flicker in his brother's eyes. Was it pain? Jonathan took one step toward him.

Richard raised the pistol. "Stay where you are." His voice cracked.

Jonathan stopped. There it was again, the flicker of the boy Richard used to be, the brother whom Jonathan loved and had lost somewhere in the past. Jonathan's voice grew soft. "You don't have to please Father anymore. We're free of him. You can live your own life, and I can live mine. Forget him, Richard." His eyes beseeched his brother from across the room.

"Forget him? You never knew, did you, Johnny?" Richard's voice raised to a strained pitch. "Father sent for his heir before he died. I came to him. But he didn't want me. He wanted you. You, his favorite son, his only son!" He choked on the last word.

Shock ricocheted along Jonathan's nerves.

Sweat broke out on Richard's forehead and dripped down his temples. He wiped it away with the back of his hand.

Jonathan shivered as Richard's eyes turned hard, masking the boy that Jonathan hoped he'd seen. Archibald's grip tightened on his shoulder.

Richard continued, his face now red with the intensity of his memories. "He despised me. He would have left me with nothing. Said I wasn't his son. That you were. He called me illegitimate, a ba . . . bast . . ." Richard couldn't speak the word. His breathing grew heavier, his eyes glazing with a queer madness.

"So that's the secret." Jonathan heard Archibald's words spoken softly beside him.

"But I showed him. He was weak, dying. This time I had the power. I took the pitcher that stood at the side of his bed and hit him, just like he had always hit mother and us. I hit him again and again and again." Richard focused for a moment on Jonathan's face. "Does that surprise you, Johnny? He never woke up after that, you know. And the doctors called the bruises a result of the fall."

Jonathan remained silent, his stomach roiling with nausea. Suddenly he understood. Violence replicated itself like a disease, passing from father to son, not through blood but through anger, through the helpless fury that craved the power to fight back. And when Richard had his chance, he succumbed and became the monster he wished to destroy.

Richard's voice cut through him again. "All those years when he hurt us, I told myself that someday I would be Lord Grant. I would be the one with the power. I couldn't let anyone take that away. Not him, not you, and not Mother."

Jonathan drew a quick breath, his eyes widening with newfound insight. "Mother was going to tell, wasn't she? That's why you banished her, to keep her from telling the truth about you, about your true father."

"I had to silence her." The gun shook in Richard's hand.

Jonathan took a step toward him.

Richard tightened his grip. "Another step and I'll shoot you now."

Jonathan halted. "You don't have to do this, Richard. I won't protest your inheritance of the estate. Just let me go. You are Lord Grant. Not me."

"I'll never truly be Lord Grant as long as you're alive. I know that now." Richard's voice carried an edge of crazed fury.

"I don't care if Harlan Grant was your father or not," Jonathan whispered.

"Don't you see, Johnny? I care. I just wanted to show that I could be the son he wanted. But you wouldn't let me do that, would you? No, you had to come to the colonies and show Father that you didn't need his title, his wealth. Why couldn't you just go back to England? Why couldn't you let me be Lord Grant, the one with the power? But you had to defy me, to show Father that you are better than me, that you are the real son." Richard's voice lowered to a deadly whisper.

The sound sent a shiver of dread through Jonathan's heart. He stepped back. "Father is dead, Richard. Dead."

Elizabeth's quick intake of breath sounded from the doorway.

Richard lowered his weapon until the muzzle pointed directly at Jonathan's chest. "Dead?" His eyes narrowed. "Not to me, he isn't."

As if in slow motion, Jonathan saw his brother pull back on the trigger.

"No!" Archibald shrieked the warning. The shot exploded in the air. Before Jonathan could wince, his uncle threw his body in front of the blast.

"Uncle!" The word burst from Jonathan's lips.

Elizabeth screamed.

Archibald fell to the floor. His hands clutched his shirt. Blood seeped from between his fingers as his head rolled up toward Richard.

Jonathan knelt and took his uncle in his arms. Blood covered his hands and chest as he looked into his uncle's eyes, cloudy now with the onset of death. He glared at Richard. "What have you done?"

Richard stood above Archibald, his pistol still smoking. Shock washed over his features. "Uncle?" His body began to shake. He dropped the gun. It skittered across the rug and stopped.

At the sound of the shot, servants came running from the far side of the house. Jonathan turned his head toward the door. Elizabeth was gone. The servants stopped in the empty doorway and gasped, their eyes fearful and questioning.

"Get a doctor," Jonathan commanded. "And bring some water and clean linens."

No one moved.

"Go!"

The servants scattered, their hurried footsteps echoing on the tiled floor.

Archibald blinked, his gaze focusing for a moment on Jonathan. "You're safe?" he whispered.

The compassion in his voice penetrated Jonathan's heart. "Yes, Uncle."

Archibald nodded once, his breath coming in ragged gasps. "I thought it was too late, but now . . ." Archibald choked, his voice sputtering. His mouth twisted over the final words. "I am . . . free . . . at last."

Jonathan took his uncle's hand in his own. "Shhh."

Archibald smiled and fell silent. Blood trickled from the corner of his mouth. He closed his eyes.

"Jonathan?" Archibald's eyes flew open.

Jonathan squeezed his hand. "Yes."

"You must . . . stop the cycle . . . of sin." His voice caught.

"How?"

"Forgive. Richard." The words slurred. Then Archibald's head tipped up, and his eyes glazed in the blank stare of death.

With gentle care, Jonathan laid Archibald's head on the floor and closed the man's eyelids.

A servant entered the room. "The water, sir, and the linens."

Jonathan looked up, his eyes scarcely seeing the servant's face. He shook his head. "It's too late."

The servant dropped her head and scuttled from the room.

Jonathan rose and turned to Richard. "You will hang for this."

Richard didn't move. His eyes never left Archibald's still form. Nothing in his face altered to show that he had even heard Jonathan's words.

"You wanted to be like Father. You wanted his kind of power. Now how does it feel?" Jonathan's voice crackled with condemnation. He looked at Richard. Remorse showed in his brother's brown eyes. Pity stirred through Jonathan. The mask of their father had fallen away from Richard's face, leaving him defenseless.

Jonathan softened. "You've never killed anyone before, have you?"

Richard glanced at him. His face blanched. He dropped his gaze to the floor and remained silent.

Forgive Richard. Jonathan took a deep breath and walked to the window, purposely turning his back on the scene behind him.

Neither man spoke.

Finally Jonathan turned. "Go home, Richard." His voice was quiet.

Richard raised his head, his eyes questioning.

Jonathan's features remained steady, revealing none of his inner turmoil. "Go back to England and take Elizabeth with you." His voice grew hard. "But if you set foot in these colonies again, I swear you will pay for what you have done here today."

Richard nodded once. Without a word he turned and left the parlor.

Jonathan watched him go. Silence descended like a shroud around him. A lump lodged in his throat as he looked down at the body of his uncle. Archibald had taken the bullet meant for him. Jonathan trembled.

Could God really change a man so much?

FORTY-ONE

Kwelik scraped the bone over the bear hide again. Back and forth, back and forth, with mesmerizing accuracy. Nothing existed but the task. No past, no future, no fear. She studied the way the bone shone in the afternoon sun, the soft *whoosh* it made as she pulled it over the hide, the pungent smell that rose from the dead skin. Anything to distract her thoughts from the purpose of her actions. *To tan the bearskin for my wedding bed.* The truth whispered through her mind. She closed her eyes. The bone shook in her hand. She must not think of it, must not remember, must not look forward or back. Only this one moment mattered, only the steady scrape of bone against hide. She must discipline her mind to see only today, never tomorrow, even as the days brought her closer to her delayed marriage.

The summer solstice had come and gone during the delirium of her illness. But as soon as she was well enough to walk, Taquachi had reminded her of her pledge to marry him. She had hoped, even prayed, that he would be shamed enough by his actions to free her from such a bond. But she'd hoped in vain. Since their encounter at the homestead, he seemed even more determined to make her his possession.

Now only the need to complete her traditional wedding preparations kept her from his grasp. And no matter how slowly she worked, every day brought her closer to the dreaded night. Soon even God would not be able to save her from the horror of Taquachi's embrace. How would she endure it?

Kwelik rubbed one hand over her forehead, feeling the pucker of a scar over her right eye. She took a deep breath, aware of the dull pain that still nagged her. She gripped the bone until her knuckles turned white. *Back and forth. Back and forth. Think only of the bone. Forget the future. Forget the past.*

Footsteps sounded behind her. She did not turn.

"*Bonjour*, kitten." The greeting tore through her senses.

Kwelik turned. "Hook Nose!" Her mind whirled in dizzy confusion as the face of the French lieutenant loomed before her. She took a step back, a wave of nausea engulfing her. Suddenly she could see nothing but the bitterness of memory—the gray smoke of her village burning, the dark eyes of her people wide and unseeing in death, a knife at her brother's throat, a bullet and blood, Lapawin dead at her feet, and the pit, rank, airless, black. And in each image stood Hook Nose, laughing with spite and malice, just as he laughed at her now.

"Are you surprised to see me, *ma petite chatte?*"

Kwelik caught her breath, her voice refusing to answer as a hundred questions dashed through her mind. What was the Frenchman doing here in this village? Did these people know who he was? Did her brother know that the man who killed her people was here? The thought terrified her, choking words from her throat. "You!" she sputtered. "Snake! *Nakowa!*"

The lieutenant stepped closer, his hand uplifted. "I have heard that word before, kitten. And I didn't like it then."

Kwelik closed her eyes and braced herself for the blow. Instead, she felt his hand lifting her chin with two fingers. She opened her eyes.

Hook Nose clucked his tongue as he turned her face to the left, then right. "Life has been harsh to you, *chatte.*" His finger traced the edge of a bruise that had still not completely faded.

She pulled her head away. "Don't touch me!"

His fingers gripped her arm as he drew her closer until she could smell his breath on her face. "You escaped me once, kitten," he whispered, "but not this time."

Terror flooded through her at his words. She screamed and sank her teeth into his hand. His shout of pain brought Taquachi from the longhouse. From the corner of her eye, Kwelik saw him striding toward them, his face dark with anger. "Get away from her, Berneau," he yelled.

A hysterical laugh rose in Kwelik's throat at the vision of Taquachi as her rescuer. She swallowed the sound.

Berneau turned, a smirk evident on his haughty features. "I will give you ten muskets for the woman."

Taquachi stepped forward, his eyes narrow. "She is not for sale."

Berneau shrugged his shoulders. "Twenty then."

Kwelik trembled as the bartering continued.

"She is to be my wife, Berneau. I will not take even a hundred guns for her."

The lieutenant sighed. "As you wish then, friend." He winked at her, a malicious smile spreading over his features. "Though I will never find another as lovely." His fingers brushed her cheek.

Kwelik batted away the touch. Berneau turned and walked toward the longhouse, sending only one backward glance in her direction. She locked fierce eyes on Taquachi. "Do you know who he is?"

Taquachi remained unaffected by her fury. "He is my ally."

"Ally?" Kwelik sputtered the term, her anger evident despite her fear of him. "How can you say that? He is the one who led the attack on my village."

"I know." Taquachi spoke the statement with calculated precision, without even a flicker of emotion to betray his intent.

Kwelik's breath stopped in her throat at the import of his words. "You know? How can you know?"

He turned toward her, his eyes like the coldest winter. Kwelik felt her blood turn to ice as he answered. "I was there."

She stumbled back, knocking the hide to the ground, her eyes wide with disbelief. "You?"

Taquachi regarded her with cold purpose. "Your people bedded with the enemy, beloved. They invited him into their midst, made him one of their own." He folded his arms in front of him. "Traitors, all of them. Your village was a scourge on our people, a disease that would infect us all."

"What are you talking about?" Kwelik's head whirled with confusion and disbelief. "What enemy?"

"The English God is the enemy. As well as their culture, their beliefs, their people." Taquachi spoke the words without inflection. "Those who preach those beliefs must die, as must those who allow the Englishman in their midst." He turned, one hand waving toward Berneau, who stood talking to Snow Bird. "The Frenchman only helped us to eliminate the infestation."

Kwelik caught her breath. Understanding coursed through her like black bile. "Papa. You're talking about Papa."

Taquachi did not answer.

Kwelik's voice raised to a frantic shout. "He never did anything but love you, Taquachi! He believed in you. He was the only one who cared when smallpox ravaged your village. He took you in as his own son when your father was sick with the disease. And you said you believed in his God. You prayed with him and read the Scriptures. I was there. I remember."

Taquachi remained unmoved by her passionate speech. "A lie, my love." He stepped toward her and placed a finger over her lips. "It is unwise to speak of the dead, *Manito-dasin*. And your father is dead. I made sure of that."

"*You* killed him?"

He stepped closer to her. "But we saved *you*, *Cheri*."

Kwelik backed away, unable to comprehend the magnitude of his words. She tripped over the hide and fell to the ground. "Why, Taquachi? Why?"

"Didn't he tell you?"

Kwelik trembled at the cold fury of his tone. "Tell me what?"

Taquachi leaned over her, his eyes black and merciless. "The day before we attacked your village, your father came to me. I thought he had come to finalize plans for our marriage. I was so happy to see him. I remember hurrying out of the longhouse, my arms open to receive him. But do you know what he said?" He did not pause for her to respond. "He said that there would be no marriage. He told me that he had been praying, and his God did not want you and me to be married." Taquachi's face hardened into fierce lines. "Oh, he acted sorry enough. But I knew the truth. I wasn't good enough for him or his God." He leaned closer. "But he paid for that mistake, didn't he? And his God will pay too."

Kwelik felt her breath coming in short gasps as she scooted away from him, her hand outstretched to hold him at bay.

Taquachi continued, "I thought a few weeks as a prisoner in a French fort would make you grateful when I rescued you. But you escaped. And even when I did rescue you, you still did not thank me. You are no better than your father. But soon we will be married, and then I will have what your God hoped to deny me."

"No, Taquachi!"

"Kwelik!" Her brother's call rang from the far side of the village. She heard him coming toward her, but she kept her gaze fixed on Taquachi. Then her stomach heaved with horrifying realization.

"Sister." White Wolf's voice filled with concern as he reached down to lift her to her feet.

She tore her eyes from Taquachi's mocking face and looked intently at White Wolf. "Did you know?" Her voice did not break from a whisper. "Did you know that Taquachi and the Frenchman killed Papa, murdered our people?"

White Wolf lowered his eyes, shame spreading over his face. For a moment he stared at the ground, unable to meet her gaze. Then he turned and walked away.

"Tankawon?" Kwelik's heart constricted with dull horror.

White Wolf did not turn back.

~

The room rumbled with excited chatter as Jonathan entered and tossed his hat to one side. The morning sun illuminated the faces of the prospective settlers, men and women of all ages, sizes, and backgrounds. But one thing was similar. Each countenance shone with bright hope and determination. Jonathan scanned the room and then shut the door behind him.

"Jonathan!" He turned at his name to see Sam beckoning him to a group of men hovering over a wide table. A crude map, held back from curling by four eager hands, spread over the oak surface. Jonathan approached the group, his eyes glancing from the map to the faces around it.

"We were discussing the best trail for travel, my friend." Sam clapped Jonathan on the back as he pointed to the map. "Perchance you can enlighten us. Shall the group cross the river here?" He indicated a place north of Pennsylvania. "Or here?" His finger moved south.

Jonathan took the map and rolled it into a tight tube, setting it on the floor beneath the table. "Neither."

Sam frowned slightly as Jonathan grinned at him. "I will lead the settlers myself."

A laugh leapt from Sam's throat. "I knew you wouldn't fail us, friend. Did you hear the news, brothers?" Sam's voice raised to include everyone in the room. Their conversations hushed as they turned their attention to Adams. "Jonathan Grant will lead you." He rested his hand on Jonathan's shoulder and squeezed. "There is no better man for the task in all the colonies, or the civilized world, for that matter."

Jonathan heard a low murmur behind him, followed by shouts of "Glory be to God! Alleluia!" He smiled. Such courage, such confidence, such joy. Jonathan watched the emotions play off the faces of the settlers. He would not disappoint these people, he promised silently, or himself either.

Sam lifted his hand from Jonathan's shoulder to motion toward a tall, lanky man of middle age. "This is Tom Piely, Jonathan. He's the minister and leader of the group."

Tom took Jonathan's hand in his firm grip. "God bless you, sir. Thank you for your commitment to our group. They'll be about thirty of us." His eyes never left Jonathan's. "The rest arrive tomorrow. Come, I'll introduce you." He led Jonathan to a short, chubby man with thinning hair and a smile that spread wide to show missing teeth. "This here is Mr. Blacker and his young wife, Sarah." Sarah's face pinkened at the introduction. She lowered her eyes as Mr. Piely smiled at them. "Mr. Blacker is a farmer and gunsmith by trade." He turned to his right. "And this young Scotsman is Mr. Timothy McKnighton. He brings no wife, but does bring a fine knowledge of woodworking and carpentry." Jonathan nodded at the enthusiastic youth before Mr. Piely directed his attention elsewhere. "Over there," he waved his hand toward the far wall, "are our bricklayer, two more farmers, a trapper, and a merchant skilled in Indian trade."

Jonathan raised his eyebrows. "A diverse group," he commented.

Tom laughed. "Though we have no fine blood, you'll find that God has made us well suited for the venture at hand."

Jonathan's brow furrowed into a grimace. "The skills you mentioned are useful, Mr. Piely. But how many of you are competent with a musket? That will be the true test of survival."

Tom's face fell. "We will do well enough on that score, Mr. Grant, God willing and in His strength and power."

"Will He be willing if you must use those guns against the red man?" Jonathan pierced the man with a questioning glance.

Tom's voice grew quiet. "We will do what we must to survive." He paused, his eyes studying Jonathan before he spoke again. "Are you a Christian, Mr. Grant?"

"He be a good man, husband," spoke a woman from behind them. "Honorable and fair-minded. He's God's own gift to us, mark me words."

Jonathan spun around as he recognized the familiar voice. A vision of graying red hair and a teasing smile met his gaze. An answering smile broke over his face. "Rosie?"

She laughed. "Aye, lad. And a bonny day it is when I can look upon your handsome face again." Her wide grin penetrated to his heart like a healing balm. He swept her into his embrace, hugging her in his arms until her breath came in delighted gasps.

Jonathan swung her around again and then set her in front of him. His eyes sparkled as he held her at arm's length. "I have never seen a prettier sight! What are you doing here?"

She smiled again and put her hand on Tom Piely's arm. "I got me a husband and a new life now. God has blessed me mightily since ye last laid eyes on me." She chuckled. "Just when I thought me old life was done and gone, God Almighty looked down on me with mercy and gave me everything I could ever dream to have." She cast adoring eyes up at her husband before returning her gaze to Jonathan.

He grinned. "I can't say as I ever thought to see you on the frontier, Rosie. But I think it's a fine idea. You'll love it there." All his doubts about the mission evaporated with one look at her face, flushed with the excitement of upcoming adventure.

"Aye, I heard you speak of it enough. Now I'm going to see it for myself." Her voice quieted. "But what of you? What happened to the pretty little Indian girl? Did you set her free?"

Jonathan's face grew dark. "I didn't have the chance to." He cleared his throat. "But that is a story best left to another time."

"Does she live yet, laddie?"

Jonathan stifled a sigh, wishing he could ignore the truth of his next words. "She lives. And with her, deceit and treachery."

Rosie frowned. "I wouldn't be so sure of that. She was a fine lass."

"You don't know, Rosie."

She thumped his chest with her forefinger and cocked her head up at him. "Don't I now? We'll let God be the judge of that." As she spoke, a song burst from the lips of the New Lights around them. The hymn filled the air and swirled around Jonathan with the vigor of their belief: "'A mighty fortress is our God, a bulwark never failing.'"

Rosie stepped up to his side, standing on tiptoes to whisper in his ear, "Listen to the words, Jonathan. 'Tis a hymn o' truth. Two Germans in our group translated the first verse for us."

"I've seen a mighty fortress fall, Rosie, and a bulwark fail," Jonathan responded. "Is God any different?"

Rosie shook her head, perplexity filling her eyes. "You haven't made your peace with Him yet, have you, lad?"

Jonathan's voice fell flat. "I don't know how."

She frowned, her hands on her hips as she challenged Jonathan with her gaze. "You surrender to Him, that's how. You give Him your life, and He gives you His."

The blunt statement struck at his soul. Surrender. Give. That's what his uncle had done. His uncle had found his peace with God. And he had given his life. That noble sacrifice was almost enough to convince Jonathan to follow his uncle's God. So why didn't he? If only Kwelik had remained true, if only Nahum had lived, if only his family had not clothed their evil schemes with a false mantle of piety. Jonathan sighed. There was still too much grief, too much pain, too much betrayal in his past for him to trust anyone, even God, with his life.

Jonathan's eyes dropped away from Rosie's fierce gaze. The year he had been away hadn't changed her. She was as stubborn as ever—and her words as piercing.

Rosie patted him on the arm, her eyes dark with understanding as the silence grew between them. "I'll keep praying for you, lad. Someday soon you will have to choose between anger and life. You'll have to stop letting your past snatch away your future. And, mark me words, on that day God will be there with you. You'll see. The day will come."

Somehow Jonathan hoped she was right.

FORTY-TWO

Pennsylvania frontier, August 1745

Yellow light from the campfire flickered off happy faces as the New Lights roasted quail, rabbit, and fish. Jonathan smiled. It was a feast by anyone's standards, a rare occurrence in the wilderness. But tonight was special. They had crossed the Susquehanna without incident. The weather was perfect, food plentiful, and hope so thick it seemed to shimmer in the air.

Jonathan rubbed his boot over the dirt and leaned against a fallen tree trunk. From the place where he sat, a little removed from the others, he watched the children laugh and tumble together in the glow of the fire while men made grand plans for their future town and women chatted about farming and quilting. His eyes met briefly with Rosie's as she sat on a log beside her husband. A look of contentment filled her face. He looked away. It was true that his fear of becoming like his father had receded since he had learned Richard's secret. Yet the type of contentment that filled Rosie still eluded him.

Laughter floated through the warm night and swirled gently around him. On the far side of the fire, young McKnighton told his stories of Scotland to a tiny group of children gathered around him, their expressions eager as they sat enraptured by the tale. Jonathan breathed deeply, smelling the rich, charred scent of roasted meat and listening to the sound of contented sighs from those who, like him, had already eaten. The sharp crackle of wood filled the air as the fire spat out a few sparks, like tiny fireflies taking wing to illuminate the night.

Jonathan leaned his head against the tree trunk. Above him stars twinkled merrily, filling the sky with the promise of another clear, cool day on the morrow. With a friendly glance in his direction, Tom Piely started a song. Jonathan smiled. "A Mighty Fortress" again. How they loved that song. It was as if they believed they would discover a real fortress at the end of the journey, so vigorously did they sing.

As the hymn rose to triumphant heights, hope whispered through him in a way it hadn't in so long that he scarcely recognized the feeling. Was it just the infectious joy of those around him? Or was it something more? Jonathan listened to the music, almost joining his voice with that of the others.

But instead he sighed and stood, unable to join their praise. Jonathan watched them for a moment longer before turning his back.

The settlers continued their evening singing, as they would for hours into the night, praising their God in prayer and music. Every night was the same. They would sing, then kneel around the fire in prayer. Sometimes they prayed for him.

Jonathan grabbed a blanket and headed for his sleeping place. They were so innocent, these New Lights, so full of dreams, of hope, of faith. They believed that God would save and protect them. But would He? Jonathan squeezed his blanket in one hand and glanced back at the ring of contented faces around the fire. If only he could protect their hopes, their dreams, and make sure their faith remained innocent and intact.

He crept away from the happy sounds, threw himself on his bedroll, and pulled the blanket under his chin. Beyond him the fire maintained its own private song, popping and whispering to the night. He had heard that sound before a hundred times, but only one time came to his mind as he listened to the flames. It had been a night much like this one. The fire had danced against the night sky, spilling gray smoke over him and Kwelik. That night the savages had come to kill them both. He would not have believed then that she would later destroy him, his home, his future. He did not think she would steal his heart and flee. The future had been full of new promise, and he had been happy with her at his side and Nahum and his homestead waiting at the end of the trail.

The settlers' song faded to a subdued whisper as their nightly prayers began. Jonathan listened to their muted tones, a strange yearning filling his soul. He closed his eyes and buried his head in his arms. Would he ever understand the peace of the New Lights? Was it the peace of knowledge or only the blindness of ignorance? He wished he knew.

In the silence of his memories, Jonathan heard Rosie's words again. *Someday you will have to choose . . .*

In the distance a wolf howled.

~

"Serve us, woman!" Taquachi turned glittering eyes to Kwelik as he held out his cup for more water.

Kwelik felt a pang of dread knife its way into her heart. *Three days, three days, three days*, the words chanted through her mind. She glanced out the longhouse door toward the horizon to watch the sun dip below the vast mountain range. Her eyes followed the red curve as the orb disappeared, scattering its purple and golden light across the western clouds. Three days more before the sun would arch through the sky to mark the day of her marriage. The thought lodged like a stone in her stomach. She gripped the water pitcher in both hands.

In the middle of the longhouse, a council fire burned within its enclosure of stones. The light from its flames did not quite reach the walls where several tomahawks and two muskets hung beside a dozen ears of drying corn. Kwelik allowed her gaze to travel to the peaked roof supported by several beams down the length of the room. There tiny flecks of dying sunlight sifted through the cracks. She dropped her gaze to the speckled pattern of light on the dirt floor.

"*Manito-dasin!*" Taquachi's demand came again.

Kwelik averted her eyes, unwilling to look into the faces of the men gathered around the fire—Taquachi, Tumaskan, Gray Bear, White Wolf, and Berneau. Since their encounter, Taquachi had taken great pleasure in flaunting her before the Frenchman. Kwelik felt the fire of fury again spark in her chest. But any defiance now would only lead to pain and reprisal three days hence.

Kwelik bit her lip, stilling the words of anger, as she poured the clear liquid into Taquachi's cup. His eyes caught hers with cold insinuation. "You serve well, beloved." He turned toward the others. "I have chosen well for a wife, have I not, my friends?" For a moment all eyes turned toward her, perusing, probing, taunting. Then a low chuckle of agreement issued from each throat. Except White Wolf's. He stared into the fire, his eyes avoiding hers, as the men returned to their business.

Taquachi tipped his cup to his lips and took a long drink before turning to Gray Bear. His eyes deepened with intensity. "Have the settlers arrived at the old trading post yet?"

Gray Bear shook his head. "They are a day out. We must leave tonight if we wish to meet them with the tomahawk of death."

Kwelik drew a sharp breath.

"Hold, Gray Bear." Berneau lifted a hand to stop the story. "Listening ears may spoil our plans." He glanced significantly at Kwelik. "Speak in French."

Gray Bear grimaced. "*Oui*, Berneau." The French words came awkwardly to his lips.

Kwelik continued to pour water, her eyes downcast in feigned submission, her mind spinning over the words Gray Bear had spoken. Would the bloodshed never end?

Taquachi nodded his agreement to Berneau's words. "We will all speak French. The *Manito-dasin* does not understand it, does she?" He turned toward White Wolf.

Kwelik saw White Wolf look up at her as he opened his mouth to speak. She caught his eye with a hard stare. *Do not tell.* She willed the words to speak through her eyes. *Do not betray me again.*

White Wolf closed his mouth and again dropped his gaze to the flickering fire. Slowly he shook his head.

Taquachi nodded toward Gray Bear. "Go on then, Brother. What did you discover?"

"I listen in woods all night," Gray Bear continued, stumbling over the difficult French words. "The English had council of war. They sang and spoke with eyes closed. They spoke to their God."

Berneau leaned forward, his face illuminated by the fire's orange glow. "What did they say?"

Gray Bear shook his head. "My English not good. They sing of strong fortress and *bulwark*. I do not know what that word is."

Berneau rubbed his hand over his chin. "In French it is called *un rempart*. It's a wall for keeping out enemies, a defense for war."

Gray Bear's eyes grew wide. "We will give them war. They say their God will build fortress and bulwark. Here." He stabbed his finger toward the ground. "On our land."

At this, Taquachi leaned forward, his face fierce in the dying light. The French words rolled quickly from his tongue. "It is as I told you. After they have built their fortress and bulwark, they will attack our village, rip open our women, kill our children, and steal our land. If we allow these few to settle, more will come, until we are wiped from the earth." He swiped his hand across the fire, then clenched his fist. "We must kill them now!"

Tumaskan pounded his fist in anger. "My son is right. English are evil. Take our land, kill our brothers. We will fight. We will kill the English."

Taquachi threw a stick into the fire. "We will leave tonight and attack as the moon rises tomorrow." A spray of sparks burst up and died in the air. "Their God will make no fortress nor bulwark here."

The words penetrated Kwelik's mind, tickling a memory from years back. *A fortress, a bulwark, and God.* They reminded her of a hymn Papa had used when trying to teach her German. Kwelik cast a suspicious glance at Taquachi and then again focused dutifully on the ground at her feet.

The savage hatred in Taquachi's face confirmed the worst of her fears. Those settlers were Christians, and Taquachi knew it. He wanted not only to destroy the white man, but also to kill her God, the God whom he felt had rejected him. But it was the blood of innocent settlers that would run thick and red from his vengeance.

Kwelik closed her eyes against the vision of imminent battle. She could not allow the settlers to be attacked unaware. She gritted her teeth and clutched the water jar to her chest. If only she could escape Taquachi's ever-watchful eyes and run to warn the settlers. But with their marriage three days away, that would never happen.

Surely God would not want her to stand by and allow those people to walk blindly into death.

Oh, God, she whispered silently, *do not let those people die. Show me a way to warn them.* As she finished her prayer, Kwelik lifted her eyes to catch sight of a girl slipping silently from their wigwam, a girl who had learned to walk like an invisible breeze.

Kwelik smiled.

FORTY-THREE

Jonathan put his hands on his hips and surveyed the meadow that would become their home. With the West Branch of the Susquehanna River running behind it, and the hills nestled to the north, it would make a fine home for the settlers and for himself.

He squinted his eyes and looked into the fading sun. Then his gaze dropped to study Ned McCoy's abandoned trading post as it glowed in the last rays of sunlight.

Jonathan jogged across the clearing and threw open the doors. The smell of dust and decay rose to his nostrils, and he coughed in the stale air. Wooden shelves covered the walls and tottered from nails high above. On the nearest shelf, a cracked jar sat abandoned, an intricate weave of spider webs sweeping from the rusted lid. Jonathan ran his finger over a plank and sneezed. It had been a long time since Ned had been shot by French fur traders and his post left empty. No one had bothered with his land since then. Until now.

Jonathan rubbed his hand under his nose and again stepped outside into the sunny clearing. He shut the door and squatted to grab a fistful of rich earth. Then he stood and allowed the dirt to run through his fingers before he turned and called to the group at the edge of the meadow.

"Good land, this." He grinned and motioned toward the building. "The post's a bit musty, but it will make a sturdy shelter for the women and children until we can build our cabins."

"Aye, Jonathan," called Tom. "It's a fine place to settle. Better than we'd hoped." He drew Rosie into his embrace as he spoke. "It's God's gift of the promised land."

Jonathan nodded. *If only we can protect ourselves from the savages.* He spoke the words to himself and let out a long sigh. At least they should have a few days to begin building before any outlying Indians became aware of their arrival, a few days before his friends discovered that they would have to protect their paradise.

Jonathan started when he heard a movement in the trees behind him. He turned, his eyes searching the woods. There! He held up his hand to shade his eyes and caught a glimpse of a small face peeking from the underbrush. Wide eyes framed with dark red hair peered back at him from the leaves. Then the face vanished as quickly as it had appeared.

Jonathan rubbed his eyes. Had he only imagined the piquant face? Before he could question further, a girl emerged from the forest and took a deep breath, her chest heaving with the effort. She studied him a moment, then hurried toward him, her bare feet flying over the grass as her buckskin skirt flapped around knobby knees. She flung herself toward him, stopping only when her determined face turned up just below his own.

Jonathan stared in surprise at the freckled, pale-skinned features below him. Before he could speak, the child threw her shoulders back and pointed a small finger at his chest. "Are you the leader of these settlers, sir?"

Jonathan's brow furrowed at the abrupt inquiry. He squatted down to look at the child more closely.

At the sight of a white girl dressed as an Indian, the other settlers hurried toward them. Jonathan could hear their heavy footsteps and whispered questions behind him. He did not turn as they came to halt a few feet away.

The girl glanced briefly at the others before her gaze again fixed on Jonathan. Her breath continued to come in short gasps as she glared at him. "Well?"

Jonathan allowed a smile to brush over his lips. "Sit down, child." He patted the grass in front of him. "Catch your breath."

The girl shook her head vigorously. "I ain't got no time to sit. Now I need to talk to the leader right away. Would you be him or not?"

Jonathan's face sobered. "I am."

"Well, then, I come to tell you what they got planned for you." She nodded quickly for emphasis.

Jonathan frowned. "What who's got planned?"

The girl cast her eyes up at him with an inscrutable expression. "Why, them Injuns. Who else?"

Jonathan motioned for the others to come closer as his gaze focused on the child. "Who are you, girl? Who sent you?"

"I ain't got no time for that now."

Jonathan repeated the questions.

She let out a hearty sigh of exasperation. "My name's Annie, and *she* sent me." Jonathan noticed how the girl breathed the word *she* with respect and reverence.

"Who is this 'she'?"

The girl paused for a moment as if considering her reply as the other settlers gathered around them. "The *Manito-dasin* sent me."

Jonathan nodded his head. "It means Spirit daughter." He spoke without turning his eyes from the child.

Annie took a deep breath. "She don't want you to die. And you will 'less you do something quick. The war party ain't but half an hour behind me. They'll be attacking as soon as darkness falls."

Jonathan stood abruptly, his arms tensing with anticipation. "How many warriors, Annie?"

"'Bout twenty, I reckon. Little more than you've got."

"Guns or arrows?"

"That French weasel's got one gun, and Taquachi's got another. Other than that, maybe one other musket, and the rest's got bows and knives and stuff."

Jonathan knelt on one knee and put his hands on Annie's shoulders. "Thank you, Annie. You've saved our lives today." He stood and turned toward the group. "Rosie, take the children and some of the women inside the building."

Annie turned to leave, but Jonathan called after her. "You too, child. Your life won't be worth much if they find you wandering in the woods."

Defiance streaked through her eyes. Then she nodded her consent.

Timothy stepped up beside Jonathan, his usually merry eyes somber. "What will we do, friend?"

Jonathan looked down at him a moment before answering. Would war never leave him alone? Would the torch and tomahawk always await him at the end of the trail? Jonathan sighed. "We ambush them."

"Tom," he motioned to the taller man, "you take a couple of the older men and heartier women over by the fire. Keep your muskets loaded and hidden at your feet. You are to look like a group of settlers innocently enjoying the night. The rest of us," he pointed to the other men, "will hide among the trees." Jonathan placed an assuring hand on Tom Piely's arm. "Be alert, Tom. When they burst into the clearing, you must pick up your guns and shoot. You will not have much time. Then we'll attack them from behind."

Timothy tightened his fist and shook it in the air. "They won't find us unprepared. Let them come," he shouted.

Jonathan laid a restraining hand on his shoulder. "The battle will still be fierce, my friend. Much blood will stain the ground this night, make no mistake."

Timothy sobered and lowered his eyes as Jonathan gripped his musket and held it high. "To the woods, men. The battle awaits."

FORTY-FOUR

One Indian brave, then another, slipped silently toward the beacon of the settlers' fire. Jonathan watched them creep by him like a black mist, undetectable except for a faint outline in the moonlight. A twig cracked beneath a savage foot, so quietly that Jonathan would not have heard it had it not sounded just a few feet from his hiding place. He held his breath, not daring to allow the air to escape his lungs, lest his own breath betray him to the enemy.

A man shifted to Jonathan's right, rustling the leaves underfoot. The brave halted mid-stride and turned, his eyes probing the bushes that hid Jonathan from view. *It is nothing. Only the wind.* Jonathan willed the Indian to move on, to ignore the sound. With a final glance, the warrior continued toward the clearing. He pulled his tomahawk from his belt as his arm brushed the branch that covered Jonathan. The wicked blade glittered in the moonlight.

Another warrior passed, his bow already taut with a long arrow. Jonathan gripped his musket in fierce fingers. His blood pounded in his ears as he waited for the moment of attack.

Silently the warriors approached the clearing, their weapons brandished, their faces painted with black streaks of war. A sharp battle cry split the air. The sound raked along Jonathan's nerves. He felt the hot breath of his companions coming fast and fearful in the darkness. *A moment more. Wait. Wait.*

Before their war cry faded from the air, the Indians leapt into the clearing. Tom shouted. As one, the settlers around the campfire gripped their muskets and dove for cover. Their shots exploded into the night air. Four of the attacking warriors fell. The rest continued to plunge toward their victims.

"Now!" Jonathan shouted the command as he rushed forward, blasting his weapon at the back of another brave. His men burst from the trees, their muskets firing. Another brave whirled and fell at Jonathan's feet. He leaped over the inert form, wielding his bayonet as a gray-haired warrior lunged toward him. The old brave parried Jonathan's blow with a tomahawk.

Jonathan ground his teeth, unable to maintain his grip as the Indian wrenched the bayonet from his hand with an expert twist. Time drew a stilted breath while Jonathan stared into the black-painted face before him.

He grabbed the Indian's wrist, halting the tomahawk's next blow. With a grunt he pulled the brave to the ground. The two men rolled in fierce combat. Each man's fingers dug into the flesh of the other. A blade shimmered in the firelight. Jonathan squeezed tighter, ducking his head as the man's hand broke free. The tomahawk descended. A tongue of hot agony sliced across Jonathan's shoulder as the weapon tore through flesh and fabric.

Jonathan felt the Indian's tendons stretch and pull beneath his hand as he again caught the man's arm. He buried his fingers deeper into his enemy's flesh. A cry of fury echoed in his ear as the tomahawk tumbled from the warrior's grip. Jonathan rolled over and lifted his foot to the Indian's chest. He kicked the man away from him and scrambled to his feet, grabbing his bayonet. With a desperate lunge, the old brave retrieved his tomahawk from the dirt. Quickly Jonathan plunged the bayonet into the Indian's chest.

A scream ripped through the night behind him. Jonathan whirled to see Sarah rushing toward her husband. Her face twisted with horror and grief. An arrow protruded from Blacker's back.

Jonathan turned grimly away from the sight. Already death had come swiftly and without remorse. Before he could reload his musket, Blacker's killer threw down the bow and came directly toward him. The brave pulled a knife from his belt, his eyes intent on Jonathan.

Jonathan backed toward the trees. Somewhere he had seen this face before. And that time too was in battle. He gripped his musket in both hands, pointing the bayonet toward the advancing Indian.

A small blur flashed across the corner of Jonathan's vision. Annie! He grimaced but did not allow his gaze to waver from the warrior before him. Yet from the edge of his sight, he could still see the girl race with fierce fury toward a man dressed as a French lieutenant. "You monster," she screamed as she tried to plunge a knife into his chest. The man easily deflected the blow. Jonathan grimaced. He could not save her now. Silently he cursed her for not staying with Rosie.

Jonathan stepped to the left, keeping equal distance between himself and his newest adversary. Now he could see the Frenchman and Annie just behind the warrior.

Jonathan took a step forward, then halted as the Frenchman grabbed the child and threw her to the ground, his fist upraised. The Indian before him closed the distance, his knife bright in the night's darkness.

Annie screamed.

Jonathan ducked under the Indian's swing, his attention jarred from Annie's battle to his own. He slashed at the warrior's arm with his bayonet. The knife fell to the ground. Before Jonathan could swing his weapon again, the warrior grabbed the other end of his musket.

For a moment they stared at one another over the musket's long barrel. Jonathan felt a chill creep through him as he looked into eyes as black as death. Then with a fierce push, he shoved the Indian away from him and stepped on the knife with one foot.

The brave stumbled backward. His eyes glanced at Jonathan, then moved to the knife that now lay beyond his reach. He hesitated.

Jonathan did not move.

Then, as one, both men's gaze traveled to the tomahawk still clutched in the older warrior's dead hand. The Indian lunged for the tomahawk. Jonathan rushed forward.

The Indian grabbed the tomahawk and threw it at Jonathan's head. The blade grazed his cheek, then spun off into the night. Jonathan felt blood ooze from the wound.

"Come, let's end this now," he whispered, beckoning the warrior with one hand.

The brave's eyes narrowed. He crouched low to the ground.

Jonathan lowered his bayonet.

The Indian crept back, his eyes never leaving Jonathan's face.

A musket fired into the night. From the side of his vision, Jonathan saw a brave in full headdress spin and fall to the ground.

As the man fell, the Indian attacking Jonathan stood suddenly. A guttural curse echoed from the warrior's lips. His face twisted in black fury. He turned and ran toward the fallen chief.

As he left, Jonathan whipped around, his eyes searching for Annie. He spotted her on the ground near the fire. The light from the flames outlined the Frenchman's slim form leaning over the girl. His hands were at her throat.

Annie's fists flailed at the lieutenant's arms as she tried to break his grip. Jonathan could see the rage in her fire-lit face as the man squeezed. Before Jonathan could move, a knife flew through the air toward the Frenchman. Its silver blade glinted in the firelight.

The lieutenant clutched his chest and fell forward, the knife's long handle sticking from his back. A young warrior stepped from the shadows to yank his knife from the man's limp frame.

Annie jumped to her feet, her eyes mirroring the Frenchman's surprise as she gazed up at the warrior who had saved her. Then she turned and spat on the Frenchman before disappearing into the woods. The young brave watched her go and then looked with eyes of contempt on the dying Frenchman. "For my people, my sister," the Indian stated, his words spoken not in the Algonquian tongue but in English.

At the same moment another Indian screamed a command. The other warriors grabbed their dead chief and withdrew into the forest.

The settlers, shouting their defiance, followed the retreating band to the edge of the woods. A whoop of victory rang from their lips as the Indians fled.

Jonathan watched them go. Then he pushed his heel into the Frenchman, shoving the body until it stared at the sky with unseeing eyes. "This time," he whispered to the corpse, "the battle is ours." Jonathan dropped his head. They had beaten the enemy, for now at least, because of the child and the *Manito-dasin*.

Jonathan's eyes traveled to the sliver of silver moon above the trees. Perhaps God did not hate him after all.

FORTY-FIVE

Kwelik knelt beside the flowing stream, her face buried in her hands. In her mind she could still see the painted faces of the warriors who had left the village the day before—faces filled with hate, dark with war. Grim, merciless, and determined. Faces that bespoke the battle to come.

Kwelik's hands trembled as she prayed. "Oh, God, save those settlers," she whispered. "Save my brother. Save me." Her voice broke. It was the same prayer she had prayed yesterday, last evening, and through the night. Yet she could get no further before her throat closed around the words and stifled her plea. Somehow the prayer always ended there, as if it too waited for events that would soon unfold. She shuddered.

A soft breeze swirled from the east and tossed a tendril of Kwelik's hair across her hand. She lifted her head. At her feet tiny wildflowers of purple and gold dotted the stream's edge. Kwelik sighed as she brushed her fingers over the velvety petals of a bright-faced daisy. How could her surroundings be so at odds with the fears of her heart?

With that thought, she raised her eyes to the water's surface. There reflections of sycamore branches danced across the creek's waves. And above them white clouds floated across the sky as if to mock her anxiety. Rocks, green with moss, peeked from beneath the lapping waves as the water rushed and bubbled over them. Everything was bright, beautiful, full of hope. Everything but her. Kwelik shook her head. Today the sight of nature's beauty could do nothing to assuage her dread. She tilted her face toward the sky. "Oh, Lord," she murmured, "why did You make the world so beautiful today?"

As the question escaped her lips, the sound of drums, deep and mournful, thudded from outside the village. Kwelik shivered. The drum sounded again, the beat shaking her very soul. It was the rhythm of death.

She turned, her knees still set in the soft earth as her eyes scanned the village. Dozens of women hurried from their wigwams and stopped, their children clutched in their arms. Behind them the flaps of wigwam doors swung in the breeze unheeded. Fear reflected from every face as the drum continued, beating out its message of doom. No one moved. No one spoke. No one voiced the fear of them all. *For whom did the drum beat?*

Slowly Kwelik rose to her feet and turned toward the sound. Silence hung over the village, broken only by the eerie thud of stick on leather. *Thump, thump, thump-thump. Thump, thump, thump-thump.*

Then as the last beat echoed through the air, the warriors emerged from the trees. Kwelik caught her breath in a low gasp just as a high-pitched wail rose from every woman's throat. A child cried. Sayewis screamed. Every eye turned to the body of their chief laid across the shoulders of the warriors.

Slowly the braves advanced, each foot placed carefully in front of the other, every head bowed, every eye steady on the ground beneath. The sight tore through Kwelik until she could hear nothing but the hammering of her own heart. Chief Tumaskan was dead.

The women's wailing intensified. Time stretched to agonizing proportions as the men drew closer, one step, then another, slow, precise, and silent amid the villagers' mournful cries.

Finally, the warriors reached the village center and lowered the body of their dead chief to the ground. No one dared speak as the people gathered around the braves. Only the voice of Sayewis rose above the keening sobs to punctuate the villagers' loss.

"My husband, my husband," she cried as she threw herself onto the chief's limp form. "Cursed be your killer."

The villagers murmured their assent, each swaying back and forth in rhythm to mourn their chief. A minute passed, then five, then ten.

Suddenly Sayewis stood, her hand reaching up to grip the beads around Gray Bear's neck. "Where is my son?"

The question sent a chill through Kwelik.

"Here." Taquachi's shout sounded from the village edge as he stepped from the trees. Sweat glistened from his brow. He raised his head, his voice carrying easily over the assembly. "See what I found near the enemy camp." As he spoke, he pulled his arm from behind him.

Kwelik heard a cry issue from her own lips. "Annie!"

There Annie stood, her arm pinched in Taquachi's fierce grip. Kwelik could see the girl's tear-streaked face wrinkled into a fierce frown. Guilt and defiance chased each other over the child's features as Taquachi thrust her in front of him.

Without a glance toward the villagers, Taquachi's gaze locked on Kwelik with cold fury. He headed toward her, ignoring the body of his dead father. His hand remained tight on Annie's arm. At his side a musket bumped in its leather holder, its barrel shining black and deadly in the summer sun. With long strides he closed the distance between them. He did not stop as his left hand raised to point directly at Kwelik. "You!"

Kwelik felt the heat of his accusation pierce her.

The gaze of every villager followed him as he halted before her, his features frozen with condemnation. "It was you, wasn't it?"

A hundred eyes, confused and questioning, turned on her. She could sense their doubt, their fear.

Again Taquachi's voice bit through the air. "You warned the settlers we were coming, didn't you?" He threw Annie to the ground at her feet.

Dark foreboding clutched Kwelik's chest. For a moment her eyes met Taquachi's before she dropped her gaze. A hand touched her skirt. She reached down and helped Annie to her feet.

"I'm sorry." The girl whispered the words, then scuttled like a hunted rabbit toward the wigwam door.

Kwelik turned back to Taquachi and opened her mouth to speak.

But Taquachi continued, "Admit it. You betrayed us."

Kwelik swallowed hard, the words forming slowly on her lips. "Yes, I warned them. I had to."

A sharp cry tore from the lips of the village women. Then a single, eerie shriek rose above the cry.

Sayewis rushed toward Kwelik, hands extended like hawk's talons, her face twisted into an ugly mask of hate. She gripped Kwelik's neck in her strong fingers and shook.

Kwelik's head snapped back and forth with the violent motion as she tried to loosen Sayewis's hold.

"Murderer! Murderer! Murderer!" Sayewis's voice shrilled in her ear.

Kwelik gasped for breath. Sayewis's grip tightened. Kwelik's vision tunneled.

"Stop!" Taquachi's command penetrated Kwelik's senses.

Sayewis dropped her hands.

Kwelik drew a ragged breath, sucking in the cool air as if she would never get enough. Blood throbbed in her temples as Sayewis whirled toward her son.

"Why do you stop me?" the woman shrieked. "By her own words, she confirms her guilt." She turned toward the villagers. "The hand of the gods fell heavy on us," she screamed. "The Great Spirit has cursed us for harboring a betrayer in our midst." Sayewis paused dramatically. "Look upon the dead body of your chief. My husband! Then look at his killer!" She thrust her finger toward Kwelik.

Kwelik rubbed her hand over her neck and glanced at the villagers. As one, they turned toward her, their eyes wide, fear and suspicion emanating from every face. Murmuring, they backed away from her. Their whispers confirmed that no one would step to her defense.

"She was never one of us," someone hissed.

"White man's blood runs through her," responded another.

"Sayewis speaks truth."

Kwelik dropped her head. For months she had worked beside these people, helped them, cared for them, shared her heart with them. But none of that mattered now. In one brief moment, everything had changed. All that mattered was that Chief Tumaskan was dead.

Taquachi crossed his arms over his chest as his mother turned and spoke directly to him, her words loud enough for all to hear. "You are chief now. You will lead us."

A slow smile spread over Taquachi's face and froze there. He lifted his head. His jaw clenched.

Sayewis's voice grew low. "Think, my son. The gods have revealed the *Manito-dasin's* black heart. She is a pawn of the white man's God. If you let her live, she will be the death of us all."

At the words "white man's God," Taquachi's face hardened until his features appeared like granite.

Sayewis lifted her chin. Her eyes narrowed as she regarded her son. "Yes, my son, she belongs to the white man's God. She serves the enemy." Sayewis drew a deep breath. "The betrayer must die."

"No!" Kwelik cried.

"Silence, devil-woman!" Sayewis spat.

Taquachi turned toward Kwelik. Anger laced his tone. "All I wanted was for you to be mine. But instead you betrayed me. You betrayed us all."

Kwelik shook her head. "I could never be yours, Taquachi. Not like you wanted. You knew that."

"Did I?" Taquachi's eyes never left her face.

Kwelik met his gaze. "You could have my body, but you would never have my soul. Sayewis is right about one thing. I belong to Jesus Christ."

"Do not speak that name!" Taquachi shrieked. His face reddened as he stepped toward her. His hand raised.

The villagers gasped.

Kwelik ducked.

Taquachi paused. His eyes snapped with evil intent. "If I cannot have you, *Manito-dasin*, body *and* soul, then," his voice raised to a shout, "neither will your God!" He pointed his musket toward the western mountains. "Tonight when the moon rises behind that ridge and darkness covers the sky, then, *Manito-dasin*, you will die!"

Kwelik felt cold horror wash through her.

Taquachi turned to the warriors. "Gray Bear, bring the ties. Long Brow, gather the wood. The women will collect the sap for the fire.

The flames of sacrifice will burn hot tonight!" He leaned toward Kwelik, his voice dropping to a whisper. "Where is your God now?"

Kwelik swallowed hard and closed her eyes. *Tonight you will die.* Her body trembled. She opened her eyes and tried to speak. Fear stopped her.

Taquachi's eyes narrowed into thin slits. His voice filled with bitterness as he spoke to her alone. "I loved you, Kwelik. I would have given you everything you wanted once you were my wife."

His words loosened her tongue. "Everything except my freedom," she whispered.

His fists clenched when he heard her response. For a moment he stared at her.

Neither moved.

Then a cold sneer spread over Taquachi's face. "As you wish then, my love." He turned toward the others. "Wait!" He raised his chin and fired his gun into the air. The blast echoed into sudden silence.

The villagers stopped and stared, their faces fearful and questioning.

Again Taquachi turned toward Kwelik. His voice raised to a shout. "As *sachem*, I will give the *Manito-dasin* one chance to save herself."

Kwelik remained silent, not daring to hope.

Taquachi removed his wampum belt. He held it toward her.

"The wampum binds your oath." The purple and white shells glittered in the sun as Taquachi's command rang cold and clear over the village. "I will give you what you want, *Manito-dasin*. Forsake the white man's God. Never speak His name again, and I will let you go free." He thrust the belt toward her.

Free? The word fluttered through Kwelik's mind. What did it mean to be free? She lifted her eyes to Taquachi.

He smiled. "I will let you walk out of this village and take Wakon with you. I offer you your freedom. All you must do is speak the words."

Kwelik glanced at the people around her. Silence hovered over them as each villager held his breath. Her eyes traveled to Snow Bird, to Gray Bear, to Sayewis, and last of all, to White Wolf.

Taquachi's voice cut the silence. "Choose, *Manito-dasin*. Freedom or death?"

Freedom . . . A dream danced across Kwelik's vision—a butterfly flitting through a meadow, its lavender wings shimmering in the summer sun. She could see herself following it, free to go where she pleased, do what she wanted, unfettered by promises or fear. *Freedom*. It was all she longed for during those dark weeks in the French fort. It was what she had dreamed of when standing on the platform of the slave auction. It was what she thought she had lost forever when she agreed to marry Taquachi. But now freedom was finally within her grasp.

She dropped her head. The moment had come, as she knew it must. This was the moment her mother foresaw. But how could she give up her dream and choose death instead?

Endless minutes crept by as the dream of freedom swirled through Kwelik's heart. She glanced at the wampum. What would she give to be free?

As the question echoed in her mind, a voice, quiet and gentle, whispered through her thoughts. *For whosoever will save his life shall lose it: but whosoever will lose his life for my sake, the same shall save it.* Kwelik trembled. Was she brave enough to believe the words?

Slowly her hands lifted to take the wampum from Taquachi's grip.

His eyes challenged her, mocked her, demanded that she speak her denial. Kwelik saw his smile deepen as she raised the shells over her head. She drew a deep breath. Her eyes swept over the villagers. Then she spoke her pledge. "The Lord, He is God." The words resounded with fierce clarity as Kwelik tilted her head toward the sky. "Jesus Christ is the one who saves me. He is my freedom!"

FORTY-SIX

"Bind her!" Taquachi's command cut across Kwelik's nerves.

She turned, her fists still clenched over the wampum, her chin raised with the triumph of her words. For a moment her eyes met Taquachi's. A wisp of doubt flickered across his features. Then it was gone, replaced by the cold fury of his hate.

"Do it!" Taquachi spun toward the other warriors.

Gray Bear plunged forward, his face dark and unreadable.

Kwelik whirled away, but hard hands clamped around her wrists.

"Do not fight me." Gray Bear's quiet voice spoke in her ear. He pulled her arms behind her back. Sinewed ropes bit into her wrists. "You are a brave woman," he whispered as he released her. "Is your God really worth so much?"

The question echoed through Kwelik's mind. She clamped her lips shut. Taquachi strode toward her. His eyes bored into hers. "You have chosen poorly, *Manito-dasin*. You are a fool. You could have been my wife. You could have been free. Now you will die." Taquachi swept his foot toward her, catching her behind the knees.

Kwelik gasped as her legs were knocked from beneath her. She fell forward, straining at the sinews that bound her hands behind her. Before she could twist to soften the blow, her face hit the ground with a hard smack.

"Her legs too." Taquachi's voice reached Kwelik through a blur of confusion and pain. Thick ties made of deer hide cut into her ankles.

"Gather the wood! Collect the pitch!" Taquachi kicked dirt across her face as he turned and pointed to various villagers.

The villagers hesitated.

"Do as you're told," Taquachi shouted. "I am chief now!

Whoever disobeys me will burn with the traitor. Do you understand?"

Whispers of confused fear rose from the people as they scattered to their appointed tasks.

Just beyond her, the wampum belt lay discarded in the dust. *Wampum binds the oath*. She heard the words again, and her mouth twisted into a pained smile. *So be it*, she thought. *They can do no more than kill me, no more than what was done to Christ*.

As if disputing her thoughts, Taquachi spoke again. "Tonight the traitor will pay for her devotion to the white man and to his God." He stepped over to her and buried his heel in her back.

Kwelik groaned under the pressure.

"Hold, Taquachi." White Wolf's voice penetrated Kwelik's senses.

Taquachi lifted his foot and turned toward her brother. "Do you oppose me, Waptumewi?"

Kwelik rolled over, catching a vision of her brother's black expression as he faced Taquachi. White Wolf held his chin high in the air, his fists clenched at his side. "For my sister's sake and the village's, I do. You cannot do this thing."

"White Wolf." The name slipped with unveiled contempt from Taquachi's lips. "Do you side with the enemy and his informer?"

White Wolf's voice grew cold. "You are the one who eats and drinks with the white man, Taquachi. You are nothing more than his trained dog."

Taquachi stepped toward White Wolf, his face twisted in fury. "I have heard enough of your sniveling, Little Cloud. You are as much a fool as your sister."

"You may take my name from me, but you will not take Kwelik. Let her go!" White Wolf's voice echoed through the village.

"Never." Taquachi's lips pulled into a cold smile. "Your demands have no power, Little Cloud. Your sister dies tonight."

White Wolf pulled his tomahawk from his belt and widened his stance for battle. "You will have to kill me first."

"So be it. Let everyone see what happens to those who defy the new chief."

Before Kwelik could cry out, Taquachi stooped over and grabbed a second musket from the hands of a young warrior at his side. Her eyes followed the gun as Taquachi raised it and pointed it at her brother's chest.

The villagers gasped.

White Wolf's eyes grew wide, then narrowed again, never wavering from Taquachi's face. "I reject you, Taquachi." He spoke the words without emotion, without fear. "Both you and your gods. So do what you must."

The shot exploded from Taquachi's musket. Kwelik screamed. Smoke filled the air. Through the haze, she saw White Wolf spin and fall from the impact.

"No!" Kwelik's sob tore from her as the smoke cleared to reveal her brother lying motionless on the ground. Long seconds passed in silence. White Wolf's body did not move. Kwelik waited, breathless. Agony shot through her soul at the sight. "No, no, no," she moaned, her head rocking back and forth in denial of the scene. "Not Tankawon. Not my brother."

Taquachi turned and spat on White Wolf's still frame. "Take him to the woods." He ground the words from between clenched teeth. "Throw his body to the wolves."

Gray Bear and two other warriors picked up the limp body and carried it away.

Tears blurred Kwelik's vision as the men disappeared into the trees. "Tankawon, oh, Tankawon," she murmured, her voice hoarse with grief. She closed her eyes.

"Take the betrayer to the sweat lodge. Tonight she joins her brother." Taquachi's voice ripped across her mind like the call of the devil himself.

She did not open her eyes as three braves approached her, grabbed her, and dragged her to the tiny hut on the far side of the village. She felt the cruel sinews bite into her wrists as they bound her to the lodge's center post.

Without a word, the men left the hut. The flap thumped into place, leaving her in darkness.

Kwelik leaned her head back on the post and opened her eyes.

"Tankawon, my brother. I would have died for you. But you should not have died for me."

Would you have chosen differently had you known the cost? whispered the insidious voice of doubt. *A few words could have saved your brother and you.*

Kwelik did not answer the question. Her eyes searched the blackness above her. *All dead.* Her father's words came back to her with haunting clarity. Even Tankawon. Tears stained her face as a sob caught in her throat, refusing to be released. In the end she could not save her brother after all. It had all come back to this—death, destruction, and darkness.

"Oh, God," she whispered, pushing the words past the hard lump in her throat, "be with me now. Have mercy on my brother's soul and on mine. You are all I have left. Everyone else is dead."

Kwelik wept silently, her head bowed, her hair trailing over her face like a shroud. This was not the way she had imagined her life would end. This was not the adventure she dreamed of while dancing through the meadow. This was not the way she had hoped God would answer her prayers. But the dreams had ended. The prayers fell silent.

Kwelik lifted her face and whispered into the darkness, "Is this the future you saw for me, Mother, when you spoke on your deathbed? You asked me to be brave enough, and finally I was. Yet what kind of future is this?" Kwelik leaned her head back. She listened to the quiet question as it echoed in her ears, and she knew the answer. God was with her, beside her, within her. She had felt Him there when she gripped the wampum and chose her fate.

"Wampum binds my pledge. The Lord, He is God." Kwelik spoke the words aloud in defiance of the darkness.

Silence answered her.

She raised her head and focused on the roof above her. A tiny ray of light sneaked through a crack in the mud and thatch, making a bright trail to the ground beneath. Kwelik's eyes followed its path, watching the tiny dust particles dip and tumble in the slim shaft of light.

See the dust, child. The words came with quiet clarity in Kwelik's mind. She caught her breath, recognizing the voice that she had heard only a few times before—the voice of God.

"I am scared, Lord," she whispered in response.

God's voice came again, quiet, gentle, and firm. *Be the dust.*

Kwelik's forehead furrowed with doubt, her eyes returning to the slender path of light. Within it the minute bits of dirt glowed with the brightness of the sun as they continued their quiet dance, despite the darkness, despite the shadows, despite the oncoming night. She studied the flow of the particles. Though tiny, insignificant, and surrounded by blackness, the dust floated in the embrace of the sun. It was beautiful, as long as it stayed within the light.

Kwelik frowned. *Within the light.* She tipped her head back, her chin pointing toward the sky. *How can I be the dust, Lord? How can I stay within the light?*

God's answer came. *Follow me into the flames.*

FORTY-SEVEN

Sunlight washed over the meadow and crowned the distant mountains like the glow of hope and glory. Jonathan put his hands on his hips and gazed over the land, his thoughts dark and doubtful despite the day's beauty. When would the Indians return? Could they fight them off again? Could he protect these people in spite of their belief that they needed no one but God?

Behind him the New Light settlers talked over the victory of the previous evening as they chopped trees and dragged them to the places where the cabins would soon stand. Snippets of their conversation swirled around Jonathan, prodding his worries.

"God intervened, my friends. He has given us this new land in certainty now."

"Aye, Tom," answered another. "Though I mourn for Sarah and her boy."

"God has not forgotten them, Brother. Nor have I. We will build their cabin first."

"Won't be seeing no more of them savages, I'm thinking. We gave them a good scare, we did." Jonathan frowned at Timothy's comment as the man swung his axe through a tall pine tree.

"Thanksgiving be to our God, men," Tom replied. "He's given us an inheritance of hope and peace."

Jonathan's brow furrowed at the comment. He knew how vain hope was and how short-lived peace could be. What would these settlers do when the Indians swooped down on them again? Next time they might not receive a warning from the mysterious *Manito-dasin*. Jonathan sighed, his thoughts traveling to the night before. How had the Indians come so quickly? How had they known the settlers had arrived? Who was the *Manito-dasin* that had saved their lives? Why did she risk her life and the life of the child to warn them? And what had happened to the girl after the battle?

Jonathan picked up his axe and began chopping the oak that stood before him. Too many questions. His blade bit into the hard wood as he glanced into the forest where the Indians had disappeared. The only thing he knew now was that they would return. The other answers lay somewhere beyond those trees. And somehow he must find them.

Jonathan rubbed his hand over his chin and stared into the woods. If the settlers were to find their peace, he would have to find a way to guard against the savages. He would have to find out how far away the village lay, how large it was, and how many braves would come against them next time. And that would mean silently tracking the war party back to their village, a task he could only do alone.

"Blacker died well, he did, defending his home and family," came Timothy's voice again. "'Twas a death worthy of a Christian."

"It was indeed, my friend," Tom's voice raised in response. "And by God's grace, brothers, may we all live and die so well."

You will, Jonathan thought, his expression turning sour. *You will. Unless I can stop the Indians*.

Jonathan reached into his breast pocket and pulled out the leather necklace he kept there. The bit of antler turned from left to right as he held it before his vision. Slowly he closed his fist around it, his eyes on the distant horizon as he walked toward the woods.

~

The tiny ray of light still shone through the hole above Kwelik. She sighed, her eyes focused on the light. Hours before she had worked at the ropes that bound her, pulling and twisting to no avail. Now nothing was left but the light.

She heard shuffling behind her as the flap pulled open and someone stepped inside. Kwelik turned her head, her eyes searching the darkness.

"It's just me." Kwelik recognized Annie's anxious whisper. "I've come to bring you some tea. Taquachi and the others are busy in the longhouse. Gray Bear's just outside, making sure you don't escape. He let me in though." Annie stepped closer and squatted in front of her.

Kwelik looked into the girl's face. Annie's eyes were still red, and her cheeks remained blotchy from crying. Kwelik's brows drew together in concern. "They haven't hurt you, have they?"

Annie shook her head. "Naw. No one's stopped to think much about me. They're all too busy preparin' for tonight. Besides," her lips quirked into a mischievous smile, "I've been hiding in the woods all day." In a moment the smile faded, and her brow furrowed to match Kwelik's. "I looked for Waptumewi's body while I was out there, but it was gone."

"Are you sure?"

Annie nodded her head vigorously. "I searched everywhere. Maybe someone took it away."

Kwelik's voice lowered. "Maybe."

Annie shrugged, then scooted over to Kwelik and lifted a cup to her lips. "You drink this," the girl muttered.

Kwelik took a sip, tasting the bitter liquid. She spat it out. "What is it?"

Annie frowned. "A little bit of tea to help you sleep, that's all. You won't feel nothing tonight if you just drink it."

Kwelik shook her head. "I will go awake and alert to the flames tonight, child. Do not think you will deprive me of that."

"Don't say such things," Annie sputtered in response. "I can't bear it." A tear slipped down her pale cheek. Furtively she wiped it away, but Kwelik could see her lips tremble with the effort to fight back her sobs. She lifted her chin bravely, her voice quaking as she spoke. "The wood's been gathered and placed all around the stake they're tying you to. Made me sick to watch them do it. Looks to me like they ain't plannin' to burn you but to cook you alive."

Kwelik turned her head to the roof above her, her eyes searching for the light. "That's the way they do it, you know. My mother told me about it. They place the fire just far enough away so that their enemy's skin blisters and peels, cooking their victim from the outside in." Despite her resolve, Kwelik shuddered.

"You don't want to be awake for none of that, do ya? Drink the tea." Annie held up the cup to Kwelik's lips again.

Kwelik turned her head away. "I won't drink it. I want to go to my death as Christ went to His. Don't make it any harder for me."

Annie sighed and sniffled. "I told Chilili you wouldn't drink it. Here, you can have this." She pulled another wooden cup from behind her back. "It's just water."

Kwelik eyed Annie suspiciously.

"It's plain water," Annie assured her. "I promise on my daddy's grave."

Kwelik nodded and drank the cool, clean liquid. Water, untainted. She smiled. "You risked much to come to me, Annie. And I thank you. Now go. I will be all right."

Annie scowled, rubbing a hand over her reddened nose. "All right? Ain't nothing gonna be right ever again!"

Kwelik's eyes filled with compassion. "Be brave, child. God will not abandon you even if I must."

Annie stuck out her lower lip. "I don't want God. I need you."

"Less than you think, child." Kwelik heard the echo of her mother in her words. "Jesus Christ is enough. Listen." She smiled gently at Annie. "I have discovered the secret of the dust."

Annie screwed up her face in a disagreeable expression. "They kept you in here all alone for too long. You're talking nonsense."

"No, finally I am talking sense," Kwelik answered.

Annie set the cup of water at her feet and folded her arms across her chest. "Well, I know about dust," she said. "That's what happens to us when we die. That's what's gonna happen to you unless I can do something about it."

Kwelik smiled. "No, the dust stays in the light of God's will, wherever it leads. To a meadow kissed by the sun, to a city covered with cobblestone, to a forest, to a tribe, to a tiny sweathouse, and even to a fire. And I must stay in that light too." Her voice grew quiet. "I must be brave enough."

Confusion covered Annie's face. She cleared her throat and sat on the ground beside Kwelik. "I don't see no light in this dingy little hut 'cept for what's coming through that wee hole above."

Kwelik ignored Annie's comment as she continued. "Freedom is in the light."

Annie snorted in response. "Ain't no point in talking 'bout freedom now."

Kwelik leaned closer to the girl. "Real freedom is following Christ, choosing His will. Only fear binds us, only doubt and error. But I don't have to fear anymore. What more can man do to me?"

"This still don't look like no kind of freedom to me, God's will or no." Annie's brow scrunched into a fierce frown.

Kwelik chuckled. "It wasn't my idea of freedom either. But maybe I was wrong." She paused, her eyes gently searching Annie's as she spoke. "I wanted to be the butterfly, flitting here and there under my own will and power. But God has shown me that I must be the dust, aloft only by His power, glorious only when illuminated by His light."

Annie sniffed and ran the back of her hand over her cheek. "What does that have to do with being free?"

Kwelik sighed. "When do you suppose Jesus was the most free?"

Annie chewed her lower lip as she answered. "When He was in heaven, I suppose."

Kwelik shook her head. "I don't think so."

"Then when?"

"I think it was when He had the power to save Himself but chose the nails instead." Kwelik whispered the words with quiet awe.

Annie wagged her head from side to side in confusion.

Kwelik smiled softly. "I am here by my own choice to follow God's will," she continued. "I was always longing for this and that, dreaming of adventure, never seeing God's will for the here and now. I was always looking for 'someday.' But someday has come. Someday is today." Her words trailed off and fell silent in the darkness.

A sob choked from Annie's throat. "Oh, Kwelik, I can't say as I understand a thing you're saying to me. I don't know nothing 'bout no dust or light. All I know is, this ain't right." Annie turned and poked her head out the flap that covered the doorway. In a moment she pulled herself back inside. "You go ahead and hang on to your

God, but I won't be standing by and watching you cook." With that statement, Annie disappeared into the dusk.

Kwelik watched her go. The light above her had grown dim with the approach of night. Yet that didn't matter now, for she had found a freedom that could not be taken, could not be killed. Kwelik dropped her head, her eyes closing in prayer. *If possible, Lord, take this cup from me. Yet not my will, but Thy will be done. I will follow You, even into the flames.*

Gray Bear thrust his head through the opening of the door, his eyes unable to meet hers. He spoke only three words as darkness consumed the day's light.

The words rang in Kwelik's soul.

"It is time."

FORTY-EIGHT

Kwelik stepped from the sweat lodge, her hands bound behind her. The flap slapped back into place, sending an echo of fear through her. She blinked into the night sky. Clouds, like silent witnesses of her imminent execution, blotted out the starlight. Gray Bear grunted and pushed her forward.

Kwelik raised her head. The village lay shrouded in darkness, its huts like gray mounds against an ever-blackening night. Near the center of the village, a torch flickered from Taquachi's hand, casting wicked shadows over his face. Behind him a pile of wood encircled a single pole, leaving four feet of earth between the logs and stake. Despite herself, Kwelik trembled. Annie had been right about the method of death. Soon the ring of wood would become a cage of flames.

Kwelik clenched her hands firmly behind her to stop their shaking as Gray Bear led her toward the stake. She lifted her chin, her eyes turning from the place where she would soon meet torture and death. Before her, shadowed figures stood silent, watching, waiting. Slowly Kwelik walked between them. No one looked into her eyes. No one whispered a word. Each head fell as she passed, hiding faces filled with shame and fear.

Kwelik averted her gaze and listened to the silence, broken only by the whisper of the flame in Taquachi's hand. She no longer felt the ropes that bit into her arms nor the cold malice that emanated from Taquachi's eyes. Nothing mattered now but to follow in the steps of God's will, to be brave enough to go to her death with the dignity befitting a child of God.

"Yea, though I walk through the valley of the shadow of death,

I will fear no evil, for Thou art with me." Kwelik's words pierced the silence.

A shiver passed through the villagers. She heard someone's quick intake of breath. Gray Bear's hand descended on her shoulder, compelling her forward. There not three steps from her, the massive pile of logs and sticks lay black against the cold earth.

She stepped within the ring of wood and stood at the tall pole. Without a word Gray Bear pulled her against the stake. Ropes scraped against her wrists and ankles as he bound her. He pulled the ropes tight and tied them. She could feel the splinters of wood digging into her back. Suddenly her body turned cold, then hot again. She clenched her jaw.

The smell of pitch penetrated her senses. The pine sap would instantly catch fire, burning hot and fierce around her, cooking her through the night. Fear lodged as a hard knot in her gut as faceless warriors added the remaining wood to the circle around her.

Kwelik listened to the sharp thwack of log hitting log. "Help me, God," she whispered, turning her face from the braves. Her gaze focused on the clouds above her. She could see them moving as the wind's hand pushed them across the heavens. In a moment a tiny patch of sky peeked from between the clouds, revealing a trio of stars. They winked and twinkled as if promising a future that could never be. She closed her eyes. *Even to the flames*, she repeated the words silently.

As the warriors completed their task, Taquachi stepped into the ring of wood. The flame flickered from his hand. He held the torch toward her, waving it beneath her chin as he spoke. "I give you one last chance to forsake your feeble God. Deny Him now, *Manito-dasin*, and I will free you." Taquachi thrust the torch closer.

The flame touched the skin of Kwelik's neck. Pain shot through her. She bit her lip to keep from crying out.

Taquachi's eyes narrowed as he again raised the torch above him.

Kwelik's gaze slid from his face to rest on those of the other tribe members. Gray Bear looked away. Snow Bird trembled. Long Brow crossed his arms as Sayewis grinned with unconcealed glee. No one spoke.

Taquachi lifted the torch higher, illuminating a huddled figure on the edge of the village. Kwelik's eyes caught Annie's, noticing the girl's blotched and puffy face and her shoulders shaking with silent sobs. "Remember." Kwelik mouthed the word, then turned back to Taquachi. Her fear melted. "I *am* free." Her voice echoed, calm and assured, in her ears. "I do not fear you who can kill my body, and after that do no more. Into God's hands alone do I commit my spirit." Kwelik lowered her voice, her eyes piercing Taquachi's. "Do as you will."

Fear flickered across Taquachi's face. The flame wavered in his hand. And for the briefest instant, Kwelik saw Taquachi's defeat.

Then he turned away. "So be it, my love."

FORTY-NINE

Jonathan drew a deep breath and studied the village laid out before him. All day he had trailed the Indians to this spot. Now night had fallen, covering his approach. Round wigwams threw black shadows over the earth, making a dark path hidden even from the scant starlight.

Jonathan silently crept forward. Like a piece of the night, he stole from shadow to shadow, until the clearing in the middle of the village was in view. There the Indians gathered, warriors and men too old to fight, women and grandmothers, children and babes, all staring at a single brave, a torch held high above his head. Behind the man Jonathan saw a woman tied to a pole, her chin raised to the sky.

Suddenly the brave spoke chilling words that Jonathan could not understand. Then he lowered the torch, and the wood caught fire. The sticks sputtered and smoked as they blazed to life. Before Jonathan could take another breath, orange flames leaped in a circle around the woman.

Oblivious to danger, Jonathan rushed forward. "Stop!" he shouted as the darkness fell away behind him. Somewhere to his right, Annie screamed. Her cry ended in a bitter sob. The flames crackled and grew taller, their light casting wicked shadows over the silent villagers. And beside the fire the tall warrior stood waiting, the torch still burning in his hand.

The Indian turned and raised the flame toward the sky. "It's too late." His tone filled with bitterness as he spoke in accented English. Then he threw back his head. A war cry burst from his lips.

Like a sharp arrow, the sound pierced through Jonathan. The warrior reached for his tomahawk. As if released by the brave's action, the villagers rushed toward the intruder.

"No, Taquachi!" Annie yelled, her words garbled by tears. From the side of his vision, Jonathan saw her grab a deer hide and run to the fire.

Before him, the Indian called Taquachi raised his weapon, his voice ringing over the threats of the advancing villagers, "Stand back! This fight is mine. Mine alone." An eerie laugh echoed from his lips.

The villagers halted.

"Stop this madness!" Jonathan shouted at them.

A hundred dark eyes stared back at him. Like phantoms they stood now in the darkness, watching, silent, waiting for their leader to make his move.

Jonathan drew closer to Taquachi. His eyes traveled from the brave to the *Manito-dasin*, her face blurred by the smoke. Beneath her Annie tried desperately to beat down the flames, but her efforts were futile. The woman writhed as the fire licked higher, obscuring Jonathan's view.

Jonathan clenched his fists and focused on Taquachi. Only a few yards separated them. He could see the firelight flicker in the man's eyes. Twice he had faced this enemy, and twice each had walked away with the battle unfinished. This time one would die.

"The *Manito-dasin* pays for her betrayal, white man." Taquachi's voice oozed over him with malice. "Now you will die with her." As he spoke, his arm whipped forward, throwing the torch with furious might. The fiery stick spun end over end through the night air, striking Jonathan's chest. Heat seared through him. Smoke stung his eyes. His shirt caught fire. A shout burst from his lips as he ripped the garment from his frame.

Taquachi leapt toward him. "Let us finish the fight," he screamed as he flung his body into Jonathan's. "No lightning will save you this time."

Jonathan hit the ground hard. His breath escaped in a pained gasp. He twisted to face his enemy as both men grappled to gain the upper position. His hand gripped the Indian's wrist. They rolled together over his burning shirt. He felt the fire sear his flesh as it smothered beneath him. And around him, the villagers still watched and waited as the bonfire gained strength.

Terror flashed through Jonathan's heart. The *Manito-dasin* must not die. He must be strong enough to save her and to save himself. He felt his grip weaken. He gritted his teeth.

Suddenly Taquachi was above him. The tomahawk shimmered in the smoky air. Jonathan's fingers dug deeper into Taquachi's skin. He could feel the Indian's hot breath on his face. Sweat dropped into his eyes. His vision blurred. The features above him twisted, then altered. Jonathan blinked. The image of the Indian melted away, replaced by that of his father. Then it shifted again, becoming the face of his brother. Jonathan's eyes narrowed. Fury flamed through him. Suddenly he was no longer fighting just the warrior but all the demons of his past.

A log tumbled in the fire behind him, sending vicious sparks into the night. The crackle of flames roared through Jonathan's senses. He tightened his grip until he drew blood from the warrior's wrist.

Taquachi's teeth sank into his forearm, loosening Jonathan's hold. A laugh echoed in his ears. Taquachi's face loomed before him. "You cannot beat me, white man."

Spittle flew across Jonathan's cheek. With one violent move, he pushed Taquachi away from him and stumbled to his feet. His heart hammered in his throat. He plunged toward the fire, his hand outstretched to save the *Manito-dasin*. The heat of the flames scorched his skin.

With a wicked war cry, Taquachi lunged at Jonathan from behind, knocking him to the ground. Jonathan's chin hit the dirt. He attempted to turn, but the steel grip of his adversary stopped him. He could feel the Indian's weight pressing into his back. Taquachi's legs squeezed around him, pinning his arms to his sides. Cold dread spread through Jonathan. He couldn't move. He couldn't twist free.

Taquachi grabbed Jonathan's hair, forcing his head back. The tomahawk flashed above him. The warrior's grip tightened. For a brief moment, Jonathan's eyes met the woman's across the flames.

"Jonathan!" Her scream tore through the night air with sudden anguish.

Kwelik. His lips formed the word, his mind spinning. *Oh, God, no!* Horror clawed his heart. The agony of his own defeat surrounded him, enveloped him, crushed him, filling him with a feeling so familiar from childhood. He was helpless to save the woman he loved. Again he was powerless. Again afraid.

Taquachi's voice cut through him. "Now you die, white man." As he spoke, he jerked Jonathan's head further back, lifting his chin from the dirt beneath.

At that moment the moon moved from behind a cloud. Jonathan's eyes caught the light, and he knew what he must do. He closed his eyes. "Oh, God," he shouted, "I need You. Save us." His cry tore through the night.

Jonathan could almost hear the whoosh of air as the tomahawk plunged toward him. Before the weapon could find its mark, Taquachi sucked in his breath. Jonathan's eyes flew open. The Indian's grip loosened. Jonathan twisted around to see his adversary's face grow white in surprised pain. From the Indian's chest, a spear protruded, its shaft sunk deep into its victim's back. Taquachi's hands gripped the tip as he fell facedown on top of Jonathan.

Desperately Jonathan shoved the Indian's body off him. His eyes searched the shadows. There a young brave stood, tall and fierce. One arm hung loose at his side, his shoulder bloodied and torn. The warrior's gaze fixed on the body of his victim. "Burn in hell, Taquachi." The words spilled from the Indian's lips in perfect English.

As one, the villagers glanced at the young warrior and then at the body of Taquachi. The brave stared back at them, challenging. Without a sound, they melted toward their wigwams.

"White Wolf?"

Annie's hoarse whisper sounded behind Jonathan as he rolled to his feet, grabbed the tomahawk, and raced toward the fire. The flames and smoke blurred his vision. "Kwelik!" he screamed.

"Save her!" Annie cried.

Jonathan pulled the deer hide from Annie's hands, beat back the fire, and plunged through the circle of flames.

"Oh, God." Jonathan felt his breath stop in his throat as he saw

Kwelik slumped against the stake. Carefully he wrapped her body in the hide. The fire roared around him. The air shimmered with the intensity of the heat. He drew a ragged breath, gripped the tomahawk, and slashed the ropes that bound her wrists and ankles. Kwelik's body fell toward him. The tomahawk clattered to the ground as he gathered her in his arms. Her skin was hot beneath his touch. Shielding her with his body, he vaulted through the wall of flames.

"Kwelik, Kwelik," he groaned as he laid her on the cool ground. His eyes searched her for any sign of life. Her charred hair gave off a rank smell. He brushed the ash from her face and leaned over her. "I thought you had betrayed me." His voice stumbled over his anguish. "I thought God betrayed me. I didn't know. I have been such a fool." Jonathan paused, his eyes never leaving the precious face beneath him. "Oh, God, don't let her die." His words dissolved into a choking sob.

Annie knelt beside him. Tears ran down her cheeks as she clutched her hands in front of her. "It's too late, ain't it?" she whispered.

Jonathan did not answer. He held Kwelik gently in his arms, all too aware of her injured flesh. Even now a blister was rising on her cheek. At the sight of it, the magnitude of his error washed through him. Why had he not sought her, searched the wilderness until he found her and saved her? Now it was too late. The agony of the thought tortured his mind.

"Does she live?" A voice stiff with fear spoke from over Jonathan's shoulder.

He glanced up.

The young brave stood beside him. Jonathan could see the Indian's eyes glistening with unshed tears as anguish and guilt stained his features.

Jonathan felt his chest constrict. He dropped his gaze.

The brave sank to the ground beside him. "The others will not challenge us now. They know my right."

"She is," Jonathan forced the words from his lips, "your wife?"

The warrior glanced at him. "She is my sister."

Jonathan turned back to Kwelik. He bent over her, listening for her breath. He heard nothing. "Oh, God, save her," he pleaded.

Kwelik lay motionless. Moments passed. Only the whisper of flames broke the silence. Anguish clutched Jonathan's heart. He waited and hoped and feared.

Then Kwelik drew a shuddering breath.

"She's alive!" Jonathan's eyes met the young brave's as his voice filled with awe. "Thank God!"

"God?" Shame darted across the Indian's features. He stepped back. A shadow fell over his face.

Kwelik's eyes fluttered open. "Jonathan?" her voice rasped, her blue eyes reflecting the light of the fire behind them.

"Kwelik!" He drew her to him, careful not to touch her burns.

She reached up a trembling hand to his face. "You came back for me."

"Hush." Jonathan laid his finger over her lips, unable to tear his eyes from hers.

Annie pushed closer. "Waptumewi is alive," she whispered.

Kwelik's eyes widened. "My brother?" Her words were scarcely audible.

"He's right here." Annie turned. Her voice cracked. "He's gone."

Jonathan glanced up. Nothing but darkness met his gaze. "He saved me." His eyes dropped back to Kwelik. "And God saved you."

A quiet smile lit Kwelik's face. "God saved us both. I will not leave you again."

Jonathan leaned closer, barely catching the words. He gently kissed her forehead. "Nor will I leave you. God has set us free."

She smiled up at him, her skin pulling tightly across her blistered cheek. "If the Son therefore shall make you free, ye shall be free indeed." Her words washed through him like the promise of a dream renewed.

"And so we are," Jonathan whispered, his lips brushing hers.

Behind them the flames danced and leapt beneath the moonlit sky. And the wolf was silent.

AFTERWORD

On October 18, 1748, England signed the Treaty of Aix-la-Chapelle with France, officially ending King George's War. As part of the agreement, England returned the captured Fort Louisbourg to the French in exchange for British control of Madras, India. This decision angered the American colonists who had risked their lives to capture the supposedly impregnable French fort. The loss of Fort Louisbourg would become only the first in a long list of colonial grievances against an imperious English government.

Watch for book two of
The Winds of Freedom series
and experience . . .
White Wolf's redemption,
Annie's release from revenge,
Jonathan and Richard's reconciliation,
and Kwelik's new life with the man she loves.

About the Author

Besides being a freelance writer, MARLO M. SCHALESKY (B.S., Chemistry, Stanford University) is a partner in a mechanical engineering firm in California. She has published more than 350 articles in prominent Christian magazines and is working toward a Master's of Divinity at Fuller Theological Seminary. Marlo enjoys many outdoor activities such as hiking and horseback-riding. She and her husband, Bryan, have been married for 11 years and are expecting their first baby.